THE C

CW01620078

First Published in Great Britain 2021 by Fleur de Lys Publishing

In this work of fiction, the characters, places and events are either the product of the author's imagination or they are used entirely fictitiously.

British Library Cataloguing-in-Publication Data

A catalogue record for this book is available on request from the British Library.

ISBN 978-0-9560298-8-1

www.fleurdelyspublishing.com
www.judeauthor.com

THE GOLD

by Jude Calvert-Toulmin

FLEUR DE LYS

www.fleurdelyspublishing.com

"The most beautiful things are those
that madness prompts and reason writes."
André Gide

For Bruce Robinson

1
Upside down

THE WATER COMES AS A SHOCK, THAT'S FOR SURE. It's all around him where a second ago there was air and now he's swallowing the stuff and choking and breathing in more and flailing his arms around and the water is everywhere, it's deep. It's the pool. He's in the pool. Water. His chest is exploding. Pain. Blue sky, somewhere, out of reach. Breathing. Water. Pain. Exploding.

❧❧❧

'Um, I think he's dead.'

'Really?'

'Yeah. As a fucking dodo.'

'Are you serious?'

'Well if he's not dead now he soon will be. He's face down in the pool and not moving, right?'

'Yeah. Look at him. Look at those little strands of hair floating around his head.'

'Like little sea anemones.'

'Yeah.'

'Yeah. Fuck yeah.'

'What are you gonna to do?'

'You mean what are *we* gonna do? Get the fuck outta here.'

❧❧❧

His body sways gently with the movement of the water. Face down, arms outstretched.

From beneath, his face, floating in the water, looks calm, at peace, his eyes closed, mouth open but making no sound in the silencing body of water engulfing him.

The sky above is clear, crystal blue, shimmering through the refractive surface of the pool water. A tiny white cloud drifts aimlessly in its heights, besmirching its expansive, blue purity. It is a beautiful and peaceful scene, a silent ending to years of cacophony and horror.

2
CLACKETY-CLACK
A Year Earlier...

'GINA, LOOK AT ME WHEN I'M TALKING.'
Gina looks back at her phone.

'I look terrible.'

Lara sighs, heavily. 'It's just the light.'

'And the fact I'm sixty next year and refuse to have surgery. Big mistake. I should have gone down the plastic route a long time ago. Look at me. I look like something that's fallen out of a bin lorry.'

'You don't. You look great. Anyway, where were we?'

'You were telling me about your chickens. Which isn't as interesting as the horses. But never mind.'

'How long do you think we've been chatting?'

'No idea. An hour?'

'It's gone very quiet outside. I wonder if Bruce is OK. Hold on.'

Gina looks levelly at her friend with barely concealed disapproval.

Lara walks to the front door and calls across the courtyard.

'Bruce?'

No answer.

'Do you mind if I just go and check? He's been writing today.'

'Oh, a *good day.*'

'A good day.'

'When you hear that clackety-clack coming from the barn…' says Gina, lighting up a cigarette, inhaling deeply and then noisily blowing smoke from the side of her mouth. 'Must be reassuring that he's not passed out amongst his *folios* again.'

Lara stands up, still holding the phone.

'I'll just have a quick look.'

She walks out of the house and across the little bridge and cobbled yard towards Bruce's workroom, a book-lined study in an adjoining barn. Several chickens appear from another barn and run after her, clucking expectantly in the hope of food.

She pushes open the door to the barn and stops, surveying the scene in front of her. Her husband of thirty-five years, Bruce, is slumped at his desk, his face buried in the keys of an ancient IBM Selectric typewriter from which extends a blank sheet of A4 paper.

Lara looks back at the phone and sighs.

Gina smiles, raising her eyebrows, questioningly.

'Is he alive?'

'Of course he is. Don't be so crass, Gina.'

'God, I can hear him snoring from here.'

'It's an illness, Gina. It's not funny.'

'Snoring's always funny. Like farting.' Gina takes a deep drag of her cigarette.

'He only snores when he drinks.'

'Oh, hardly ever, then,' says Gina, archly. 'What's he writing, anyway? Still toiling away on that screenplay?'

'I'm popping you on the desk for a minute, Gina.'

Lara props the phone up next to an empty bottle of wine.

'All I can see is his fucking ear. I'll ring you back later, darling, I can see you've got your hands full.'

Lara bends down, looks into the phone and smiles, wanly.

'OK darling. Talk later.'

3
DREAM HOUSE

'HAVE THEY GONE?' ASKS JULIETTE.

'Flea took a while going, but Moon and Cypher went right off,' answers Adriana, brightly.

'Did you read them the safari book?'

'Yeah, and they've got their meditation lullaby playing now.'

'Great. That's great. Quiet time. Rest. Great. I need this.'

Juliette, amber-eyed, flame-haired, full-lipped and permanently on edge, slides onto the huge white faux-leather couch and gazes absently at the ocean, swelling with an unusually loud roar beyond the open panels of glass at the far end of the living room.

'Make it quieter, Adriana, the sea's too noisy,' she says, airily, waving a hand towards the windows.

Adriana picks up a discarded exercise sock from the vast expanse of twinkling gold-flecked marble floor and smiles at Juliette.

'I can't change the sea.'

'You can do *anything*,' Juliette purrs. 'You're my sanity touchstone.'

Juliette thrusts her hand before her face, spreads her fingers wide and stares mournfully at her nails. 'I'm not using gel anymore. Ruins your nails. Book me an appointment with Janice, will you? I'm getting my nails done tomorrow.'

'Sure, boss. Are we gonna sign off on sand play by the ocean with the kids after lunch, before we head back to LA?'

'No. I've changed my mind. I'm keeping them out of the sun for now.'

'Am I allowed to disagree with you today?'

'Yeah. What are you going to say about the sun? That it's suddenly not dangerous?'

'Well no, but, despite all being blonde, the kids *are* Syrian.'

'But they didn't spend a whole lot of time in Syria before they were rescued, did they? They didn't see much *actual sun*. Mostly they were exposed to clouds of smoke from bombs, I guess. They're casualties of war.'

Juliette takes a deep breath, looks down at her voluptuous, hourglass figure, hugged into a tight red pantsuit, and sighs, heavily.

'I'm fat.'

'You're not fat.'

'I don't pay you to tell me I'm not fat. I pay you to tell me the truth. I. Am. Fat. And my breasts are too big.'

'C'mon, breasts like that cost thousands of bucks and yours are all natural.'

'I know. But they're still too big. Get me a glass of that Jérôme Prévost, Adriana. There's a few bottles chilled in the fridge, right? The sun's setting. I need a drink.'

Adriana click-clacks across the floor to the kitchen area, removes a bottle of achingly fashionable growers champagne from the fridge, pops the cork, pours the fizz into a tall glass and hands it to Juliette, who knocks back half of it in one long slug.

'Besides, your figure is world famous. You don't look like a stick,' adds Adriana.

'Or a lollipop. Like Gillian Carrington…'

'Like Gillian Carrington. You're "all woman" as they say. You should be proud of it. You're gorgeous. The most beautiful woman on the planet, even.'

'Some anonymous little Twitter troll said that I was fat the other day. Actually used the "F" bomb about me.'

'People throw rocks at things that shine,' coos Adriana. '*Assholes.*'

Juliette glowers at the sea.

'Where's Micky? He's never around when it's time to put the kids to bed. What is parenting if you can't even put your own kids to bed?'

'I think he's in the den.'

'Call his cell, will you? Tell him to get his ass down here. We need to chill together. That's why we're in Santa Monica, isn't it? And he fucks off to his den as soon as we arrive.'

Adriana obediently rings Micky.

'He's not answering.'

'That son of a bitch. He's probably reading. What kind of loser reads books when there are movies?'

Adriana smiles. 'Shall I draw the drapes?'

Juliette chews on the inside of her cheek, a nervous habit developed in an adolescence fraught with fighting off her predatory Uncle Fred.

'Bella George fired her chef the other day,' she suddenly announces.

'Really? Wasn't he the best?'

'Well, so I'd heard. But she asked for foo yung and he served it in a folded up mess with *no sauce.* Apparently that's how they eat foo yung in *England.* But we're not in *England.*'

'No sauce. That's crazy.'

'I won't say who, out of confidentiality, but someone very close to me who can be trusted was at Bella's town house in Brooklyn recently…'

'Amy?'

'Yeah. And she told me that there were cigarette butts in the pot plants. How can people live like that? Gross.'

'I wouldn't be so surprised boss. Behind closed doors are where everyone's secrets lie. No-one is as they seem.'

Juliette springs up from the couch and marches purposefully towards the open windows. She stares dramatically at the ocean beyond, throws her head back and smiles.

'I *love* that. "Behind closed doors are where everyone's secrets lie. No-one is as they seem."'

She repeats the sentence over and over, with a different emphasis every time. '"Behind *closed* doors are where *everyone's* secrets lie. *No-one* is as they seem." Where did you get that Adriana? Where's it from?'

'It's not from anywhere. It's just something I think, from time to time. That nobody's as they seem, that we're all merely false constructs, that everyone's playing a game, hiding, wearing a mask.'

'Well, I wear a mask at work, of course. It's my freaking *job.*'

She looks at Adriana suspiciously. 'Unless you mean, like, all the time. *Do* you? Is that what you mean?'

'There's more to people than meets the eye, that's all I'm saying.'

'You mean I'm a phony?'

'No boss, of course not. You're genuine compared to everyone else in this town. I mean life is complicated.'

Micky slopes into the vast, luminescent chamber of the living room, his white towelling robe completely open at the front, parted over his belly and revealing the top of his pubic hair. He ambles languidly to the couch and sinks down into it, tossing a paperback book onto one of the peacock blue silk cushions lining its plump contours.

Adriana makes her way to the kitchen area, subtly avoiding looking in Micky's direction.

Juliette turns sharply to look at him.

'Where have you been?' she demands. 'This is meant to be *quality family time.* The kids are already in bed. You can't just press rewind on time with the kids, Micky. It only happens once. You'll never get another chance, *this* chance, *right now*, this *evening*, to put your kids to bed again in *quite the same way*. Tomorrow is a different day, it won't be the same! *The boat's sailed without ya!*' She wafts a manicured hand at the ceiling.

'I see you've started on my Prévost.'

'It's not yours.'

'Jérôme sent me that case himself.'

'It was for *us*. He loves me, actually. *Adores* me.'

'Yeah, well, everyone loves you. Until they know you.'

'Oh, I see. It's going to be one of *those* evenings, is it? Adriana, I won't need anything else. Just fetch me over another bottle of *Micky's* Prévost before you go.'

'Sure. I'll be upstairs in my room if you need me.'

'I won't. It's fine. If I do, I'll call you.'

Micky, without thinking, follows the twenty-five year old blonde's backside with his eyes as she leaves the room.

'Don't. Even. Think about it.'

'What am I meant to fucking do? The girl's got a great ass! So I'm meant to pretend she doesn't *exist?* It doesn't mean I wanna bone her! Jesus!'

'You're meant to be paying attention to *me*,' says Juliette, huskily, her voice softening as she sashays towards him, her eyes flashing mischievously and her hips swaying slightly.

'OK. OK.'

She sits on Micky's lap, straddling him, her legs draped either side of his hips, and runs her fingers through his mop of blonde hair. At forty-three he's only just starting to go bald, and despite the slight puffiness of his body he's still beautiful, his boyish looks, piercing blue eyes, wealth, power and fame making him irresistible to women, and the slight bridge of his nose from a long-ago car smash which he stubbornly refused to have corrected in surgery merely making him a more bankable talent for action roles.

Juliette slides her hand towards his crotch but he casually brushes it away.

'I'm beat, honey,' he pleads, limply.

'Not too beat to read fucking poetry! Just too beat for *me!*'

He pushes her from him and stands up, breathes in deeply, reaches into his robe and scratches his balls, then ambles over to the window. He stands quietly, looking out to the ocean beyond.

'It was Rumi,' he says, casually, as if that explains everything.

'Oh, *that's OK then.* Fucking *Rumi! Fuck* Rumi! You may as well! You never fuck *me!*'

He swivels on the spot to face her, his expression suddenly a mask of fury. 'What you don't seem to understand is that I fucking *need* poetry and literature to *keep me fucking sane!* I *need* Lorca. I *need* Voltaire. I *need* Joyce. So I'm too tired to fuck! So fucking what? Use a dildo. Get that idiot beefcake masseur round here to give you one if you're on heat. *I need fucking culture, Juliette, not ass!*'

'You're either gay or you're on Oxy again. Which the fuck is it?' she spits with disgust.

'Oh, here we go. Here the fuck we go again on this tedious old merry-go-round of you feeling so neglected, boo-fucking-hoo because you're so fucking spoilt and needy with your fucking narcissistic personality disorder.'

Micky walks over to Juliette and bends down slightly, lowers his face towards hers and sneers 'You hang on Adriana's every word whilst she simpers to you and tells you *exactly* what you want to hear and it's all *an absolute crock of BS.* She doesn't mean any of it, you *needy freak!* You've adopted these kids and now you're bored, because not enough men are slavering over you which is the only thing that seems to make you function!'

He stands up again and points his index finger at her face. 'So *now* you're accusing *me* of going back to *Oxy.* Well you listen to me. You take a good long hard look in the mirror at yourself - which should not be a challenge for you as that's all you ever fucking do anyway

- and face up to what you fucking are, which is a fucking *lush*. You can't *wait* to get those kids in bed so you can get fucked every night so don't start lecturing *me* about fucking Oxy!'

Juliette jumps up from the sofa, stands inches from him and jabs a perfectly manicured pink fingernail in his chest.

'You're using again. I fucking *knew it*. You fucking *promised*, Micky, you promised when we adopted those poor abandoned kids that you would *stop* with all that shit!'

'Like I said, take a good fucking look in the fucking *mirror*,' he hisses.

He strides towards the sofa, grabs his Rumi and marches out of the room, stopping before the sweeping open staircase. He takes his phone out and barks into it. 'Gary? Get me another dozen cases of Prévost. My fucking *lush* of a wife is *draining all my resources*.'

'Asshole!' shouts Juliette at his retreating figure as he stomps off upstairs in pursuit of his solitary den.

The room is now silent but for the quiet roar of the ocean beyond. A small, blond-haired boy appears at the end of the couch, a fluffy green dragon clutched to his chest.

'Mommy. Me and Dragonbobs want a cuddle.'

'Flea, baby, let's put you and Dragonbobs back to bed, it's sleepy time now.'

Juliette picks up her phone from the glass table in front of the couch, presses the screen and says wearily,

'Adriana...'

4
INTOXICATION

'IT'S LIKE A LOVE AFFAIR. ONLY WITH FUCKING PROSECCO.'

'Well where do you think it came from? This "love affair", as you put it?' asks the therapist, turning a black, shiny ball point pen around in her fingers.

'I think it all started when I was a teenager. At the dinner table with my stepmother. And in the middle of one of our typical rows, i.e. her belittling me and me trying to stand up for myself, she smeared squirty cream all over my face - that vile stuff you get in a tube.'

'I see,' says the therapist, now watching Ella intently.

'She squirted a bit on her finger, looked at it, then reached over the table and pressed her finger in the middle of my forehead. You know, where the third eye's meant to be. And she wiped her finger down my nose and slid it over my lips. Ended up with her finger on my chin and she like, whirled her finger around a bit in the dimple. All greasy, covered in squirty cream. I don't know what was more revolting. Her or the cream.'

'And how did that make you feel?' asks the therapist.

'It was almost as bad as when I got raped. In fact I *felt* like I'd been raped.'

'I support that,' says the therapist, nodding gently.

'It just stays with you. Stuff like that.'

'Was this humiliation a regular occurrence?'

'That was just one of dozens. It makes you feel worthless. And then a few years later you discover sparkling gold Prosecco that takes away all the pain and makes you feel great again. It's a panacea. Self-medication, you know.'

'I support that too. Alcohol consumption is widely regarded as a form of self-medication.'

'As I said, I'm not an alcoholic,' says Ella, lifting both forefingers up in protest.

'I didn't mean to imply you were,' answers the therapist, gently.

'I'm just partial to getting off my tits on Prosecco and falling downstairs, that's all. I don't, like, hide bottles of vodka behind the couch.'

'Do you see your "love affair" with alcohol as a problem?'

'Well, I'm a writer. Who's an alcoholic. Fancy,' says Ella, gazing out of the window at the little mock-Tudor building in the middle of Soho Gardens. 'Only I'm not an alcoholic.'

Ella glances at her watch.

Zack won't be home for at least another three hours. Wine o'clock.

She walks away from the little terrace, glances at the goldfish in the pond, and returns to the house, heads straight for the kitchen and plucks a chilled bottle of Prosecco from the fridge. She slowly unwraps the black foil, untwists the wire cage around the cork and feels a tingling of anticipation in her stomach as the cork pushes up slightly under the pressure from within.

She holds the cork with one hand and with the other, twists the chilled bottle against the cork, which squeaks slightly with the friction. The cork pops from the neck of the bottle with a satisfying thwump, and the cool, fruity aroma hits Ella immediately. Cold gas hisses from the bottle in a tiny little puff of effervescence.

She takes a large wine glass from the shelf, holds it at an angle and carefully pours the Prosecco, lovingly watching as the glass starts to fill with sparkling golden liquid.

Taking the bottle and glass out to the terrace, Ella sits on the stone bench next to the pond, raises the glass and takes a deep slug of wine.

Immediately, the cool drink takes effect and a glowing warmth spreads throughout Ella's body. She closes her eyes and sighs.

This is life. Life is perfect.

She surveys the little terrace, studying the jewel-like flowers of the red geraniums, then follows the mosaic pebbles laid in concentric circles around the pond, where Nin, her cat, is sitting staring at the fish. She can hear the chickens clucking contentedly from beyond the gate to their run. A deep satisfaction with the world envelopes her.

She takes another swig of Prosecco and her thoughts start racing.

I should be making some notes for the next novel. What's the next novel even the fuck about? No fucking idea. God, it's all so thrilling. I'm so happy. Life is perfect.

Life is so perfect that she feels herself drifting away from reality with each fresh gulp of wine until half way through the second glass she's far away from the sunny little terrace, her head brimming with zany ideas, the fleeting peace she felt with the first taste of wine now vanished into a seething chaos of spontaneous, unfocused enthusiasm.

It's fucking eight o'clock already! Zack will be back soon. How did those empty bottles get there?

Ella returns to the house to fetch another bottle of Prosecco and catches sight of herself in the lounge mirror.

I look way older than forty-seven. No mistaking those bags under the eyes. And the skin. Slightly waxy, with an unhealthy pallor. I'm starting to look like a fucking pisshead.

She glances at the two empty bottles in her hand then looks back at her reflection.

Make-up. That's what I need. Drink first though.

Forgetting that she was on her way to the fridge, she lies down on the sofa, guiltily ignoring the open laptop on her desk where she knows she should be working.

Short nap before I open another bottle.

Zack looks over at Ella, lying on her back, her dark wavy hair spread over the white pillow, bottom lip trembling slightly as she gently snores.

She is amazing looking, there's no doubt about it. Especially for her age. And she's a fantastic fuck. But fucking hell she can put it away.

He shakes her shoulder, gently.

Ella's eyes slowly open and she looks up at Zack, dazed and foggy.

'What? What time is it?' she mumbles.

'Seven. I have to get up.'

'You've only just got home.'

'It's seven in the morning Ella.'

'Yeah.'

'You really thought it was still last night?'

'No. Yeah. No. It's the morning. I know,' says Ella, blearily.

'I've godda go. Got a meeting at nine with Benjy.' He kisses her briefly.

She props herself up on one elbow and watches Zack as he gets out of bed and stands up straight, stretching, raising his arms in the air and looking sideways at himself in the full-length mirror attached to the wall. He runs a hand through his thick, brown curly hair and yawns.

He's gorgeous. I wish he wasn't so fucking vain though. Still. Only thirty-seven. Another decade'll knock the vanity out of him. By the time he's fifty that strong youthful promise will have deliquesced into a middle-aged puddle. So do I even care?

'Why the fuck has Benjy arranged a meeting at nine o'clock in the morning?' asks Ella, irritated.

''Cause Benjy's a fucking cunt.'

'Well why is he still in your band, then?'

'Because, as I've told you a zillion times, he's even more of a fucking amazing axeman than I am, and we need him.'

'You should have put your foot down, Zack. Told him later. Nine o'clock is a fucking ridiculous time for a band meeting.'

'He's working at midday. And going round for dinner at his mum's later. So it's gotta be nine.'

'Right. Just that I thought we could have a leisurely morning together,' says Ella, flopping back onto the pillow.

Zack pulls on some jeans and looks over at her, half smiling.

'Surprised you're even awake to be honest.'

'I wasn't. You woke me up.'

'Hangover?'

'No, why?'

'You were pretty wasted last night.'

'I wasn't. I was fine. I was tired.'

'You had three bottles of Prosecco, darlin'. You were out cold.'

Zack leans down and kisses her on the lips.

'Gotta get ready.' Taking a fresh t-shirt from the wardrobe, he puts it on and leaves the room.

Ella sits in her pyjamas, staring at the laptop still sitting open on the table on the other side of the lounge. She knows no writing will be done today. Like yesterday.

Zack wanders into the lounge munching on a piece of toast. He holds it between his lips whilst he pulls on a vintage denim jacket.

'What you gonna do today, then?' he asks casually, as though not really interested.

'I intend to write.'

'Do you intend to carry on being in a foul mood all day?' he says, putting the last remnant of toast into his mouth. 'Coz that's not good for writing, is it?'

'I'm not. I'm just tired.'

'Hungover. Shouldn't drink so much. I keep telling you to take it easy.'

'I don't need to be told what to do. I'm fine. What about you and all the coke you shove up your nose, anyway?'

'That's recreational. Goes with the lifestyle. It's not a fucking problem,' he says, lifting his chin and smiling smugly.

'You're a dick. Go to your meeting.'

After the door slams, Ella breathes a deep sigh of relief.

He's a fucking idiot half the time. Maybe I'd be better off alone.

She brings the laptop over to the sofa.

'I can't write. I feel shit. Today is shit,' she says to the screen.

'What was it my mother said last time we spoke? "Life is short. Do something every day to make yourself happy." I'm going to do something nice. Watch a film I haven't watched for years. A favourite film.'

Ella glances out through the French windows at the garden. Nothing moves but a slow flick of orange in the pond.

Withnail and I. I remember seeing it as a teenager. I'll watch that.

Here we go, found it. The fag end of the sixties. Just before I was born, the summer of love fucked to oblivion.

She finds the film online and starts watching it, totally engrossed.

I'd forgotten what an oleaginous leech Uncle Monty is. And Marwood, so innocent and terrified. The gentleness beneath the humour. And Withnail. Oh God, the heart-breaking pathos. Withnail in the pouring rain reciting fucking Hamlet to the wolves. Fuck me it's tragicomedy at its very best, I'd forgotten how fucking brilliant it is.

I've got to find out more. Written and directed by Bruce Robinson. Google him. YouTube. The Ruby Wax Show, TV show back in the nineties. Bunch of artistas getting wankered at Ruby's dinner party.

That's him.

Bruce.

Oh my God.

He's amazing.

Totally arseholed.

And utterly fascinating.

I love him.

Women's breasts exploding on airplanes. Is that even politically correct? Probably not. Being sexually assaulted by film director Franco Zeffirelli. Fuck. I'd heard Zeffirelli was a total perv. So that's where Uncle Monty comes from. Withnail and I is partly real. Well of course it is. Like so much fiction.

He's written an autobiographical novel. The Peculiar Memories of Thomas Penman. A stepfather torturing a young boy called Thomas. Bruce, of course. Protest crapping all over his parents' house. All that parental abuse. Just like my life. I need to know more.

Fuck. It's five in the afternoon and it's sunny outside.

'Where did the afternoon go? Wine o'clock.'

5
SUNDAY LUNCH

JAMES ROBINSON LETS OUT A HUGE SIGH AS HE LOOKS around his studio. His synths and guitars are stacked out of harm's way in a corner, covered in dust sheets, whilst the rest of the room has exploded into sawdust. The wall mounts for the speakers are skeletal timber frames and the half-assembled oak floor reveals perilous drops to the cellar below.

He knows that he couldn't get this done in London. If it means still living at home in the middle of fucking nowhere in the Yorkshire Dales, then it's a small sacrifice for having his own space to make music. And Leeds and the rest of the band are only a couple of hours away.

His dark, curly hair flops over his face as he looks out of the tiny window of the barn, across the field towards the house.

He picks up his phone and voicenotes his friend.

'Tom, I know I said I was gonna help you today, but Mum's organised some family meal. I can't get out of it, my sister's coming. We'll carry on tomorrow, yeah?'

He puts the phone down and peers out of the window once more, just as his sister's white van draws up in the courtyard. He leaves his studio and, hands in pockets, walks along the track across the field, towards the house.

A slim young woman kneels on the front seat and leans into the back, rummaging around.

James stops by the van.

'Hazel?'

Hazel scrabbles back over the seat and emerges from the van.

'Hi, James. I thought they'd like this.' She holds up a bottle.

'What is it?'

'Elderflower champagne.'

'Dad won't drink that.'

'Well Mum and I will. What have you been up to?'

'Building the studio. And gigging. It's all on my Instagram. You never look at my stuff,' he says accusingly.

'You know how busy I am.'

'Rescuing foxes,' he mocks, eyes rolling.

Hazels shoots a glare at James as they walk towards the house.

'They need me.'

'The foxes…'

'Correct.'

Hazel stops to pet the chickens milling around, who instinctively flatten their backs as she bends towards them, then follows James across the little bridge leading to the main house.

'Every time I cross this bridge, I feel like I'm home. It's not like any other bridge.'

Lara appears at the front door, grinning and opening her arms wide to embrace Hazel.

'*Darling!* I heard your van.'

Hazel proffers the bottle.

'I brought this. It's alcohol free.'

'Oh, thank you,' says Lara, brightly. 'How thoughtful of you, darling.'

'Well *I* want a beer,' mumbles James, squeezing past them and into the house.

Bruce sits at a long wooden table by the window of the large farmhouse kitchen, a lamp suspended from the oak beams above casting a warm glow in the thin November light. He's poring through *The Observer*, flicking the pages with an ever increasing frown.

As James walks in Bruce looks up over his reading glasses.

'How's it going, Sprout?'

'I was gonna help Tom today. Doesn't matter. I just want to get it done.'

'Building sites settle into their own semi-permanence and never seem to progress. That's their nature,' muses Bruce, gazing out of the window across the courtyard and towards the fields.

'Any beer in the fridge?'

'Help yourself, Mum got you some of that craft beer you love so much.'

'Cool. Hazel's brought some elderflower zero alcohol shit.'

Bruce looks up, smiling affably.

'Lovely.'

James cracks open a can of Salty Kiss, returns to the table and slowly pours the beer into an elegant stemmed glass.

Bruce looks at the pouring procedure with mirth.

'I still can't get my head around anyone drinking beer out of a stemmed glass like it's fucking wine. Next thing you'll be wearing nerdy NHS specs and growing a big bushy beard. Fucking St Ives was full of them.'

'They're called hipsters, Dad.'

'They're called wankers.'

'Here, have a taste. You tell me whether it should be drunk from a stemmed glass like wine or from a big pint tankard like old man's beer.'

Bruce takes the glass, sips some beer, rolls it around his mouth and looks at the ceiling, thoughtfully before smiling back at James.

'It's very you. But I'll stick to the vino, ta.'

Hazel walks into the kitchen and smiles at her father, who stands, grins and gives her a huge bear hug.

'*Pickle.* It's been too long. Harrogate's only up the fucking road.'

'I was here at the end of summer, Dad. Only a couple of months ago,' protests Hazel, shrugging off her jacket and throwing it over the back of a wooden chair.

'What's been happening in fox world?'

Hazel sits down and looks at her father, levelly.

'You haven't seen today's papers, then?'

James grins, silently.

Bruce gestures towards his copy of *The Observer.*

'I'm reading them.'

'I mean the gutter press.'

'Well, obviously not. I don't read that shit. Why?'

Hazel smiles, then reaches over and takes an apricot from the fruit bowl in the middle of the table.

'Wait till Mum's here. It's kind of terrible, but kind of hilarious too.'

Lara walks in, notices Hazel's jacket, picks it up and walks out of the kitchen with it before returning without it. She walks over to the Aga, puts on a scorched old oven glove to open the hot oven, inspects the lasagne she's baking then shuts the oven and walks over to the table, taking her place at the far end, opposite Bruce.

Hazel picks up her phone and glances up at her mother.

'I tried to ring you this morning, Mum, but it went to voice mail.'

'Sorry, darling, I was out exercising the girls.'

'You care more about those horses than you care about us,' says James, who grins and takes a long swig of beer.

'Well I didn't want to text you, I wanted to tell you in person…' begins Hazel.

'Dad's in *The Sunday Gazette*,' blurts out James, cracking out laughing.

Bruce looks up from his *Observer*, eyebrows raised.

'Don't tell me. St Ives Arts Festival.'

'In one,' says Hazel.

Lara blinks very slowly, then takes a deep breath and exhales in a long, slow, sigh. She reaches for the bottle of Château de Camensac sitting next to the fruit bowl and pours herself a glass.

'Go on, Hazel.'

'Shall I read it out? Or do you want to read it?'

'Just read me the headline. I won't need to read the rest. It's all the product of some junior hack's fevered imagination, anyway,' sighs Lara, resignedly.

'Well this sounds like fun,' smiles Bruce, draining his glass of red and immediately pouring another one. '*I* want to read it.'

'You don't have a smartphone, dad. That's why you haven't already seen it. It's all over Facebook.'

'Well I'm not really interested in Facebook. What does the headline say then?'

'Shall I do the honours, James, or do you want to?' asks Hazel.

'Feel free,' says James.

Hazel takes a deep breath, looks down at her phone, looks back up at the three faces all staring intently at her then reads aloud:

'"Drunken Foul-mouthed Luvvie, Film Director Bruce Robinson Calls Festival Audience a Bunch of UKIP Cunts."'

James splutters on his beer, bursts out laughing and bangs the table with his fist.

'Dad! *Legend!*'

Hazel glances at him disapprovingly.

The colour drains from Lara's face.

'Please tell me you're joking, Hazel.'

'Erm, no,' says Hazel, handing her mother the phone.

Lara glances over at Bruce, who is still grinning broadly.

She looks away from him and worriedly scrolls through the article, before handing the phone to Bruce.

'I didn't know the West Country had overwhelmingly voted to leave the EU,' she muses, glancing at Bruce.

'Well, that's pretty much as you described it to me when you rang from the hotel the next morning. *Except* for the part about calling the audience "a bunch of UKIP cunts",' says Lara, her mouth tensing as though she's unsure whether to laugh or cry.

'I told you what I'd said as soon as someone told *me* what I'd said,' protests Bruce, indignantly. 'And I apologised to the audience the following day. What do they want? Blood? I got pissed and sounded off a bit. Hardly the crime of the century, is it? Anyway, let me read this crap.'

Bruce adjusts his spectacles and slowly reads the piece, a benign smile plastered on his face all the way through.

'Well. There you go. We are where we are. No-one reads this shit anyway. It's not The Guardian or The Washington Post, is it? Therefore it's irrelevant. It's utter *bollocks*.'

'I'm with you, Dad,' says James, smiling. 'They *are* all a bunch of UKIP cunts down there anyway. They're all buying up property for second homes. And Cornwall has the highest suicide rate in the UK because out of season it's fucking dead down there. All these houses standing empty owned by a bunch of right-wing cunts from Bayswater.'

'You really are your father's son,' sighs Hazel. 'I've got to say, Dad, that I don't think it reflects very well on you.'

'Well, it's not the *best* press he's ever had. But as your dad says, we are where we are and it's not the end of the world,' coos Lara, soothingly.

'Er, you haven't seen the comments, yet, Mum,' replies Hazel.

Lara's face falls. 'Oh God. Are they bad?'

James picks up his own phone, finds the article and scrolls down to the comments.

'I'll give you some edited highlights. There's 947 comments.'

'Fuck me I'm popular,' quips Bruce, smiling.

'Here we go. "A drunkard with a mullet, whom I've never heard of."'

Bruce's eyes light up as he bursts out laughing.

'Brilliant!'

'Apparently, you're a "Fucking four-eyed fannyhole". Another one, "Button it doughball. Nobody gives a toss about the rantings of a drunk". And this one, er…hold on…oh yeah here it is, "A has been alcoholic living on the streets" followed by "Who does this special snowflake think he is living in his gilded luvvie castle looking down on us plebs?"'

'Well which am I? In the gutter, or living in a "gilded luvvie castle?" I can't be both. What a bunch of wankers, honestly.'

'Wait! And this one, "I have never heard of the films he claims to have directed",' continues James.

'I didn't direct *The Rum Diary*, then…'

'Nope. Just a figment of your imagination.'

'Can we stop reading this crap, please? Seriously, these people are not worth wasting your energy on,' interjects Hazel, looking exasperated.

'It's hilarious!' replies James. 'And Dad needs to know what these arseholes are saying.'

'Dad doesn't need to know, James,' says Lara. '*I* don't need to know, either.'

'Yes, Mum, he does.'

'I'm quite enjoying this,' says Bruce, the grin never leaving his face. 'More entertaining than the crap they write about me on the bloody Ripper forums.'

'Here's one that's sort of supportive, Dad. "I remember *Withnail and I* from my university days. I've never laughed so hard at any film in my life, before or since. Terrible language, mind you, but brilliant writing. And now he's written a riveting book about Jack the Ripper!"'

'Brilliant writing. There you go. All is forgiven,' says Bruce.

'"I named my son after him, he is a shining star of an example of a decent human being. After reading this I will light another candle and pray for him at my shrine",' quotes James, triumphantly.

'And, "The drunken man says what the sober man only thinks."'

Bruce raises his wine glass, looking from Lara to Hazel and James and gives a broad grin, his eyes alight with mirth. 'I'll drink to that.'

Lara's eyes flash at Bruce before she gets up from the table, goes over to the Aga and takes out the lasagne.

Hazel shakes her head. 'I can't believe there are so many nasty people in the world. Well, I can. I see the way they treat foxes. But once they get behind the anonymity of a keyboard, human beings can be vile.'

Lara removes four hot bowls from the Aga and places them on the table, then returns to fetch the lasagne, placing it on a large serving mat in the centre.

'It's cruelty-free, darling,' she says to Hazel. I've used the vegan cheese you like for the sauce,'

'Thanks, Mum.'

'Mmmm, smells delicious, darling,' says Bruce.

'Yum, Mum, in my tum,' says James, grinning.

Lara smiles. 'You've been saying that since you were three years old, Sprout,' she says fondly.

'I know. You always tell me. That's why I say it. I know you love it.'

Lara ruffles his mop of unruly dark hair with her hand before she sits down, and he smiles up at her.

'Help yourselves, everyone.'

After silently stacking the last of the crockery in the dishwasher, Lara positions herself at the table, opposite Bruce.

'Is James upstairs in his room?'

'No idea,' murmurs Bruce, having returned, after a three hour lunch and with Hazel now departed back to Harrogate, to reading *The Observer.*

Lara stands and walks over to the door leading out to the hall, closing it gently, then sits down again, staring intently at Bruce.

'What the fuck, Bruce? I mean, what the actual fuck? *Why?*'

Bruce looks up at her and grins, then shakes his head.

'I don't know. It was a shit audience. Arrogant arseholes with stone-faced silicone-injected women banging on about their philanthropy and how many fucking yachts they owned. It made me want to puke. Or drink. Or leave. So I carried on drinking and ended up wankered. And told the fuckers what I thought of them.'

'But why does the whole world have to know? It's in the fucking *Sunday Gazette*, Bruce. I don't want the whole world thinking you're some drunkard who can't keep his shit together. It's *humiliating.* It's embarrassing for me, *and* the children.'

'James thinks it's funny.'

'Well Hazel and I don't.'

'Look, I'm sorry. I can't remember any of it.'

Bruce stares at the grain in the oak table and then looks up at Lara.

'Sorry. You know I don't want to hurt you.'

She shakes her head.

'We've been through this so many times over the years, Bruce. I leave you to get on with your writing, I don't disturb you, I don't hassle you about drinking...'

'I couldn't ask for a more reasonable wife. You're right. Most women wouldn't put up with me...'

'It's just...so *public.* I've got five missed calls on my phone from various people. Including that,' Lara shakes her head, frowning. 'That *cow* from the board of governors, no doubt ringing just to *gloat.* It brings out the worst in people, this kind of thing. It's not just about you. Or us. I just don't like this whole *public* aspect of it. I really don't.'

Bruce reaches over the table and takes Lara's hand in his. 'I'm sorry. It won't happen again.'

'How many times have I heard that?' Lara says, wearily, looking at Bruce with exasperated love.

'By the way, I meant to tell you. Wayne Montana's been in touch. He wants to produce a movie of *Jack,*' says Bruce.

'Wayne Montana? You hate him, don't you?'

'He's a total cunt, yeah.'

'So what are you going to do?'

'Nothing. It doesn't feel right. I'm in a good place with the writing, I don't want to go off in another direction. Fuck him.'

Lara stands up from the table and murmurs to herself '"Fucking four-eyed fannyhole". It just beggars belief, Bruce. The whole thing, it really does…'

6
INNER CRITIC

JULIETTE WAKES WITH A START. THE ROOM IS STILL DARK. She picks up her phone. 1.30am. Four hours sleep.

You haven't had enough sleep. You need at least five hours when you're shooting a movie. It's gonna show.

'I've got to swim. I've got to get my head straight.' Julia says out loud, flicking on the phone camera and examining her face.

There isn't time. You need more sleep.

'I am off book - I know all today's lines. I need to swim.'

A photo of Juliette and Micky holding Flea, Moon and Cypher sits on the bedside table, silently taunting her. Her family. Her children. None of whom are with her, but on the other side of the world, in Croatia, with Micky and their new nanny, Frances.

Juliette walks into her dressing room, selects a swimsuit and puts it on, ties her hair back and pulls a white swimming cap decorated with rubber flowers over her head to protect her hair. She looks at herself in the mirror.

Fat.

Juliette walks downstairs, under the vaulted, beamed ceilings, past the white stucco walls decorated with huge, framed close-ups of flowers, down the broad wooden staircase and into the kitchen with its tall, arched windows overlooking the terraced gardens, haunted all the way by a thinner vision of herself.

The fridge is as wide as the bedroom she grew up in. She removes a quart jug of gazpacho juice, freshly made the night before, and pours herself a large glass which she quickly drinks.

Seventh day of shooting, seventh day without alcohol and on a mostly juice-based diet.

You'll faint if all you have is juice. You need one of the kids' donuts. Or six. There they are, at the back of the fridge, dripping with sweet frosting.

Shutup. Juice is not fattening. Plus it's refreshing. Nutritious. Cleansing.

She opens the French windows to the garden beyond. The swimming pool is floodlit in a wash of gold. Recessed spotlights illuminate the palm trees surrounding the pool and the gardens beyond. The night sky is a deep, inky blue.

Juliette places her phone on one of the family of sun loungers sitting alongside the pool, puts on her yellow reflective swimming goggles and walks down the pool steps and into the cool water.

She reaches out with her arms, sinks below the surface and swims a few strokes underwater, undulating her body, then surfaces, breathes and gets into a rhythm as she swims up and down the pool.

You are nothing. You are fat.

Juliette's breathing is deep and regular now, her face bobbing in and out of the water as her arms and legs work together in unison.

The doom-laden voice slides out of her mind along with all the other mental detritus.

My mind unfurls and stretches into every crevice of the universe. I am calm. I am free. I am zen.

Juliette pushes against the water, breathing out a stream of bubbles then taking a deep breath of night air each time she surfaces.

I worked hard for this. I believed in myself. I belong here. This is my life. No-one can take this away from me. I am not a terrible person.

Juliette inwardly repeats the mantra as she glides through the cool water, completely alone and totally calm, her breathing deep and regular.

I am complete. I am purified. I am in the present moment.

At the end of the pool, Juliette performs a flip turn almost triumphantly, then dolphin kicks underwater before surfacing again, her mind trained and focused.

There are women out there far less qualified than me, doing what I should be doing, because they believed in themselves more than I do. Take Freya Stephens, for example. Freya Stephens is not more beautiful than me. She may be slightly thinner. But her breasts are way smaller. And all men love big breasts.

Breathe, arm reach, push away, kick, smooth glide, cool water.

And she's had way more work done than me too. Her face is plastic and immobile.

Splash, calm, glide.

She is an icon of wax to her God of surgery.

Breathe.

She could melt under the lights.

Glide, turn, breathe.

Juliette stops swimming, stands in the water, pulls her goggles away from her face and dips them in the water to rinse the mist from them then resumes.

Breathe, glide, push, breathe.

I hate her.

She rises from the water and stands stock still in the middle of the pool, the early morning breeze rustling the palm trees, the occasional bird twittering from hidden shrubbery.

She stares at the beautiful, illuminated garden around her.

'If she lays one finger on him, I'll fucking kill her,' says Juliette out loud.

She wades to the pool steps and exits the pool, frowning. She removes her cap and goggles, unties her hair and towels it dry before picking up her phone. 2am. On schedule.

In the kitchen, Adriana is up, dressed and making coffee.

'Nice swim, boss?'

'I am zen. And focused. And prepared, thank you.'

'Half an hour before Brandon gets here.'

'Have you checked Micky's Twitter yet?'

'I have. Nada,' announces Adriana, popping a slice of bread into the toaster.

'I don't trust him. Correction. I trust him. It's *her* I don't trust. He's such a pussy around beautiful women.'

'Freya's had so much shit written about her, she wouldn't dare to rock the boat by trying anything around Micky.'

'I have to clear this crap out of my head. It's bad for me. I'm not gonna think about him again until I Facetime him this afternoon.'

'It's gonna be fine.'

As the car sails from Los Feliz down a mercifully quiet freeway towards the studio, Juliette quickly does a Twitter search for #juliettejanesson, then, disgusted with herself, shuts down Twitter, puts her headphones in and plays her favourite pre-work music, *Bajo el Sol Jaguar* by Jorge Reyes. It sends her into a peaceful trance, focused and prepared for war.

Adriana fields all the previous night's messages, then peers out of the window at the people in cars whizzing past. Blurry snapshots of everyone else's lives, doing something, going somewhere in a tiny sliver of time that has melted away as soon as it's appeared.

Juliette lets out a loud snore and her head drops. She jerks awake and opens her eyes, staring ahead, then glances slyly at Adriana, who pretends not to notice.

By the time they get to the lot and Juliette's trailer it's bang on 3am. Three hours till sunrise. Almost certainly another eighteen hour day, interrupted at some point with a video call to Frances and the kids but also, most importantly, fourteen hours until she's due to Facetime Micky.

In make-up, Juliette stares at herself in the mirror as she becomes incrementally more beautiful with every applied product.

On set, she nails every take. She is polite as always to the crew and the rest of the cast.

But she is separate from all of them. Inside, her stomach is so tense it's almost painful.

By 4pm she is very, very tired. She understands why others feel the need to pop various meds to keep them alert during the day and knock them out at night, but after seeing the way Micky's Oxy habit has come to grip him, she is avoiding that path.

At 4.10pm, lying on the couch in her trailer, aimlessly scrolling through Google results of her name, she sees it.

'10 Hollywood A-Listers No-One Wants to Work With. #8. Juliette Janesson.'

She sits bolt upright. Published that morning on the gossip site *Bing Bong.*

'Another actor no-one in their right mind wants to work with is temperamental time-bomb Juliette Janesson. Notorious for her no holds barred screaming fits at crew and co-stars, the fiery redhead takes no prisoners. "She reduced me to tears on set with her constant demands and criticism" we were told exclusively by a runner who wishes to remain anonymous. Known for demanding multiple vases of fresh white lilies in every room of her trailer, the actor also refuses to eat with the rest of the cast and crew, choosing to grab a meal to go at lunch and eat alone in her trailer.'

'Bull-*shit*!' yells Juliette to no-one in particular. Adriana, sitting outside the trailer on a fold-up chair, knocks at the door.

'You OK boss?'

'Hell no! Have you seen this?'

Juliette thrusts her phone at Adriana, who reads quickly through the article. She hands the phone back to Juliette and gestures at three large vases of lilies.

'Yeah it's like a regular botanical gardens in here. What a bunch of *horseshit*.'

'I'll fucking *sue* them!' shouts Juliette, jumping up from the couch and pacing up and down, angrily. '*Assholes!*'

'It's pathetic. I've never known you shout at anyone on set.'

'I never shout at anyone, *ever!*' screams Juliette. 'I don't shout, *period!* It's not in my *nature!*'

'It's not something I witness on a regular basis, it's true,' coos Adriana. 'Or…even an…*occasional* basis. The people who write this shit are just massive jerkoffs.'

'They can suck their own balls. Assholes!' screams Juliette.

'I'll ring Robert and get him to fire off a legal threat to Bing Bong Bill.'

'Nobody takes that douche seriously, he is a *parasitic leper!*'

'You're right boss. He is. A total sleaze-ball,' says Adriana, nodding her head, thoughtfully.

'He's a piece of *shit!*' answers Juliette, catching sight of herself in the mirror then turning to Adriana and whining pitifully, 'I'm a horrible person. Look what they're doing to me! Turning me into a horrible person who's fucking angry all the time! Assholes!'

Adriana lowers her eyes and leaves the trailer, her phone already to her ear.

Freya Stephens, almost six feet of supreme intellect, drive and physical beauty, reclines languidly on a couch surrounded by a sea of hastily discarded clothes, her head in Micky Valance's lap, sipping champagne from a paper Starbucks cup and stretching her toes in post-coital satisfaction. She sighs, deeply.

'This is easily the most fun shoot I have ever done.'

Micky idly strokes her hair whilst scrolling through his phone.

'You know why?' she tilts her head up at him, coquettishly and smiles.

'Mmm?' grunts Micky, continuing to scroll.

'Because of *you*. Because I just *love* being with you. On set and off. The whole thing. It's just...time wisely spent. I feel fulfilled. Mentally, physically, spiritually. You fulfil me.'

Micky raises his eyebrows slightly and smiles, vacantly.

'What time is it?'

'I have no clue. And I could care less. We're done for today, and I am having fun. Who cares what time it is or what the rest of the world is doing? The world can go fuck itself!' she adds, expressively, before draining her glass and pouring another one.

'It's just that I have to...erm...I have an...appointment right now.'

'Who with?'

Micky sighs heavily. 'Juliette. In LA.'

'*Really?* Can I talk to her too?' asks Freya, sitting up and draping herself over Micky's naked body.

'You are kidding me. Yeah, she's gonna love that. C'mon honey, I've gotta get dressed.'

'Oh, poo. I don't want anything to drown my sparkles.'

'Well...' says Micky, gently pushing Freya away, 'Needs must.' He stands and stretches before scratching his balls.

His phone rings with the familiar Facetime alert.

'Fuck. She's early. Freya, sweetheart, you're gonna have to split, babe. If she finds out you're here, we're busted.'

Freya gathers her clothes from the floor and reluctantly starts getting dressed again.

The phone continues to ring. Micky ignores it and frantically pulls on his sweatpants and t-shirt, examines himself briefly in the mirror, unruffles his hair and replaces the black spectacles he's been wearing in his role of Detective Shrader. He stares at Freya, questioningly. She picks up a script and waves it in front of his face. The phone goes silent.

'We've been going over tomorrow's lines together, OK? C'mon, Micky. I wanna say hi to her, it's no biggie.'

Micky's phone rings again and he answers it. Juliette's face looms in close up, her face masked in a frown, before she realises the call has connected and she pulls back, poses and pouts as she examines her image on the screen.

'Hi, I just rang you and there was no answer,' she says, accusingly.

'I know, I heard it. The cell was on charge in the other room, I didn't get to it in time.'

Freya leans in over Micky's shoulder and giggles at Juliette.

'Hiya, Juliette! That was my fault, sorry. I nabbed your husband. I asked him to go over our lines for tomorrow. I forgot my lines so many times today, it was embarrassing. I bet that never happens to you.'

Juliette's face stares placidly from the screen with no outward sign of emotion.

'It's great to kind of meet you at last! I'm a huge fan of your work you know!' gushes Freya.

'Thankyewww' coos Juliette with a frozen, cold-eyed smile.

'So…I think we're done here, anyway, huh Micky? I'll leave you two love birds to it!' trills Freya. 'Bye for now. I can't wait to meet you in the flesh. So to speak!'

Juliette's face with its icy smile remains frozen in hidden torment.

'Likewise.'

'See ya Freya!' yells Micky, cheerfully, waving at Freya as she leaves the trailer, before turning back to the screen.

Juliette flashes a look of pure hatred.

'What. Is going on?' she demands.

'Whaddaya mean? Nothing's going on! I've been helping her out! She's a airhead, you know that, everyone knows it.'

'Yeah, she's such a airhead she majored in law from fucking Harvard. Has she been coming onto you Micky? Because if she has, I wanna know about it. I tell you everything that happens on the lot when I'm working and you promised you'd tell me too.

'Well you wouldn't believe she majored in law from Harvard or anywhere else for that matter. She's a bubblehead pain in the ass is what she is. You just witnessed it. "I forgot my lines *so* many times today"' he mimics in a high, whiny voice. 'And I have to work with her every day for another three fucking weeks! Gimme a fuckin' break!'

'So you don't think she's hot?'

'No, I do *not* think she's *hot*. Why would I want *that* when I have *you?*'

'Because I'm not there and she's *convenient*.'

'Yeah, she's *conveniently* very fucking *irritating*.'

'Anyway. How are the kids? You spoken to them today?'

'No. Have you?'

'No. I haven't had a chance. It's been crazy over here. I miss my babies.'

'I know, honey. I do too. And I miss you.'

'You get to see them every day, I don't.'

'You'll see them next week in Malawi, for a whole three days. It'll be magical.'

'I'm over there for work, Micky. This ambassador gig's going to be a monumental ball-breaker.'

'You'll have Frances and Adriana. I wish I were going.'

'I know you do, honey.'

'Anyway, babes, check *this* out. Wayne Montana's been in touch. He wants me for this crazy project, a movie about Jack the Ripper. I'd play Jack. Naturally.'

Juliette feels an icy chill all over her skin.

'The *Pork Chop*'s been in touch? That *predator?* He's a fucking *asshole*.'

'Yeah. But…Jack the Ripper!'

'Someone even worse than him. Hard to find. Who else is on board?'

'I dunno yet, The Pork's keeping schtum about everything to do with it. All I know is it's based on a bio Bruce Robinson's just written about the Ripper.'

'Who?'

'Bruce Robinson. *Withnail and I*.'

'*The Rum Diary* Bruce Robinson?'

'The very same.'

Juliette shrugs.

'Go for it. You can do dark.'

'Yeah. I'm excited.'

'I've gotta go.' says Juliette, wearily. 'Julian's throwing a little wrap party at the Brasserie.'

'OK babes. Call me when you get home, OK?'

'Sure,' says Juliette, blowing Micky a sullen, unenthusiastic kiss.

In the golf cart on the way to La Brasserie, a fluffy *Folies Bergère* affair behind Stage 32, Juliette adjusts her Versace evening gown, fidgeting with the straps.

'Call Brandon would you Adriana? Tell him I want three bottles of Cristal in the cooler for the ride home. It's gonna be 90 minutes of traffic hell.'

'Sure.'

They ride in silence for a couple of minutes, bouncing along the studio's Main Street before swinging round to the back of the lot.

'He's fucking her,' says Juliette.

'What makes you say that?'

Juliette cranes her head and sprays her neck and wrists with Chanel no 9.

'I just know it. "I forgot all my lines. It was embarrassing. I bet that never happens to you, Juliette". Kissing my ass. Calling us "love birds". Patronising, sanctimonious bitch! I need a fucking drink.'

Adriana steers the cart round a final corner and stops outside La Brasserie, where various members of the cast and crew are milling around, chatting.

'Don't worry about it now, boss. C'mon, this is your chance to break loose and have some fun!'

Juliette casts a withering look in Adriana's direction. 'At a *wrap party*. Sure. All those runners who've been secretly lusting after you for weeks on end downing enough booze to summon up the courage to actually approach you and start dribbling down your cleavage. I sure am gonna break loose on *this one*.'

Adriana smiles indulgently at Juliette as they climb out of the golf cart together.

Juliette lifts her chin, smiles radiantly and sashays towards the gathered crowd at the entrance, her white, voile, lace-trimmed dress flouncing and glittering with every step as it catches the California sun.

'Here she is!'

'We wondered where you were!'

'You look divine!'

'Thankyewww!'

'Radiant!'

'Thankyewww!'

'Oh *Juliette's* here!'

'Hiiiiii!'

Adriana steers Juliette into the restaurant where a small group of people by the bar all turn their heads towards her.

Rupert Penrose, the first assistant director, spots Juliette, walks over and gives her a warm hug. A crisply uniformed server passes by, bearing a silver tray laden with glasses.

Rupert swipes a flute of champagne, passing it to Juliette. 'You've been fabulous, darling, it's been *such* a pleasure working with you,' he oozes in the plummiest Oxford English.

'Thankyewww. You too, Rupes, I've had a blast,' coos Juliette, then notices the glass. 'Oh, no champagne thanks. I'm off alcohol!' she declares loudly.

'You sure? Don't you think you deserve a wee drink? You've worked *so* hard.'

'I'm good, thankyewww.'

Juliette plucks a glass of iced mineral water from another server's tray then elegantly swishes around the room, stopping to talk to various cast and crew members.

She sips at her water, laughing along with people, smiling her practised smile and exuding glamour.

Then she sees him.

Montana.

The first thing she notices are his lopsided eyes, scrunched into their default routine malevolence, boring into her from across the room.

What the fuck is The Pork Chop doing here? He's had nothing to do with this movie.

The huge bulk of lard strides purposefully towards her, clearing everyone from his path with his aura, insidious surface charm and sheer girth.

Her guts feel as though they're about to vacate her body taking everything in their path with them.

I remember. That first time alone with him. Me asking about the script. Him unzipping his pants. Exposing himself to me. That was meant to be a private script reading, Wayne. I was young. Naive. Unknown. Powerless.

She can't get the image of that penis out of her mind. Small. Egg-shaped. Distorted. And the bloated belly looming above it. The puffy red face. Terrifying. Managing to avoid him in private ever since. Deliberately refusing to thank him in her Oscar speech. *Bing Bong* dining out on it ever since. Scenes from that night forever seared on her memory. Photos of the night forever embedded in the fabric of the internet. Juliette, poised in her shiny spangled gold evening dress, him with his clammy fat hand gripping the exposed flesh of her arm. His ogreish face grinning along with her at the cameras, his masking his grubby secrets and hers masking her hidden pain and loathing for him.

I wanna leave, now.

'Hey. Long time no see, Juliette.'

'Yeah. Long time.'

Not fucking long enough, ya fat fuck.

'You're looking radiant, as always. Has Micky told you I want him for this Ripper movie?'

'Yeah.'

'So you're gonna encourage him and no other movie is going to get in the way of Micky taking this part, right? He's keen as fuck... so *you're* keen as fuck, too. *Right?*'

'We'll decide between us, Wayne. As we do with everything. Now we're a married couple,' she adds, smiling in as nonthreatening a manner as she can.

His eyes harden even further. Stepping close, he slides his hand round her waist and grips her ass so hard that it hurts. He moves his face in towards hers and hisses into her ear 'Don't forget who gave you your first break, you little bitch. There are stories going round about your pussy-on-pussy fun driving your poor husband right into his co-star's wet little cunt. Want that in the press?'

Juliette pulls away from his grip, picking up a whiff of expensive aftershave.

I remember that smell. That's how the rape smelt.

She looks desperately around the room before catching Adriana's eye and gesturing with her eyes towards the door.

'I have an appointment. I have to go,' she says quietly.

She turns away from Montana's sweating bulk and floats across the crowded room as though nothing were amiss, hooking up with Adriana near the door.

'What's up?' asks Adriana as they emerge outside.

'*The Pork Chop* is up. Didn't you see him?'

'No...'

'I'll tell you later...'

Juliette and Adriana stand in the shade of the canopy awaiting Brandon's arrival.

'Thankyewww!''Oh thankyewww!''Thankyewww!' simpers Juliette to various well-wishers.

You need a drink. No wonder you feel disgusted. You should be ashamed of yourself. You should have grabbed him by his balls, twisted them until he squealed, then hissed at him that you'd like to hack them off and stuff them down his gullet until they choke him to death. You had your chance and you blew it, loser. You're pathetic, spineless and weak. And he knows it.

At last, Brandon pulls up in the studio SUV. He opens the back door for Juliette who gratefully slides in, followed by Adriana.

As Brandon swings the door shut behind her, Juliette reaches for the cooler and grabs a bottle of Cristal and two glasses, offering one to Adriana.

'I'm good, boss,' she says, holding up her hand.

'Whatever. I need a drink,' replies Juliette, wearily.

'What did he say to you?'

'Called me a bitch. Reminded me how I got to where I am. Threatened that if I don't persuade Micky to do this Ripper movie he'll tell his buddies in the press that I'm a fucking *lesbian!* And basically told me Micky's fucking Freya Stephens. And for once, didn't flash his revolting little dick at me.'

'Asshole.'

'*Total* asshole. I loathe every fibre of his being.'

'Don't we all.'

Juliette pours herself a glass of the cold champagne and quickly gulps the contents down before pouring herself another. As the SUV joins the solid block of traffic choking the freeway, she smiles to herself.

Fuck the traffic. Fuck the Pork Chop. Fuck LA. Who gives a fuck?

She picks up her phone and tries Micky's number. No answer.

'You don't think Micky's fucking Freya, then?' she asks Adriana.

'I dunno, Juliette. If he is, he's freaking *nuts*. You're one in a million. He'd be crazy to lose you.'

'That is *exactly* what I think,' agrees Juliette, draining the second glass. 'Crazy.'

Sensing that Adriana is maybe tiring of hearing about her problems with men, Juliette messages Susan Sarandon, her friend and confidante of several years since appearing together in *Red and Yellow Tulips*, the Golden Globe winning TV series about the Dutch underground resistance set during World War II.

I think Micky is up to something with Freya Stephens. And I had a run in with The Pork Chop. Really need to talk...

Four minutes later, the phone bleeps and Susan replies:

I'm with the kids right now can I call you later?

Juliette doesn't bother to reply.

The journey back to Los Feliz takes two bottles of Cristal and 93 minutes.

Adriana steels herself as Brandon pulls through the security gates and up to the house.

'Home!' yells Juliette, joyously throwing her arms apart and blearily gazing out of the window.

She yanks open her door, tumbles out of the car and weaves unsteadily towards the house.

'D'ya wanna come in, Brandon?' asks Adriana, pleading with her eyes.

Brandon looks dubious but smiles and shrugs.

'Sure.'

'I could just maybe do with some help, here. She's not in a good way. Generally. She's...under a lot of pressure.'

'It figures. No problem, Adriana. Let's do it.' He grins at her in the rearview mirror and she smiles back, eyes filled with gratitude.

Adriana jogs up to Juliette and catches her arm to stop her swaying.

'Let's get you inside, boss, yeah?' she says, gently.

'I am *fine!*' shouts Juliette, shaking her arm away and staggering towards the entrance. She holds onto the white trellis portico as Adriana opens the front door.

Inside the house, Adriana dumps the bags and end-of-shoot presents on the hallway couch.

'Are you sure you're cool for a while?' she says to Brandon.

'Yeah. I've got a gig down on the Strip at midnight. But, until then...' He raises his eyebrows.

'Oh, you're playing? In your band?'

'Yeah.'

Adriana looks up and Juliette has disappeared.

'Holy shit! Where the fuck *is* she?'

'She went through that door...'

Adriana runs towards the kitchen and through into the gardens, followed by Brandon.

Juliette, still resplendent in her shimmering, floaty white dress, is swaying drunkenly towards the pool. 'Wayne Montana is a fat ugly *asshole* and I am going *swimming!*' she shouts, as she walks straight off the side of the pool and disappears into the blue water.

7
Ripperology

TEN AM. ONE BOTTLE OF RED DOWN, BRUCE PACES UP and down the worn red carpet of the barn floor, gesticulating passionately as he delivers the lines from his screenplay-in-progress, *The Block.*

'Just hand it to me, fucker,' he growls, menacingly, before turning on his heels and pacing back down the carpet.

'Just hand it to me, fucker!' he shouts, angrily.

'Just hand it to me, fucker,' he intones, casually.

He stops and stares out of the window at the apple tree, flush with white flowers.

I've been writing this fucker for twenty years. Fuck knows whether it'll ever see a screen, but this is my baby. I'm not handing this one over to get eviscerated by some Oxbridge cunt with a degree in fucking law.

Bruce doesn't keep wine in the barn. Restocking his working supply requires a return to the house, a self-imposed discipline which theoretically provides a barrier to his opening bottle after bottle in quick succession. After hours in the dim cocoon of his workroom, he emerges squinting into the blinding sunlight of a warm, spring Saturday morning.

As he crosses the yard, a strange car pulls into the driveway. A woman gets out, opens the boot and lifts out a green plastic pet carrier. Bruce can hear Lara, talking to the horses in one of the stables.

He continues his voyage over the foot bridge and the tinkling stream towards the house.

He walks across the kitchen, through an old oak door and down a flight of cold stone steps, each tread worn over the centuries into a concave dip.

Bruce pulls out the last remaining dusty bottle of Château Haut-Brion and stares at the rest of the wine racks.

They're fucking empty! We never run out of wine! When has that ever happened? Never! This is a fucking catastrophe!

He returns up the worn steps to the kitchen and through into the hall, at the end of which, in a dim recess, an iMac and printer sit on a table lit by a chrome and green glass-shaded lamp.

He spends as little time in the recess as possible.

He puts the bottle on the table next to the iMac.

I've got to email my publisher.

Fuck him.

He opens the bookmark for *ripperology.com*, the most active of the online Jack the Ripper forums.

Those armchair cunts have been dissecting him and his book, *They All Love Jack* on there for the past five fucking years, long before the book was ever published. He's so used to it that it barely registers now. Page after page of faceless keyboard warriors ripping apart and analysing him and his work in post after post, simply because he had the temerity to write a book about their pet obsession - the century old unsolved Jack the Ripper case.

He's going to print off some of this bile for his forthcoming talk at the bookshop on Charing Cross Road. He scans the forum threads, selecting the most vitriolic posts, copying and pasting them to a new document. He ends up with five pages of mouth-frothing insults about him and his work.

Once the printer has noisily disgorged its contents, Bruce collects the sheaf of papers and walks outside, the bottle of wine under his arm, heading back to his sanctuary.

The woman he saw before is still in the yard, wandering around aimlessly, still carrying her plastic pet carrier. She notices him and walks towards him.

'Hello, dear. Do you work here?'

'Yes.' Bruce smiles benignly.

'Oh I'm so relieved! I thought I'd come to the wrong place. We lost our little Gretal at the weekend.' Her voice tightens. 'She went over the rainbow bridge.'

The woman glances down at her feet then back up at Bruce, her eyes bearing a decidedly watery look.

'When her frail little body stopped convulsing, I knew she was gone. I knew. I said to dear husband, "Fly free, little one. Fly free." She was loved.' She shakes her head sadly, chin quivering with emotion.

'I'm sure she was,' says Bruce, wondering who she is and what on earth she's going on about.

'I know we can't replace her,' says the woman, mournfully. 'Nothing can replace her. But at least by doing this, we're handing another little soul the keys to freedom.'

Bruce is surreptitiously monitoring the face but can't see any actual tears, although the voice is definitely choking up.

'So you're here for…?'

'Any of them! I'm not fussy! As long as she's a rescue, has two wings and a beak, I'll give her a new forever home!'

'*Chickens!*' announces Bruce, triumphantly.

Lara emerges from the stables behind the woman and walks towards them, wiping her hands on her apron and smiling.

'Hi, are you here for the eleven o'clock rehomings?' she asks.

'I am!' cries the woman. 'I was just telling your farm hand about how my Gretal flew off to the chicken cloud of goodness last weekend.' She resumes her air of tragedy.

'Oh, I'm *so* sorry,' says Lara. 'Come and have a look at our rescue girls. They're just through that stable door, they're in a bit of a state, they've only just arrived from the factory, so don't be surprised at them looking a bit oven ready.'

'They won't be going in *my* oven!' squawks the woman.

'It's just the clipped beaks and lack of feathers makes them a pretty sorry sight...'

'Bless!' cries the woman, righteousness surging through her veins as she turns around. She heads urgently towards the stable, the pet carrier swinging in her hand.

Bruce looks at Lara questioningly. Lara looks back at him evenly and sighs.

'British Hen Welfare Trust. That's why I went off to Harrogate at the crack of dawn, I picked up forty of them. I *told* you I'd volunteered for us to be a rehoming point.'

'Was I pissed when you told me?'

'Oh God, I don't know, Bruce. Probably. Today's shaping up to be a bit of a nightmare. I think one of the horses might be poorly. She's gone off her feed. It's Comet, as well. I've been worried about her all week. I'm going to have to call the vet out.'

'Which one is Comet again?' asks Bruce.

'The *chestnut filly*. How's it going in there, anyway?'

'I've printed off a load of bollocks those 'Ripperologists' have been spouting about me in their ridiculous bloody chat rooms.'

'Why?'

'Thought I might include some of it in my talk next week at the bookshop.'

'Well don't let it get you down. These keyboard warriors have all got one thing in common and one thing in common only.'

'They're all cunts?'

'They've all got too much time on their hands. Don't take it to heart, darling.' She touches his cheek and smiles. 'I'll see you later. And don't forget Richard's popping in for dinner tonight on his way to Scotland.'

Bruce retreats back into the solitude of the barn, opens the bottle, pours himself a glass, takes a slug and then paces up and down, holding the printed sheets in front of him and reading the Ripperologists' postings out loud in voices of whiny theatrical bitterness, then answering them in his own rather bemused voice.

'Brent V: Ripperology Mag: One is now under the obligation to ask oneself whether Mr. Robinson has not, as with so many armchair Ripper theorists before him, so utterly convinced himself of his suspect that he has completely blinded himself to the flaws in his theory, circa 1,000 pages or not.'

'801, actually, "Brent V".'

'Jason Forest - Author, Researcher: Why are we even wasting our time discussing Robinson's pet theory when it's yet another steaming heap of opportunistic bollocks?'

'What is "opportunistic" about it? *What?* Nothing!'

'Janice DeLoro - True Crime Journalist: Robinson's long-winded attempt to untangle this complex case is continually undermined by head-rushes of explosive, crazed invective. Is he on drugs?'

'Hole in one, Janice! I'm an alco-fucking-holic! Which has no fucking bearing *whatsoever* on your point. Whatever it is.'

Bruce's voice now rises to a high-pitched mocking whine.

'Bindi F - Author: Attributing lack of proof to evidence of a cover up is the path that leads to madness. Really, the more information that emerges, the harder it is to make sense of Robinson's gibberish.'

He takes another gulp of wine.

'Cheers, Bindi, *Author*. I mean, thank you, from the bottom of my fucking heart, for your erudite and perceptive analysis of my work!'

'Brent V - Ripperology Mag: Robinson is no better than those flat earthers, railing hysterically against NASA. He has an agenda. His own. He's only written this book in order to make a film out of it. He thinks us Ripperologists are stupid? Well we've cottoned on to your little game, sunshine. Busted.'

'I'm a fucking *screenwriter, you odious little cunt!* It's what I *do!* Write fucking screenplays! I've written *dozens* of the fuckers! For fuck's *sake!* If I wanted to write a fucking *film* I'd have *written* a fucking film, not spent fifteen years and half a million quid of my own bread writing a *fucking book!* You couldn't make this bloody shit up!'

A spider drops on a thread down from a beam in the ceiling, repairing its web in a shaft of sunlight pouring through the window.

'What do you think, spider?' asks Bruce, looking up at the tiny animal. 'You make more sense than any of these fuckers, honestly. I'm not sure if I even want to inflict this shit on my audience. *Fuck 'em!*'

He throws the sheaf of printoffs down in disgust, sits back at his desk, re-reads the last few lines of *The Block* and starts hitting the typewriter keys.

Richard E. Grant's convertible white Mercedes draws up into the courtyard of Lilythwaite Farm en route to Scotland, conveniently halfway between his home in Surrey and the flat in Edinburgh which he keeps for The Fringe, and which he lends out to friends should they need somewhere to stay whilst in the city, in return for a sense of philanthropic wellbeing.

His friendship with Bruce, ignited through *Withnail,* then deepened and enriched over the intervening thirty years, has reached a point where each knows and trusts the other completely.

Richard climbs out of his convertible white Mercedes and strolls across the yard, every inch the dapper English gentleman in his Hush Puppies, cream chinos and blue cotton short-sleeved shirt, a cricket jumper casually draped over his shoulders, the arms tied loosely at his chest. He carefully picks his way around the chicken shit, avoiding the hens who look at him curiously whilst they chunter to one another as though discussing this vaguely familiar visitor.

He crosses the little bridge over the stream to the open front door and walks in.

'*Hellooo!* I'm here! Bruce?' he calls out, in his trademark quintessentially crisp Public School English.

Bruce appears at the door of the kitchen looking dishevelled and bleary-eyed.

'You OK?' asks Richard, hugging his friend warmly.

'Bit of a disaster earlier on,' replies Bruce, grinning. He fetches a jug of chilled orange from the fridge and places it, along with a confetti glass tumbler, on the large wooden table, where Richard takes his usual seat alongside the window.

'Freshly squeezed,' says Bruce.

'By your lovely wife, no doubt. Where is she?'

'Having a bath. She'll be right down.'

'So what happened?' asks Richard, pouring some orange juice and toasting his glass to Bruce, who pours himself another glass of wine and hazily lifts it in Richard's direction, grinning.

'We ran out of *vin rouge.*' He ruefully holds his glass up to the light to examine its contents.

'You *never* run out of wine.'

Well, *Lara* ran out. She has the odd glass, occasionally. Probably *she* made it run out more than me, actually.'

'Bollocks. You've been on a bender. You look fucking awful.'

'Well it's hardly fucking surprising, is it? I've spent all bloody morning wading knee-deep through the utter *shit* and *bile* these fucking *cunts* are spouting about me in their bloody *chat rooms*, which is enough to turn *anyone* to drink.'

'*Forums.* Nobody goes on "chat rooms" anymore. The special interest boards online are called *forums.* Well to be correct I suppose it should be *fora.* But Latin's gone to pot these days.'

'Well, whatever the bloody things are called, they're cesspits of venom, populated by vile little grubs scrabbling around beneath the floorboards of decency and decorum.'

'Since when were you bothered about decency and decorum?'

'They're a bunch of cunts, Richard, they're just not very nice people. You have to wade through this guff to actually see how bloody unpleasant they are. And how arrogant. With such monstrous egos.'

Richard laughs 'Well you should be at home with *that* part.'

'No I mean it, they're spiteful. It's actually quite upsetting.'

'Well, these special interest boards aren't very pleasant places to be, sometimes, which is why I avoid them.'

'*Bollocks.* You're the vainest man I know. I bet you're googling yourself silly every day trying to find out which chat rooms are talking about you.'

'*Forums.* And no, I'm not. I simply don't have the time, Bruce, I'm too busy fucking *working.* Aside from the day job I launched my own *signature fragrance* a couple of years ago, don't forget.' Richard bristles slightly at the suggestion of vanity.

'I know. And it's bloody lovely,' says Bruce, taking a large slug of his wine and grinning. '*Jack.* Named after my Ripper book.'

'Named after the Union Jack. Anyway, go on then, you had a running out of wine disaster. Don't tell me you ran out of 1999

Château Beychevelle and had to resort to necking a box of Aldi *vin ordinaire*.'

'Ran out altogether. Catastrophe.'

'So you drove to the off-licence. Sober? Or, no, let me guess... drunk...'

'I drive better when I'm drunk. As you know.'

'As I don't know. I will never get in another vehicle with you at the wheel again. So what happened?'

'I took Comet.'

'Lara's horse?'

'Yeah. I couldn't be arsed to take the horse box off the back of the Land Rover. Assumed it was empty.'

'And she was still in it?'

'Yeah. And then en route I glance in the mirror and some bloody silver lorry's tailgating me. Brake suddenly to piss it off. Poor Comet got a bit shaken about. And now she's not talking to me.'

Bruce grimaces uncomfortably.

'Poor thing,' says Richard.

'Yeah, she gave me the filthiest look when we finally got home and I let her out. Horses do have a way of letting you know they think you're an arsehole.'

'Whereas most of us keep it to ourselves,' says Richard, bursting out laughing and looking at Bruce fondly.

'So what did Lara say?'

'I didn't tell her,' he says, guiltily.

'Ah. OK, Mum's the word.'

He takes a deep breath and smiles, but there is a warning flash and a sadness in his eyes.

'You are a crazy motherfucker, Bruce.'

'Well at least I got the red,' smiles Bruce, raising his glass to Richard. 'I'll shout Lara that you're here. Think we're having a broccoli bake or something. Are you hungry?'

'Starving. I love your wife's cooking.'

8
Plan

'BRENT V - RIPPEROLOGY MAG: ROBINSON IS NO BETTER than those flat earthers, railing hysterically against NASA. He has an agenda. His own. He's only written this book in order to make a film out of it. He thinks us Ripperologists are stupid? Well we've cottoned on to your little game, sunshine. Busted.'

'What a bunch of absolute bellends. He's a fucking screenwriter for God's sake! If he'd wanted to make a film, he'd have written a fucking *film script* you *arseholes!*'

Zack scrolls through his phone, completely ignoring Ella.

'You wouldn't believe some of the utter *shite* these wankers come out with.'

She looks up at Zack, still immersed in his phone.

'Zack.'

'Mmmm?'

'Are you listening to me?'

'Yeah.'

'What am I talking about, then?'

'Um. Tell me again.'

'So, you're not listening.'

Zack looks up and stares at her, a blank expression on his face. 'What? Just remind me. I mean, tell me. I didn't hear you.'

'I *said,* that the Ripperology forums are full of absolute fucking *dicks.*'

'Why the fuck are you even on there, then?' asks Zack, accusingly, looking back down at his phone.

'Because I'm researching Bruce Robinson.'

'Why?' asks Zack, looking up at her again.

'Because he's fascinating.'

'What, 'cause he made *Withnail and I?*'

'Plenty of great films have been made by absolute arseholes. Bruce is not an arsehole. He's one of the coolest men I've ever stumbled across. And an incredibly interesting person.'

'Right,' says Zack, continuing to scroll down the screen.

'And...I think I want to write a book about him.'

Zack freezes mid-scroll and looks up at her, pointedly.

'What sort of book? A biography? You don't write biographies. You haven't got the patience.'

'Cheers. No, a novel.'

'Why?'

'Have a look at this.'

Ella finds the *Ruby Wax* on YouTube and passes Zack her phone.

Zack watches half-heartedly as Bruce Robinson comes onto the screen, bantering with Ruby Wax before sitting at a dinner table.

'Yeah. Right. OK. So?'

She pauses the video and takes back her phone.

'See? See what I mean? He's like a fucking *rock star.* He's cooler than Evan Dando.'

'So you wanna fuck him. That's it.'

Ella rolls her eyes at him.

'No I don't want to fuck him. But he's *brilliant*. Can't you see that? And these *dicks* on the Ripper forums are slagging him off, calling him all the names under the sun. Basically 'cause he's written a book about Jack the Ripper and they fucking haven't! It's jealousy! It's pathetic! Here...'

She holds out her phone again.

'Watch. There's more.'

Zack looks disinterestedly at the screen.

'Yeah. So she's telling him he's debauched. And he's totally fucking pissed.'

'So? It's a fucking *dinner party*. They're serving *wine*.'

'In a TV studio?'

'It was the nineties, Zack. Before political correctness ruined the world.'

'He looks like a total pisshead,' says Zack. He looks up at Ella, suspiciously. 'Hold on, he's not a pisshead, is he? Is *that* what the attraction is?'

'You can really be a cunt, sometimes, you know that? He is a self-confessed alcoholic, yes.'

'Not really surprising considering everyone in *Withnail*'s practically an alchy,' says Zack.

'They're not. Marwood isn't an alcoholic by any means. Withnail might be on the way. But Marwood is just dabbling.'

'Right. Dabbling.'

'Like you with coke.'

'Oh, I wondered when we'd get round to that one. Cheers. Never miss an opportunity to have a dig, do you?'

'Anyway, Bruce has had long periods of sobriety. Six and a half years at one point.'

'Well he's not sober there, is he?' Zack points at Ella's phone.

'Obviously that wasn't filmed during one of them. But even when he's arseholed he's utterly riveting.'

'Right. But he's a movie director. Ergo he's an arrogant control freak. They all are. Arseholes rammed with fawning minions.'

'For fuck's sake, Zack, what a ridiculous cliché. And he's had a terrible childhood. Can you imagine your father shouting at you, "Shut up. You're just a loud-mouthed little cunt!" when you're fucking *fourteen?* Well no you can't because you had a perfect fucking childhood stuffing your little face with Danish pastries on that commune in København.'

'My childhood was far from perfect.'

'You know what I mean. Relatively perfect. Compared to Bruce's. As a child he was so traumatised he took to protest shitting around the house. No wonder he's a fucking alcoholic.'

Ella stares at the image of Bruce, paused on the screen.

He's a tortured genius. He's God. I adore him.

'He's unfathomably sensitive.'

'You're unfathomably *gullible* falling for all that "sensitive" shite.'

'I'd rather be naive than a hardened cynic. How are you ever going to be happy with such a bitter, suspicious heart?'

'I'm not bitter and suspicious. I'm practical and rational. And you're being ignorant and stupid.'

'A man calling me "stupid". How fucking *original,* Zack.'

Zack stares at her evenly.

'OK. So what's the point of this novel, exactly?'

'There isn't a *point.* It's a *novel.* Novels and films don't change the world. They're *entertainment.* Why does it need a *point?*'

'So you think a novel about some pisshead Ripperologist who made a cult film, what, over thirty years ago, is actually going to interest anyone, do you? Really? I hate to piss on your chips, babe, but...'

Ella stands up and walks towards the kitchen, turning round to see Zack following her with his eyes, grinning smugly.

'You can be really nasty sometimes, Zack. It's not endearing. It makes me want to write this book even *more,* not less. You're just pissed off that Bruce Robinson is more *interesting* than you. That he isn't even a fucking musician and yet he's more rock 'n' roll than you are. You're *jealous.* Just like those wankers online. Fucking *pathetic.*'

Zack glares at her. 'I'm not jealous.'

'Yes you are. And was I jealous when you and Curtis wanted to work with Beth Orton and you started stalking her on Instagram like a love-sick puppy? Oh, let me see if I can recall exactly. Ah. Here we are. *No I fucking wasn't.* I didn't even *care.* Because it was about your precious *music.* Your oh-so-fucking-important *career.* In fact, I fucking *encouraged* you if I remember correctly. I even fucking messaged Beth's producer for you. In service to you! Bowing before the feet of the gods. Zack, Benjy and Curtis, the holy fucking trinity.'

'Curtis Christ. There you go,' says Zack, coldly.

'I still don't believe it's his real name.'

'It is. Get over it.'

Ella walks into the kitchen, slamming the door behind her.

Zack hears the familiar sound of the fridge door opening, the gentle muffled popping of a cork then the clinking of glassware.

Well that's Saturday afternoon down the pan. Thought we could have a leisurely shag but no, Ella's upset so Ella has to jump aboard the fucking Prosecco train. She's a fucking joke. I dunno why I fucking bother.

He reaches into his pocket and feels the small, plastic zip-lock bag between his fingers.

The phone rings in the kitchen and he hears Ella answer it.

'Hi, Jem. No, nothing really, just chilling with Zack...'

He takes the packet out, opens it and tips a small pile of white powder on the glass table in front of him. Taking a credit card from his wallet, he energetically chops at the pile, efficiently reducing it to a nice, even powder, before dividing the pile into two long, fat lines.

He takes a tenner and rolls it into a thin tube, then bends over towards the lines. With one finger he blocks his right nostril and snorts the powder into the other nostril through the tube, then swaps over to inhale the other line. He rubs the remaining powder on the table with his finger and wipes it across his bottom gum, then quickly replaces the card, tenner, and bag, and walks over to the mirror on the wall, inspecting his nose for tell-tale signs of coke.

A cool rush spreads throughout his head and immediately he feels grounded, aired, chilled, alert, and infinitely superior to fucking Ella, all at the same time.

Good gear.

Ella continues clanking around in the kitchen, chattering to Jem, and he sinks back into the long discussion he was reading on his music subreddit, 'Why Oasis are the greatest rock band in the history of music.'

Maybe not such a bad Saturday afternoon after all. Ella can fuck right off.

The doorbell sounds. Zack reluctantly goes to answer it. Ella can hear voices in the hall, talking quietly.

Curtis walks in and smiles shyly and endearingly.

'Hi Ella.'

'Hi Curtis. How's things?'

'OK,' says Curtis, taking a seat on the chair opposite Ella.

'Cup of tea?'

'I gave up, remember?'

'Oh yes, sorry. So are you still on that raw diet? I admire you so much for that.'

'Yeah. Feel so much better.'

'He doesn't eat enough, do you mate?' says Zack, returning to the sofa.

Curtis smiles, enigmatically.

'A kebab shirker.'

'For fuck's sake, Zack,' says Ella glancing over at him.

She turns back to Curtis. 'Zack tells me you might be going to Japan to record the new album.'

'Yeah,' says Curtis, looking out at the garden, thoughtfully.

'You don't wanna come though, do you?' says Zack, pointedly, looking at Ella.

'I've got my own ship to sail. I don't jump on other people's,' says Ella, staring back at him. 'Nothing against anyone else who wants to go with you, though. I'm just too busy, that's all.'

'Well Carrie isn't going either now,' says Curtis, sadly.

'Why not?' asks Zack. 'I thought she was up for it?'

'Things are a bit…we're going through a hard time.'

'Mate. You should have said,' says Zack.

'How long have you been together? Must be seven years or something,' says Ella.

'Eight.'

'Fuck. I'm sorry, Curtis. You're not gonna split up, are you?'

Curtis shifts uncomfortably in his chair and adjusts his glasses, looking at the carpet.

'Oh dear, really? That bad?' asks Ella.

Curtis looks up at her. 'Sometimes things don't turn out the way you expected. We're not in control. Nobody's in control. It's all madness.'

Ella smiles at him, kindly. 'Yup.'

9
Philanthropy

JULIETTE STARES, WIDE-EYED, OUT OF THE WINDOW OF the South African Airways Airbus.

'You OK boss?' asks Adriana, handing a pack of baby wipes over the aisle to Frances.

'I am trying to contain myself. I am exhausted. My head feels as if it is about to explode into a thousand pieces. Those kids *have not stopped* since we left LAX,' Juliette hisses.

'It's been over a day's journey, the poor little guys are pooped,' says Adriana, sympathetically.

Frances is cradling baby Cypher in her lap. The tot's bottom lip is sticking out as she sleeps. Toddler Moon has buried herself in Frances's bosom and is snoring gently. Flea, five years old, is quietly looking out of the window, his expression blank, his eyes full of fear and confusion.

'Whining, bickering and moaning since the minute we left,' continues Juliette in a low whisper to Adriana. 'We shoulda *drugged 'em.* Or me.'

'Well, we've agreed it's going to be a booze free trip, we've got a lot to get through in only three days.'

'I wasn't actually asking for drugs. I don't *take* drugs.' Juliette's eyes widen in exasperation.

'I know you don't, boss.'

'A chilled bottle of Cristal is all I'm talking about. Why can't we just do this?' says Juliette, looking out of the window.

'They ain't gonna have liquor stores here. Or much of anything else. This ain't really a mall and nail parlour kinda town, boss. This town's built on tobacco and religion. It's all about the big guys grabbing the small guys by the balls and ripping their souls out through their asses.'Cause they ain't got much else than soul worth taking.'

'Well that's why we're here, huh?' Juliette perks up, suddenly recalling her reason for this whistle-stop visit to Malawi with her entourage in tow. 'This place is going to be the root of my future success as an ambassador of goodwill and woman-of-the-people philanthropist.'

'Have you updated the blurb for the promotional YouTube vid yet?' asks Juliette.

'I did it at LAX.'

'Read it to me.' Juliette gazes back out at the featureless blue void.

'OK, hold on,' says Adriana, opening her laptop and locating the text.

'Juliette Janesson, as LongaVita's newest goodwill ambassador, has spoken. Who can ignore the fact that so many millions are suffering? Women, children, babies, and men too. I have to do something. I'm not that different to anyone else. I'm just like you. There's a flesh and blood human being behind the shimmer of the silver screen. I have the same feelings and desires as all of you out there. Don't we all want the same things? Justice. Equality. Meaning in our lives. To be loved. To be respected.'

'*To eat.* You got that in there? These guys out here don't have enough to eat, right? Mention food. And medicine. They need drugs, right? And bandages and stuff? And injections? All that jazz?'

'That's just the passion blurb. I get to the business bingo lingo next.'

'OK. Go on...'

'"By championing effective grassroots programmes and strategies to advance women's health, curb HIV and alleviate hunger and poverty, Janesson is fast becoming a global voice for women."'

Juliette nods curtly in acknowledgement, her eyes distracted by Frances's lap, where Moon is curled up and fidgeting in her sleep, her legs kicking and twitching.

'Frances,' whines Juliette, impatiently. 'Moon looks uncomfortable. Can you, like, adjust her, or something? Move her around a bit?'

'Sure boss, I think she's dreaming. Just don't wanna wake her now she's finally gone.'

'Right back atcha,' says Juliette, smiling flatly and turning back to Adriana.

'Yeah. So, "Janesson is fast becoming a global voice for women." Thing is, I haven't started yet. Won't that sound kinda weird?'

'No. Remember what I'm always telling you, boss. Think yourself into it. *Become it. Then do it.* Like acting,' she adds with a smile.

'OK. Yeah.' Juliette pauses then adds glumly 'Micky's been ignoring my messages since we left LA. A whole day.'

'There'll be a reason.'

Juliette lowers her voice. 'Yeah. Smashed out of his skull on Oxy or banging Freya Stephens. Those kinda reasons.'

'Mommy,' whines Flea, turning his face towards Juliette and Adriana across the aisle. 'I wanna cuddle.'

'Come here, baby,' coos Juliette, opening her arms to him. He droopily ambles towards her, curls up in her lap and immediately falls asleep.

'He sure is a cutie,' says Adriana.

'He sure is,' murmurs Juliette, looking fondly down at his curled up form and stroking his blond, curly hair.

❧❧❧

The passengers disgorge from the plane and walk across the still hot tarmac into the airport which, at midnight, is eerily deserted. Crickets chirp in the darkness.

'We're gonna get clearance to just walk through without having to go through all that security shit, right?' asks Juliette.

'Don't think they're playing ball on that one, boss. I checked. We have to go through customs and security just like everyone else.'

'But we're *not* everyone else. *I have three kids.'*

Adriana suppresses the smirk which is desperately trying to escape from her lips.

'And. *I'm Juliette Janesson,'* pleads Juliette, wearily, knowing that here, at least, that fact opens no doors.

By the time they get through customs and security, Juliette realises with disappointment that none of the other passengers has recognised her.

Their welcome party comprises a single uniformed guard from the Malawian Defence Force, who stands at the arrivals gate, holding up a sign saying 'Boulange. Adriana.'

Adriana and Juliette approach the guard, followed by Frances, carrying Cypher in a baby sling and pushing Moon in a buggy whilst Flea trots alongside them.

'Adriana Boulange,' says Adriana, smiling sweetly.

'You have arrived. Welcome to Africa,' answers the guard, grinning broadly. 'My name is Mac Donald. May I please see your passports?' He holds out a hand. His other still holds the name board.

Juliette glares at the guard as she hands her passport to Adriana to pass over.

'All good,' he declares with satisfaction, snapping the passports shut one by one. 'Come with me, please.'

The party follow the guard to a large SUV with blacked out windows, parked right in front of the sliding doors of the small arrivals terminal. Mac Donald holds the door open as Juliette climbs in first followed by Adriana. Frances passes the children into the SUV then embarks upon the unwieldy process of moving the buggy from pavement to vehicle. Juliette looks on, pityingly, as Frances removes changing bags and unpacks luggage from the buggy's storage rack, tucking in play beads on strings that keep pinging around with a life of their own, before finally managing to fold the damn thing up.

Beads of sweat shine on Frances' forehead in the humid, hot night. Juliette turns and stares into the chirping darkness. *So this is Africa.*

When the party finally arrive at Latitude 13, their hotel on the outskirts of Lilongwe, it is quiet and still under a black sky abundant with twinkling stars.

'I will meet you here at 10am to take you to Christ Blood School,' says Mac Donald as he closes the doors of the SUV behind them. 'Please sleep well.'

'Thanks Mac. See you tomorrow,' says Adriana.

'Donald. Mac Donald. Not Mac. Mac Donald. Like the famous burger,' says Mac Donald, patiently.

'Of course. How could I forget? The famous burger. Thank you, Mac Donald. We will see you tomorrow.'

As they enter the hotel, Frances nods in satisfaction and surveys the interior. The floodlit swimming pool shimmers through the windows of the large reception hall, whose white walls are hung with stylish art, craft pieces and iron artefacts. A chandelier formed from a huge fountain of copper discs is suspended from the ceiling and an elaborate filigree wrought-iron room divider separates off the spacious empty dining room.

A weary-looking young concierge in a blue uniform trimmed with gold embroidery, standing behind a long glass counter, smiles as the party arrive at the check-in desk. The concierge types their details into his computer as Juliette leans over the counter, her silver bracelet rattling on the glass.

'I just want to check that you're fully stocked with *champagne,'* she demands. 'In case I want a *drink,'* she adds, unnecessarily.

Adriana glances at Juliette and flashes her a warning look with her eyes.

The concierge glances from his computer to Juliette and smiles broadly.

'Of course, madam. Our bar is fully stocked at all times of the day and night for your enjoyment.'

'Thankyewww,' she gushes, ignoring Adriana.

After checking in, the concierge takes Frances and the sleepwalking children to their room then accompanies Juliette and Adriana along a cool veranda to their adjoining rooms.

'I like it. Thanks, Adriana.' Juliette stands, looking around the room. A huge king-size double bed, draped with a white mosquito net, dominates the far end of the vast bedroom, whose white marble floor shimmers in the honeyed glow of the wall lights. Juliette drops her handbag on a spherical wicker chair facing a large, shiny, pebble-shaped coffee table.

'Yeah, I knew it would be stressful for you, boss, so I wanted to get the best.'

'My sanity touchstone,' coos Juliette, getting out her phone and connecting to the hotel's wifi. Her phone pings almost immediately.

'It's him. Micky,' she snaps. 'Finally.'

'What's he said?'

Juliette begins reading in a whiny voice. '"Babes, exclamation mark, on location all day in some godforsaken hellhole corner of

Bulgaria, exclamation mark, no signal, exclamation mark, love you to bits, exclamation mark, will try to get signal tomorrow, exclamation mark, it's like the bona fide Wild West out here, exclamation mark." That,' ends Juliette flatly, a mask of fury sliding onto her face. 'So. In a word. Fucking.'

'Boss, he may be telling the truth. They're, like, in the middle of nowhere, right?'

Juliette paces up and down, tearing her travel clothes off in fury and flinging them to the floor, leaving a trail of scattered garments in her wake.

'We're in the middle of fucking *Africa* and they've got fucking wifi. It's the age old excuse, right? "No signal?" No signal means he's fucking her. End of.'

'Talk to him tomorrow when you've had a good night's sleep.'

'I need a drink,' Juliette moans. 'I don't just *want* one. I mean I *need* one. I *have* to have a glass of champagne.'

'Am I allowed to disagree with you today?'

'No.'

'You made me promise to make you stick to no booze this trip.'

'Yeah, well, I changed my mind, OK? Like that was totally unnecessary overkill on my part. I was being cautious, that's all. Now I want a glass of champagne. Right now. From the bar. They said they're fully stocked. Would you order me one, please? Actually a bottle. No, make that two. Cristal. And those old-fashioned champagne glasses like Marilyn had in *The Last Sitting*. No flutes. Chilled. Everything. Champagne. Glasses. Everything chilled. The works.'

Juliette is pacing up and down the marble floor as she scrolls through Micky's Twitter feed looking for evidence of any online activity.

'His Twitter is silent. The douche.'

'So...' ventures Adriana, cautiously. 'How about we do straight to bed and a good night's sleep? Because, yanno, we've got the photographer booked in tomorrow to do the pap shots, boss.'

Juliette glares at Adriana. 'Get. Me. Some. Champagne. *Now.*' She raises her eyebrows and points towards the door.

Adriana suppresses a heavy sigh then smiles warmly at Juliette. 'Absolutely no problem, boss. I'm on it.'

10
SHAKESPEARE'S

THE SERVER PLACES AN ESPRESSO ON THE WOODEN TABLE in front of Ella.

'Thank you,' Ella smiles up at her.

Ella picks up her phone and studies a photo of Bruce, evidently taken some years ago, in which he's holding a half-burnt cigarette and staring calmly into the camera lens against a backdrop of bookshelves.

She scrolls to a more recent photo by acclaimed photographer Donald MacLellan. In this one Bruce reclines in a crimson velvet armchair, wearing a brown, diamond-patterned cardigan, his face lined with wearisome experience.

Scrolling down, Ella re-reads one of Bruce's quotes, about a screenplay he's been working on for several years, provisionally titled *The Block.*

'The lead character is an American, astonishingly cynical, kind of gruesome, uptight, claustrophobic freak. i.e. he's me. Except I'm not American.'

Oh God he's just so funny. So witty. Can I adore him any more than I already do? Probably not. He's perfection. I totally love the bloke. There is just something about him. And I'm going to meet him. In about half an hour.

She feels sick with anxiety at the thought of their impending meeting and giddy when she stands up. She walks to the toilet, shuts the door behind her and stares into the mirror above the sink.

Stop being ridiculous. Fucking get it together, Ella. He's just some bloke who pisses and shits just like everyone else on earth. You're behaving like some kind of love-struck super-fan. This is not you.

She takes a deep breath.

'Yeah. It's not me. It's my book,' she explains to the mirror. She adjusts her hair and stares at herself admonishingly, as if daring her reflection to contradict her. 'You can do this.'

Emerging from the café into Old Compton Street, Ella turns left and heads towards Charing Cross Road. She barely notices the people sitting outside cafés in the sunshine. All she can think about is the bookshop.

Turning right onto Charing Cross Road, she sees it up ahead, on the other side of the road.

Shakespeare's.

I wonder whether he's already there.

The black gloss paint on the front door is peeling around its rusty hinges. A shop still in tune with Soho's rapidly vanishing Bohemian authenticity, its windows display antiquarian books bound in faded covers of varying colours, jostling for space on hand-made wooden shelves. Ella feels immediately at home.

She crosses the threshold of chipped Victorian black and white chequered floor tiles and enters the shop. The musty aroma of old books hits her immediately.

Ahead of her, around twenty people are taking seats at the back of the shop, facing a lamp-lit table piled with copies of *They All Love Jack.*

Suddenly, he's there. Walking past her with an impish, sprightly gait which belies his age. He looks shorter than she'd imagined, and somehow frailer.

He starts talking quietly to an elderly, bespectacled man, presumably the bookshop owner. At seventy, Bruce is technically elderly too. But unlike the slightly stooped bookshop owner, he still emanates a youthful vitality.

Bruce finishes his murmured conversation, turns around and walks slowly back in Ella's direction, away from the audience members, some of whom are still taking their seats. He stops next to her, deep in thought, one hand to his face, his thumb against his lips.

He's carrying a sheaf of A4 papers in one hand.

On impulse, Ella turns to him. 'Are those printoffs from the Ripper forum?'

Bruce looks across at her, surprised. 'They are, actually.'

'I've read the entire thread. All fifty-odd pages of it. Bunch of arseholes.'

Bruce's eyes light up as he suppresses a smile.

'Don't take any notice of them. Tossers,' she adds.

Bruce smiles broadly without saying anything then notices the bookshop owner giving him a little wave.

He turns to Ella, apologetically. 'Better go on I suppose. Was going to nip outside for a fag but it'll have to wait.'

'Break a leg.'

'Cheers.' He walks towards the little wooden table piled with copies of his book, around which the audience are seated in a horseshoe arrangement.

He sits down, looks over his glasses at the people gathered expectantly before him and pours himself a glass of water from a large glass carafe.

He casually adjusts his worn brown leather jacket. His clothes seem to be a part of him. The denim shirt has never been slung over the back of a chair, the trainers have never lain upturned in the middle of the carpet and the jeans never folded neatly at the bottom of a wardrobe. His clothes are like the second skin of some ageing, world-weary rock star.

He faces the audience with an endearing grin and starts talking about his book *They All Love Jack.*

'You know, this whole Jack The Ripper thing was a complete accident. I had no real intention of ever writing it. But I was living in Los Angeles, and Raymond Chandler, in one of his books he talks about the Ripper crimes being impossible to solve…'

Ella already knows the story and finds herself simply watching his body language and listening to the tone of his voice, so that his words float in and out of her consciousness. 'I come back to London… intrigued…Scotland Yard…you're not *the* Bruce Robinson are you?'

She wills herself to listen to what he's saying rather than simply soaking up his presence.

'…so he says to me, "Nobody's ever gonna bust this thing," and I say, "I'll bet you five pounds I could." So, researching and writing this book has taken fifteen years of my life. I never got the fiver,' he finishes, laughing.

On cue at the gag, the audience laughs along with him.

This human being is the one I want to write into a book. It's not just his work that shines, it's him.

At the end of the talk, the small audience bursts into an enthusiastic round of applause, punctuated by the odd whistle. An orderly queue of fans forms in front of the small wooden table.

Most of the audience would have been in their twenties when *Withnail and I* was made. Now they're fifty-somethings, clutching their books in anticipation.

I don't have a book. Fuck. I can't just go up and talk to him without a book to sign.

Yes you can Ella. He's not some mythical God. He is just a fucking bloke writing his name on some books, just like you've done in the past at your own book signings.

Yes, but he's Bruce Robinson and I'm just Ella Quinn.

Shut up. Do it.

A woman in her mid-fifties with bleached blond hair carefully teased into a messy bun approaches Bruce, her eyes aflame with worship, and hands him a copy of *They All Love Jack.*

He opens the book and waves a gold fountain pen in the air, glancing at her and smiling, boyishly, as he asks her name.

'To Susan. Love Bruce,' he announces loudly, signing the book with a flourish and giving Susan a charming grin before she walks away, clutching her book and smiling radiantly.

Ella hangs back until, at last, the one remaining fan walks away from Bruce's table.

He reaches for the carafe and pours the rest of his water into a chunky glass tumbler. Taking a final sip, he adjusts his glasses then gathers his things together and stands up to leave.

She walks over to him, ignoring the heaving nausea in her stomach. He looks up as she approaches.

'Hi Bruce. I didn't introduce myself earlier. Ella Quinn.'

'Hi, Ella,' he says, raising his eyebrows expectantly.

'You didn't quote from those forum arseholes then,' she laughs.

'No. I considered it, but...'

'Well it was a really entertaining talk.'

'Thanks, glad you enjoyed it.'

'Um...look...there's something I want to ask you about...'

'Fire away.'

'I'm an author, OK? And I'm planning to write my next novel with you as the protagonist. I mean with the main character actually being called Bruce Robinson...'

'Marvellous. I *love the idea,'* says Bruce, his eyes lighting up.

'Well, that's great. Do you want me to give you the general gist?'

'Sure.'

'Well, it's about the Bruce Robinson character falling in love with this gorgeous young American journalist. It all goes tits up and he goes back to his life in the sticks.'

'Sounds great. Do it,' he says, grinning.

He thinks I'm crazy. That's OK, Ella. Just keep going. As if nothing were amiss. Smile.

'I, er…I might have a few questions.'

'Email me. Have you got some paper? I'll give you my email address.' He casually unscrews the top of the fountain pen.

Ella frantically rummages around in her bag for her notepad.

It's not there. For fuck's sake, Ella.

She grabs a paper napkin left on the edge of the table.

'I carry a notepad everywhere, normally,' she explains, weakly, handing him the paper napkin.

Bruce writes his email address on the napkin and hands it back.

haweswaterres@gmail.com

She stares at the black, spikily scrawled words.

That's Bruce's handwriting. For me.

'Cheers.'

Bruce gestures towards the door of the little bookshop.

'Think they're waiting for me out there, I'd better go.'

'OK. Bye. And thanks.'

She watches as he walks out of the bookshop and closes the door behind him.

Bye Bruce, I fucking love you!

He's gone. Ella stares at the old wooden door.

That's where he went. Through that door.

She stands rooted to the spot, going over the last few minutes of her life.

For fuck's sake, Ella. Why couldn't you have said something intelligent, like 'A novel about obsession, addiction, creativity and love'? Talk about L'esprit de l'escalier, you dick.

She stares at the door, and the realisation suddenly hits her.

He said yes.

He's OK with it.

He likes the idea.

He's given you his email address.

In his own handwriting.

With his gold fountain pen.

Get the napkin out, you fool, and look at that fucking writing.

His email address.

You did it, Ella.

Everything is fucking great.

Ella steps out through the door onto Charing Cross Road and the heartless cacophony of London's streets.

No sign of Bruce, long gone, yet only moments before.

A black cab sounds its horn at a bike courier who speeds past people crossing the road.

Everything's changed.

11
Pool Boy

SUMMER HAS GENTLY SWUNG INTO LIFE AND A SLOW embracing warmth has enfolded England.

Bruce takes a slug of red and gazes absent-mindedly out of the open window of his barn before looking back at the typewriter.

The voices. I can't hear the fucking voices. It's been a week now. Even with the red. Still can't hear them. I can't write without the voices and I can't hear the voices without the red and now even with the red I can't hear the fuckers.

'Fuck it!' he says. He stands up from the typewriter and paces the length of the barn.

Turning on his heels, he marches purposefully to his desk, sits down in front of the typewriter and stares at the line of dialogue on the page.

He starts typing.

And suddenly, he can barely type fast enough to transcribe the words pouring onto the page in front of him.

Lara puts her phone down as James walks into the kitchen.

'Hi darling.'

'Hi Mum. I'm starving. Is Dad back?'

'Yes, he got back a couple of hours ago. He's in the barn, working. There's some sushi in the fridge, you can finish that off if you like.'

'Nice one. How was his trip?'

'OK I think. He seemed to enjoy it. Said it was a good audience. Went for a nice curry afterwards. And some author wants to put him in her book. Or something.'

'Cool.' James rummages in the fridge. 'Where is it?'

'The sushi? On the top shelf, at the back.'

James's friend Tom walks into the kitchen. James looks apologetic. 'Oh, sorry, Mum, I forgot to say, Tom's here.'

'Hi Tom. Tea? And there's some sushi if you'd like.'

'I'm fine, thanks.' Tom shoots her a disarmingly charming smile. Tom is thirty-seven but barely looks out of his twenties.

Lara looks away, reminding herself that Tom is just James's friend, to whom she always proffers tea and food, a hospitality which is invariably declined, as Tom always brings his own flask and sandwiches when he's here working on James's studio.

Lara reads a message that's just popped up on her phone.

'Damn. That is a bloody nuisance. Jonti's come down with some ghastly virus and can't do the pool this weekend. I really wanted it sorting. It feels like there's a heatwave coming on, don't you think so?'

'Yeah.' James talks through a mouthful of sushi.

'The forecast for next week is wall to wall sunshine, up in the thirties.' Lara shakes her head. 'You don't know anyone who does pools, do you Tom?'

He smiles mischievously. 'I do know someone, yeah, actually.'

'Oh, could I have their number? I think the nearest company that does it is in Leeds, it's such a pain, that's why we've always used Jonti.'

Tom laughs. 'It's not someone else, it's me. I do our neighbour's pool. Got all the chemicals and everything.'

Lara's eyes widen in appreciation. 'Oh. That's fantastic. It's round the back. I could show you if you like?'

James continues eating his plate of sushi and scrolling through his phone, disinterestedly.

'I know where it is,' says Tom, grinning. 'I see it en route to James's studio every time I go there.'

Lara wipes her hands on a tea towel and looks at Tom, distractedly. 'Yes, of course. I suppose you will have.'

'James and I have finished for the day. Got to wait for some parts arriving before we can do anything else. So we could have a look at the pool now? If you want?'

'Brilliant,' says Lara, smiling. 'We won't be long, sweetie,' she says to James, as she and Tom leave the kitchen. James continues to munch on his food whilst scrolling on his phone.

Bruce is in the zone. The writing is going so well that he doesn't want to be interrupted. He fetches two more bottles of red from the house, returns to the barn and plonks them on his desk, ready for if and when they are needed. He starts typing again, so fast he can barely keep up with the torrent of words flowing like liquid gold from up there somewhere, through him and onto the page.

He's laughing like a drain now as he types.

This is good. This is great. This is all that there is. Nothing else exists beyond these words. This is pure, distilled beauty, blood and heart.

The gold.

Lara's plaid cotton shirt is tied loosely at the waist, above her faded blue Levi's. Her long hair is up in a loose bun and escaping tendrils of silver drape down her neck and fall loosely onto her shoulders.

Tom watches her as she walks towards the back of the farmhouse. She possesses that elusive combination of free-spiritedness and refined elegance, so rare to find together in one person. He's noticed her beauty before, but never really had the opportunity to study her at close quarters like this, as he follows her into the green field.

She's got a lovely arse. In fact, she looks fucking amazing for her age - she must be in her sixties. But she's James's mum. Happily married. And so out of bounds she may as well exist in a different universe.

Lara glances behind her as they reach the field where the pool is situated.

'So, this is it,' she says, gesturing towards the still covered pool.

Tom looks her in the eyes. 'I'll have to clean the leaves off the cover before I remove it. If you've got a long brush I can do it now...'

Lara fetches a long-handled broom from the pool hut which sits under a stand of ash which have just burst into leaf. She hands it to Tom, who methodically sweeps the accumulated leaves from the cover surface, whilst Lara stands quietly watching him.

'It's not been touched since last summer. I've got no idea what's underneath. I normally just let Jonti get on with it,' says Lara, to break the silence.

'If it's been covered it'll be fine.'

Tom walks around the periphery of the pool, kicking the springs from the grommets holding the cover in position.

He glances across at Lara, who shifts her weight from one foot to the other as she stands, poised, hand on hip, head cocked slightly to one side, looking at him.

'I can help if you want. I don't mind. Shall I do the ones over this side?'

'It's fine. It's a one man job, honestly.'

With the cover released from its holding springs, he starts to peel it back, folding the fabric into even sections on the grass at the end of the pool and gradually revealing the shining expanse of water underneath, which glistens blue and gold in the sun.

Tom stands back, on the opposite side of the pool to Lara. They both look at the water, then at one another.

'It looks so tempting, doesn't it? I'd love to just dive in,' muses Lara, half to herself, looking back down at the water.

'It does,' says Tom.

Lara sighs. 'I guess it needs treating first, right?'

'Yeah. I can bring my stuff round tomorrow, if you want me to get started straight away?'

'That'd be great.'

'It takes a few days to get the chemical balance right. Always a bit tricky.'

❧❧❧

Bruce stops typing and glances up and out through the window once more. The apple tree has shed most of its blossoms and a carpet of sugar-pink petals lies beneath it on the green grass.

Beyond the tree, Lara comes into view from beyond the trees, heading towards the back of the stables and the swimming pool field, closely followed by Tom.

She's beautiful, my wife. I love the way she walks. Who's that with her? That mate of James's.

The page. Get back to the page.

Bruce bows his head slightly, focuses, and disappears once more into his work.

❧❧❧

Tom walks round the pool to where Lara is standing. He stoops down and unscrews the top of a large white plug set into the ground.

'I'll just check the water level in the skimmer,' he explains, removing a bottle of anti-freeze and peering into the hole at the gently bobbing water within. He replaces the bottle, screws the top back on and stands.

'Water level is fine, anyway.'

He smiles at Lara, who smiles back.

How come I've never noticed how fit she is before?

'It's a really nice pool. How long have you had it?'

'Oh, I don't know. About twenty years. It was great when the kids were growing up but now Hazel's gone and James never really uses it.' She looks at the water wistfully. 'Bruce still loves it though, when it's warm enough. He always says "Stephen Spielberg paid for it."'

She glances at Tom and laughs, lightly.

'It's his little joke. Well, it's true, actually,' she adds fondly, smiling.

'Perks of the job, I guess,' says Tom, looking from Lara back down into the water.

'Yes. Well, one of them.'

She gestures with her hand over the field towards the farmhouse.

'I wouldn't have all this if it weren't for Bruce's work. My sculptures don't bring in much. I'm very lucky, really.'

Lara looks over at Tom, who is still looking into the water.

He's beautiful. Young and therefore almost certainly daft as a brush. But he is beautiful.

'Your studio's in that far barn, isn't it?' asks Tom.

'Yeah…'

'I'd love to see your work sometime. Always loved sculpture.'

'I'll show you. Soon. I'm in the middle of a project for an exhibition.'

'What sort of project?'

'An alabaster statue. Of a child. You know about DACA?'

'Nope…'

'It stands for the Deferred Action for Childhood Arrivals. So-called "Dreamers". Trump's planning to deport thousands of these kids who were illegally brought into the U.S. I'm sculpting one of them.'

'Wow, cool. I'd *love* to see that.'

'Well, I'll show you, soon.'

Lara looks at Tom, thoughtfully.

'How old are you? If you don't mind my asking?'

'Thirty-seven.'

'Oh, I thought you were about James's age,' she laughs.

'So you mean I don't look my age?' he glances up at Lara, catching her eye and grinning.

'Well, I guess you don't. Do you have kids?'

A fleeting tension forms in Tom's face. He looks up at her.

'We were going to. Me and Francine, my girlfriend...'

He tails off and looks down into the water, which ripples lightly with the summer breeze.

A palpable tension hangs between them as they both stare at the water in silence.

'She got breast cancer. And she didn't make it.' Tom shrugs.

'Oh. Oh, I'm so sorry.'

'She was four months pregnant when she died.'

'Oh, I'm so sorry, Tom. How awful for her. And for you. How... terrible...'

'Yeah,' says Tom, tonelessly, still staring into the water. 'It was ten years ago now.'

He glances up at Lara. 'Don't think I mentioned it to James. I do consider him a mate. But it's more on a work footing, really. We don't really talk about...about stuff like that.'

'Did you ever consider trying again? I mean, has there been anyone else?'

'Yeah. There've been others. A lot of others. None that I'd want to settle down with. Certainly none that I'd want to have kids with. Francine was my soul mate...'

He stops talking and again stares down into the water before continuing.

'I found her pretty early on in life I guess. And then I lost her. *C'est la vie.* You win some, you lose some. I won the lottery of love, you might say. Then lost it all.'

He stops talking, folds his arms, and looks up at the sky.

'Can you hear those magpies, chattering? I love magpies.'

'Yes, cheeky little things, aren't they?'

Tom turns to look at Lara again.

'Guess you won the lottery of love, too, finding Bruce.'

Lara glances away, looking slightly uncomfortable at the intimate turn the conversation has taken.

'I have. We're very happy. He's a wonderful man. He's a one off, that's for sure.'

The magpies cackle in the ash trees and they both look up simultaneously.

Lara smiles, with relief more than anything, that the silent spell between them has now been broken.

Bruce finishes writing the section he's been working on and stops. He can hear voices through the open window, coming from the direction of the pool.

He pops open his third bottle of red of the day, pours a glass and drains the thing almost in one go. The resultant warmth spreading through his being brings an equilibrium, easing him into a comfort zone of balanced giddiness.

He pulls the last sheet of A4 through the typewriter and reads through it, laughing out loud in several places before adding it to the pile of papers on the desk. He picks up the pile, holds it in his hands and feels the texture of the paper, silently treasuring the thousands of words concealed between the sheets.

The earlier vision of Lara and Tom heading towards the pool suddenly seeps back into his consciousness.

He stands and crosses to the heavy door, pulls it open and walks out of the barn into the sunlight, carrying his wine, following the path behind the stables and on towards the pool field.

Lara and Tom are standing together, both looking reflectively into the now uncovered pool.

Lara glances over at Bruce on seeing his approach.

'Darling, we were just talking about you.'

'All good, I hope,' he grins.

'I was telling Tom here about Spielberg paying for the pool...'

'Water,' says Bruce, smiling. 'It's uncovered.'

'Jonti's got some virus, he can't do it. I thought you'd like it open. Now there's a heatwave on its way. So Tom offered to do it.'

'Thanks, Tom,' says Bruce.

'Pretty cool that Spielberg paid for it, I've got to say.'

'Yeah. *In Dreams.* Neil Jordan ended up doing the film instead of Spielberg. The script I wrote for Steve bought the pool though.'

'So, Tom's pulled the cover back. And released those springy things from their...things...' Lara looks inquiringly at Tom.

'Grommets.'

'And he's coming back tomorrow to balance the chemicals.'

Bruce walks to the edge of the pool and looks deep into the water, the surface forming shimmering patterns in the evening sunlight. He sways very slightly, mesmerised by the movement of the water.

'Then I can swim in it.'

12

Joy Down in Our Hearts

FREYA STEPHENS IS POINTING A FINGER AT MICKY Valance's head, her mouth wide open in a huge smile, her eyes sparkling with glee and her blonde hair casually trailing across her face. The caption accompanying the Instagram post says '*Get me! On location in Bulgaria with The Valance! Fun times!*'

The post has nearly half a million likes.

Juliette throws her phone across the bed where it bounces, catapults through the air and lands in the little stone fountain gurgling in the centre of the room.

'Fuck fuck fuck.' She dives out of bed and yells 'Adrianaaa!'

The door opens and Adriana rushes in, quickly surveying the room for damage from the night before. Juliette, still in her lingerie and surrounded by empty champagne bottles, is scrabbling frantically across the bed to reach her phone before it drowns and dies.

'*Adriana!* My cell! It's in the fucking fountain!'

Adriana strides over to the fountain, reaches into the water and retrieves the phone. She wipes it on her t-shirt and hands it to Juliette.

'It's still working. We better grab some breakfast, boss, it's 9am already. Mac's coming at ten.'

'Ugh. I'm fucked. I need more sleep.' Juliette flops limply back onto the bed.

'So…what time did you finally hit the sack last night?'

'I dunno. Three, or four, or something. Anyway, how am I meant to even *sleep* whilst this shit is plastered all over fucking Instagram?' She looks mournfully at Adriana and thrusts out her phone, showing Freya Stephens' Instagram post.

Adriana coolly appraises the photo.

'It could be innocent, just goofing around.'

Juliette leaps off the bed, suddenly animated.

'This is not *just goofing around!* This is full on *Netflix and chill!* They're fucking!'

She stands in the centre of the room fiddling with the thin strap of her camisole and looks at Adriana pleadingly.

'I can't take any more.' The words emerge in a tiny, vulnerable whisper. 'I've had enough. He doesn't love me. He never loved me. The only person Micky loves more than Micky is *Micky.* And the only *thing* he loves is *work.*'

'Boss,' says Adriana, tenderly.

Juliette lowers her head and momentarily stares at the floor, lost in thought, then lifts her head up again and stares at Adriana, purposefully. 'How much time are we on before Mac gets here?'

'Forty-five, boss.'

'OK. Let's do it.'

❧❧❧

Flea looks mournfully out through the huge glass panels of the breakfast room as the black SUV disappears down the road.

He pushes two triangles of toast around his plate with his little forefinger, and looks up at Frances with a hollow, sad expression on his face.

'I don't like it here. I'm tired.'

'We won't be here long, sweetie. Then we'll be going back home to see your friends at school again,' replies Frances, brightly.

'Benny? and Joel?'

'Sure. Benny and Joel and all the other guys.'

'When will Mommy and Adriana get back? Where have they gone? Can't they stay and play with us?' Flea's voice takes on a whining tone.

'They'll be gone all day honey-pie.'

'Why?'

'Because they have work to do.'

'What work?'

'Well, Mommy is visiting some children at a school.'

'Why?'

'She's going to give them money so they can get more toys.'

'Are they getting the toys today? What sort of toys? Can I play with them? I wanna go too,' says Flea, his face drooping.

'No, it won't be today, poppet. Mommy will be in meetings all day with other grown-ups.'

'So when do they get the toys?'

'There aren't any toys right now, Flea. They're just talking right now. Talking about buying the toys. The poor little children here don't have much money. Or many toys.'

Flea thinks for a minute.

'They can have some of my toys. I don't like my toys. My toys are boring.'

'You like looking at li'l creepy creatures in rock pools better than toys, huh?' says Frances, fondly, rubbing Flea's hair.

'Yeah. I wanna go to the beach house and go to the beach and look in pools.' 'Sometimes we can't do what we want to do, Flea, that's just life.'

'Why not?'

Frances sighs, heavily. 'Because there's just things we have to do.'

'Why?'

'Well, to earn money for a start. To pay for the things we want.'

Flea looks up at Frances.

'Is Mommy fetching the toys for the kids because she needs money?'

'No, she's doing it because she's a kind person.'

Flea thinks for a moment then smiles.

'I love Mommy.'

'I know, she's a good person.'

'I just wish she'd play with me more. I miss her. I want her to be here. She's always working.'

'I guess that's so she can earn money to buy you toys.'

'I don't want more toys though. I want Mommy to look in rock pools with me. But she never does. She's always on her phone. Or at work.'

'Yeah, she's just busy. I'm sure she'll look in some rock pools with you next time we're at the beach house.'

'Will you look in rock pools with me, Nanny Frances?'

'Sure I will. When we get back. Which is gonna be soon. OK little guy?'

Mac Donald stares straight ahead as he drives down the dusty road through a barren landscape dotted with baobab trees, set into red earth. The sky is heavy and overcast, bearing over a scattering of people walking along the roadside, dressed in colourful t-shirts, cotton trousers and skirts. Most are carrying loads, some in their arms, some on their heads. Old-fashioned bicycles trundle along, similarly laden with goods. The straight road is empty of other vehicles as far as the eye can see.

A woman with a huge load of fabric balanced on her head sits wearily by the roadside, a small infant wrapped in a sling nestled against her.

Juliette's eyes widen with sudden shock.

'We were meant to be bringing the kids! Where's the kids?'

'You messaged me last night to say don't bring them…'

'What? What time?'

Adriana picks up her phone and checks.

'3am boss.'

'What? I've told you before, Adriana, don't ever take any notice of anything I say at that time in the morning in case I'm, like, *wasted!'*

'Sorry, boss. You sent a few messages and you sounded OK…'

'Well I obviously wasn't OK, was I? We need the fucking *kids.* How are we going to do the pap shots without the *kids?'*

'We can do them later, after the school.'

'I want to get papped at the school, surrounded by little kids, including my own kids. Kids everywhere. And me in the middle. Being benevolent and gracious. Just *mother the fuck out of it.'*

Adriana looks sceptical.'Well, to be honest, the paparazzi aren't likely to turn up to some school in the middle of nowhere. It's going to look better if it's at the hotel. Which is an international destination.'

'I guess so,' says Juliette, sulkily. 'Maybe we can grab some kids from the hotel for the shot. Maybe the cleaners have got some spare kids with them. I want maybe twelve, fifteen kids around me besides my own kids. Is that enough? Fifteen kids? Is that overkill?' asks Juliette, narrowing her eyes.

'We'll sort it when we get back, don't worry.'

Juliette sighs heavily and scrolls through her phone disconsolately.

Fucking Micky. Nothing. He's got his fucking phone turned off.

The SUV pulls off the main road and heads up a dirt road, kicking up clouds of red dust behind it as it bounces towards Christ Blood School which appears in the distance, a long, low, single-storey brick building, painted in pale pink.

As the vehicle draws nearer, a crowd of some twenty children become visible, gathered in front of the school and all dressed identically, the little boys in blue cotton shirts and trousers, the little girls in blue cotton dresses. They are aged between five and ten and all of them are beaming with radiant smiles.

Mac Donald climbs out of the front of the SUV and opens the back door for Juliette and Adriana. Heat billows into the air-conditioned interior.

Juliette eases herself out of the back seat, careful to keep her white jodhpurs and freshly pressed white cotton shirt as pristine and crease-free as possible. She ducks her head to avoid knocking the white fedora she's wearing, and adjusts her huge, mirrored shades.

She glides with studied poise towards the children, followed by Mac Donald and Adriana, a picture of pristine and perfumed elegance.

The children are a sea of eyes full of wonder and amazement. But even as she walks towards them, they are already dancing on the spot, jogging up and down rhythmically, flapping their arms around and singing their welcome song as a united choir.

'We are Christ Blood children
We feel joy down in our hearts
We welcome you with open arms
Our shining movie star'

Over and over again they repeat the refrain, every one of them smiling at Juliette and Adriana, who stand transfixed at the outpouring of genuine love, affection and wonder flowing from the children towards them.

'This is just *beautiful,'* whispers Juliette. She removes her sunglasses and, suppressing the lump developing in her throat, bends down to shake the children's hands in turn. As they all reach for her, Adriana quickly snaps a photo on her phone.

A tall white woman, wearing a multi-coloured turban and long, brightly coloured dress, walks towards them, smiling.

'Welcome to Christ Blood School,' she says stiffly, thrusting a hand in Juliette's direction. 'Thank you for travelling so far to see us. Would you like to have a tour of the school before we head to the meeting room?' she asks, crisply.

'Sure. What a bunch of fine li'l dudes!' says Adriana, brightly.

'They are progressing enormously well. If it weren't for the funding we receive, they wouldn't have a chance in life. Our philanthropists are our life blood.'

'As well as Christ,' quips Juliette, pointing up at the crucifix which rears from the peak of the roof.

The tall bony woman bristles and opens her mouth to speak.

'She's kidding,' steps in Adriana. 'We're both huge fans of God. Great guy. Love his work. Jesus too.'

'We will proceed inside. Praise his name,' says the woman, glancing up at the cross.

The sea of children is now chattering excitedly amongst themselves in Chichewa, their eyes shining with joy and love.

'Thanks, kids, that was really wonderful. You're all little stars to me,' says Juliette, warmly, grinning down at them.

The children break out in a spontaneous cheer, waving their hands around and grinning.

As the women follow the head of school into the shade of the low building, Adriana shows Juliette the photo she's just taken.

'That is great, Adriana!' Juliette exclaims.

'Shall I insta it?'

'Yeah. Go for it!'

'You want me to @ Micky in it?'

'Nah. Fuck him.'

Moon and Cypher are already asleep by the time Juliette and Adriana return from Christ Blood School. Flea is sitting up in bed, playing on his phone, with Nanny Frances sitting nearby, also on her phone. Juliette gingerly opens the bedroom door a crack, not wanting to wake the children if they're already asleep.

Frances hastily puts her phone down, but not before Juliette has noticed.

'Is this quality time?' she snaps.

Flea looks up at Juliette and smiles, holding out his little arms.

'*Mommy!* You've been gone so long. Did you bring me any toys from the school?'

'There weren't toys, honey. It was just a boring meeting at a school.'

'Were there kids?'

'Yeah, there were kids.'

'Did they have toys?'

'No, sweetie. They're very poor. They had some books. They were studying.'

'Oh,' says Flea, looking disappointed.

'We'll go to the mall as soon as we get back home and get you some toys, OK?'

'OK,' he says, glumly, looking down and pulling at his fingers.

'How have they been?' asks Juliette of Frances, who stands up and moves a pile of clothes from one of the beds to a suitcase.

'Fine. I took them to that private nursery, the one I showed you online? They've done some fun things. Moon's been a little off colour and sleeping a lot though.'

'Is she OK?'

'Yeah, I've taken her temperature, it's normal. I think it's probably just the change of scene, you know, all the travelling. We only arrived yesterday and we're off again tomorrow...'

'Yeah...' says Juliette, disinterestedly, gazing at Moon's sleeping head, blond curls tumbling over her white pillow.

'So…the photo shoot idea with the kids…I was wondering if it was going to happen this afternoon, after the school?' asks Frances.

'I was gonna call you about that but I got tied up in this meeting. It dragged on and on and on. So boring. All these facts and figures and statistics. And the photos with the kids weren't necessary in the end. Adriana got a great shot over at the school. I don't need the kids in.'

Juliette sniffs and fiddles with her hair.

'Anyway, I value their privacy. They're not just here for some *photo op.* They're here because *I want to be near my kids.* I don't like being thousands of miles away from them. Unlike some people,' she adds, pointedly.

'Sure, I understand,' says Frances.

'Well, I'm pooped. I'm going for a shower. Night night Flea,' says Juliette, bending over to kiss him.

'Can I have a bedtime story, Mommy?' asks Flea.

'Maybe tomorrow, Mommy's very very tired after all the work she's had to do today.'

'OK,' says Flea, quietly. 'Night, night, Mommy.'

He puts his phone next to his bed and rolls over, pulling the thin quilt around his face and reaching for his cuddly dragon.

'I'll let you know if there's anything else,' says Juliette to Frances as she leaves the room.

Frances turns the lights out and leaves through the adjoining door to her own room, glancing back at the children one last time for the night.

Flea lies still pretending to be already asleep, his eyes wide open, staring into the endless void of the impenetrable and scary darkness, Dragonbobs clutched tightly to his chest.

Juliette walks past Adriana's room on the way to her own. The door is ajar, and she can hear Adriana dictating a voice note.

'How did your gig go? I'm back at the hotel so I can chat for a bit. Let me know when you're free.'

Juliette pauses but there's no other sound. She returns to her own room and slumps into the spherical wicker chair. It is hugely uncomfortable, meant obviously for show and not sitting in, so she stands and looks out of the French windows at the floodlit gardens down below.

She scrolls through her phone.

Nothing from Micky. Absolutely nothing. It's as if I no longer exist. What time is it in LA? 11am. Perfect time to ring Susan.

As well as a friend, Juliette regards Susan as a mentor and a role model. She knows that in times of crisis, Susan inevitably dispenses wise words.

'Hi Susan, it's me.'

'Juliette! Hi, honey! How you doing?'

'Oh, yanno. I'm OK. I'm in Malawi on that humanitarian gig I told you about.'

'Oh yeah. Visiting the school?'

'Yeah.'

'Great! So how's it going?'

'The little kids sang for me and Adriana today. They were awesome. So cute. Then we had some meetings, sorted some sponsor shit out. We're cool.'

'Well, that's fantastic!'

'Yeah, it's real cool, but look, Susan, I'm having a real shit time out here.'

'Why? What's up?'

'Well, it's Micky…'

'OK…'

'He's still in Bulgaria, shooting that movie with Freya Stephens.'

'OK…'

'And I think they're fucking.'

'Right…' Susan sighs.

Juliette bursts into tears.

'I'm sorry, Susan. I don't mean to cry.'

'It's OK, honey.'

'It's just that everything's going to crap. He won't answer my messages. And the bitch is posting pictures of them together on Instagram that are getting like six million likes, so the whole world knows about it!'

'Pictures of what on Instagram?'

'Pictures of *them*. Together, you know? All over each other. With her saying "Oh I'm having such a great time on location with Micky Valance!" type of thing.'

'Well, maybe the shoot just happens to be a great one. It does happen, you know.'

'She interrupted my Facetime with him the other day. They were in his trailer. "Going over lines together." Yeah, right.'

'Well, that does happen too...'

'I know...' says Freya, choking back tears.

'OK, well look, what does your gut tell you?'

'They're fucking.'

'Then you could be right. Always listen to your gut. The gut never lies.'

'So you think they *are* fucking?' whines Juliette, pitifully.

'I don't know really, one way or the other. But *you* think they're fucking. That's more to the point. What I think doesn't really matter.'

'We've only been married a year! We've only just adopted the kids! I can't fail now! We've not even had a chance!'

'It's not a question of your failing, Juliette. Relationships are organic, honey. They keep growing and changing, they don't stand still, they change as you change, and they need to grow as you grow. A lot has happened to both of you in the past year. A year ago you were this young couple with no kids on a break from work, spending all your time together. Now suddenly you've got three little kids and you're both working on big projects. Your relationship has moved into different territory, so of course it's going to change.'

'But why can't it change so we get closer instead of it changing so he's fucking someone else?'

'We both know what this business involves, Juliette. I don't need to tell you.'

'Yeah, remember Creepy Charlie on *Tulips?'* replies Juliette, breaking into a rueful smile through her tears.

'How could I forget?' laughs Susan. 'What a douche. But what I'm saying is, on location, shit happens.'

'I'm sure he's fucking her. I just know it.'

'But you know, Juliette, it's not just about him. And it's certainly not about Freya Stephens. She could be anyone.'

'She probably is. She's probably one of hundreds.'

'Well there you go.'

'So you think she is? One of hundreds?'

'I'm not saying that. What I'm saying is that even if it's only her, it's not about her. Or him. This is about you and where your boundaries lie. About what is and what is not acceptable to you. There's a moral bottom line in any relationship - this is what I will not put up with. This is what I will not accept. And, you know, maybe Micky is crossing boundaries that are unacceptable to you.'

'Like fucking other women? Well of course that's unacceptable.'

'It happens, and a lot of women put up with it in this business, Juliette. We both know countless examples. I'm not saying they should or they shouldn't. I won't judge. Everyone is different, and everyone's moral bottom line is drawn in a different area. For some women it's being unfaithful once, a one-night stand. For others it's a short fling. For others it's a relationship where it's just based on sex and your partner isn't emotionally involved. For others it's basically anything goes, like an open relationship. What I'm saying is it all depends on *you,* Juliette, and where you draw your bottom line. And that line, he cannot cross without it spelling big trouble.'

'Well he crossed it. I want to be his everything. I don't want him desiring any other woman except me. I should be enough for him. I'm beautiful, aren't I?'

Susan laughs, gently.

'Sure you are, honey, but it's not only about looks. Looks are gonna fade some day, like a peach left in a bowl for a week. There has to be more to a relationship than just looks. What you look like is only the wrapping on the box. It's what's inside the box that's important. Such a cliché, but so true.'

'Yeah, and I guarantee it one thousand percent that he's inside Freya Stephens' box, probably right now.'

Susan laughs. 'Well, maybe you should just confront him about it when you get back. When's he due for a break from filming? Is he coming home?'

'I dunno,' says Juliette, sulkily, her crying having abated into the odd sniffle of self-pity.

'Get a good night's sleep, honey. Things always look better in the morning.'

'Yeah...hey let's meet up when I get back, it's been too long...'

'Sure, honey, it's a plan. Call me.'

As Juliette hangs up, her heart surges at the unexpected sound of a text alert.

She stares at the phone, hoping to see Micky's name pop up. Instead it's 'Pork Chop' Her heart plummets into her gut.

Do more work on Micky and less on licking those pussies then get back to me. I want a yes by Friday.

Juliette shoves the words into the 'Pork Chop' box in her head and turns a key in the lock. She's not dealing with it. Things are stressful enough already.

Fuck him.

She looks outside at the big silver moon shining through a shroud of gauzy mist. Despite the warm night and the beauty of the moonlight, Juliette shivers involuntarily and her skin crawls.

⁂

As the Airbus takes off from Lilongwe and climbs through a vast bank of cloud, Juliette sits back, closes her eyes and ears to the din and chatter of Nanny Frances and the kids, and dreams of drinking chilled champagne from a tall flute, just before dinner is served in her favourite restaurant in Paris - warm asparagus spears, drizzled in hollandaise sauce. Micky sits beside her, gazing adoringly at her and tenderly holding her hand.

She seizes the vision and holds onto it in her mind.

I'm exhausted. The trip to Africa. Wayne Montana just, like, non-stop. Freya Stephens parading my husband all over social media. It's all just a phase, a dog turd on the sidewalk of my life. Things can be good again. Things are going to be just fine.

13
THE VITAMIN SHOT

BRUCE EMPTIES THE BOTTLE OF RED INTO HIS GLASS and places it back on his desk to join the other three empty bottles. He takes a gulp of wine then turns back to the typewriter.

Lara enters the barn, walks over to Bruce and puts her arms around his neck, bending forward to tenderly kiss the top of his head.

'Darling, Richard phoned earlier. I didn't want to disturb you but I guess you should give him a ring back.'

Bruce stops typing, turns and looks at his wife and smiles.

'What did the fat fuck want?' he asks warmly.

'He said the shoot for *Downton Abbey*'s been delayed. He's got a month at his girlfriend's place in Málaga. He wants us to go over and join him.'

'I'm too busy. *The Block*. It needs more work.'

'Darling, I'm wondering if maybe it might do you good. To get away for a bit. And us, too, to be honest…' she trails off, hopefully.

'Who'll look after the menagerie?'

'Gina's got a few stables empty at the moment, she'll have the girls over at her paddock...and James can look after the chickens...'

'You've already arranged it then...'

'Gina just happened to ring me. Right after Richard. And James heard and volunteered. I think he can see you need a break, too.'

'I'm cracking up, am I? It's that obvious to everyone except me?'

'No, darling. You're not cracking up. I just think we need to get away for a bit. And Richard really wants to see you. He loves you, Bruce. It'll be like a vitamin shot to your system.'

'Well, if you think so. Can you organise it?'

Lara takes both his hands in hers and kisses him on the cheek.

'Of course. Come on, let's eat.'

She walks out of the barn followed by Bruce. As he walks across the courtyard towards the main house he has the sense that he is being watched. He looks over towards the stables and Comet is hanging her head from the top of the stable door, staring at him sideways out of one eye, warily following his every move.

'Sorry,' he mouths at her and she raises her head and nonchalantly looks away from him.

Richard puts down his phone and turns to his girlfriend, Maria.

'I knew it! Lara says her and Bruce are coming over. Fantastic!'

Maria sits at a make-up mirror, illuminated around its margin with bright light bulbs. She pouts into it and finishes touching up her lip gloss.

'So I get to meet the famous *Bruce.*'

'You do. He's the most wonderful person *I've ever met.*'

'I know this, Richard. You tell me all the time.'

'Yes but you *don't understand.* He is a legend. A fucking *legend.*'

Richard stands up and starts pacing up and down the terracotta tiled floor of the apartment.

'There isn't a man walking this *earth who* has more intelligence, more verve, more *chutzpah,* more creativity!' he announces with an emphatic flourish of his hands.

'I know, I know. He is a "God amongst men".'

'He fucking *is!'*

'And this is not just because the best role of your life was in his film, of course, Richy?'

'Don't call me Richy.'

'Your precious *Withnail*?' she adds, sarcastically.

'No!' exclaims Richard in wide-eyed disdain at Maria's suggestion of self-interest. 'It's because *every fucking pore of his skin oozes genius.* He *eats genius for breakfast.'*

'But he's an alcoholic, right? It's not so clever to drink so much you fall over all the time. He's just a typical *guiri.* Wake up, drink, fall asleep in the sun, get burnt, go home on the plane and tell everyone all about your fantastic holiday,' she sneers with disgust, waving a hand dismissively.

Richard bends down and jabs a finger at the back of her mane of black hair whilst she coolly appraises his reflection through her mirror.

'You do realise that this *great man* wrote and directed what is widely considered to be *the* greatest comedy film of all time. Don't you?' he demands.

'Yes. You tell me all the time,' snaps Maria, archly raising one eyebrow.

'How can you be so dismissive?' he answers, a hurt, slightly disbelieving expression replacing his frustrated anger.

'I gave the greatest performance of my life in *Withnail and I!* In fact, I've been told that my performance as Withnail is the greatest performance in the history of cinema!' he announces, triumphantly, throwing both arms open widely and flicking his hands to emphasise the point.

'And not just by one person, either! By *several people!* People who *matter!* People who *know!* People in the *industry!*'

'You mean your little coterie of *amigos.* It's a very small world, your world of acting and films...'

'Unlike your great big world of *Instagram stardom,*' laughs Richard, bitterly.

'How many followers do you have on Instagram? 90,000?' demands Maria.

'130,000, actually,' counters Richard, smugly.

'Wow! And how many do I have? *Three quarters of a million!*' snaps back Maria, smirking at him tartly before turning her attention back to the mirror and a tiny strand of stray hair which is spoiling the hard-lined precision of her perfectly defined eyebrows.

'It's not a competition,' he whines, a genuinely hurt look passing over his face now.

Maria stands, turns round, wraps her arms around Richard and wiggles her body against him, looking up at his face and smiling, flirtatiously.

'I know. I'm just teasing you, Richy. Don't be so angry. We'll find you some more Instagram fans. We'll do more selfies together. Then *my* fans will find *you!*'

Past 11am, the Plaza de la Merced is still brimming over with people eating and drinking at the cafés and restaurants which line the square. The orange street lights glow against the backdrop of mature trees, strung with pretty white fairy lights.

Richard E. Grant sits high above the square on the balcony of Maria's apartment, typing up his diary on his laptop. The warm air is suffused with the aroma of jasmine floating up from the square.

14
CURTIS CHRIST

ELLA PUTS HER PHONE DOWN WITH DISGUST.

can't make it tonight babe. gig is on again xxx

'What the actual fuck.'

'What?' asks Jem disinterestedly. She removes the bottle of Prosecco from the ice bucket in front of her, picks it up and examines the level before pouring herself another glass and swigging half of it back in one.

'Zack. The gig that was cancelled is on again. He's not coming tonight. So I'm going to have to perform *alone.* Here, at the fucking ICA. With absolutely *no-one* I know in the audience. The fucking Institute of Contemporary Arts! There might be fucking critics! And I'll be on my own! 'Cause you're not staying, are you?' Ella looks hopefully at Jem.

'Nah babes, got to shoot to meet that bloke I told you about.'

'The one from Tinder?'

'Yeah.'

'I thought you'd deleted the app?'

'Downloaded it again. Anyway. Thank fuck it's fucking Friday!' shouts Jemima, cheerfully, raising her glass.

'I'll drink to that,' says Ella, sullenly, taking a long swig of wine, her attention caught by the brightly coloured bottles lining the illuminated white shelf above the bar.

'How's things? What have you been up to?' asks Jemima.

'I've had an idea for a new book.'

'Go on...'

'You're actually interested? You're never interested in my life.'

'No, go on, I wanna hear about it,' says Jemima, casting her eyes towards the door on the lookout for more interesting people than her friend.

'I want to write a novel with Bruce Robinson as the protagonist.'

Jem looks blank.'Who?'

'He wrote and directed *Withnail and I*.'

'Oh yeah! Him! Great film,' nods Jem.

'He was also nommed for an Oscar for his script for *The Killing Fields*. And he wrote and directed *The Rum Diary*.'

'Never heard of it.'

'Big production. Top notch crew, that sort of thing. With Johnny Depp.'

'Ooooh *Johnny Depp*. I like him.'

'Well Bruce has just spent the last fifteen years writing a biography about Jack the Ripper.'

'Great,' says Jemima half-heartedly, knocking back the rest of her glass of Prosecco and looking round the room.

'So I thought, suppose I write a love story, where Bruce meets this beautiful, enigmatic, voluptuous redhead. A...I dunno...a journalist or something. And he falls in love with her, and they have this mad passionate affair, and it all turns to shit, and Bruce goes back to his wife. Tragic doomed romance sort of thing. What do you think?'

'Do you fancy another drink?'

'I'm performing tonight. I'd better go easy.'

'I'm just off to the bar, hold on.'

Jem sashays over to the bar and returns with another ice bucket nestling another bottle of Prosecco. Ella raises her eyebrows.

'Whassup? It's fucking Friday!' announces Jemima, joyfully.

Ella sighs, heavily. 'So, anyway, in my mind, the redhead basically looks like Juliette Janesson…'

'I *love* Juliette Janesson. She's gorgeous. Wish I had her tits. I might get a boob job actually. Mine are too small,' says Jemima, running her hands over her low cut top.

'Your breasts are fine as they are.' Ella takes a swig of wine and feel a relaxing warmth spread through her body. 'So what do you think?'

'I think I should go for it! I'm never going to have kids so breastfeeding's not an issue. Should I go for a D cup or double D? Whaddaya reckon?' says Jemima, pushing her breasts together and looking at Ella questioningly.

'…about my idea for a novel…'

'Yeah it's great.' Jemima drains most of her glass of wine in one. 'Do it, babes.'

'Juliette Janesson and Micky Valance don't look very happy at the moment, have you noticed?' asks Ella.

'They're the perfect Hollywood couple!'

'There isn't such a thing. These are just human beings who fart and shit just like you and me, Jem.'

Jemima picks up her phone and googles 'Mickliette'. She tilts her head sideways as she looks at a photo of the pair at a recent awards ceremony.

'They look happy enough to me.'

'Zoom in on their eyes. Are they happy eyes?'

Jemima enlarges the photo with her fingers and frowns with distaste.

'Oh my God! How much surgery has she had? She looks like a waxwork dummy!'

'*Whatever.* That's not the point. Look at the expression in their eyes. Their eyes are grim, sad, full of anguish. That's not a happy couple. They're a really fucking *miserable* couple.'

'Maybe they just don't like award ceremonies,' shrugs Jemima.

'Maybe they fucking *live* for the red carpet, Jem, but are fucking miserable 'cause their *marriage* is in crisis. They probably don't actually get to spend a whole lot of time together. It can't be easy.'

'Yeah must be really tough. A thousand pairs of Jimmy Choos, a private jet and surgery on tap. My heart bleeds. Anyway according to this, Micky's just started filming in Croatia with Freya Stephens.'

'See what I mean? Would you really want your husband the other side of the planet frolicking around in waterfalls with some gorgeous actor? I wouldn't.'

'I'd just like a husband,' sighs Jemima, mournfully.

Ella takes a gulp of wine. 'So that's me, anyway. How are things with you?'

'*Nightmare* day. Didn't stop. Wanker Dave, that head of department I told you about? Been on my case, *again.* Wanted another "One to one" in his office this arvo. I told him to fuck right off. Well, I didn't use those words exactly, I just said I already had a conversation scheduled. He's a dirty little perv. I hate him.'

'Right.'

'Told me, *again,* that I was *hot* the other day. Actually said "You're wasted in academia. You're far too hot."'

'*What?*'

'Yeah.'

'You should have reported him to HR. That's sexual harassment. Right there.'

'I know…but he didn't mean it like that. He thinks I'm fit, that's all.'

'But Jemima, it's not *acceptable.* To talk to your employee like that. It's bang out of order. It's sexist, predatory and intimidating.'

'Yeah. I suppose it is, really,' laughs Jem.

'Fuck, Jemima, you shouldn't need *me* to tell *you* this. You're being paid sixty fucking grand a year to educate women about this shit, for fuck's sake.'

'Yeah I know. I know you're right. It's just that sometimes he can be so…*nice.* He does like me…'

'What the fuck does it matter whether he likes you or not? He can't be allowed to talk to you like that. For God's sake, Jem.'

Jem looks down at her feet. 'Yeah. I think it's just…after that time I kind of encouraged him, that's all…'

'What time?'

'Um…we went for a drink, last year, at the end of term.'

'What happened?'

'Well, I guess I was quite pissed. He had his hand on my leg. And I didn't stop him.'

'Right…'

'And, you know, one thing led to another…'

'Let me guess. His hand being on your leg led to his knob being somewhere or other.'

'Well, I went back to his, didn't I?' Jem looks innocently at Ella, her eyes widening.

'And…?'

'Well I tried to say no, and actually, well, I don't know what happened, I passed out.'

Jemima looks sheepishly at Ella and finishes her Prosecco in one long slug.

'And then?'

'I woke up in his bed.'

'Clothed or naked?'

'Naked. I don't even know what happened.'

'And where was he?'

'In the kitchen, unpacking a Deliveroo.'

'Right…'

Jem lowers her voice. 'I was a bit sore, though. You know…'

'What? *Jemima!* Are you telling me that he got you so drunk you passed out, then he *raped* you whilst you were unconscious?'

'Shhhh! *No!* Of course not! It wasn't rape!'

'Well, what the fuck else was it, then?'

Jemima looks blankly at Ella.

'Jemima, I'm not being funny. But *that is rape.*'

Jemima visibly squirms. 'Let's not talk about it anymore,' she announces, firmly.

'OK. But did you report it?'

'*No!* Of course not! I can't even remember what happened!'

'But you were *sore,* Jemima. That means he *fucked* you. Whilst you were *unconscious.* Meaning that he had non-consensual sex with you. Which means *he raped you.* How can you work alongside him every day after *that?*'

'Well, he does think I'm hot,' shrugs Jem, smiling weakly.

Ella shakes her head in disbelief and quickly drains her glass. 'Whatever. I'm going to the loo.'

She feels heady and unstable as she walks across the bar, uncontrollably swaying despite her concerted efforts to look poised and in control.

By the time she returns, Jemima has lined up yet another glass of Prosecco for them both.

Ella looks at the wine.

I haven't eaten yet. Drinking on an empty stomach before a performance does not bode well. Shit. I'm pissed.

Steve Blow, a slam poet making a name for himself on the London circuit, enters the bar. He walks straight over to Ella and grins, arms open in greeting.

'Ella! Great to see you again! Thanks so much for coming tonight!'

Stand up and hug him, you dick. Don't think I can stand up without falling over. Fuck.

Ella smiles up at him from her seat. 'Hi Steve! I'll be right with you, just finishing off here...'

A waft of vague disappointment fleetingly passes over Steve's face. He nods and wanders over to the bar. Ella turns back to Jem, who suddenly seems completely plastered.

'I dunno why I put up with it!' she almost yells. People joining the ever expanding writers' group glance over at her, disparagingly.

'He's a fucking *cunt!* I should just tell him to *fuck off!'* Jem stands up as though to go to the bar again, waving her empty glass around for emphasis.

'I agree Jem. I keep tellin' ya.'

'I fuckin' hate him! Just because he's got a fucking *dick* does not entitle him to behave like a complete *cunt!'* Jem sags against the wall behind her, eyes unfocused.

'Yeah,' says Ella. Out of the corner of her eye she notices the writers group dispersing, filing next door to the performance area. She glances at her watch.

Fuck. It's almost time to go on. I haven't even read through my poem.

Ella turns to tell Jem that it's time for her to leave, only to find that Jem has slid down onto the bench, her head slumped on her chest. A thread of saliva slowly slides from the corner of her gaping mouth. Ella nudges her and Jemima opens her eyes with a start.

'Wha'? I'm awake! Wha'?'

'Jemima, I've godda go. Are you sure you're not coming next door to see me perform?'

'Nah. Not really my thing, poetry,' slurs Jemima. 'Godda hot date.' She lurches to her feet, supporting herself against the wall.

Ella guides her to the exit, barely able to stand herself. Outside, she flags down a cab for Jemima, who tumbles in, her skirt hiked up to her arse and her knickers showing. Two teenage girls walk past, glance at her and snigger, catching one another's eye.

Ella returns to the bar and orders a pint of soda water. Bracing herself, she walks next door.

The audience are already silently seated and Steve Blow is on stage, introducing the evening.

Ella takes the only free table, right at the front.

I'm on the wrong table. I should have sat at the back. Now everyone behind me can see that I'm quite obviously completely fucking arseholed.

Eventually, she hears Steve announcing her name.

That's my name. That's my cue.

With the aid of the table Ella carefully stands upright and walks with exaggerated steadiness up to the little stage, which is illuminated with two small spotlights. She stands in the glare, facing the shadowed audience.

'I was gonna read an intr'duction but don' think I'll bother...' she starts, then realises with horror that her words are coming out slurred.

'So this is it. "*Dark S'mmers...Summers.*" Wrote it last week...'

She delivers the poem in a slow monotone. It comes out a slurred mess. At the end, she looks out at the audience.

'Tha's it,' she mutters, walking off the stage awkwardly, dazzled by the lights.

The audience claps politely for a few seconds afterwards, as if ashamed at their own hypocrisy.

Oh, look, on the next table. That's Shenelle Dickinson. Haven't read any of her work. Bet she's good though. London Slam Poet of the fucking Year.

Ella leans over and slurs, drunkenly, 'Hiya Shenelle. Love your work. I've actually read some of it. You're great, you are. *Great.* I just *love* you. Your *work.* It's fuckin' *great.*'

Shenelle's haughty, pinched face tightens as she glares at Ella.

'Thanks,' she snaps, her thin lips attempting a smile.

Ella grins back, but Shenelle has already turned away.

Probably time to go.

As Ella makes her way to the door, Steve Blow approaches and hugs her. 'Thanks for performing Ella, you were great.'

'Sorry Steve. No. I was shit. Nerves got me.'

Steve nods then puts a reassuring arm on her shoulder.

'The writing carried it, don't worry.' Ella nods and smiles gratefully at his lie.

❧❧❧

Slumped in the cab, Ella stares at the shimmering, coloured lights of the West End outside the window, streaked into abstract patterns by slashes of sliding rain.

By the time the cab draws up to her house in Shoreditch, she can barely see or comprehend anything around her.

She opens the door of the cab, gingerly climbs out, then deflates slowly, sinking onto the wet pavement. She rests her forehead on the cold tarmac, dimly aware that she needs to get in the house, as lying on the pavement at night isn't the greatest move.

A crisp female voice somewhere above her snaps, 'Are you alright, Ella? Do you want a hand?'

Ella vaguely recognises the voice as her irritating neighbour, Elaine, who has miraculously appeared from nowhere to witness the spectacle. Ella twists her head to see Elaine's upside-down face peering at her.

'I'm fine. I wanna craaaawl home. And you,' - she lifts a finger - 'you're not gonna stop me.'

Ella somehow manages to hoist herself onto all fours and starts crawling slowly towards home, with Elaine standing on the pavement behind her, staring disapprovingly, glancing up and down the street in case anyone is watching.

Ella drags herself up the short pathway leading to her house, then up the three front steps to the front door. Miraculously, her keys materialise in her hand as soon as she reaches into her pocket. She pulls herself up by the door handle, fumbles the key into the lock and falls into the house, landing on the lounge carpet, a large, wet fish emerging from the depths of the sea to lie plump, lifeless and glassy-eyed on the sand.

❧❧❧

'Ella.' Zack touches Ella on her bare shoulders but she doesn't move.

'*Ella.* Wake up.' Suddenly, he sounds frantic. '*Fuck! Ella!*' he shouts, shaking her shoulders.

There is some detectable movement beneath one eyelid and she grunts.

'Wake the fuck up, Ella,' orders Zack.

With difficulty, Ella rises slowly to the surface of consciousness and opens her eyes.

'It's light. What time is it?'

'Ten o'clock.'

She opens her eyes and focuses on Zack. 'Ten o'clock? Where have you been all night?'

Zack sits on the bed next to her.

'Curtis is dead,' he says, shaking his head. His eyes fill with tears. 'He's fucking dead, Ella.' His voice cracks with grief.

Ella props herself up on one elbow, shocked into life.

'What? What happened? How? *Dead?*'

'I dunno exactly. A few of us went round to Scarlett's after the gig.'

'Fuck. No. Dead? He's dead?'

'Yeah.'

'Which Scarlett? Notting Hill Scarlett?'

'Yeah.'

'He's dead? Fuck. I can't believe it. That's fucking terrible. What happened?'

'I don't fucking know. We were in the garden, watching the dawn, chilling, you know? And Curtis falls asleep on the grass. About five in the morning I'm ready to get back here and I go over to Curtis to see if he wants to share a cab, and he's completely out cold. Just doesn't respond. So I turn him over, like, and he's…he's fucking *blue,* Ella.'

'Jesus.'

'It was fucking *horrible.'*

'Fuck.'

'He was *dead.* Just like that. *Gone.* Fucking *gone.'*

'I can't believe it. Oh God. What did you do?'

'Tried to resuscitate him. Nothing. Called the ambulance and the paramedics were there in fucking five, man. Police cars everywhere too. Literally blocked off Elgin Mews. They've only just let us out the police station. Got to go back this afternoon to make a statement.'

'So, what, how did he die?'

'Dunno. There was some vomit on the grass where we turned him over.'

'So he probably choked on his own vomit.'

'Maybe. I dunno, Ella. It was horrible. Awful.'

'Fuck.'

'Seeing that. His face.'

'But he doesn't take drugs. He doesn't drink!'

'Fell off the fucking wagon didn't he? Found out Carrie's been banging the singer out of Doomintrolls.'

'Shit…'

'So he was knocking back vodka all night. Got on stage. Drumming was spot on. But then early hours he starts on the Tequila.'

'Oh God, no.'

'We're all telling him to take it easy. Just wouldn't fucking listen.'

'Oh, Curtis.'

'You know that fountain thing Scarlett's got? With the cherubs on it?'

'Yeah.'

'The cherub fountain, yeah. He was lying next to that. On the grass. Just…dead.'

'Jesus.'

'Worst thing that's ever happened to me.'

'Worst thing that's ever happened to *him.*'

'So when I came back and saw you, you know, lying there…'

'You thought I'd *died?*'

'Well, I don't fucking know. You didn't move when I touched you.'

'Well, I'm still here.'

'*Fuck.* Can't believe he's gone. Just like that, *gone.*'

'Oh God. Curtis. I should have talked to him when he dropped round. Something was obviously up. Why didn't I talk to him?'

'You couldn't have stopped it, babes.'

'No,' says Ella, glumly.

They both stare mutely at the floor as noise from the traffic beyond filters through the open window.

Ella sits, deep in thought, staring at the concentric circles of pebbles surrounding the pond, sipping on a pint of spring water.

Zack sits down heavily on a plastic garden chair and cracks open a cold can of beer.

'Fucking six hours down the cop shop. Fuck me.'

'Where's Curtis?'

'In the fucking mortuary, where do you think he is?'

'I just wondered. Where he actually *was.*'

'We didn't see him being taken away. He was still there when we went down the police station.'

'Right.'

'So, what have you been doing all afternoon?' asks Zack, wearily, taking a swig of his beer.

Ella turns to face him and sighs, deeply.

'I got completely wasted last night as well. Made a right tit of myself at that poetry reading. You know, I had a few drinks with Jem beforehand.'

Zack rolls his eyes. 'I've told you, she's fucking bad news that woman. Total fucking flake. Fuck knows how she holds down that lecturing job.'

'She gets used, that's how. She was telling me about it last night.'

'Well she fucking asks for it.'

'Don't say that, Zack. She's fucked up. Her father raped her as a child. She's very confused, and very damaged. That's why she drinks. It's an anaesthetic. To cope. To forget. It's the only time she feels safe, when she's drunk. Ironically.'

'Yeah well, whatever. You know what I think of her.'

'She's got a good heart.'

'No she hasn't. She uses you as a drinking buddy. End of.'

'OK. Well, she won't be doing that anymore,' says Ella, quietly. 'Because I'm not drinking anymore. Starting from now.'

Zack takes another swig of his beer and smiles, patronisingly.

'Oh, really? *You?* Not drinking?'

'Yeah. It's time to stop. It killed Curtis, didn't it?'

'*Choking* is why Curtis is dead.'

'*Alcohol* is why Curtis is dead.'

'Yeah, yadda whatever.' Zack picks up another can and examines the label.

'I've been reading up on it, Zack. All afternoon.'

'Right.'

'Alcohol causes cancer. Did you know that?'

'Don't believe everything you read on the internet.'

'I read it on medical sites, for fuck's sake. It's killing millions of people every year. It killed Curtis Christ just like it killed Jimi Hendrix. And no-one seems to give a shit. Everyone just carries on as if it's fucking *normal,* drinking themselves to *death.*'

'Jimi Hendrix didn't drink himself to death. He was *murdered.* Everyone in the industry knows that.'

'Well I'm not *in* the industry, whatever that is. And I'm not interested in conspiracy theories. But you get my *point.*'

'I get that you're *ranting.*'

'I'm not *ranting.* I'm telling it you straight. Countless women are addicts, just from drinking Prosecco in wine bars at lunch and after work. And that's what *I've* become, Zack. A wine o'clock Prosecco addict.'

Zack winces and looks deeply uncomfortable.

'Yeah. A pisshead. You neck it back a bit. But you're hardly an *addict,* for fuck's sake. You're not an *alchy.*'

'A drunk male artist is an intriguing rogue. A drunk female artist is an embarrassing, washed up old hag. I can't change society. But I can change *me.* I'm stopping.'

Zack stares at Ella for a few moments, thoughtfully.

'OK. So how does that fit in with the fact that me and Benjy are opening a fucking micro-pub, then? You're just gonna sit there and drink water and start banging on about "Wine o'clock Prosecco addicts"? That's gonna be great for business, isn't it? We've failed before we've even begun. Nice one, Ella. Thanks for your fucking support.'

'Zack, this isn't about what is good for *you.* It's about what is good for *me.' E*lla glances coldly at him then paces up and down next to the pond. 'I can't keep using booze to self-medicate away my problems. Booze isn't going to erase my terrible childhood, is it? Or stop me getting raped? Booze is just going to drag me down and possibly fucking kill me.'

She stops pacing and turns to look at Zack. 'I want to fucking stay alive, Zack. I don't want to give myself a fatal head injury from collapsing on a pavement or drown in a pool of my own sick or die slowly of an incurable cancer in some hellish hospice out in Boreham

Wood. I want to *live.* I've got a fucking book to write for a start. I'm just not doing this anymore.'

Zack stares at her as if she's gone mad.

'Never drinking again? We've all been there. You're just hungover, darlin'. And in shock. You'll get over it.'

Smirking, he takes a swig of his beer and leans back in his chair.

'Well, whatever you think, I've made my mind up. And I'm going away for a couple of weeks, Zack, I've decided,' she says, examining her fingernails, one by one.

'Oh, you're going away, are you? Where?'

'Marbella. You know my old friend, Isabella?'

'The author?'

'Yeah. She asked me if I wanted to go and stay at her villa. I think it'll do me good.'

'You haven't seen her for years. You might hate each other.'

'I've known her since we were five years old, Zack. I feel safe with Izzy. No other responsibilities or distractions. Just go over there and write. Izzy understands, being a writer.'

'*I'm a writer.* I write fucking *songs.*'

Ella stands up and looks at Zack wearily.

'Whatever.'

Zack finishes the dregs of his can of beer and stares at her, mournfully.

'Do what you want.'

15
Going

THE SKY OVERHEAD IS FILLED WITH A DARK, MENACING layer of cumulonimbus. The air is thick and muggy. The sun glints briefly then vanishes, swallowed up by the grey cloud bank.

A sudden chill stirring in the air pulls Bruce from his reverie, prone on a large navy blue towel on the grass, next to the swimming pool. He squints at the sky and rolling over, blearily reaches for the glass standing on the tiled poolside. He takes a slug of warm wine, which the heat of the afternoon sun seems to have transmuted into a quite disgusting fluid. He grimaces, finishes the glass and pours another from the almost full bottle standing by the pool, this time knocking back the entire glass in one, noting that this one is not quite as disgusting as the warm dregs he's just swigged.

A flash of lightning slashes open the clouds, blanching the landscape for a moment. A few seconds later, a crack of thunder peals from their depths and a threatening energy pervades the field where he lies, as the detonation gives birth to thudding echoes, rumbling onwards into the distance. Large drops of water fall suddenly from the still air, turning the surface of the pool into hissing spikes and instantly drenching him.

Shit.

It doesn't matter.

The rain doesn't matter.

A storm doesn't matter.

He turns onto his back and lets the rain fall on his face as he stares at the darkness above.

I've got this far. Seventy. An age I thought I'd never even reach.

He ponders, blinking against the hammering rain.

I'll always feel like a failure compared to Dickens and Beaudelaire. But what does it matter what I think? What does human opinion matter anyway when the planet's irreversibly frying in the climate crisis and our galaxy is just a speck amongst billions?

Thunder booms again and he laughs, the rain running down his cheeks.

The rain starts to fall more heavily now, and the air is almost crackling, alive with electricity.

Probably not the best place to be in an electrical storm, lying next to a swimming pool in the middle of a field.

Bruce reluctantly and laboriously stands up, picks up the wine bottle and empty glass and trudges back across the field towards the house.

The huge ash trees overhanging the field have taken on a brooding, threatening air in the growing storm, flexing their muscles against the chaos and standing stark black, silhouetted against the clouds.

The flooding ground underfoot is squelchy. Mud leaks over the tops of his Birkenstock sandals making his feet slimy.

He walks gingerly across the now perilous terrain, clutching the bottle and glass close to his chest.

A flash of pinkish lightning illuminates the sky, almost immediately followed by a deafening clap of thunder. The trees seem to scream in silence and the rain momentarily recedes. Bruce pauses and looks upwards.

Must be in the eye of the storm now.

He starts walking again.

Finally he reaches the house. He walks through the doorway into the kitchen, a sheen of rain covering his torso, his swimming trunks soaking wet and his silver hair slicked to his face in damp strands. Lara looks up from the breakfast table and stares at him, quizzically.

'What are you doing, Bruce? Where have you been?'

'I *was* sunbathing by the pool. Thought I'd better come in. There appears to be a storm.'

'It's been pissing down for twenty minutes. Why have you been sitting out there in the pouring rain?'

'*Lying* in the rain.'

'Well whatever have you been doing, *lying in the rain?*'

'Enjoying it, oddly enough.'

Lara rolls her eyes slightly and sighs.

'Have you seen James today?'

'No.'

'Well he can't get out of bed. He's running a temperature and he's been vomiting for the last hour.'

'Oh dear...what do you think it is?' Bruce says, still dripping on the stone kitchen floor and starting to feel cold.

'I've got no idea. But I can't leave him like this...'

'What do you mean?'

'I mean we're due to drive to the airport in a couple of hours and I can't possibly leave him like this.'

'Has he got a hangover?'

'No. He's not got a *hangover,* Bruce. He had an early night last night. This is food poisoning or a virus or something. Why does everything have to relate to booze with you?'

'Because I'm an alcoholic?'

'Nevertheless, everything doesn't come down to booze. Especially where the kids are concerned.'

'I didn't say it did. I just genuinely wondered whether James had a hangover. That bottled beer he drinks is enough to make anyone ill. Anyway, he's twenty-three, not ten. He'll be OK. He's got access to food and water.'

'It's not just him I'm worried about. He's looking after *the girls.*'

'Horses or chickens?'

'Chickens. The horses have gone to Gina's, remember? But James still has to put the girls in their coop at night and let them out in the morning, feed the cats and walk and feed the dogs. He can't even move, Bruce. He's got a sick bucket next to his bed. I can't expect him to look after the animals whilst he's like this. He can't even look after himself. And he looks terrible. His hair is all matted with sweat. I hate seeing him like this. I hate it when the kids are ill, you know that.'

'Well can't one of his mates come and help?' Bruce offers, glancing at the kitchen door and longing to get dried and dressed, but sensing that this is a conversation which is not to be interrupted.

'We're in the middle of fucking nowhere, Bruce, no, they can't.'

'What about that bloke, Tom?'

'I don't know...I don't know about Tom...but I don't feel right just flying off to Spain and leaving James like this. *I can't do it.* I just *can't.*'

'So it's not the animals. It's James,' sighs Bruce, wearily.

'It's everything,' says Lara, her voice rising. 'I've got *responsibilities* here. I can't just *walk out* on my responsibilities.'

'James is an *adult* darling. He's not dying. Bit of flu maybe.'

'James is *my baby* and he's *ill*, Bruce. I am *not* leaving him like this.'

'What, so I'm going to Spain alone?'

'You'll have a great time. You and Richard.'

'But I thought the idea was that *we* had a break. Us. *Together.* Which you keep saying *we need.*'

'We *do,*' says Lara, insistently. 'But not right now. *I can't.* I have to stay.'

'So why don't you just book two more flights for next week? Go then?'

Lara looks unsure but shakes her head.

'It's just too complicated, Bruce. Gina's at a show next week and you've got that speaking gig coming up at Oxford University...'

'Next week? God. Really? Is it that soon?'

'Yes. It's that soon.'

'These bastards just sneak up so quickly. One after the other.' Bruce starts walking slowly towards the hall door, shivering slightly.

'So I'll drive you to the airport, then I'll get back here. You have a week in Málaga with Richard and his girlfriend. What's her name again?'

'Maria.'

'Maria, that's it. It's just what you need. To get away for a bit.'

Bruce shrugs. 'I've got to get out of these shorts and dry myself off, I'm freezing.'

'Why did you get caught in the storm, did you fall asleep by the pool?' asks Lara as he reaches the door.

Bruce pauses in the doorway.

'It caught me unawares. Fell asleep under the sun. Woke up and the sky was black as pitch.'

As if on cue a bright flash illuminates the dark courtyard beyond the kitchen window and a deafening boom rattles the cups on the wooden dresser.

'Terrific storm,' marvels Bruce.

Lara looks distracted, frowns, and picks up a jug of water and a glass.

'I need to get James to drink something. And you need to pack,' she shouts after Bruce's retreating figure. 'We'll be leaving soon.'

After lugging his case down the stairs, Bruce looks at his watch. Due to leave for the airport in half an hour. He stops at the end of the hall, puts the case down, turns on the dreaded iMac and checks his email.

Dozens of the fuckers since the last time I looked.

He wades through them all. Thankfully none of them are from the Ripperologist cunts. The last one he opens is from the author he met, Ella, sent almost two weeks ago.

Hi Bruce,

It was so lovely meeting you at the bookshop. I hope I didn't keep you too long, waffling on about my book idea. There's so much I wanted to ask you - you don't fancy doing an interview for my blog, do you? Anyway I'm about to go to Spain to start writing the book. I'll keep you posted with progress.

Best Wishes, Ella.

Bruce thinks, frowning, then fires off a reply.

Thank you for the e and including me in book - I thought Shakespeare's was a laugh and thanks for being there best BR.

He picks up his case and walks outside towards the Land Rover.

I'm not doing an interview for a bloody blog.

Three brown chickens run up to him and start chattering loudly, looking up at him expectantly in case he's bearing food.

'Not now, girls. I'm off on holiday,' he says, kindly, inwardly chastising himself for talking to the feathered little beasts as though they were human.

He hauls the case into the back of the car and turns towards the house, where Lara is emerging from the front door, looking harassed, and Charles is draped over the back of the sofa by the lounge window, panting wildly.

'Hope the traffic's OK,' Lara says briskly, walking towards the car. 'Have you got the keys, Bruce? Are you driving? I'll drive,' she says definitively, and climbs into the driver's seat. She puts her keys into the ignition then glances at Bruce. 'Have you got everything?' she asks, looking into his eyes, worriedly.

He smiles vaguely. 'No fucking idea. Let's just go.'

Bruce looks idly out of the aircraft window as the green fields and tiny houses of Leeds and Bradford vanish below the wad of grey candy floss which now engulfs British Airways flight BA2745.

The plane bursts into clear sky and a sheet of brilliant sunshine illuminates a grey, monotonous cloud sea as far as the eye can see. Only a tower of cumulonimbus far to the west offers any visual relief.

A large man sitting next to him stares ahead through thick, black-rimmed spectacles. The seat belt light pings off and the man unfastens his evidently tight, uncomfortable strap and immediately turns to Bruce,

'Where are you going then?' he enquires in a broad Yorkshire accent, his high, nasal voice slightly incongruous to his bulky frame,

Bruce looks at him and smiles, politely. 'Málaga.'

'I'm going to Mijas Golf,' announces the man. 'Golfing holiday.'

'Ah.'

'Golf' adds the man with a wink, leaning toward Bruce, who manages to recoil slightly at the minor invasion of his body space without actually moving.

'Not a sport I've ever really tried.'

'It's not about sport. It's about *who you meet. Networking.* And the clubhouse bar, of course,' explains the man, self-importantly.

'Right.'

'So, you off on your own, then?'

'Looks like it. Meant to be with *my wife*, but she had to bail out at the last minute.'

'Nuisance when they do that.'

'Well, our son's a bit poorly...'

'Wouldn't know about that. Never had kids myself. No time, not with my business. My employees are my family. Finance. Went public this year.'

A flight attendant appears next to their seats with a trolley and offers them a drink.

'Scotch on the rocks,' demands the large man.

'I'll have a bottle of the French red, please,' says Bruce, grinning at the cabin attendant, who smiles back, her eyes sparkling.

'Not a Scotch drinker, then?' enquires the man, dubiously.

'No. Vino for me every time. Red. And French.'

The attendant delivers the drinks.

The man carefully pours a slug of whiskey onto the chunks of ice in his plastic tumbler and gingerly takes a sip. He grimaces, then aggressively flicks his fingers back and forth at the cabin attendant to summon her attention.

'Haven't you got any Bells? This J&B tastes *Irish*.'

'I can assure you it's Scotch, sir,' says the cabin attendant with a rehearsed smile. 'It's J&B.'

'Well it's got that tang of *Irishness* about it. What's been done to it? Has it been *tampered with?*'

'No, sir, none of our onboard drinks have been tampered with. They all have to pass security.'

'Well I'm not happy. Give me another one.' He thrusts the offending tumbler at the cabin attendant.

'We have a ten year old Laphroaig if you'd like it at no extra cost if we've inconvenienced you, sir.'

'Can't stand that stuff. Tastes like TCP. Have you not got any *Bells*?'

'No, sir, we only have J&B or Laphroaig.'

'I'll have another J&B, then. But not one that's been *messed around with*.'

'Certainly, sir. Would you like me to remove the one you've poured?'

'It'll do for now. Just pour the next one straight into it.'

The flight attendant unscrews another miniature of J&B and tops up the man's drink.

'More ice,' he instructs, holding out the tumbler.

'Certainly, sir.'

'Good *girl*.' He draws out the second word lasciviously.

As the flight attendant carefully plunks two cubes of ice into the man's drink, she catches Bruce's eyes which are watering with suppressed mirth. She smiles conspiratorially at him with her eyes, before standing and moving along the aisle.

The man takes a deep slug of his quadruple whisky before peering quizzically at Bruce.

'What line of business you in, then?' he demands.

'I'm a writer,' says Bruce, wearily.

'Oh. Right. A *writer*. Actually finished a book, then?'

'A few, yes.'

The man's eyebrows rise expectantly as he plays his trump card. 'Been published?'

'Erm. Well, yes.'

'Anything I might have heard of?'

'Well I wrote a film called *Withnail and I*. You may have heard of that.'

The large man looks suspiciously at Bruce's forehead and then studies the lines of his face before snapping back to his Scotch. He pushes out his lower lip and shrugs slightly.

'*Withnail*...rings a bell. Never seen it though. Written anything else? Anything popular?'

Bruce inwardly sighs and smiles as he elegantly raises the plastic glass of French red to his lips.

'Not really. I'm not really what you'd call a populist.'

'No, go on, try me. What else?'

'I wrote a film called *The Killing Fields*. The screenplay.'

'*Seen it!*' shouts the man, triumphantly, jabbing a finger. 'The one about the journalist in Cambodia!'

'The very one.'

'Didn't like it actually. Thought it was a bit slow.'

'Sorry you feel that way. Can't please everyone.'

'*Jason Bourne*. Now that's what a I call a film. Seen all t' *Harry Potters* too.'

'Fabulous.' Bruce turns to look out at the sea of clouds, stretching out to the horizon.

'You should watch those. Might learn summat,' says the man.

The flight attendant reaches across the man and places another bottle of red in front of Bruce, smiling. 'I saw *The Killing Fields* on Blu-ray the other week. Wonderful film. It was nominated for a bunch of Oscars, wasn't it? So that was you? You wrote that?'

The man looks from her to Bruce, trying to find a way to re-insert himself into the conversation.

'Yes, it was. And here I am. On a flight to Málaga, surrounded by… lovely company. Such as yourself.'

'Aw, thank you. Well, congratulations. I really did love that film,' says the woman, gently, before retreating back to her trolley and bending to collect more glasses.

The man stares at her backside before looking sideways at Bruce and smirking.

Turning his attention away from the grotesque sitting beside him, Bruce takes out a tattered red and white paperback of *Rimbaud's Complete Works.* He opens the page at a faded, creased yellow post-it note, which marks one of his favourite poems, *The Drunken Boat*, into which he can sink for the remainder of the flight.

The man glances at the book and slugs back the last dregs of his icy, watered-down Scotch.

'Can't beat a good Ian Rankin,' he sniffs.

But Bruce has already gone.

16
THE DESERT ROSE

JULIETTE POPS OPEN THE BOTTLE OF CHILLED CRISTAL, pours herself a full glass and swigs it down in one before slugging in a refill. She sinks back against the white leather seat of the SUV.

'Thank God I'm back. LA. The land of the sane.'

Brandon looks straight ahead as he cruises towards Los Feliz along the freeway from LAX, the pink and yellow lenses of his Dolce & Gabbana shades reflecting the burnished gold of the setting sun.

'Glad to be home, then, boss?' he says, over his shoulder.

'Yeah. It was hard work. And too hot. And too many goddamn *flies*. And *sooo* much poverty. Like *everywhere. So* depressing. Can't figure why everyone was like *laughing and smiling* when they've got *nothing at all* in their lives. I mean, their lives are like *totally empty.* They don't even have *cars.* I mean, how can anyone actually *live without a car?*' says Juliette with exasperation.

'You kinda seemed to have fun, Adriana.'

Adriana smiles. 'Aw, the kids there were cute. So sweet and friendly. You liked the pics I sent you?'

'Yeah. Those li'l kids at the school. Blew my mind.'

'Yeah well, I'm done with kids for a few weeks. It's Micky's turn now,' chimes in Juliette.

'I dunno what to think about Micky, insisting that the kids go from the airport straight to Bulgaria with Nanny Frances…' says Adriana.

'Micky is being a gigantic dick.'

'Well anyway, good to have you both back,'says Brandon, looking in his rear-view mirror at Adriana, who looks at him, flashing an intimate, secret smile.

Juliette scrolls through her phone with one hand, the other clutching her glass, and starts reading the article.

'Well this isn't good. Micky Valance and Freya Stephens looking kind of enmeshed here on the set of Shrader's Game, shooting in Bulgaria right now. Who took this coy little snap we don't know, but whoever it is is probably heading for the big heave-ho after leaking this little gem. Don't Micky and Freya look kinda cosy? And even, loved-up? Or is it just the camera angle? Micky's wife, Oscar-winning diva Juliette Janesson, isn't going to be very happy about this one!'

Juliette slams her phone onto the seat of the SUV.

'Fuck that fucking asshole Bing Bong Bill!' she yells. 'Have you seen this, Adriana? On *Bing Bong?*'

Juliette tosses her phone across the back seats at Adriana who catches it mid-flight.

Adriana reads the piece in stony silence then hands the phone back to Juliette.

'No-one reads *Bing Bong* any more, Boss. *No-one.* Bing Bong Bill was done years ago,' she adds, sympathetically.

'Yeah? Well 452 fucking people read this crapola. That's how many comments it's had.'

'Don't read 'em, boss,' warns Adriana, but Juliette is already poring through the vitriol.

'Bitch. Fucking *asshole!'* she exclaims as she reads each comment. 'Not one person defending me! Everyone saying *he* deserves someone better than *me.*'

'Nothing about you being a lesbian, then?'

'The Pork won't do that yet. That's his last resort. He's hoping I'll keep him sweet with Micky. He can go fuck himself.'

'And are you? Are you gonna encourage Micky to do this Jack the Ripper thing?'

'Am I fuck.' Juliette sticks her middle finger up in mid-air at an imaginary Wayne Montana.

'If Micky doesn't do the movie, Juliette, the Pork Chop's gonna poison the press with this lesbian shit. Be careful...'

'Yeah, I know...' says Juliette, her bravado evaporating. Her eyes sadden and she visibly withdraws into herself, sulkily gazing out at the multitude of lights spread across LA.

The car slows as a chorus of horns up ahead announces a traffic jam. Brandon looks out at the LA. sprawl.

All that shit. All that glory. All that deceit. All that mundanity. All those voices, jabbering, millions of them, out there somewhere, unheard.

Some of those lights will be coming from within four walls between which men are raping a child. And filming it. Others from homes where children are sleeping peacefully after kind fathers have tucked them up in bed with a bedtime story. Others from where musicians are composing on saxophones, gardeners are cleaning their tools, chefs are burning their fingers, women are weeping silently whilst others plot their revenge against the men who have raped them. And the homeless gazing wistfully from dark alleyways towards the lights.

All that human detritus. All that horror. All that love. All that humanity.

He can sense the kernel of a song rising out of the unthinkable chaos as he contemplates the hidden heart of LA and its seething population. He starts to imagine the rhythm, the timbre of the sounds weaving in and out of one another as a sad, haunting melody forms in his mind above a thick drum beat and heavy bass and he begins to hum the notes to himself as he watches and thinks and feels, his frail humanity drowning in the terrifying depths of LA's boundless joy and depravity. The horror and immensity of it all absorb him, the heaven of creation glinting from behind the oppressive clouds in his mind.

The traffic starts to move. With an effort, Brandon snaps back to the grid and puts the car into drive, trying to hold on to the half-formed song in his head.

He glances back at Juliette in the mirror. Her tired gaze has now mutated into a furious, steely glare as she addresses Micky on her phone.

'You've seen it then?' asks Micky, tentatively, his voice small and tinny on the speaker.

'Hell yeah! What the fuck are you even doing, curled up like that with *that bitch* on set? What is going on, Micky?' Juliette's voice lowers to an icy calm. 'Because if you don't tell me, I'm going to find out. And now it's on fucking *Bing Bong* for the *entire world* to see.'

'The *entire fucking world* doesn't read fucking *Bing Bong*, Juliette. Jesus. Chill the fuck out.'

'They *pretend* they don't. But they *do*. How much more of this shit do I have to put up with? Because, yanno, I'm seriously questioning this marriage. Every single fucking day of my life.'

She hisses into the phone, face inches from Micky's tiny image. 'I've been in fucking Africa and not been able to get hold of you for *a week*. What the fuck's *that* all about Micky? In fact, *don't even bother to answer*. Because I know *why*. Because you've been *fucking* Freya Stephens. Haven't you?'

There is silence on the other end of the phone.

'*Answer me*. Haven't you? Aren't you? Fucking *asshole!*'

Silence.

'Goddamit Micky. You fucking answer me *now* and tell me what the *fuck* is going on with that slack-pussied whore, you *asshole!*'

'Nothing's going on. We're just friends,' replies Micky, levelly.

'*Liar!*' screams Juliette, slugging back the remains of her champagne and thrusting the bottle and empty glass at Adriana to pour her another one. 'Lying asshole!'

Adriana stares at the empty glass and glances up at Brandon in his rear view mirror, who smiles back at her, ruefully.

The traffic slows to a snail's pace and finally grinds to a halt again as the sun slips down below the horizon, a haze of warm rust and crimson spreading across the sky. Adriana messages Brandon.

I'm free later if you wanna catch a drink downtown?

Brandon's dash-mounted phone buzzes with a Miles Davis riff. He glances over at the screen and looks in the rear view mirror again at Adriana, meeting her eyes.

'Yes' he mouths, without smiling, looking at her intently.

Adriana slips her phone into her bag, smiles silently to herself and glances out of the window at the sea of lights before her. Endless possibilities. Hope, excitement, joy and lust.

She glances back up at Brandon. He's smiling at her now, openly. Grinning. Adriana grins back and her heart surges.

'Champagne, Adriana,' demands Juliette, turning around and glaring at her assistant.

Adriana looks warmly at her boss with sympathetic eyes. 'Boss…'

The car swerves smoothly off the street, through the gates and onto the drive in front of Juliette and Micky's Los Feliz house.

Juliette has the door open before the car has even stopped. She climbs out, marches up to the front door, opens it, enters the house and slams the door hard behind her.

Inside, she rests her back against the inside of the huge, oak door, braces her feet on the marble floor and screams, shaking her head from side to side. The scream comes out as a primitive howl. Of pain. Of despair. Of shame. Of fear. She slides to the floor and curls up in a foetal position, great sobs heaving out from deep inside her, rasping her throat and blinding her eyes with tears.

Outside, Adriana and Brandon silently unload the luggage in the warm dusk, cicadas chirping in the gloom.

'Do you think you'll have to stay with her?' asks Brandon.

'Nah. She's cool, she just needs to get it out of her system.'

'So, shall we, like, just dump this stuff and shoot?'

'Yeah. Her Pilates instructor is due here in five anyway. And she absolutely promised me tonight off, after Africa. She's got her problems, but she's not a cold-hearted bitch. Unlike like some of them.'

'I know. I've grown kinda fond of her, yanno?'

'Yeah, me too. She's OK.'

'Cool. Let's do it.'

The pair smile conspiratorially at one another as they carry the luggage towards the house.

The Desert Rose Mediterranean Restaurant is mercifully quiet, with just a few midweek lunchtime diners seated here and there in the cool shade.

Juliette enters the shaded patio, which is dominated by a spectacular, twenty-foot high stained-glass rose which catches the sun, casting pink light onto the white-clothed tables.

Arriving early, Juliette is dressed incognito in grey jogging pants, a pale blue t-shirt, a white baseball cap and wearing large black Versace shades. She looks younger than her twenty-nine years with no make-up and almost unrecognisable as the A-list movie star. She sits at a discreet corner table at the far end of the terrace to wait for her friend, Susan Sarandon.

After ten minutes, she arrives.

Seventy years old, with auburn hair, large brown eyes, an ethereal beauty and a self-possessed confidence which belies her natural shyness, she attracts a few glances of recognition from the diners as she crosses the terrace.

Wearing a smart, geometric-patterned dress and flats, she smiles warmly when she sees Juliette sitting hunched nervously in the corner over a glass of champagne, scrolling earnestly through her phone.

'Sorry I'm a little late sweetie, the traffic across town is just crazy.'

Juliette stands up and the two friends hug one another warmly.

'That's OK. I've only been here a couple a minutes. Thanks for coming at such short notice.'

'I said we'd do lunch when you got back from Africa. I'm good for time this week, don't worry, and it's nice to catch up with you. Phones just aren't the same as face to face, don't you think?'

'Yeah, tell me about it. I've not seen Micky for over a month now. I'm fucking sick of seeing his face stuck in the middle of a small piece of plastic. I want him *here.*'

'Ah, Micky,' says Susan, sitting down and pouring herself a glass of water.

'Did you see it? The *Bing Bong* piece?' Juliette blurts out.

Susan rolls her eyes. 'I don't read that shit, Juliette. You know that.'

'Neither do *I.* That's the whole point. I'm stooping to a whole other level even reading this garbage.'

'You know it's garbage. Forget it,' says Susan, kindly. She catches the eye of the waiter, who comes across to take her order.

'A bottle of Pellegrino for me, please.'

Juliette looks nonplussed.

'What's wrong? You're not drinking?'

'Nah. I'm driving.'

'I got an Uber. And I am *definitely* drinking,' says Juliette, grinning and sloshing back her champagne. 'The world is a better place for me right now with champagne in it, that is for certain. I need this.'

'I dunno. I think the world would be a way more tranquil place if we just replaced booze with grass. Guys don't beat up on their wives when they're stoned, people don't fight in bars...'

'It makes me paranoid. And I do not need that shit right now...' Juliette says, adamantly.

'So anyway, what do you think? About the *Bing Bong* story? Oh, you haven't read it. Hang on. Here...' Juliette swipes through to the story on her phone and thrusts it over to Susan who scans the story quickly then sighs, heavily.

'I think you need to talk to him. Who knows what's going on? Like I said before, this could all be bullshit. He's on location a continent away. You know how tough that is. You've gotta figure out what you want from the relationship, I guess.'

The waiter appears with Susan's water and politely places the bottle and a glass with ice in front of her.

'Are you ready to order your food?' he asks.

Susan picks up a menu and scans it. 'I'll have the garbanzo and edamame salad, please.'

'And I'll have the asparagus linguini. It's delicious. Are you sure you don't wanna try it, Susan?'

'I'm good, sweetie.'

'I don't know what I want anymore,' says Juliette sadly as the waiter leaves.

'All I wanted was for Micky to love me, and act like he loves me. But it's not gonna happen. This is a joke. Both of us a world apart, working, the kids being trailed around between us. We're never in one place at the same time. And when we are, we fight. And him not being able to keep his dick in his pants...'

'Well, look, you have a choice. You could go buy a ranch in flyover country, stay home with the kids and have a nice, quiet life. But I know that's not what you want.'

Juliette looks mournful. 'Micky would never do that. He's totally addicted to his fame and the power he has over the opposite sex. I'm not addicted, though.' She looks up at the giant pink rose and adds 'I hate it, sometimes. I could give it all up tomorrow.'

'Including giving up the power *you* have over the opposite sex? 'Cause you know that's on the horizon too, right? Hitting fifty and becoming invisible?'

'Ha! I won't get to fifty.'

'Yeah, well you just might,' says Susan, laughing. 'But you get over it. You realise that being physically beautiful isn't the be all and end all. That, amazingly, there is a deep, profound happiness to be found outside of looking good. But it comes as a shock when it first hits you. That one day you glance at yourself in the mirror and you think "Fuck. I look old."'

'Yeah, well, you're preaching to the converted here. I'm already fucking old. I'm almost *thirty*.'

'It really kicks in somewhere around fifty-five. After that, it hits ya. I am actually gonna get old,' says Susan, laughing gently.

'You know something,' says Juliette, leaning over the table and lowering her voice. 'When I was like, eighteen and part of that whole Venice Girls scene, I was such a dork. I thought I was gonna remain forever amongst the privileged chosen few, "The Venice Girls," we were a breed apart, we were gonna stay forever young, unlike all those *old* people who through their own stupidity, failed to stay young and instead got *old*. And then, I dunno, around twenty-three, it hits me that I'm not gonna stay young forever and one day I'm gonna be just the same as all those other old people. I'm not "chosen". I never was. Every year I'm just gonna get older. Every year I'm gonna look worse, have more wrinkles and more saggy skin. And it's fucking depressing.'

'If you've got anything about you, which you *have*, Juliette, you roll with it and get over yourself. There's so much more to life than what a woman looks like. And that's where the joy comes in. When you realise where your real strengths lie and it's what's in *here* that counts.' Susan taps her head with her middle finger. 'And in *here*,' she adds, holding a hand on her heart.

'Looks can be a useful tool, but really they mean *nothing*, Juliette. They're the shiny wrapping paper on the box. And one day the wrapping paper loses its shine and becomes crumpled, tatty and torn. But, all along, it was *what's in the box* that really mattered.'

She shrugs and takes a sip of her water.

'Takes some people an entire lifetime to realise it. And then some people look in the box, into themselves. And they don't like what they find and spend the rest of their lives desperately trying to smooth out that tatty, crumpled old wrapping paper and spraying it with gloss to make it look shiny again. And all it ever looks like is sprayed-over crumple. Work on what's inside the box instead of trying to gloss over that crumple. Work on making what's inside the box beautiful. Then that beauty will seep through to the outside, and the whole fucking box will start shining. That's the secret. Look inside. Find yourself. Just become a nicer person. It ain't rocket science.'

'I'm already nice. Aren't I?' asks Juliette, aghast.

Susan laughs out loud. 'Sure you are, otherwise why would I be here?'

'Cause you feel sorry for me?'

Susan reaches across the table and takes Juliette's hand in hers.

'No, not because I feel sorry for you, Juliette. Feeling sorry for someone is the very worst reason to become someone's friend. Or lover, for that matter. Don't be led by pity. It's guaranteed to come bite you in the ass when you're least expecting it…'

Juliette's shoulders slump.

'I don't feel like I'm a nice person. I feel like a flake. And a phony. And a coward. And a failure.' Her eyes fill with tears.

'…says the Academy award-winning actor with three beautiful kids, who lights up any room she walks into…sure, that's totally my idea of failure too,' says Susan, gently.

She squeezes Juliette's hand. 'You're gonna get through this. Whatever it is. You're gonna reach inside yourself and find that strength and you're gonna come out fighting, Juliette. I'm not your friend because I feel sorry for you. I'm your friend because I know how strong you are and how much you've had to fight for that strength. You know, as women, we're not born strong. We have to fight tooth and nail, every inch of the way, to develop our strength. But it's in there. In all of us. Waiting for us to find it.'

'Well yeah, we all know *you're* strong.'

'But I didn't get strong *just like that,*' says Susan, clicking her fingers. 'I *grew strong.* And so will you. At the moment, you're a sapling whiplashed by winds. But you're gonna grow into a big old oak tree that even a hurricane can't touch. This is just part of the growing process. Don't cry too much at the wind, Juliette. You fight it, and you'll get strong.'

Juliette stares at Susan and tears roll down her face. 'I've never heard anyone tell it like that,' she says, quietly.

'Well, sometimes I feel whiplashed too. I feel weak too. I just don't show it too much. You're not alone, Juliette.'

The waiter arrives with their order and places the food on the table, professionally oblivious to Juliette's tears.

Acutely aware that she has just broken the golden rule of not letting her guard down in public, Juliette quickly scans the terrace. The restaurant is starting to fill up but none of the customers seem to have noticed who is sitting in the corner.

She looks down at her food and pushes it around the plate with her fork before looking up at Susan mournfully.

'Do you think it's gonna work out with Micky? I mean, what's your gut feeling on this?'

Susan sighs heavily and glances across the terrace at the customers arriving.

'I don't have the knowledge to predict an answer to that one, Juliette. Certain people come into your life for a purpose. Certain love stories almost feel inevitable, like they were meant to happen. It might end up not working out. But whatever happens, you will learn and grow from it…'

'So you think he'll run off with Freya Stephens?' asks Juliette, pitifully, her eyes filling with tears again.

'Look. Who knows what's gonna happen? But whatever does happen, you're gonna be fine. You're the strong one, here. Don't forget that.'

'OK,' says Juliette, smiling.

17
Málaga

'WHAT DO YOU MEAN, YOU'RE GOING OUT WITH YOUR friends? We have to get the apartment ready for Bruce! He'll be here in two hours! The place looks like a pigsty!' exclaims Richard, throwing his arms around in exasperation as he paces across the lounge of Maria's apartment.

'I don't know what it is, a pigsty.'

'A shit hole,' answers Richard, gesturing at the trail of Maria's clothes dropped across the floor between bedroom and bathroom.

'I can't live like this, Maria! These…these trip hazards! Going for a crap has become a life-threatening expedition!'

Maria walks across to him, reaches out and rearranges his hair. 'You love it, Richy.'

'Don't mess with my hair, I've told you a million times. I like it just so.'

'You need to go to the peluqueria. Your hair, it looks very old-fashioned. But you are still so *handsome,'* she purrs.

Richard pauses by a large mirror on the wall of the lounge to rearrange his hair back into carefully coiffed neatness.

'You have this way of making a man feel simultaneously chastised and flattered. I don't know how you manage it.'

'I am a word artist,' announces Maria, smiling smugly. 'It is my job.'

'You are a very messy young lady. Come on, we need to tidy up. Can you just, maybe, pick up your clothes? And I'll go and clean the kitchen.'

'We need a maid,' says Maria, tetchily, gathering armfuls of clothing.

'We do not need a maid. We just need a little organisation.'

The pair of them continue cleaning the apartment in separate sullen silence.

Just before ten o'clock, the intercom sounds. Richard rushes over to the apartment's front door and picks up the white plastic handset from its base.

'Hello? Is it you, Bruce?'

'Yeah. Hi.' Bruce's voice sounds tinny over the intercom.

'You made it! I'll buzz you in. Take the lift to the third floor and I'll meet you there.'

'OK.'

Richard turns to Maria, who stands examining her nails and avoids looking at him.

'Open that wine. Just put it on the table over there with three glasses. It needs to breathe. God, we should have done this half an hour ago. Never mind that, we should have met him at the airport.'

'We couldn't meet him at the airport. You had a meeting.'

'Yes and I feel bloody awful about it!' he barks, before rushing out into the hallway to meet the lift.

Maria rolls her eyes and reaches for the bottle.

The lift doors part, revealing Bruce, looking slightly bemused. He exits the lift, dragging his suitcase on wheels behind him, a leather messenger bag slung casually over his shoulder, his hair messed up and flyaway after the journey.

He grins and embraces his old friend, holding him tightly in a firm hug.

'Richard!' He laughs, openly. 'Good to see you.'

'Good to see *you!* Come on *in!*'

Maria turns from opening the wine to see Richard usher Bruce through the front door of the apartment. She is immediately struck by his aura. He exudes a lightness of spirit and natural charm as he walks smiling over to Maria and hugs her warmly.

'Hello! Maria! I don't speak any Spanish I'm afraid, but Richard tells me you speak perfect English.'

She smiles back at him.

'That's OK. I can understand almost everything. Except "pigsty". Richard teach me that word today,' she says, glancing over at Richard, who gestures behind Bruce's back, frantically drawing a line across his neck with his finger in an attempt to silence Maria.

'Now I know it means the same as "shit hole",' she adds, smiling at Bruce.

'What a beautiful pad you've got here,' says Bruce, looking around.

Antique mahogany bookcases line one wall and a large glass dining table sits in the centre of the room, lit from above with a blue Swarovski chandelier, its trailing chains of sapphire crystals glittering above the tapas of olives, stuffed artichokes, roasted peppers and patatas bravas laid out on the table.

Richard glares briefly at Maria then sweeps his hand towards the table.

'Come and eat. Would you like a glass of wine, Bruce?'

'I won't say no, thank you.'

Richard sweeps over, pours himself a glass of freshly pressed orange juice and fills the other two glasses with a 2010 Marqués de Riscal

Baron de Chirel, handing one each to Maria and Bruce, ostentatiously clinking Bruce's then Maria's glass. 'Salud!'

'Salud!' says Bruce.

'Salud!' says Maria.

As they drink, the three are united in the toast for the briefest moment of time, as life from the street below drifts up towards them. Shouts, conversation, laughter and the chinking of other people's glasses in other people's lives.

Later, sitting on the balcony drinking, Bruce is starting to slur his words, but his eyes remain acutely focused as Richard talks about their friendship.

'One of his finest moments was getting me drunk for the first and only time in my entire life,' explains Richard to Maria.

'You had never been drunk before…' says Maria, looking at him with a faintly patronising smile.

'Quite. I'd tried every type of alcohol known to man, but I hated the stuff. The character of Withnail, of course, is a raving drunk and Bruce here insisted that I experience being actually drunk before attempting to play Withnail drunk.'

Richard's eyes light up at the reminiscence.

Bruce smiles almost absent-mindedly as he glances between Richard and Maria, who, with her long, tumbling black hair and sultry Mediterranean beauty reminds him somewhat of his wife, only thirty years younger.

'So I knock back two entire bottles of champagne one evening, feel absolutely ghastly all night and arrive at this swanky hotel for rehearsals the next day with a head like a lump of lead and eyes like prunes. Notice the free bar and on impulse, fill a tumbler three-quarters full of vodka and top it up with coke. Knock it back and end up hurtling towards the French windows to spew my guts up all over the beautifully manicured lawn outside, with Bruce and my co-star, Paul McGann, laughing like hyenas in the background.'

'Wasn't laughing when I had to clean it up. Foul. I swear your champagne and vodka puke had clouds of radioactive fall-out hovering over it.' Bruce grimaces at the memory.

Even though she doesn't understand every single word, the humour and rhythm of Bruce's speech and his conspiratorial glances are enough to make Maria laugh. She can see why Richard loves him.

'Richard tells me this story many times,' she says gently to Bruce. 'It's a very funny story.'

'To your credit though, Richard, you nailed an on screen drunk better than I've ever seen before or since,' says Bruce, turning his attention back to Richard.

Richard looks smugly at Maria, who catches his eye and looks back to Bruce.

'Maybe I nailed the part, but you nailed the film. Greatest comedy film of all time and I remain eternally honoured to have been a part of it.'

Maria studies Bruce's face as he resumes talking to Richard. He has an aura, as though he's channelling some kind of current, and a casual rakishness which throws her off guard but which she simultaneously finds comforting.

With an effort, fighting slightly against the effects of the wine, she once again tunes in to Richard's and Bruce's conversation.

'There's a drawing room scene we're shooting once filming resumes...'

'Are you talking about *Downton Abbey?'* asks Maria.

'Yes,' says Richard, frustrated to be interrupted mid-flow when talking about his new TV show.

'And I'll be standing somewhere in the environs of a cabinet full of fine Edwardian glass. Candice, the girl from props has told me about all the glass they've got in there. Not only nineteenth century but gorgeous seventeenth and eighteenth century stuff! It's so...Rococo!'

He waves his right hand. 'According to the script, at some point I have to remove a piece of glass from the cabinet, examine it closely and then clean it with a glass cloth before placing it on a table.'

He looks meaningfully at Bruce for a moment. 'Well. I cannot go into that scene without being able to breathe that glass. I need that beautiful glass to flood through me. In fact I need to have already swum in the big pool of antique glass. And guess what? The Museo de Vidrio y Cristal right here in Málaga is that swimming pool! It is the glass ceiling of glass! There is nowhere higher, anywhere!'

'What about Versailles?' asks Bruce, dryly, reaching for his glass.

'You can't fit Versailles into a cabinet. I'm talking about artefacts. Wall to wall, embellished hand-blown beauty! I have to take you, Bruce, you will absolutely adore it. It's Málaga's number one visitors' attraction on Trip Advisor, I've been wanting to go ever since I first met Maria.'

He looks expectantly over at his friend.

'I'm up for it,' says Bruce, smiling.

Maria tops up her and Richard's glasses from a cold bottle of mineral water and refills Bruce's with more of the Rioja.

'It's a beautiful place, Bruce, a "sea of tranquillity" as you would say in English. I'll come with you if I'm free.'

'I'll look forward to it,' answers Bruce.

He looks back out over the square, now glowing with the phosphorescent yellow of the streetlights, and sighs with a quiet satisfaction. Lara was right. He is starting to feel more at peace than he has done for months.

18
Isabella

THE SCENT OF ANDALUCÍA HITS ELLA AS SOON AS SHE steps onto the tarmac. A rich, dry, earthy fragrance which she senses as much as smells over the jet fumes. She inhales deeply and smiles, closing her eyes.

Outside the airport building, Ella walks towards the parking lot and, right on cue, a pink jeep swerves into view, sliding to a halt in the nearest bay.

Ella's childhood friend, Isabella Rosado, jumps out of the car and walks purposefully towards her, grinning.

'Ella! Finally, you here again. It's been so long!' she says in Spanish, reaching out to hug her old friend.

'Izzy! I've missed you!'

'I miss you so much! I'm so happy that you're here!' trills Isabella, taking Ella's case and swinging it into the back of the jeep.

Ella walks to the driver's side on the left of the vehicle. Isabella looks at her, wide-eyed, jangling her keys until Ella rolls her eyes, grins at her mistake, walks round to the passenger side on the right and climbs into the jeep.

Isabella sparks up a skinny spliff, takes a deep drag then hangs her arm out the window as she draws away from the parking lot and pulls out onto the motorway for Marbella.

She glances over Ella and smiles through the smoke, her eyes creasing. Although still wearing her trademark short, blonde bob, she looks much older now. Harder, and colder.

'I can't believe it's been fifteen years,' she says archly, before exhaling a plume of smoke from the side of her mouth. 'You haven't changed, Ella.'

'You haven't changed either,' Ella lies.

'Pah!' exclaims Isabella. 'I *have* changed. *The fame* has changed me. It is a *curse*. I *hate* it. I have no *privacy* any longer.'

'Well, you could drive something a little less conspicuous than a pink jeep,' says Ella, laughing.

'I *love* my jeep. She is my *friend*. She will *never* let me down,' answers Isabella, dismissively. 'It is not my car that is the problem. It is the fans! They stop me in the street, they hassle me in the restaurants. They treat me as if I am a curious commodity. It is so boring!' she says, lifting one hand from the steering wheel and gesticulating. 'I just want to be treated like a normal person!'

'Well, you *are* still a normal person.'

'Of course I am! I am exactly the same person as I was before I was famous! Nothing has changed!'

Isabella glares straight ahead of her at the road, takes a deep toke of her spliff, then flicks the butt from the jeep.

'We go home, we drop your suitcases and get ready, then we come back to Málaga. There is a party tonight. In my honour, yes? You will love it!' she grins.

As they draw into the residential quarter of Marbella's Casco Antiguo, a feeling of trepidation creeps over Ella.

Isabella brings the jeep to a halt in front of a traditional townhouse at the end of a quiet street.

She walks up the entrance steps and throws open the front door, leading to a bright, large entrance hall opening onto the lounge, beyond which is a balcony overlooking the sea in the distance.

'It's lovely,' says Ella.

'Better than that poky little apartment I used to have, no?'

'Yes, it's amazing, I love it.'

'Here, I show you your room,' says Isabella.

Ella follows Isabella up to the second floor and a large white attic room lined with windows in each wall, which opens onto a spacious roof terrace. She takes in the 360 degree view up to the mountains, across the flat roofs of the old town and beyond to the sea and along the coast where little white houses glitter in the distance.

After a quick shower and change into a summer dress, she waits outside at the bottom of the steps for Isabella under a streetlight which casts a golden light onto a hedge of cerise bougainvillea in front of her house.

Isabella appears at the front door then clanks it shut behind her. She's wearing a white trouser suit and high heeled black Laboutins, their signature red soles clicking on the steps as she gracefully descends them.

Ella climbs into the front of the jeep and applies her lipstick in the sun visor mirror as Isabella pulls out into the street.

'So, how have things been?'

'That boyfriend I told you about? The film producer? Ernesto? He is a tragic shit.'

'A "tragic shit"?'

'Our relationship is a tragedy. And he is a shit.'

'What's happened?'

'I am certain that he is married. He is always flying to Paris. What is exciting about Paris? Nothing! The last time I was in Paris I had a *terrible time!* I *hate* the place! And I think he has a *wife* there.'

'I think Paris is great.'

'If Paris contains a wife of Ernesto then Paris is not so great, wouldn't you agree?'

'I guess so, yes. Why do you suspect Ernesto has a wife?'

'Because he makes excuses. All the time. Not to travel with me. Because he has to go to *Paris*. He says it's for his *work*. But I know. I *know!*' shouts Isabella at the windscreen, her face screwing up into lines of fury. 'It is for his *wife!*'

Isabella sparks up a new, pre-prepared spliff, takes a toke and airily blows out a plume of smoke, glaring ahead of her as she overtakes a minibus.

A white taxi travelling towards them sounds its horn loudly in warning.

'Hijo de puta!' shouts Isabella and slams her hand down on her horn in response.

'Taxis,' she mutters with disgust.

'Maybe you should finish with him, then,' says Ella, ignoring Isabella's terrible driving and trying to be helpful.

'Finish with him? Don't be so stupid! Of course I'm not going to finish with him! He is in love with me! I know it!'

'Maybe you should stay with him, then.'

'And put up with all his crap? What do you think I am, a masochist?'

'Well, there's no easy answer, I suppose, Isabella.'

'I am not his doormat. He will not treat me like this!' Isabella shouts at the windscreen, putting her foot on the pedal and accelerating, her face set in grim determination and bitter resentment.

Ella remains silent for the rest of the journey.

Isabella draws into a parking lot screeching her tyres in the dust as an elderly man shuffles over to collect his parking fee. Isabella gets out of the jeep and resentfully slams a euro into his outstretched hand whilst avoiding looking at him.

They cross the quiet street and El Balneario, the former majestic Victorian spa, comes into view. A white building sits on a promontory jutting out to sea, its neo-classical pillars illuminated in violet blue and the Cypress trees fringing it glowing with green fairy lights. Beneath a billowing white canopé sits an array of white-clothed tables, framed by more strings of twinkling lights.

Isabella strides confidently past the restaurant terrace packed with diners, one or two of whom turn to stare at her, whispering behind their hands. She continues into a private party area, a large, white marble-floored room with a long bar at the far end.

Small groups of guests are dotted around laughing and talking whilst crisply uniformed, smiling waitresses mingle amongst them proffering morsels of fresh tapas and chilled glasses of Cava.

Isabella pulls out a large, white fan, heavily embellished with blue sequins, holds it aloft and sweeps into the room, a beaming smile frozen onto her face as she radiates energy at the guests, who, one by one, smile and coo on seeing her entrance. The sequins from her fan shimmer in the light, scattering sparkling blue reflections onto the palm fringed walls as she sashays across the floor.

On entering the room behind her, Ella spots Rafael, Isabella's brother, whom she has also known since childhood. He turns around, sees her and grins, flinging his arms open and throwing them around her in a warm embrace.

'*Ella!*' he shouts with joy, squeezing her tightly and kissing both cheeks.

'Rafa, how lovely to see you!' says Ella in Spanish.

'How long are you here for?'

'Just two weeks.'

'You should stay longer! We miss you, Ella, you are family!'

'I know, it's only a few hours away.'

'It's been so many years!'

'Yes, I know. I got hijacked by my life…'

Rafa laughs, warmly.

'Isabella tells me you are also an author now, like her.'

'Well, not quite like her. I've written a few books. I'm not famous like Izzy.'

'I am sure they are wonderful books. Are you writing one right now?'

'Yes, I'm writing a novel partly set here, in Málaga.'

'Cool. What's it about?' he asks with genuine interest.

'It's about a writer called Bruce Robinson. He wrote and directed one of my favourite films, it's called *Withnail and I*.'

'With…what?' asks Rafael. 'I don't know it,' he says, tilting his head to one side, questioningly.

'It's very well known in England…' says Ella, apologetically, wondering why she feels the need to apologise.

'I translate your novel into Spanish for you when you finish, OK?' says Rafael, smiling broadly.

'Sure,' says Ella, suspecting he'll never get the time.

Isabella turns around from greeting various guests and notices her brother talking to Ella, walks across and joins them. She greets her brother perfunctorily with a kiss on either cheek.

'You look tired,' says Isabella, accusingly.

'I know, I've been working late every night this week on a new project.'

'You shouldn't work so hard.'

Rafael looks away from her, suitably admonished.

Isabella spots someone she knows across the room and waves, smiling, her eyes crinkling and her teeth showing white.

A middle-aged man in jeans and a black t-shirt approaches and tentatively smiles at Isabella.

'Excuse me. I have just finished reading *Gazpacho en Verano*. I just wanted to say that I love it. It is your best novel yet,' he says humbly. 'You are a genius.'

Isabella's smile freezes over in a flash and her body stiffens.

'Thank you for your support.' She takes a sip of her drink, not engaging eye contact with the man, who stands there, hopefully, waiting for some warmth or social intercourse. Quickly realising he isn't going to get either from his heroine, the man slinks away, looking slightly embarrassed.

Isabella turns back to Ella and rolls her eyes.

'I don't like the fans. I can't deal with them. I have no patience anymore,' she says, gesturing with her hands towards her head. 'What is it in English? They are doing in my head!' she says, laughing, momentarily switching back to English.

'Bit cold, Izzy. "Thank you for your support." You may as well have told the poor bloke to fuck off.'

'I get rid of them as soon as possible. They disturb me.'

Ella takes a sip of her drink and tries not to laugh at her friend's rudeness.

The room quickly fills as more and more guests arrive. Ella walks outside into the warm, jasmine-infused, sea-salted air, to listen to the waves in the darkness.

A man stands alone next to the sea wall, just beyond the furthest few of the diners, staring out to sea.

He's silhouetted perfectly against the glittering reflections of the moon on the water. Ella pulls out her phone and takes a photo, then looks at it. The man is just a black silhouette but, framed against the sea, the sky and the moon, the photo is beautiful. She looks back up at him and grins. He turns around and looks back, quizzically. He's about late twenties, with dark, curly hair and a soft, kind face.

'I took a photo...' explains Ella in Spanish, holding up her phone.

The man smiles and walks over to her. 'May I see?'

She shows him the photo and as he continues to smile, he looks up from Ella's phone and straight into her eyes.

Fuck. Gorgeous.

'It is beautifully composed. Really, you are an excellent photographer.'

'Thanks. Do you want me to send it to you?'

'Of course. Please. Yes,' he says. He catches Ella's gaze again and holds it a moment too long for casual friendliness. His eyes are large and brown, framed with long, dark eyelashes. Ella glances down at his mouth then quickly back up at his eyes.

'My name is Francisco. Here, I'll give you my number. Add me on WhatsApp,' he says, gently, taking out his phone.

Ella sends him the message and he studies the photo. 'Ella Quinn. Such a lovely name.'

'Thanks.' She looks up at him again. He's still staring intently at her face and into her eyes.

'You speak such perfect Spanish. Do you live here? In Málaga?' asks Francisco.

'No…no…I'm only here for two weeks, on holiday…'

'But you know Isabella Rosada…I saw you with her earlier…so…?' He looks at Ella quizzically, head cocked to one side.

'Very old friends.'

'Ah, I see.'

'So…do you live here?'

'Yes. I'm a cellist. I play with the Málaga Symphony Orchestra.'

'Cool.'

'I also play in a classical group. For the tourists, you know? In the hotels of Pedregalejo.'

'It's lovely round there. So, who's your favourite composer?'

'Oh, Schumann for sure. Obviously. He is the master. I am *obsessed* with him. I *adore* him. I *love* him. The others are silver and bronze. But Schumann! Schumann is the gold.'

'For me Mozart is the gold.'

'Are you a musician too?' he asks, smiling politely.

'No, a writer.'

'What do you write?' he smiles at Ella, still looking into her eyes.

'Books.'

'What kind of books?'

'Just, you know, general fiction. Men, women, pain…' she laughs.

'Like, the bondage thing you mean?' he asks, laughing, his eyes widening in mock surprise.

'No! Nothing like that. I mean, the pain of being human. Just, everyday stuff. You know, life being mainly shit.'

'So, depressing stuff, you mean? First you are a bondage queen and now the princess of suicide diaries!' he continues, his eyes twinkling.

'I hope I'm neither,' she laughs.

'I see. So are you a reader, too?'

'I am.'

'In that case, who is your favourite writer?' asks Francisco, smirking mischievously.

'Bruce Robi…oh…someone you've probably never heard of,' says Ella, shaking her head and looking at the ground. 'Just…a writer. Just…someone…English. Not famous over here…'

'If you like his work, then I'm sure so would I. I will seek the work of Bruce Robby.'

'Bruce Robi...' Ella starts to explain, but her words are drowned out by Isabella, who appears at the door of the hall, waving frantically and demanding, 'Ella! Where are you? Come here, *now! We're going to dance the rumba!*' She vanishes back towards the music.

'I'd better go.'

'She behaves like a possessive lover,' says Francisco, nodding over towards the hall.

'She does a bit. Well, we're not lovers. I've got a boyfriend.'

Francisco smiles complacently. 'But of course. A woman as beautiful as yourself would never be single for long.'

'He's a dick, though.'

Francisco laughs.

'And a coke head. In fact, it's probably going to end soon. I'd go so far as to say that I actually fucking hate him. I don't know why we're still together.'

Ella looks out at the sea, avoiding Francisco's gaze. 'No idea why I told you all that. Sorry. Too much information.'

'On the contrary, it is very good to know. So you are looking for love?'

'No, not at all. No. Not looking for love.'

'So, you're not lonely?'

'No! Of course not! I'm just telling you that my boyfriend is a tool. Telling you, far too much, probably.'

'Because you are sensitive. And beautiful. And in pain,' says Francisco, gazing at Ella intently.

'Ella!' shouts Isabella, returning to the doorway. 'I told you to come *now!* We are dancing the rumba! Stop talking and *come and dance!*'

'It's been lovely to meet you, Francisco. I'd better go,'

'Enchanted, Lady of Ella,' Francisco replies, smiling. He leans in to kiss Ella's cheeks and the fragrance of his skin makes her feel slightly heady.

'I hope we'll meet again,' he adds.

Ella smiles at Francisco, walks away from him and back into the hall where Isabella, in the centre of the room, is now throwing her head back with joy, flapping her large white fan and dancing with a short, thickly set black man, sporting a long grey beard and a turquoise blue kaftan.

Ella plucks a glass of sparkling mineral water from a tray and glances back towards the terrace, the twinkling lights and the moonlit sea beyond, but Francisco has gone.

19
QUEEN OF THE ANDES

BRUCE AND RICHARD'S WHITE TAXI BEEPS LOUDLY AT a pink jeep travelling in the opposite direction.

'I've always fancied having a jeep,' says Richard, glancing out the window of the taxi.

'My kids wanted me to get one when I sold the Aston.'

'Not really you, though, is it?'

'Nor you.'

'Driving like a fucking lunatic, that jeep. Now that *is* you.'

'Thanks.'

'No problem,' Richard grins.

⁂

The bougainvillea-draped exterior of Casanis Bistro, a chic French restaurant in the old town of Marbella, twinkles with fairy lights in the dusk.

'Isn't it gorgeous?' says Richard, as the taxi draws up outside the little restaurant, its balconies, heavy with geraniums, overlooking the diners seated at the candle-lit, white-clothed tables on the pavement outside. 'I told you it'd be worth the drive.'

'Well you've taken me to some shit holes before, let's hope this is worth it.'

'Ha. *You've* taken *me* to some shit holes. *And* made me work in some.'

'Which has led to your considerable public acclaim, I should add,' says Bruce, dryly.

'Bonjour. Have you got a quiet table somewhere?' asks Richard when the Maître D', dressed in classical French black and white apparel, appears to greet them.

'Mais naturellement, upstairs there are no other guests. You have the floor to yourselves, monsieur.'

He ushers the pair up a winding flight of stone stairs, past Tin Tin murals and an immense Monstera deliciosa, up past a series of spectacular driftwood chandeliers to a light, airy first floor with windows overlooking the street below.

As soon as they are seated, Richard's phone pings. He reads the message and looks slightly agitated, a pained expression settling on his tanned face.

'Ah. Maria's got home to find we're not there and is not best pleased.'

'Didn't you invite her?' asks Bruce.

'I thought she was working till late. Apparently not.'

'Do these Instagram influencers or whatever they're called have office hours, then?'

'She was doing a shoot for some branding or something, I'm not sure.' Richard plucks a menu from the table and starts studying it in earnest. 'The Kenyan green beans are amazing.'

Bruce picks up a menu and scans it. He glances up at a waiter who has just appeared from nowhere.

'A bottle of the Gevrey-Chambertin Faiveley, please.'

Richard pours two glasses from the fresh jug of water on the table.

'The entrecote was Maria's favourite before she went vegan. Are you still off the meat?'

'God yes. Disgusting stuff. Who in their right mind would want to eat the reheated flesh of a murdered *corpse?*'

'And so unhealthy,' adds Richard, nodding his head.

'What makes absolutely no sense to me is people whining on about the Chinese skinning live cats, when there's animal concentration camps three miles down the road from them. Auschwitz! Treblinka! For pigs, and chickens, and cows. *Disgusting*. "Oh but our ethically sourced local produce farm, it's like a luxury holiday for the animals, we pamper and coddle them and they eat fresh fucking heavenly-scented grass." Well what sort of fucking holiday is it if instead of packing your bags at the end you get an electric rod shoved up your arse and your throat slit! Eh? Even Butlins wasn't that bad in its heyday. Ethically sourced meat my arse. What is ethical about brutally murdering an innocent animal? Nothing! "Yes but they're slaughtered humanely!" Oh, that's OK, then, so I'll gently stab you in the neck with a knife, ever so humanely. Fucking *ridiculous*.'

The waiter reappears with a flourish. He expertly opens the bottle of wine and then, one hand behind his back, pours a sample into Bruce's glass with the other.

Bruce takes a sip of the wine then smiles at the waiter.

'Lovely.'

With a light deftness, the waiter pours a full glass for Bruce, whilst Richard covers his own glass with one hand and shakes his head briskly. 'Non. Merci.'

The waiter departs and they resume their conversation.

'You're right of course. And let's not forget that animal agriculture is contributing to the climate crisis. We all need to stop eating meat!' says Richard.

'I'll drink to that' says Bruce, grinning, raising his glass and draining it in one.

Richard sips his water whilst looking levelly at his friend and smiles, gently.

'Look. I do have limits,' says Bruce.

'I've yet to see them,' answers Richard, laughing.

'I've never drunk wine straight out of the bottle…'

'OK...'

'No matter how wankered I was. I've always poured my wine into a glass,' says Bruce with a flourish, refilling his glass. 'Missed the glass a few times, though. Tried to pour it from a still corked bottle as well. But never actually *drunk from the bottle.*'

'Bollocks. That's pure snobbery. Like a smackhead gloating about the fact he only ever uses clean syringes to inject his *balls.'*

Bruce splutters, laughing.

'…not that I'm comparing you to a *smackhead,*' laughs Richard.

A silence falls between them for a few moments before Richard continues, 'So…what's this about this author who's putting you in her book, then?'

'Oh, I don't know, nothing really. Just someone who approached me after a speaking gig. Said she's basing a character on me in her novel.'

'Has she been published?'

'Yeah, written a few novels.'

'What's she called?'

'Ella Quinn.'

'What, her real name? Or a nom de plume?'

'Real, I believe.'

Richard puts on a pair of reading glasses, picks up his phone and looks across at Bruce, raising his eyebrows and smiling mischievously.

'Let's have a look at her, then.'

He opens Instagram and searches for 'Ella Quinn.'

'Ella Quinn,' he says, slowly. 'Sounds like a detective. There's loads of them. Aha. This is her. Ella Quinn, author.'

He silently scrolls through her photos.

'They call this "stalking". The youngsters. Merely looking through the content of someone's freely uploaded social media content is now known as "stalking". *Ridiculous.*'

Bruce looks vaguely embarrassed. 'Well, as you know, I don't do mobile phones or smart phones or whatever you want to call them. Loathe the things.'

'Very fucking useful little things, though…' murmurs Richard, still looking through Ella's photos. Her smiling on a restaurant terrace in Málaga. Her with her arms around some musician. Her earnestly sat in front of a laptop and captioned *#writerslife*.

'I must say, she looks very well for forty-seven.' He holds up the phone for Bruce to see. 'Mind you, they all do on Instagram. Maria looks about fucking seventeen with all the apps she uses. Who needs Botox when you can have an instant *Facetune?*'

'What the bloody hell is a "*Facetune*"?'

'Oh, just some app they use to remove the wrinkles and skin blemishes. Like airbrushing a portrait.'

'I don't even know what an "app" is. You don't use these "app" things on your own photos then?'

Richard pulls a face of mock shock and laughs 'Of *course* not. I don't need *an app* to make me look young and wonderful.'

He continues looking through the photos in silence, then stops abruptly. 'Ah, there's one here that mentions *you*. It's a selfie of her, radiating love at the camera.' He grins at Bruce.

'"Working on my new novel about legendary writer and film director hashtag Bruce Robinson." She obviously *adores* you.'

'I don't think so. She's a writer appreciating another writer's work, that's all.'

'*Adoration.* I can see it in her face. Mind you, her eyes are a bit wonky.'

Richard scrutinises the photo on the phone even more closely. 'I think she's used some kind of filter on this one,' he announces, suspiciously. 'It's making her look more *loved-up*.'

He places his phone on the table and removes his glasses with triumph. 'So maybe you win. She doesn't really adore you after all. The worship is all *cerebral*.'

The waiter approaches again and takes their order.

'I'll have the tagliatelli avec legumes frâiches from the Menu du Jour, please,' says Richard.

'Sounds lovely. Same for me,' says Bruce in French, as the waiter tops up his wine glass.

'Bien sûr, monsieur,' says the waiter, bowing slightly.

Richard waits until the waiter has disappeared, then leans forward earnestly.

'You know, I was thinking about this very thing just the other day. About how difficult it is to really *know* someone. I mean, admiring someone from afar, you're obviously going to get it wrong most of the time. That person will never really be how you see them from the perspective of a stranger. But what about people you actually *know?* How well do we actually really *know* anyone?'

'Well, we don't. We don't know ourselves most of the time so how can we ever know anyone else?' answers Bruce.

'What about, say, when you admire someone who happens to be a *total cunt*, and you're in denial about it? You don't *want* them to be a cunt. So you kid yourself that if you believe hard enough that they're *not* a cunt, then by some magic they won't be. Your belief and will can transform them into a lovely person - decent, honourable, honest and self-sacrificing...'

Bruce listens intently as Richard warms to his theme and starts gesticulating with increasing emphasis.

'And then every time they behave like the cunt they really are it's a *mortal blow* to the unreal, smooth and perfect false *them* you've created in your head, gradually denting and twisting your perfect creation, until eventually they've hammered and beaten the character you've created in your head into a horribly accurate reflection of themselves, with its gnarled twists of deceit, ugly gashes of cunning, dents of manipulation, slashes of selfishness and *great rips of betrayal.* And as you mournfully gaze at your *ruined creation,* you marvel at how *mean* they could be to cause such *wilful damage* to something so innocent, beautiful and perfect as *your vision* of them. And you think to yourself, *"What a cunt."* That's what I mean,' finishes Richard, grinning triumphantly.

'You're not talking about me, are you?' asks Bruce, grinning mischievously.

'Of *course not.* I'm talking about when you know deep down that someone's an absolute cunt of a cunt, *a monster.* But you keep pretending otherwise, because to admit they're as much of a cunt as you know they are is just *too much to bear.*'

'Maybe the author would feel like that about me if she knew me better,' laughs Bruce, taking another swig of his re 'I'm sure you'll always remain an *alabaster statue* to her,' says Richard, smiling and rolling his eyes.

'Some are born cunts. Some become cunts. And some have cuntdom thrust upon them,' says Bruce, wistfully.

Richard laughs. 'Bravo. But seriously, don't you think this industry can encourage cuntishness of monstrous proportions sometimes?'

Bruce reflects for a moment. 'I don't think it's necessarily just *this* industry. Personal demons latch onto power, fame and wealth as an opportunity to create havoc in *any* walk of life.'

'Yes. Brilliant. Exactly.'

The waiter brings their food, discreetly placing the large round bowls of pasta in front of his diners.

'Merci beaucoup,' says Bruce, giving the waiter a dazzling smile.

'Oui, merci' adds Richard, nodding at the waiter and smiling.

Richard twirls tagliatelli around his fork and as he moves it towards his mouth, his phone bleeps again.

Sighing, he puts his fork down and opens the message.

And it is our restaurant! And now it is too late for me to join you! I have an appointment early tomorrow morning! I think you are being very mean, Richard! I don't see Bruce very much at all since he arrive, are you jealous?

Richard hastily types out a reply then puts the phone back down on the table and continues eating.

'I know they're intrusive. Mobiles

'One of the many joys of throwing the damn things out of the window. No-one can interrupt you anymore,' says Bruce, putting a forkful of pasta into his mouth.

'It's Maria. She says she's hardly seen you since you arrived. She's obviously *bored* with my company. I've only been here two weeks.'

'Maybe she just wanted to join us. As you say, it *is* a lovely spot,' says Bruce, kindly.

'*Our* restaurant, she calls it,' says Richard, bristling. 'I just think that sometimes…three's a crowd. And there's the language barrier… and her age…'

'I can see what a heavy burden it is, having a beautiful, intelligent young Spanish girlfriend,' says Bruce laughing.

'I'm not being funny. It really can be a genuine *chore*.'

'Maybe you're not meant for each other, then.'

'Is anyone really meant for anyone? I'm not sure whether I believe in the notion of soul-mates. That out there, amongst all those millions of people, there's only person who's right for you, only one person whose heart can meld with yours in the most beautiful way imaginable. Only one person with whom one is completely in tune. Thinking the same way, imagining the same dreams, laughing at the same things. Looking out of the window at the clouds and knowing that they're somewhere out there, and they're thinking about you too at that very same moment. Just knowing. And then, your phone goes. Wherever you are. In the middle of the desert, on top of a mountain, in the middle of fucking Tribeca at a film festival with a million people up your arse. And you look at your phone. And it's them. And they *were* thinking about you.'

'Unless you don't use mobile phones,' adds Bruce, dryly.

'OK well yes but it could happen with *landlines* too. Or going even further back in time, the postman delivering a letter just as you were deep in thought about its writer. You know the score. Whatever the technology involved, it's that concrete proof that you're both flying on the same invisible thread through time and space, like...like...two little spiders, each weaving a web on opposite continents and suddenly your webs collide in another dimension...'

Bruce looks at Richard intently as he finishes his last fork of pasta and then places his cutlery neatly in the empty bowl.

'Have you met somebody else?' he asks.

'No. Of course not. I *love* Maria.'

'So was it ever like that with her? Phones simultaneously *pinging* from Cadiz to Toronto in beautiful tandem? Modern love, eh?' quips Bruce.

'No. But I imagine that meeting someone and instantly feeling this kind of volcanic energy between you could happen at any time, and with any number of people.'

'But it doesn't,' counters Bruce, pouring another glass of wine. 'It's rare. Like a rare flower. Like the Puya raimondii.'

'The what?'

'Puya raimondii, Queen of the Andes, a bromeliad which only blooms once in its life.'

'Ah, yes. I've heard of that.'

'Produces thousands of flowers on a huge, fuck off thirty foot spike. That's the kind of incredible energy which occurs naturally between people so rarely. It's pure...and it's beautiful...and it gives rise to... creation...the creation of life...either literally...or figuratively...'

Richard takes a sip of his water and looks across the room, wistfully, as Bruce continues...

'And that magical connection is the holy grail. The pot of gold at the end of the fucking rainbow. It's what power and money and fame can't buy, that kind of connection. And those who haven't got it, they'll just fucking snatch what they can. Your body. Your spirit. Your pride. Your sense of *self.* They'll suck *the very fucking soul out of you*, like *vampires*, leaving you a *frail husk*. But it's never enough, they can *never get enough*, this horrific theft always leaves them *hungry*. Because they're devouring *poison* instead of food. What they really want is what they can never have, the creativity, the love, beauty and passion that emanates from a true meeting of souls. The heavenly creation. *The gold*. Totally out of their fucking reach. And they know it.'

Richard nods thoughtfully, as Bruce continues. 'If you look at what's inside these predators, under the surface, where no-one else can see the full picture, it's a Goyaesque fucking war zone. An abomination. And these miserable, grasping monsters are everywhere. Desperate, haunting ghouls, prowling for souls amongst the fallen, empty corpses from which they've already devoured and sucked the life-blood. Abusive fathers, megalomaniac film producers, fucking serial killers, whatever. They all want *the gold*. And they can never have it. Miserable fucking wretches and a scourge on humanity, the fucking lot of them.'

Richard nods, sagely. 'You're right.' He looks at his friend intently, then glances away, looking across the room.

'Thousands of flowers on a huge, fuck off thirty foot spike. Once in a lifetime. That was *Withnail*. That was the gold.'

20
The Glass Museum

ISABELLA LIES NAKED AND SPREAD-EAGLED ON THE ROOF terrace sun bed, the dark, bare mountains to her right, the glittering blue sea to her left, the hot golden sun above her head, her eyes closed, smoking a large spliff whilst swaying her head erratically to El Camerón's *Como el Agua* blasting from inside the house.

Ella sits wrapped in a sarong in the shade of a large potted palm, writing notes in pencil in an exercise book.

Her phone pings with a message.

I cannot stop thinking about you since I met you. Can we meet again? x

Ella smiles smugly to herself. Francisco.

I'm free on Wednesday if you want to meet up for a coffee. x

Almost immediately, he answers.

But I do not have a car. Or somewhere to go…

'What the fuck?' says Ella out loud.

Isabella ignores her, eyes closed and head swaying from side to side in bliss at the music.

'Isabella?'

'What?' she replies, tetchily, exhaling a plume of smoke up towards the sky.

'You know that bloke I photographed at the gig at El Balneario?'

'No.'

'You know, the one standing outside. The one standing by the sea. I showed you the photo I took of him.'

'Oh yes. What?' She continues swaying her head to the music.

'He's messaging me. Wants to meet up. I said I was free Wednesday. And he replies, "I do not have a car. Or somewhere to go." What's he going on about? Why do we need a car to have coffee? I can get the train.'

'He's talking about somewhere to go to fuck you,' Isabella answers, matter of factly, taking another deep toke on her spliff.

'Fuck me? But I'm old enough to be his mother!'

'That is precisely why he wants you.'

'But…but I'm living with someone!'

'Does he know that?'

'He knows I've got a boyfriend, yes. But not that we're living together.'

'He wants to fuck you anyway. They're all the same. Men. They just want to fuck. Especially with the *guiris*. And even more with the *old* guiris. The old guiris are all *desperate*.'

'I'm not desperate. And I'm not a *guiri*.'

'You're English. And here on holiday. Therefore you're a *guiri*. To him you're a stupid tourist, a *guiri* who will be easy to fuck.'

'I'm here to *write*. Not fuck. Or be on holiday,' says Ella firmly, tapping out a reply.

We don't need a car or 'somewhere to go' to have coffee.

He he of course not. x

And I live with my boyfriend, by the way.

We meet for coffee anyway, yes?

Ella puts her phone down, her moment of joy dissolved.

'I wouldn't meet him,' says Isabella, airily. 'You have Zack already. He should be enough for you. This Francisco is just a silly little boy. A waste of time.'

'I know. Fuck him,' she replies, glumly.

'No more talking now. I listen to *El Camerón!*' announces Isabella, wiggling her body on the sun lounger in time to the music as she reaches out to extinguish her spliff in the ashtray and misses, stubbing the soggy, tar-speckled butt into a tub of coconut body butter on the table beside her.

Ella winds her way through the back streets of Málaga, along side streets where little cafés harbour locals drinking black coffee and light beers, and roadworks fill half the street with clouds of dust and brooding workmen.

On the northern outskirts of the city centre, in a tranquil triangle of buildings on the Plazuela Santísimo Cristo de la Sangre - Holy Christ of the Blood Plaza - facing San Felipe Neri church, a long derelict former merchant's residence has been recently restored and behind the deceptively plain facade now lies Málaga's beautifully curated glass museum.

Just inside the heavy oak entrance doors, an elderly man sits quietly in the shadows on an elaborately carved wooden chair in front of a floor length red velvet curtain, waiting for visitors to arrive.

He's wearing a pink taffeta shirt and pressed cream cotton slacks. Bald, bespectacled and elegant, he has a refined, world-weary and vaguely patronising air about him, seemingly out of time and place in the modern world.

Once Ella has paid her entrance fee, he approaches her, smiling politely.

'Good afternoon, Señorita. My name is Inocencio de Espinosa. I will guide you around this beautiful museum.'

Inocencio leads her through the elegant villa and into the central courtyard, festooned with hanging plants cascading from the balconied walkways on all four sides.

From the courtyard, doorways lead into endless, sumptuously furnished stone-floored rooms, all lined with cabinets displaying exquisite glass pieces from ancient Egypt to twentieth century Italy.

Inocencio, almost a living part of the museum himself, slowly guides her through the rooms, explaining the histories of each display and pointing out particularly spectacular or significant pieces.

Finally, after an hour or so, they arrive back in the airy courtyard.

'You may, of course, feel free to explore the museum further on your own, now that I have guided you through its beauty and richness,' states Inocencio, matter of factly, after his tour. He bows, slightly.

Ella smiles a thank you and Inocencio returns to his seat by the entrance.

Re-entering the museum, Ella wanders over to a cabinet of exhibits where her eyes are caught by a pink Lalique fluted vase. She stares at the beautiful object, entranced by the delicate folds of glistening opaque glass.

Viewed in profile through the glass cabinet, she looks strikingly familiar. She's wearing a white voile top and denim shorts, her hair in Dutch braids on either side of her head.

She puts a phone to her ear and says, in English, 'I'm still in the museum, I'll ring you back. Yeah, it's amazing.'

Suddenly aware that she's being watched, Ella glances to her left and notices a man peering at her through the Laliques.

'Bruce!' she exclaims, emerging from behind the glass cabinet.

'Um, Ella, isn't it?'

'Yes, it is. What on earth are *you* doing here? I can't believe it.'

'I've...come on holiday.'

Ella grins. 'Not gonna say it, Bruce.'

'What?'

'*By mistake*. The line from *Withnail*. "We've come on holiday by mistake." The one everyone always quotes,' she says, still grinning.

'I almost have. Not really the holiday I planned...'says Bruce, trailing off.

'Well, I didn't plan this one either. Gave up booze and my boyfriend turned into a gigantic dick about it overnight. So I'm staying with a friend. Isabella. She's an author. Only a successful one. She has a pink jeep.'

'Saw one of those on the way to Marbella the other night.'

'That could well have been us. Was it heading in the opposite direction?'

'It was indeed.'

'We were on our way to El Balneario.'

'I'm not familiar with it...' Bruce says, politely.

'It's an old Victorian spa just up the coast. It's beautiful. It's a restaurant now. Right on the sea. All lit up with strings of trailing lights,' says Ella, waving her hands around as if conjuring up the lights before them.

'It sounds lovely. My *wife* would like that.'

'You should take her...'

'Well, not this time. I was meant to *be here* with my wife. But our son's been taken ill. She's stayed at home to look after him.'

'Oh God. I'm so sorry. I hope it's nothing serious.'

'Well, it's just flu. So no, not really. But he couldn't be left.'

'I guess I wouldn't leave my children if they had flu, either. Well, if I had children. Which I don't. Actually I think I already told you that in an email...'

'Did you? I'm sorry. I'm not very good with emails and the internet. Can't stand them.'

'No, well, I can see. I write you an essay, you reply with a line of lower case text speak,' says Ella, laughing.

'Email. Hate it. I told you,' he says, grinning a charming smile and at ease now.

There's a short silence between them.

'Have you seen the piano room? It's fantastic,' asks Ella.

'Oh. Where is it? I'd love to see it, yes.'

Ella guides him through several rooms, across herringbone-tiled floors furnished with plush velvet sofas, overlooked by formal portraits and mirrors framed in thick rococo gilt frames.

They reach an annexe room with a grand piano topped with a vase of geraniums and a small standard lamp, giving the room a warm orange glow. An upholstered red velvet stool sits in front of the piano.

'Isn't it just lovely?' says Ella, admiringly, running her hand along the engraved wood of the piano's lid. 'It's the same model that Mozart played. The guide told me.'

'Can you play?' asks Bruce.

'Not really. I started learning as a child. But my father only wanted me to learn scales and set pieces so I could pass the grades. He went ballistic when I started writing my own music.'

'That sounds familiar.'

'Yes, I read that Vivian McKerrell, your flatmate, the one who inspired Withnail? That he resented you writing...'

'Yeah. He *hated* me writing. And my father hated every ounce of creativity in my bones,'

'I know, Bruce. I read your novel, *Thomas Penman...*'

'It's all autobiographical...'

Ella sits at the stool, opens the lid of the piano and glances back up at Bruce.

'You can tell it's autobiographical. It had to be...' she says, as she begins picking out individual notes on the keyboard.

A voice booms from beyond the door to the piano room.

'The *piano!*'

Innocencio looms into view and loiters in the doorway, his face a mask of irritated disapproval.

'Please. The piano is only for the use of *professional artists*,' he says, enunciating each word carefully, wrapping his mouth around each syllable as if each is a rare delicacy to be savoured and explored with his tongue.

'I'm so sorry,' says Ella, crestfallen. She stands up from the piano and closes the lid.

Inocencio inclines his head. 'If you would like to hear the piano being played, we have regular concert nights, with guest pianists from all over the world. But we cannot, of course, have visitors *interfering* with such a *magnificent instrument*.'

'I wouldn't dream of interfering with such a majestic beast,' says Bruce, deadpan, his eyes widening.

'And I regret doing so, Señor de Espinosa. Please accept my humble apologies,' adds Ella.

Inocencio bows slightly and smiles, his face emotionless.

'I appreciate your cordiality. The English, always so polite.'

His phone sounds with the opening bars of *The Ride of the*

Valkyries and he scurries away, holding the phone close to his ear and talking in confidential tones to the caller.

'We are not *artists*,' says Bruce, smiling warmly.

'No. Evidently not,' says Ella, smiling back and then glancing down regretfully at the now silent piano.

'To think, Mozart played on a piano just like this. I wish I could have been there, sitting alongside him, watching him play. Just imagine, sitting beside Mozart whilst he's playing Piano Concerto no 20 in D Minor.'

'The first romantic piano concerto ever written...'

'Apparently so. I love it.'

'So do I.'

A silence falls between them as they look at they both look at the piano.

'I occasionally have imaginary conversations with Charles Dickens,' says Bruce, thoughtfully.

'Yes, I read that in an interview with you. What do you talk about, with Charles?'

'Everything. He's my therapist. I named my dog after him.'

'My cat's named Nin.'

'After Anaïs?'

'Indeed.'

'One of my favourite writers.'

'And mine,' says Ella, smiling.

After strolling around the rest of the museum, they wander out together into the bright late afternoon sunshine, past a seated Inocencio, who nods goodbye to them as they leave.

'I was meant to be coming here with my friend, but we kind of *lost* one another somewhere in the city centre,' says Bruce.

As if on cue, Ella looks up and sees a tall, casually refined, middle-aged man walking towards the entrance of the museum, his arm around a beautiful young Spanish woman. Ella recognises him instantly and smiles to herself. Richard E. Grant, Withnail himself. So that's Bruce's missing friend.

'We lost you, Bruce,' says Richard, walking towards them.

'Indeed you did. I've already been in. This is Ella,' says Bruce.

'Hello, Ella,' says Richard with a charming grin stretched across his face. 'Lovely to meet you.'

'Lovely to meet *you* Richard. Big fan of your work. Thought *Prêt-à-Porter* was massively underrated. Big fan of Altman generally, actually,' says Ella, gushing against her will.

'Oh, as am I. A *dear* friend of mine as well, until his sad passing. Um, this is Maria.' Richard stands back to introduce his girlfriend.

'Hola, Maria.' The women instinctively greet each other with a kiss to each cheek. 'I'm called Ella,' says Ella in Spanish.

'You speak Spanish!' exclaims Maria, looking surprised.

'Yes, I've got friends here.'

Richard and Bruce exchange glances.

'Well I'm lost, for one!' announces Richard, jovially.

'Sorry, we speak English now,' says Maria, reverting to English.

Richard raises his eyebrows at Maria and smiles. A silence falls over the group.

'Well, I'd better go' says Ella. 'I…I still have so many questions,' she says, turning to Bruce. 'You have my mobile number already, I think. I emailed it to you, right?'

'Did you? I don't have a mobile, though. Hate the things. I don't know how we'd contact one another really, I'm not staying at my own place. I'm at Maria and Richard's,' he adds, glancing at Maria.

'You can have my address, Ella,' says Maria, taking out her phone.

'Thanks, Maria. Is that OK, Bruce?'

'Sure, of course. Pop by any time. You know where I am.'

'OK. Well, lovely to bump into you,' says Ella, kissing Bruce lightly on each cheek. 'Lovely to meet you Richard, and you too, Maria.' They kiss on either cheek.

'Hasta luego!' says Ella and walks away across the square.

Richard focuses his gaze on the retreating Ella, the stranger he'd assumed had just bumped into Bruce in the glass museum.

I know where I've seen her before. She's that author. From Instagram. The one writing a novel about Bruce.

'So, shall we go for some tapas?' asks Bruce.

'Lets. I'm starving,' says Richard.

Richard lets Bruce walk ahead slightly, then turns to Maria and looks at her, levelly.

'I really don't like strangers knowing my address, Maria, you know that,' he half whispers.

'It is *my* address, not yours,' replies Maria, coolly.

'Yes, but I like to keep my life *private,*' he objects.

Maria laughs out loud and elbows Richard in his side, jokingly. 'You! Who puts photos of your bathroom on Instagram!'

'Yes but I don't even *know* this woman. I know *nothing about her*, except for the fact that she seems to be writing a novel about Bruce! And now suddenly here she is, in Málaga, *at the very same time as us!* I mean, *what the actual fuck?*'

'She is probably just on holiday, like you and Bruce are. English people come to Málaga on holiday all the time. And anyway, she is not interested in you Richard. She is interested in *Bruce,*' says Maria, matter-of-factly, smiling triumphantly at him.

Bruce turns around and looks at Maria and Richard, bickering quietly behind him, out of earshot. 'Where are we going, anyway?'

'No idea,' says Richard, glumly.

'I take you somewhere *fantastic.* You will *love* it. They have the *best* tapas in Málaga,' says Maria, smiling. 'This way.'

21
Ageless

LARA WASHES HER HANDS AT THE SINK WHILST CHARLES, the rescue dog, sits obediently on the floor. Part Terrier, part Springer Spaniel and with a perennially scruffy coat, he looks up at her hopefully with big, appealing eyes, his tail swooshing across the floor energetically.

'Walkies soon, Charles. Let me finish up here, first.'

The front door sounds with a gentle knock and Charles jumps up, excitedly, his tongue lolling. He eagerly follows Lara as she opens it to find Tom standing there, looking slightly perplexed.

'Oh, hi, Lara. I've been trying to get hold of James. We've been waiting for some parts to be delivered and they've finally arrived. Only James's phone is off…I was a bit worried. I've brought them over, anyway. Is he OK?'

'James is ill in bed with flu. Come in, Tom.'

Tom follows Lara into the kitchen, followed by a disappointed Charles, who sniffs at the hem of Tom's Levi's for interesting new signals from the world beyond.

'Would you like a cup of tea?' asks Lara. 'While you're here?'

Tom nods. 'Yeah OK. Cheers. I wasn't planning to stay long, really. I was just going to drop this stuff off and go but yeah, a cup of tea would be really nice, thanks.'

He sits at the table and tries not to look at Lara as she walks around the kitchen, putting the kettle on and reaching into the fridge to bring out a tray of chocolate brownies. He glances out of the window at the forecourt of the house, where chickens and ducks are strutting around happily in the sun, immersed in their own world.

Lara puts two mugs of tea on the large, wooden kitchen table along with a dish of brownies and two plates, then sits down, brushing a strand of hair from her eyes.

'I'm sorry I wasn't around for you treating the pool.'

'It's OK. I had everything I needed.'

'I did plan to be here…to supervise…but my friend Gina needed some help with her new gelding…'

'Honestly, it's OK, no worries,' says Tom, smiling. 'Those look lovely,' he says, looking at the brownies.

'Have one. I made them yesterday. I don't know why. No-one to eat them. James is ill and Bruce is away in Spain.'

'Ah, right,' says Tom, carefully removing a chocolate brownie from the pile on the plate. 'So has Bruce got, like, a screening out there or something?'

'No, it's a holiday. I was meant to go too, but I decided to stay and look after James. So he's staying with Richard…Richard E. Grant. They're still good friends…'

'Cool.'

'So…I'm here…with the chickens and the sunshine…'

'Well, here's not such a bad place to be…'

'No…'

'I mean, you have got a lovely place…'

'Yes…thank you, we love it here.'

A silence hangs between them for a second.

'So…when does he get back? Bruce?'

'In a few days, he's only gone for a week.'

'Sweet…'

Lara pauses, then adds, 'It's kind of a nice break, actually…' She looks down at her tea.

'Right…' Tom nods, slightly awkwardly.

'Well, you know…' Lara says, glancing up at Tom and looking away quickly.

'Yeah...'

'Just…'

'You mean, like, his lifestyle?'

'Kind of…'

'Yeah.' Tom ponders for a moment, frowning slightly. 'It must be lonely sometimes. You know, with him off in that barn, writing all day. I mean, I don't mean just him, I mean, like, living with a writer. Like any writer. Must be difficult, I mean. With them writing all the time. Kind of thing,' he trails off.

'Yes…well no, no it's not lonely. Not really. I pop in and chat to him quite often. And I'm very involved in my own work…I didn't mean...'

She looks at Tom and he looks back into her eyes, waiting for her to continue.

'Not that…it's not lonely…not as such…'

'No…'

'I just mean, sometimes…you know…'

'Yeah…'

'His…'

'Yeah…'

'We don't really talk about it…' says Lara, looking away again.

'No, of course not. I didn't mean to…'

'You didn't…' She smiles, gently.

Tom watches the thick strand of silver hair swing back across her face again, sheltering her eyes.

She is so gorgeous. She's wasted on him.

'So…does he go to, um, AA, or anything?'

'Yes, yeah…well, I do too..for partners and family,' she adds quickly.

'OK. Right…but…he doesn't drink that much, does he?'

Lara looks straight at Tom, directly into his eyes, as she elegantly sips her mug of tea.

'I've literally got no idea how much he drinks. A couple of bottles of wine a day? Maybe more? Maybe four? Probably not that many, that's pretty exceptional. Less.'

Tom studies her face as she talks, her soft lips, her gentle, expressive eyes.

'I really don't know,' she continues. 'I stopped counting bottles a long time ago. There's no point. I'm not his guardian. You learn eventually. That it's not your responsibility. It can't be.'

'Wow, four bottles of wine, that's, like, more than a bottle of vodka…'

'Yes, I know,' says Lara, defensively, the creases around her eyes narrowing imperceptibly. 'We don't really…I think if he thought about it like that…but he thinks of it as just wine. And wine can't really hurt you…'

'You must be worried sick…' says Tom, with a look of concern on his face.

Lara shakes her head. 'I'm fine. We're fine. Everything's fine. We have a lovely life,' she adds, crisply, smiling broadly.

'Yeah, of course…' says Tom. He sips his tea.

Her face looks so fragile and beautiful. She's ageless. And so vulnerable, sitting there, drinking her tea. I want to fuck her.

He attempts to dispel the thought from his mind whilst it lurks at the periphery of his consciousness.

'I mean, from the outside, speaking as an , you and Bruce seem to have it all.'

'There isn't such a thing as having it all. No-one has it all. Nothing is perfect. Or complete. Or pure.'

'No, of course not. I guess not.'

'The thing is, Tom, if you scratch the shiny surface of any seemingly perfect family, underneath, there's always turmoil and pain,' says Lara, matter of factly. 'Always. That's just families. And...people. And life, really.' She smiles softly.

Tom frowns. 'But...some people do seem to get everything they want in life, whereas others, no matter what they do, never get what they want...'

Lara sighs and looks out of the window, deep in thought. Charles takes the cue and runs over to the window seat, leaps up and puts his paws on the window ledge. He starts to pant, excitedly.

Lara smiles at him. 'In a minute, Charles.'

He looks disappointed and sinks his head into his paws, looking longingly out of the window.

Lara looks back at Tom.

'The thing is, that people who always focus on what they can *get* out of life are destined to be permanently unhappy. They focus on getting, say, money and power. And no matter how much they get, they always want more. Then they find out, usually too late, that all the riches and power in the world are never going to fill that bottomless void. Which is the desire to get it all. And that money and power can't get you happiness because the only thing that brings real happiness is love. And you can only get real love if you focus on *giving*, not getting.'

Tom's face breaks into a wide smile.

'Sweeeet. So true. I've never really thought about it like that. I love the way you think. You're so intelligent and perceptive. You think, like, totally out of the box, don't you?'

Lara smiles at his endearing naivety.

'Well, one thing that's genuinely wonderful about getting older is the way your mind changes...'

'You're not old.'

'Well, middle-aged...'

'Middle-aged is in the future when you're like, fifty or something.'

'I'm sixty-five. What does that make me, then?' asks Lara, laughing out loud.

Tom looks straight at Lara and smiles. 'You're ageless. Like a fine piece of hand-blown glass.'

'A "fine piece of hand-blown glass". Nice. Never been called that before.' She smiles.

'Sorry. I...um...meant it as a compliment.'

'I know. It's fine. It's lovely. It's a...a really nice compliment. Thank you. Very much.' She smiles warmly at him and he smiles back, his confidence returning.

Lara looks away, then finishes the remains of her tea. 'I suppose I should get on.'

Tom stands up. 'Yes, don't let me keep you. As I said, I only popped round quickly to drop this stuff off. I hope James feels better soon. Tell him to give me a bell once he's up and about.'

'I will.'

'And maybe next time I drop round I could see your studio?'

'Oh yes. I completely forgot. I...er...well look, next time, OK?'

Charles looks from one to the other of them, tail wagging, then leaps at the back of a chair where his lead is still dangling temptingly from the morning's walk. He grabs it in his mouth, then runs to the front door, claws clicking on the tiles.

Tom and Lara follow him in silence. Lara opens the door and Tom walks out then stops. He pauses then turns around to face her. They hug one another momentarily and Lara closes her eyes for a second. It's too much of a shock, the feeling of his arms wrapped around her, even so briefly. When she pulls away, she feels exposed, vulnerable, and confused.

'Thanks for the brownies. Delicious. And I…'

'My pleasure.' Lara cuts him off, looking past him to where Charles is now sitting in the yard, lead hanging from his mouth, waiting patiently. As Tom turns away and walks to his van, Lara suppresses the urge to shout after him,

'You're not an outsider.'

22
The Pork Chop

'HERE'S THE THING. THERE'S A MOVIE COMING UP which you'd be perfect for. *Perfect.* You'd be great in it. But…'

Juliette sighs heavily and blinks in slow motion as she studies his face. The receding hairline, the putty-like skin, anaemic, pudgy lips and unshaven double chin. The mean, lopsided brown eyes, one of them open slightly wider than the other, almost squinting at her, pleadingly. A hollow, ugly man, devoid of grace and with all the oleaginous charm of a used-car salesman.

'…it's not gonna work out unless you do what I say. That's the bottom line. You know how this goes…' He looks at her meaningfully, a slight smile playing on his plump lips.

Juliette, in white jeans and a red t-shirt, her auburn hair tied back into a tight bun, sits bolt upright on the lounger, legs crossed and hands clasped tightly in her lap. Her eyes are hidden behind a large pair of black Dolce & Gabbana shades.

Wayne Montana is wearing nothing but a pair of baggy blue swim trunks, overhung by the heavy sac of his freckled, hairy belly.

He makes me wanna puke. The entitlement of the powerful male, to look like a piece of shit and not give a fuck, eh Wayne? Burgers and Krispy Kremes not looking so well on you, ya fat fuck.

Juliette has not come alone. At Montana's insistence on the strictly confidential nature of their so-called 'meeting', both Adriana and Brandon are waiting out the front in the SUV.

Juliette is vaguely aware of noises coming from the house, possibly the housekeeper, milling around inside. Montana's wife Emma doesn't seem to be home, which puts Juliette even more ill at ease, suddenly feeling a need for safety in numbers, trapped alone with him in the gardens of his huge colonial-style Spanish mansion.

'Don't you think the bougainvillea are looking swell?' asks Montana, sweeping his hand towards the white wall alongside the swimming pool, blanketed in cascades of brightly clustered pink flowers.

Juliette stares at him from behind her shades, uncomfortable that he's changing the subject and not quite knowing what to say.

'I guess. Yeah. They look cool.'

'The gardening crew have done a great job with them this year. Best gardening crew in Beverly Hills, I tell ya. You want their number? Want me to fix you up with them? They're in demand. Everyone wants them. English guys.'

'I'm good, thanks.'

'You sure? Really, they are so recommended, they are the *best.* The crème de la fucking crème of fucking horticulture out here.'

'I am good for the landscaping, really.'

He's gonna make me ask him about it. Asshole.

'So what's the movie?' asks Juliette, trying to sound casual and nonchalant.

'The movie? You don't wanna talk about flowers, huh? I thought all women liked to talk about flowers. Guess you're not all women,' he says, smirking.

'No, Wayne, I am obviously not all women. Tell me about the goddamn movie.'

'OK, OK, take a chill pill,' he says, holding the flat of his hand up to her in admonishment.

'It's called *Gungirl.*'

'*Gungirl*,' repeats Juliette, raising her eyebrows.

'*Gungirl.* The lead is a so, so strong female role, perfect for you to reflect your many, many strengths.'

'OK…' Juliette forces a smile.

Montana holds his pudgy hands in front of his face, palms outwards, and gesticulates apropos of the plot summary.

'Nurse goes on a gun rampage. She's stunning. The only way this nurse forward slash rampage thing is going to work is if she looks fucking *incredible.* So goddamn *hot* you can't take your eyes off her. Celluloid fucking Gorilla Glue. You've got that, baby, and the numbers prove it.'

Juliette involuntarily feels a pang of pride. As he knows she will.

'There's a fucking gigantic bloodbath, blood everywhere, spurting from every limb, this is *real* violent, Tarantino shit, OK? She fucking *wastes* this whole cabal of surgeons who've been behaving, let's say, a little *inappropriately*, yanno.'

'Raping her?' asks Juliette, flatly.

'Yeah, yeah, sexual misconduct, that kinda thing.' Montana rolls his eyes. 'She has this life-changing epiphany in the slammer and starts with all this feminist campaigning for gun control. Becomes a libtard heroine. It's a very strong role, really strong. It's gonna be a *liberal feminist masterpiece.*'

'OK…and what do you want me to do for this role?' asks Juliette, warily.

'Apart from lose ten pounds?' Montana's face is deadpan.

Juliette stares at him, evenly, before he continues.

'Micky is holding off on saying yes to this Ripper movie and *you need to change his mind.* It's *very, very simple.* Even *you* could understand it,' he adds.

'Micky? He's been out in the sticks somewhere in Bulgaria, filming with Freya Stephens. You know that, Wayne. The signal hasn't been great. I've hardly had any contact with him myself,' protests Juliette, removing her shades and looking at him with anguish.

Montana glowers at Juliette in silence as her mind races…

What the fuck are you even doing here Juliette? You know what that asshole's like. You're established enough without needing his help to get parts. And now look at yourself. You're pathetic, reduced to freezing like a deer caught in the headlights of a juggernaut. Fuck.

Montana hauls himself up from the lounger and jumps to his feet, surprisingly athletic for a man of such huge bulk. He stands towering over Juliette as she sits staring up at him with a growing sense of fear. An ugly vermilion flush is visibly surging up from his neck and into his face.

'*I don't think you're trying hard enough to persuade him!*' he yells, the flush now reddening his entire face. Juliette looks down and notices tiny crumbs of food, stuck in the hair on his paunch.

'Look at my fucking face when I talk to you! You use *whatever you got* to persuade him! Use those *sweet little titties* of yours, that *cute ass*, I don't give a *fuck* how you do it but it is *your duty* to make sure Micky knows that saying *no* to this movie is simply *not a fucking option!* And saying no to *me* is *never a fucking option!*' He jabs his forefinger at her threateningly.

Something about the phrase 'sweet little titties' cuts through Juliette's fear and propels her to stand and face him, her mood darkening to match his as bile floods her stomach with raw anger.

She moves her face closer to his and yells back.

'These "sweet little titties" as you put it, are not what got me a fucking Academy Award. *My talent did. And you fucking know it!* I've got *influence* in this town!'

'You won a gong for *The Cashier* because *I made it happen, you cunt! Me!* The fucking Academy board members do what the fuck I tell 'em!' he screams at her.

'*No*, I won it because my portrayal was *fucking beautiful*, you son-of-a-bitch! I made people *cry* at fucking movie theatres from coast to fucking coast!' screams Juliette. 'They *related* to me! They wanted to *be me*, the lonely heiress, working her ass off at fucking Walmart to find a man who believes in her and loves her for herself! It's what every woman wants! To be loved for who she is and not for *what she fucking looks like* or *how she can fucking help a man* and it's fuckers like you who are too fucking *stupid* and *twisted* to realise it!'

Her face snarls with loathing and contempt. 'I know what you do behind Emma's back. I know you're fucking other women. We *all* know. The whole fucking *town* knows! You're a fucking *pig!*'

Montana takes a deep breath then lowers his head, pushing his face so close to Juliette's that she can smell last night's whisky on him. The reek and the closeness of his flesh make her want to retch.

'That's right! I've fucked 'em all! Gillian Carrington! Bella George! Micky's little piece of snatch, Freya fucking Stephens! They fucking *love* me! All of 'em!' he yells.

He grabs Juliette's arm and drags her across the terrace towards the house.

Too shocked to scream, she focuses on not falling as he yanks her through the huge floor to ceiling glass doors in the east wing of the house and into a vast screening room.

On the walls are large framed prints of a dinner-suited Montana at various award ceremonies, each one an almost carbon copy of the other but featuring a different beautiful actor. Montana presenting a huge grin to the camera, his chin thrust forward proprietorially with his pudgy fist clamped around the bare arm of each smiling, spangled beauty, cooing adoringly into his big, fat face.

He shoves Juliette forward roughly and jabs a finger at a photo of himself and Freya Stephens, who is standing coquettishly clad in a backless, flowing gold designer gown against a backdrop of wall to wall Golden Globes logos. In the photo, Montana's hand rests on the small of Freya's back, just above the swell of her buttocks.

'See? Look at them! I'm not called "God" for nothing!' He sweeps his arm to take in the photos across the wall. 'Yeah, they get their Academy Awards, but they also get shown the *best fucking time!* The Baftas, Cannes, red fucking carpets everywhere, magazine covers, the best hotels, the finest fucking restaurants, designer gowns, limos! I make 'em into stars! And I make 'em laugh. *I'm funny.* I'm a funny guy!' He turns her to face him, still gripping her arm. 'The bottom line, sweetheart, is *the cunts can't fucking resist me!*' He leers into her face.

'Get your hands off me,' Juliette orders quietly, her voice dropping an octave, the words seething from between her teeth.

Wayne drops his hand away from the grip they have on Juliette's upper arms, leaving crimson marks on her pale skin.

'I'm leaving. Now. You are behaving very, very badly. And not for the first time. How *dare* you grab me like that?' she hisses, acidly. 'I haven't forgotten what you did to me when I first arrived in this town. I will never forget it. You should be *ashamed of yourself.*' She practically spits out the final words, jabbing a finger right into the soft, hairy flesh of his protruding belly.

She replaces her sunglasses, turns on her heels and marches towards the glass doors, stepping through them with her head held high, hiding the huge wave of relief she feels at being outside, and free again.

'Juliette!' pleads Montana as he runs after her. 'Juliette! Come on now baby. Don't be like that! You're embarrassing me here! You're blowing this *way* outta proportion! We were just *talking!* It's called

business! The art of negotiation! Don't you understand *business?* Don't make it *personal!* You're escalating this *way out of line,* this is *hysterical!* Why are you being so *unreasonable?* Is it that time of the month, sweetheart?' The anger has evaporated, replaced by the whine of a spoilt child.

Juliette marches around to the front of the house where Brandon is sitting at the wheel of the SUV, reading a paperback of Dostoevsky's *Crime and Punishment.* Adriana lies stretched across the back seat, a Yankees cap pulled down over her face, taking a nap.

'*Guys!* Let's split!' shouts Juliette as she approaches the vehicle.

Adriana jumps up from her prone position and opens the back door. Seeing the look on Juliette's face, the colour drains from her own. This is not good.

Juliette climbs into the vehicle next to Adriana and turns to face Montana who has now caught up with her, standing there in his swimming trunks and flip flops on the gravel forecourt.

Juliette leans out of the open window and says to Montana in a steady, low voice, 'The "cunts" as you so delicately put it, all fucking *hate* you, *Wayne.* We all do. And you know what we do behind your back? We take the fucking piss out of your body.' She holds her little finger in a crooked shape and wags it towards him, mockingly. 'Your little egg-shaped dick is almost as famous as you are.'

Montana glances at Brandon, who stares impassively forward, belying the smirk behind his eyes.

Juliette smiles elegantly and raises the dark-tinted glass window to cut Montana off.

'Go for it,' she barks at Brandon, who guns the engine and sprays gravel in all directions as they roar out of Montana's driveway.

Adriana peers out of the rear window to see Montana storming across the forecourt, his face visibly contorted with rage. She turns to look at Juliette.

'*Wow,* boss. Just *wow.* Like, I've never seen you like that before. Like *total wowserfest.* What the *fuck* just happened back there?'

Brandon calmly glances through his rear view mirror, his face an impassive mask.

Juliette looks at Adriana and removes her shades.

Slowly, her body begins to convulse, and then she starts uncontrollably shaking. She grunts, then lets out a heaving sob and wraps her arms around her body, desperately clinging to herself, rocking backwards and forwards, backwards and forwards.

23
Ladies who lunch

LARA WEARILY REMOVES THE CAKED MUD FROM HER green wellingtons on the iron boot scraper recessed in the farmhouse wall, just by the main entrance. She stops and looks at its worn surface, patinaed from the cleaning of thousands of boots since the house was built in 1650.

She senses movement in the periphery of her vision, looks up and sees James through the kitchen window, shuffling around in boxers and t-shirt, looking miserable.

She removes her boots, enters the kitchen, walks up to James and hugs him.

'Darling. You're up! Are you feeling better?'

'No. I feel like shit. I'm going back to bed. I just came down for some food. What is there?'

'There's some French onion soup and some pumpkin seed bread I made this morning. Will that do?'

'Yeah, thanks. Would you bring it up? Feel like I'm going to pass out.'

'Baby. Of course I will, darling. I'm going to Ripon to meet Gina for lunch in a bit, will you be OK?'

He nods, wearily. 'Yeah, I'll be fine. Going back to bed, Mum.'

'OK.'

Lara watches her son retreat upstairs and her heart constricts with maternal love. She has to constantly remind herself that he's a man now, even though at some level he will always remain, in the depths of her subconscious, her newborn baby boy.

She warms the soup and takes it with the bread up to James's room, but he's asleep. As she leaves the tray next to his bed, she notices the screen of his phone is still lit up. So he must have only just dropped off. A picture of his girlfriend, Winter, occupies the screen.

He must miss her, with her working in LA. Never shows it though.

She changes into smart navy jeans, a clean white t-shirt and her favourite oatmeal pashmina shawl, which she wraps around herself as she looks at her reflection in the full-length mirror. It feels nice to get out of wellies and work clothes.

Britain's third smallest city, Ripon, where the watch is still sounded by horn to the four quarters of the medieval market square at 9pm as it has been every night since 886 AD, is, as usual during the summer months, busy with tourists.

Lara has arranged to meet Gina at Svensk, a Scandinavian-themed restaurant on a small backstreet just off the market square. Its cool, tiled flooring and minimalist pine furnishing provide a welcome respite from the tourists swarming around the Thursday market and nearby cathedral.

As soon as she walks through the door, Lara spots Gina, seated at a table by the far wall of the restaurant, peering at her phone over the top of her reading glasses, her hair hanging over her eyes as she concentrates.

She looks up as Lara approaches, grins and stands up to greet her old friend.

'You made it! Traffic bad?' asks Gina as she hugs Laura and kisses either cheek.

'No, no, fine, hi. Just, sorry…sorting things out at home. Am I very late?' asks Lara, looking worried.

'Twenty minutes!' announces Gina, looking at her watch as she sits back down.

'Sorry.'

'It's OK.'

'You know I hate being late,' Lara replies, adjusting herself into her seat and smiling.

'So! Phones away! Blasted things!' says Gina, putting her phone back into her pocket.

Lara laughs 'I was going to leave mine at home. Only brought it because James is ill.'

'Can we nip outside for a fag?' interrupts Gina.

'Sure.'

A server approaches the table wearing a casual denim skirt and t-shirt, her blond hair braided neatly into Dutch plaits.

'Are you ready to order?' she enquires, politely.

'We're just going outside for a fag, actually,' says Gina.

'You are,' says Lara, gently, smiling.

'I am. She isn't. But she's coming too,' says Gina. 'Would you bring our drinks outside? What do you fancy, Lara?'

'Well, I'm driving. I'll just have a latte with soymilk please,' says Lara, smiling at the server.

'I'm not driving so I'll have a G&T. Ice, no lemon,' barks Gina, grinning at the server.'You've not been here before, have you, darling?' she looks sideways at Lara.

'Nope.'

'There's a lovely little enclosed courtyard out the back.' She narrows her eyes and peers through the mullioned window at the overcast sky, illuminated from above by a brief gleam of sunlight. 'Rain's stopped. We could eat out there if you like. Supposed to brighten up later.'

'Fine by me.'

'You're so easy-going. One of the many reasons I love you,' says Gina, warmly, grinning as the pair leave the interior of the restaurant to head outside.

'Have to be,' begins Lara, but her words evaporate as Gina marches ahead towards an empty table in the corner of the cobbled courtyard.

Seating herself, Gina places a turquoise snakeskin briefcase on the table, opens it and removes a long shiny box of Vogue Superslims and an engraved silver Zippo from the top inside pocket.

'Please tell me that bag isn't real crocodile or snake or whatever it looks like,' says Lara.

'Of course not darling. It's faux. Calvin Klein. If you're interested in the designer. Which you won't be.'

'I'm not,' says Lara, picking a pistachio from a bowl the server places before them, expertly shelling it and popping the green nut into her mouth.

Gina draws a cigarette from the packet and places it between her pursed lips, flicking the top of the Zippo open as she does so. She inhales deeply and exhales a plume of smoke, sitting back in her chair with satisfaction as she clicks the lighter shut.

'So…first things first. How are the girls?'

'Fine. Comet's much better, Luna is full of it as always and Apple is just delightful, sweet, my baby. How are yours?'

Gina draws on her cigarette, then lifts her right leg and waggles her foot. 'Trimming Claudius's hoof yesterday and he stomped on me. Don't think he broke anything.'

'Didn't you get it checked out? He's a big lad.'

'Nah.' Gina waves her cigarette, dismissively.

'Weren't you wearing safety boots?'

'Nope. Silly me, eh?'

'For fuck's sake, Gina. How many times has that horse broken your toes?'

'Seven. Possibly eight. I've lost count. Comes with the territory.'

'None of mine have ever broken any of my toes…' says Lara, gently, shaking her head.

'Yet…' Gina replies pointedly, then takes another long drag on her cigarette, her cheeks sucking inwards, before exhaling another plume of smoke from the left side of her mouth.

Lara looks at Gina levelly, slightly raising her chin. The edges of her mouth crease in an almost imperceptible smile.

Gina frowns.

'Don't start on about smoking. I know I know, I said I was going to try vaping. But some of those bloody vaping contraptions. Awful things, stink like a sweet factory,' says Gina, defensively.

'Have you ever actually tried one?'

'No. They look utterly ridiculous,' says Gina, taking another drag and then elegantly raising her hand, emphasising the long, thin shape of her cigarette. She moves her face closer to Lara and lowers her voice, conspiratorially. 'Why do people have to be so fucking *furtive* about it? Whipping these ugly contraptions out of their pockets, sucking on them then hiding them again. Drives me mad. Give me fags any day.'

'I'm so glad Bruce gave up smoking. Used to stink the entire house out,' says Lara, matter of factly.

'You know I only *ever* smoke outside,' contests Gina. She pauses. 'How's he getting on in Spain, anyway?'

'Fine. I think. It's impossible to get hold of him though. At the moment I'm reduced to sending messages via Richard which is bloody useless. I don't mean Richard's useless, he's lovely. But when you've been married thirty-five years you don't expect to be sending messages through your husband's best friend.'

'It's ridiculous,' snorts Gina. 'Why can't he just get a *bloody phone* like *everyone else?'*

'Because he's not *like* everyone else.'

'Of course not. He's a *genius,'* says Gina, trying very hard not to actually roll her eyes.

'Ouch. That's a bit harsh, Gina.'

Gina stubs out the half-smoked cigarette in the black, burn-marked plastic ashtray on the table and squashes the long filter in half with her thumb and the end of her forefinger.

'Sorry, darling. I just mean that we make allowances all the time for men when they have talent. Allowances that are not made for women. If we, as women, inconvenience people, no matter what our position in society, we're either being *incompetent* or just a *bitch.* If a *man* inconveniences anyone we're expected to *understand* and make *allowances* for him. Because of his authority, or fame, or wealth, his colour, his genius or even his bloody place on the autism spectrum.'

'Or all of them,' smiles Lara.

'Quite. And I get *bloody sick of it.'*

'We all are.'

'But we all keep buying into it. We all keep *making allowances* for them. I mean, I'm not having a dig, but you and Bruce are a prime example.'

'Gina…I'm not in the mood.'

'Well it's got to be said, sometimes, love.'

'No it doesn't, Gina,' says Lara, gently.

Gina ostentatiously removes another cigarette from the shiny blue packet and flicks it alight, sucking on it and blowing the smoke out of the side of her mouth.

The server approaches their table and places a tall glass of gin and tonic before Gina and a large latte in front of Lara.

'Sorry about the wait, are you eating and ready to order?'

'I'll have the smashed avocado on ciabatta with chilli flakes, please,' says Gina, without even looking at the menu.

'Um...' says Lara, pulling a menu towards her and studying it intently, 'The pancakes with lingonberry coulis and whipped coconut cream, please.'

'No problem. Thank you,' says the server, whisking the menus from the table and disappearing back into the restaurant.

'I'm not having a go, I promise,' says Gina, taking a sip of her G&T. 'I mean, look at me. I know I should cut down.'

A slightly chill breeze has sprung up after the rain. Lara elegantly adjusts her shawl, protectively pulling it closer around her shoulders.

'How's the studio?' asks Gina, in a warm, conciliatory tone.

'Still working on my refugee.'

'Is it still causing you turmoil and self doubt?'

'Massively.'

'Still? How, darling?'

'Just....should I be even be doing this? What kind of statement am I trying to make about conditions for refugees fleeing warfare and persecution? Am I making it forcefully enough? Is the stone going to speak, to shout, to explode with pathos? Or will it remain inert and cold? It's terrifying, sculpting. Coaxing the spirit out of a block of alabaster, chip by chip.'

'I can only imagine.'

'The studio is very photogenic though. On social media I look like I have the perfect life,' says Lara, smiling ruefully.'Anyway, are you going to ask about the children?' she adds, a crisp edge creeping into her voice.

'Of course, darling, of course. Look, I didn't mean to be funny, earlier...'

'It's fine.'

'OK. So how are they?'

'I don't want to tell you, now,' says Lara, impishly.

'Go on,' says Gina, rolling her eyes.

'Hazel's working herself to the bone on Fox Vox, you know, her *Giving a Voice to Foxes* campaign. She looked exhausted last time I saw her.'

'Well good for her, good for her! You know I think that's a very worthy cause, I've said it before. And James? He's still ill, you said? He's such a darling,'

'Yeah. Well, I think he's on the mend, now. The studio's going well, he's hoping to have it finished by the autumn,'

'Fantastic.'

'Then as soon as it's built he'll probably move out to Leeds or London or somewhere, wouldn't surprise me.'

'Do you think he's ready to go?'

'I do, really, yes. I don't want him to, of course. He'll be the last one to flee the nest. But yeah.'

'Is he working on it on his own now or has he still got that mate helping him?'

Lara looks at Gina and smiles, enigmatically.

'Oh, I *see.* It's like *that,* is it?' laughs Gina.

'Like *what?'*

'Go on, then, spill the beans,' says Gina. She looks at her friend and grins in anticipation.

'It's nothing. Nothing, really,' says Lara, fiddling with her shawl and adjusting it nervously around her shoulders.

'*What?* Tell me!'

'Well, he came round the other day to deliver some part for the studio or something. And I invited him to have a cup of tea. As I always do, in fact. You know, just being polite. And normally he declines. But this time, he accepted. I don't know, maybe because Bruce is away and James was ill in bed. I think he probably felt sorry for me because I've been on my own...'

Gina snorts, dismissively. 'Sorry my arse. I think he probably *didn't* feel sorry for you,' she says, laughing.

'Anyway, he stayed and we had a bit of a chat, and, well, he was flirting with me.'

'Flirting with you. *Again,* you mean. Like when he was looking at the pool?'

'That wasn't flirting. He was just checking the pool over.'

'Not from how you described it on the phone. It wasn't the pool he was checking over.'

'He was, literally! Just checking the pool over. And telling me about his late fiancée and how much he was still grieving…'

Gina takes a long drag on her cigarette, exhales the smoke and then immediately takes a gulp of her G&T and looks away.

Lara pauses and plucks another pistachio from the bowl, peeling it expertly with her long, slight fingers.

'Sorry, Gina…' she says, glancing up at her friend.

'It's OK. It's been two years since Grey…'

'I know, but it's extraordinary, it feels like yesterday when we were all last having lunch together, you and Grey and me and Bruce. Time passes so quickly...'

'I know. It doesn't seem a minute since Grey was even first diagnosed. And then he went so fast. And now it's two years. Just like that. Anyway…so…what's his name again? James's friend? Tim, wasn't it?'

'Tom.'

'Tom. So what was he doing then? In your kitchen. With you.' Gina smiles lasciviously. 'Come on. Tell Gina everything.'

'Nothing in particular. I just kept getting the impression he was flirting with me. You know, the way he was looking at me. And then he said I looked like a…like a fine piece of antique glass or something.'

'He *what?'* Gina throws her head back, laughing uproariously. '"A fine piece of antique glass"? Where did he dig that one up from?'

'No idea, but…'

'An antique, no less!'

'No, actually, I wasn't a piece of antique glass. I was a piece of hand-blown glass.'

'Hand-blown,' says Gina, archly, raising her eyebrows. 'Where on earth do you *get* these men from?'

'He's James's friend. Nothing to do with me!' laughs Lara, nervously.

'So, what are you going to do about it?'

'What on earth do you mean?'

'I mean, what are you going to do about it?'

'You mean, am I going to encourage him? No!'

'Why ever not?'

'Because I'm *married!'* splutters Lara.

'And that's the only reason you wouldn't allow this intriguing situation to develop any further? Because you're *married?* Well, we've established that you fancy him, then.'

Lara sighs, heavily. 'Don't be ridiculous,' she says, fidgeting with her shawl. 'And it's not a "situation."'

Gina smirks and takes another swig of her G&T.

'You do fancy him. Admit it. I know you do. I can tell.'

'*Gina.* You are behaving as if we were still at uni together and you are being *utterly ridiculous.* Please stop it…'

'You've already told me how gorgeous this Tom is.'

'Look, he's young. He's hot. OK, he's nice to look at.' She pauses, choosing her words carefully. 'But I think of him as I'd think of a…a work of art or something. Aesthetically pleasing. On a purely artistic and unemotional level.'

'Great. So he thinks of you like a piece of antique glass and you think of him like a work of art. And you don't want to fuck him? Get outta here!' says Gina, grinning.

'Look, *objectively speaking*, he's gorgeous. And I can't deny it has affected me somehow. But no, I'm not going to do anything about it.'

Gina looks directly into Lara's eyes. 'You should,' she says flatly.

'There is *no way.* You mean, have an *affair?'* says Lara, aghast at the suggestion.

Gina sits back and coolly appraises her friend's shocked expression. 'That's precisely what I mean.'

'*Gina!* Of course I'm not going to have an affair! Don't be so utterly *ridiculous!'*

'I still don't see why not.'

'*Because,* as I've already *said,* I'm happily married!'

Gina widens her eyes and looks at Lara, smiling.

'No, Gina! It's not going to happen! Absolutely not! Why on earth would I want to risk everything I've worked so bloody hard for, for a quick shag with some young *boy?'*

'I thought you said he was thirty-seven? That's not a boy. Not in my book. That's a man.' She examines her fuchsia-painted fingernails.

'Well he's a boy to me. He's almost thirty years younger than me. It's completely out of the question. It would cause mayhem. Imagine if Bruce found out. He'd be devastated! I'm certain he's never been unfaithful. He's not the type.'

'So? Maybe affairs have never motivated him. It depends where your motivations lie.'

'And anyway,' continues Lara, ignoring the slight, 'Young people are notoriously lacking in tact. They talk. They can't keep secrets. What if something happened, just hypothetically, between Tom and I, and he told James? What would James think of me? It would destroy my family! No way, it's just not worth the risk.'

'So you have actually got as far as thinking this through, then?' asks Gina.

'No, I haven't. I'm just going through it now, in my mind, in response to you and your reprehensible notions.'

'So, you haven't actually *thought* about Tom? In that way…not once?'

The server approaches with their food.

'Smashed avocados on toast with chilli flakes?' she asks.

Gina puts one finger up and the server places a large, square, white plate in front of her. A small square of ciabatta sits in the centre, mounded with avocado and chilli flakes.

'And the pancakes…' says the server, placing a similar plate in front of Lara.

The women wait for the server to depart beyond earshot.

'I'm not doing it, Gina. Bruce and I have an honest relationship.'

'I'm sure you do. As far as you can.'

'The key to the success of our marriage is honesty. We've always been honest with one another. I'm not going to start being dishonest now. Not after all these years.'

'But you'd like to,' says Gina, smirking triumphantly as she cuts into her ciabatta.

Lara looks down at her pancake then carefully cuts off a triangle. She drags it slowly through the lingonberry coulis so that it glistens scarlet, then pulls it through the whipped coconut cream and puts the forkful of food into her mouth. The slightly bland richness of the pancake is shocked into stark life by the tart sweetness of the lingonberry.

'He's got nice eyes. And lips,' says Lara, matter of factly.

Gina eats her food and looks at her friend, levelly.

'And I know what you keep getting at, about Bruce's drinking,' says Lara, testily.

'Ah, that. The elephant in the room which we're not allowed to talk about.' She looks up at the clouds, drifting slowly across the blue sky.

'Look. No-one has any idea of what we've been through Gina. Not even you. Nobody reveals everything about themselves. There are always secrets. It's not that it's an elephant in the room, as you put it. It's just that there are other things to talk about. It's an uncomfortable subject for me.'

'So you've always been honest. But there are always secrets. I get it. Whatever you say, sweetie,' says Gina, dismissively.

She finishes her avocado toast and then almost immediately reaches for her cigarettes. She lights up and takes a drag.

'So, are you going to shag this Tom, or not, then?'

24
Stories

HALF PAST TEN AND THE SUN IS ALREADY SCORCHING hot. Bruce walks out of the lounge onto the balcony, puts a glass of orange juice and a bowl of cereal on the patio table and rests his hands upon the wrought iron balustrade, looking down into the square of Plaza Merced. Through the trees lining the square, he can make out a figure, sitting on a bench. It looks like it's made of bronze.

Richard joins him on the tiny balcony, looking at his phone.

'Do you ever put that damn thing down?' asks Bruce, glancing over at him and smiling.

'I'm *co-ordinating*,' says Richard, looking worried.

'Co-ordinating what?'

'That interview I'm doing for the *Sunday Times* magazine. *Artists in the Med*. It's today,' he says, his brow furrowing as he continues scrolling.

'Well, enjoy it. I'm sure it'll be fun,' says Bruce.

'It shouldn't take too long. Although they want to drag me to some little town up the coast for a photo shoot. Nerja. White houses and blue sea. Looks beautiful, actually,' Richard glances back into the lounge then lowers his voice to a conspiratorial tone and looks at Bruce earnestly.

'Maria wanted to come along. I'm sure the main reason is because she wants to meet Javier Ojeda, the photographer. She's already following him on Instagram. Someone else to take yet more pictures of her. The well of her need for attention is seemingly *bottomless*. I utterly *despair*, sometimes. Do you mind *awfully* if I leave you both here for a few hours?'

'Of course not. I don't expect to be entertained. You know me.'

'I'd better go. I'll see you later on at some point. We could go to El Pimpi this evening if you want. Lovely place. Fantastic terrace, a nice little stroll from here. Antonio Banderas's favourite haunt when he's in town, apparently.'

'Sounds great. I'll see you later.'

Bruce stands for a while watching the people below as they emerge into the sunlit gaps between the trees and then disappear again into the deep shadows. Maybe after breakfast he'll sit at a bar in the square, alone. He hasn't had a chance to do that since he arrived. The need for solitude gnaws silently inside him like an unfulfilled hunger.

He sits down at the little table and eats his cereal in silence. He can hear the *tap tap tap* of Maria typing on her laptop in the lounge, then the front door slamming shut as Richard leaves.

The tapping stops. There is silence, the only sound the white noise of the city in the background.

Bruce finishes his cereal, sips his orange juice and sits looking at the square through the balcony railings. A diminutive French Bulldog pisses against a tree.

Maria appears at the balcony doors, smiling.

'Is it OK if I join you? I am so tired of working. Always I am working. So many of the messages to answer and people to talk to, all of the time. They think it's so glamorous, being an Instagram influencer. But no!'

'Sure, have a seat.' He smiles at her, privately wishing that she weren't there.

She cocks her head to one side and smiles, slightly flirtatiously.

'Do you know what I am going to do tonight?' she asks.

'I have absolutely no idea.'

'I am going to watch this *Withnail!* Richard talks about it all the time. I think he had a very special time, working with you.'

'I think so too. It *was* a special time. Once in a lifetime, I guess.'

'Of course is not that I am an ignorant person of the old English cinema!' exclaims Maria. 'I love your Laurence Olivier in that film from many years ago, *Marathon Man!* The Nazi dentist causing the pain in the mouth!' she wraps her arms around herself and makes a shivering motion.

'We used to have a picture of him, on our wall,' says Bruce, looking at the bulldog's pissing tree below, where now two pigeons are flapping in and out of the branches.

'In a place I lived, in Camden, in London.'

'I have been there! I *love* Camden Market!' says Maria, joyously.

'Yes, well, I haven't been there for quite a few years, actually. But years ago I used to live there with this bloke called Vivian. He was partly an inspiration for one of the characters in *Withnail...*'

'Oh! How *fascinating...*' says Maria. She leans her elbows on the table, rests her chin in her hands and gazes intently at Bruce as he speaks.

Solitude forgotten, Bruce warms to his enraptured audience of one, slipping easily into the role of raconteur.

'So we're living in this awful bloody hovel and Viv comes back one night with this *drink*. Two pints of it. *Yon white stuff* he called it. Like pure white kerosene. And we start drinking this *disgusting fluid* and decide that what we need to do to make our lives happier is to get rid of the pustules on the bathroom wall...'

'Pustules?'

'Vile little lumps on old walls, blisters that look like they might burst at any minute and ooze some vile liquid...' explains Bruce, smiling, his eyes widening.

'Oh...' says Maria, fascinated.

'Anyway, in the bathroom, there's this picture of Lawrence Oliver, as Othello, and the pustules are actually coming through his face. Bloody disgusting. Just the sight of that blistered face every morning made you want to retch. So that night, Viv finally decides enough is enough, finds this sledgehammer in a cupboard somewhere,'

'What is it, sledgehammer?' interrupts Maria.

'Bloody great big thing you hit things with. So Viv takes it into the bathroom and starts whacking Olivier's face with it.' Bruce simulates a wild hammering motion with his right arm.

'Whack, whack, whack, like this. And suddenly, the entire back wall of the house collapses into the garden. And we're both standing there in the moonlight, completely wasted, just looking out through a great big bloody hole. Literally straight out into the garden.'

'Oh, Bruce! How *terrible!*' says Maria, holding up her hands to her face and laughing in horror.

'And less than a week later he bloody moves out, doesn't he? Scarpers off to the provinces to star in some play, leaving me alone in this god-awful bloody *slum* with half the bloody back wall missing!'

'It sounds like an adventure, your life!' says Maria, her eyes alight with admiration.

'It hasn't all been fun, I assure you.'

Maria frowns slightly and leans forward.

'Tell me. Tell me of the tragedy as well as the comedy,' she says gently.

Bruce looks at her for a moment in silence, deep in thought.

'The progress of time has this quite *magical* quality to it, of transmuting - changing, you know - many a tragedy into comedy. Only, some of it is very *black* comedy,' he laughs.

'It was just that Richard, he mention something that happened to you when you were making *Romeo and Juliet*. He didn't say what. Just that you had a very bad time making the film. Because of the director, Franco Zeffirelli.'

'Well, yes. It wasn't the best of times, I have to say.'

'Tell me. I want to know,' says Maria, her eyes widening attentively.

'God, *Romeo and Juliet*,' he says, shaking his head and looking into the middle distance as he remembers.

'He was such a bastard, Zeffirelli. I'm straight out of drama school. Fresh as a daisy, as we say in English. I get cast in *Romeo and Juliet*. Never even been on a plane before, and suddenly there I am in Rome, in this amazing apartment on the Via de Due Macelli.'

'The Via de Due Macelli?'

'Yeah. Smack in the centre. You know it?'

'But of course. It opens into the Piazza di Spagna, where are the Spanish steps.'

'That's the one. So I walk in there and he's surrounded by about a dozen young men, all very cutely dressed, with these little Gucci handbags. And Franco sort of brings me in to introduce me. And as I walk in these guys with the handbags are like "Ma Franco, chi e questo uomo? Incredibile!" You know, "But Franco, who is this man? He's incredible! I was gorgeous back then," says Bruce, laughing.

'You still are,' says Maria, grinning.

'I'm not. But whatever. So Zeffirelli says to me "Oh you must be very *tired*. You have a *shower*." And the next thing I'm in the bathroom having a shower and the door opens and there he is, standing there looking at me. "I'm going to give you a kaftan," he says – he'd just come back from Cairo, beautiful blue silk kaftan – so I get dried and put on the kaftan. And he dries my hair.'

'He dries your hair?' asks Maria, looking shocked.

'Quite. "Bit odd," I think. "Maybe he's being paternal, you know, he's just cast me in his film, I'm his protégé, straight off the plane in a foreign country, don't speak the language, he wants to look after me," sort of thing. But at this point I'm starting to feel *a bit nervous.* So we go back into the room where all the Gucci boys were swanning around, cooing like doves. Only they've all gone. Melted away. The room's empty. Just the sound of car horns from the street below. It was all so *insidious.*'

'Insidious? My English, sorry, it's not perfect. You mean, little bit, little bit, so you hardly notice what's going on?'

'Quite. All of a sudden the room's empty apart from Franco. And me. He waves his hand for me to sit down. On a huge chaise longue. Upholstered in yellow satin. "What do you want to drink? You want something to drink? Bit of whisky?" I don't drink fucking whisky. Never have done. "I'm fine, Franco," I say. And that's when he looks down at me and he fixes me with this look. Like I'm a little *morsel* just perched there on his *satin throne.* And he says "Are you a sponge? Or a stone?"'

Maria raises both hands up to her mouth in shock, then crosses herself with her right hand. 'Dios mío.'

'Now I'm bloody petrified. Totally paranoid. I've got absolutely no idea what's about to go off. Only I know it's going to be bad. I've got no idea what he's talking about, a sponge or a stone. So I make a joke out of it, you know, to try and lighten the situation. "A bit of both, Franco," I say, laughing. And before I know it he's on me. Pinning me down with these huge arms. Great long tongue rammed down my throat. Thick as a tree trunk. Reeking of fags. That sour taste, filling my mouth and all the way down my throat. And those pudgy hands all over me, groping at me. I'm fighting him off, pushing him away. Feeling so sick. I didn't know what to do...'

He looks across the Plaza de Merced and stares at the trees, deep in thought.

'Oh, Bruce. That is so disgusting. Pobre sito. So did he?'

'No. No, I managed to get away. But I was in shock.'

'It was bad enough. A *rape kiss.* How terrible for you, Bruce.'

Bruce glances back at Maria and drains his glass of orange juice.

'The next morning, the producer and his entourage are all hanging around in this beautiful baroque hallway. And he's got white patent leather shoes on, a white patent leather belt, pink hipsters, an open blue shirt with a big gold bauble bouncing on his chest. Completely obvious but I didn't know! Had no idea what was going on! I go up to him and I say, "You're never going to believe what happened to me last night," and he says, "What happened?" And I start to tell him and he says "Ooooh *reeeeaaaally?"* like he's got a huge ball bearing in his mouth. And what I don't know, what I'm too fucking naive to realise, is that this producer, this director, all these giggling minions, they're *all in it together*. It really didn't sink in for a long time. That they'd done this before. It was their *routine*. And all these years later, I still wonder, how many others like me were there? How many didn't escape? How many lives were *completely ruined?*'

'Bruce, this is so terrible. That was…it was…*sexual assault*. You know that, don't you?'

'I do now. At the time I didn't have a clue what the fuck had happened, Maria.' He shakes his head. 'So fucking naive. I was a baby, really.' He pauses and gazes out over the square again. 'When I think of my own son at that age…it's so young. You know nothing of life at that age. You're just a *snack* for these *grotesques*.' A sadness passes across his face before he looks up at Maria and grins.

'So, there you are.'

Maria reaches out and squeezes Bruce's hand.

'Bruce, I know you are so funny, you make me laugh, but this is so terrible a thing to happen to you.'

'Well, it was many years ago now. I guess it all went in my work, didn't it? The very next year I wrote *Withnail and I*. It was catharsis. That's how I dealt with it. By writing about it. And once I'd written *Withnail* I started drinking. Only not whisky. *El vino*. So. It shaped my life, for better or worse. And there's your Uncle Monty. Oh…I forgot, sorry, you haven't seen the film. Well if you see it, you'll maybe understand where some of it came from.'

'I watch it tonight, I promise. Do you think I will understand all the English?

'Well you seem to understand my ranting, so I'm sure you won't have a problem.'

The apartment buzzer sounds. Maria disappears inside to answer it. She picks up the handset and answers the caller in Spanish.

'Yes, hello, Miguel. Yes, OK, come up.'

She opens the front door and waits, peering out into the tiled hallway. Footsteps sound and shortly, Miguel, a waiter from Tita Conchi, the café bar at the foot of the apartment block, appears at her door. Dressed in black trousers, white shirt and a black apron, he smiles and holds out his phone to Maria.

'Hello Maria! For you! Voice messages! In English! They must be important!' says Miguel, looking slightly perplexed.

Maria plays the messages then stares at the phone, looking slightly confused.

'Can I?' she asks, gesturing towards the interior of the apartment.

'Of course!' says Miguel, smiling.

Maria walks back out to the balcony, Miguel's phone in her hand.

'Bruce. Someone has sent a message for you. To the bar downstairs. I don't understand what he wants. I play it for you.'

Wayne Montana's voice booms from the phone.

'Yeah, get this message to Bruce Robinson, upstairs at numero fourteen, wouldja? Apartment of Maria Aranda. *Maria Aranda*, yeah?'

'Bruce, baby, long time no see. Wayne here. I've heard you're in Málaga. Get back to me aysapp about this Ripper movie. We're putting everything together at this end and Micky Valance is in for the Ripper. Totally committed, OK? I'm zooming with him for the next hour but call me back straight after that. Do not forget to call me! It's gonna make an *incredible* movie, Bruce! *Incredible!*'

Bruce raises his eyebrows but otherwise his face is blank.

'Many thanks, Maria...'

'Who is he?' she asks, looking concerned.

'Well, whoever he is, he seems to think we're the best of friends, doesn't he?'

'Have you met him before?'

'Once. Years ago. At an awards ceremony...'

'Is he...a producer, or something?'

'Let's say he wields a dark wand of power.'

'He sounds like he is not a very nice person if I'm honest, Bruce.'

'He's an arsehole,' says Bruce, levelly, smiling up at her.

'Anyway, I make sure he doesn't disturb you again. Sorry for that.'

'That's OK.'

As soon as Maria disappears back into the apartment again to return Miguel's phone, her own phone vibrates against the slatted wood of the patio tabletop and rings with a haunting song - Cecilia's *Un Ramito de Violetas.*

Bruce listens to the tune, intrigued, never having heard the song before. Maria rushes back out to retrieve the phone before it stops ringing, her hair falling over her face in thick black curls.

'Sí...?'

'Hi. Maria? I'm really sorry to interrupt you, I'm Hazel, Bruce's daughter. I begged Richard for your phone number, I hope you don't mind. It's just that I urgently need to talk to my dad and I was hoping he may be still at your flat and hasn't gone out...'

'Oh, hello, Hazel! Your father is here, he hasn't gone out. Would you like to talk to him?'

'Pleeeease,' says Hazel.

Maria hands the phone to Bruce.

'Is your daughter. Hazel,' she says, smiling.

Bruce takes the phone.

'Pickle! How are you?'

'Well, not good, actually, Dad.'

'What's happened?'

'So I went to this fox rescue, about an hour ago, and the people there were *so* weird, Dad, you literally wouldn't believe it. This vixen was under their decking, she was terrified. And there's a man, and a woman, I don't know if they were married or what, and I'm outside, trying to coax this vixen out of her hiding place, right? And the man, he's in the kitchen. And he starts shouting at the woman. Really weird stuff like "No-one's ever going to find out unless you tell them, you stupid bitch!" and stuff like that. And she's shouting back, like "I said I wouldn't tell anyone! Why would you think I'd tell anyone! Even if they found out, no-one would believe you'd done it! And we cleaned up the blood anyway, they won't find nothing here!" It was totally crazy. They must've thought I couldn't hear them!'

'Right…' says Bruce, his face clouded with worry.

'But then the woman comes out on the decking and I look up and she's standing there, just staring at me with this *look* on her face. Super *weird*. And the poor vixen starts whimpering. And I'm struggling, trying to open the trapping cage, and this woman says in this really cold voice, staring down at me, "Did you hear that?" Oh my God. I was literally almost shitting myself, Dad. It was *so* terrifying.'

'What did you say to her?' asks Bruce.

'I pretended she was asking about the vixen. I said "Yes, I've been right under the decking, I heard her whimpering, it was louder before but she's quietened down now."'

'And what happened then?'

'She just kept looking at me *super* strange. I felt so scared, like she was going to do something to me. Like literally kill me or something. So I managed to get the vixen into the cage and I said to this woman, "It's OK, I'll see myself out. Thanks for letting us know," and I left by the side gate. No way was I going back into that house. Super creepy. Then I ran all the way back down the lane to the van, carrying the little vixen in the cage. I've literally never been so scared in my life, Dad!' Hazel's voice trembles as though she's about to burst into tears. 'And the vixen was terrified too.'

'*Darling*. You're OK. You did the right thing. Well done.'

'I just wanted to talk to you, Dad,' she says, pitifully. 'It was like a horror film.'

'It's OK, I'm here. Talk away.'

'You don't think they'll like, track me down, like I'm some sort of witness to whatever it was they did, do you? Track me down and like, kill me or something, do you?'

'Of course not. Forget it if you can. Where did it happen?'

'Outskirts of Croydon.'

'Croydon. Well there you go. Inbreds. Just your average backwater crazies. Don't worry about it,' says Bruce, laughing.

'OK.'

'OK, Pickle?'

'Yeah...'

'OK.'

'Dad?'

'Yeah?'

'I really wish you'd get a phone. It's a total pain not being able to message you or anything,' says Hazel, her voice hardening almost imperceptibly.

'I'm not getting a phone. I threw the last one away,' he says, firmly but kindly.

'But how am I meant to contact you?' she whines.

'Through your mother.'

'But what if you're away and I want to talk to *you?*'

'You can email me.'

'I tried that. You literally *never* check your email!'

'OK. Well, I'm sorry…'

'But it's a *joke,* Dad!' says Hazel, accusingly.

'Well darling, I'm sorry that my life isn't organised in a way that's 100 per cent convenient for you, but that's the way it is. I am not getting a mobile phone or any other bloody contraption, OK?'

'*Fine.* I *knew* if I rang up for sympathy I'd just get a *lecture.* What kind of father are you, anyway? *I shouldn't have bothered!*'

'Hazel…' says Bruce, but she's hung up.

He hands the phone back to Maria, who smiles sympathetically.

'Trouble at home?' she asks.

'Not really,' he sighs. 'My daughter. She rescues foxes. And gets herself into all sorts of situations.'

'Rescue foxes? In Spain we don't do this.'

Bruce sighs heavily. 'No, in England we tend not to, either…look, I think I'm going to go downstairs, to thank that waiter. It was very kind of him to bring the phone up.'

'That's Miguel. He's lovely. I already thanked him…'

'Still, I'd like to thank him myself.'

'OK…well, I'd better get back to work. Ciao!'

'Yes, work…' says Bruce, looking back out to the square, where the two pigeons are now settled on a tree branch, side by side, calling softly to the world.

Bruce avoids the lift, having harboured a perennial distrust of the things for as long as he can remember. He descends three flights of cool, marble steps to Tita Conchi, situated right under Maria's apartment block. The white awning and white plastic tables on the terrace adjacent to the street belie the quirky, bohemian interior. A black filigree wrought iron spiral staircase in the corner of the main bar leads incongruously up to the ceiling, where it comes to an abrupt halt against a brightly painted mural of flamenco dancers in scarlet, turquoise and emerald dresses.

Antique, leather-bound books are propped on every tread of the staircase, amongst plants trailing from brightly painted ceramic pots.

Miguel is standing at the bar, his head down, focused on polishing glasses with a large white cloth. He looks up and smiles at Bruce.

'Hello, once again, señor!' he says brightly, a hint of a gold tooth glimmering as he smiles. 'May I get you a drink?'

'I'll have a look at the drinks menu if it's not too much trouble.'

'Of course,' says Miguel, handing Bruce a laminated card.

'I'll just have a bottle of the Rioja Reserva.'

'Claro, señor, please take a seat.' Miguel sweeps an arm to indicate the empty café .

'I'll be outside,' says Bruce. 'And thank you for earlier. Very kind of you.'

'No trouble at all, señor,' says Miguel, smiling.

Bruce takes a seat outside, under the canopy, in a position where the sun is still shining on one of the seats. He adjusts his sunglasses and silently basks in the joy of much-needed solitude.

Miguel brings the wine, pours Bruce half a glass, and returns inside, leaving the bottle. Bruce takes a drink. The red flows through him like warm liquid gold. Alone and with a drink, he finally feels at peace. He opens his copy of *Rimbaud's Complete Works*, adjusts his glasses and begins reading.

25
UNTWISTED

I HAVE TO SEE HIM AGAIN. I'M TOO SCARED TO SEE HIM again. I'm too scared to approach him. He won't want to see me, he'll think I'm some ghastly nuisance fan who won't leave him alone. I can't call in on him out of the blue. Oh God, what am I going to do?

Stop being so fucking self-pitying Ella. He told you to look him up, didn't he? He liked you. So just find his address and go and fucking see him. What's the worst that can happen? Get a fucking grip, woman and get the fuck on with it.

Ella retreats back into the cool darkness of her room, sits at the window overlooking the sea, and opens her laptop. She types the address into Google Maps. 2, Calle San Juan de Letrán. The apartment is right there, overlooking the Plaza Merced, inside a tall Gothic block fronted with wrought-iron balconies and bay windows.

So that's where Bruce is staying. Half past seven. I'll visit him this morning, before it gets too hot.

Bruce wakes at 7.20am, his head thick and fuzzy. His mind slowly surfaces into wakefulness, where it immediately starts to reassemble the events of the previous evening, an incomplete jigsaw puzzle with each memory floating into place, gradually revealing the complete, ghastly picture with pinpoint accuracy.

Maria looking worried. Maria saying, 'We'll have to get you to bed.' Me saying 'I love you Maria. You're so good for Richard. You make such a good couple.'

Maria holding me up as I try and stand.

Some arsehole laughing and pointing his bloody phone at me.

Maria taking me upstairs.

My lovely bed.

He looks at the clock. Half past seven.

By eleven o'clock the sun is blisteringly hot. Ella leaves Málaga Centro metro taking a route along shady, narrow back streets, avoiding both the tourists and the sun until she reaches the Plaza de Merced.

At the corner of the square, she looks up.

That's it.

She gazes up at the apartment building, then crosses the road in front of the apartment block to enter the deep shade of Calle San Juan de Letrán.

She tentatively peers around for the entrance and then suddenly sees it, a double-fronted glass door with a blue and white glazed ceramic tile embedded on the wall next to it, bearing the number two.

She steps up to the door and stares at the small metal rectangular buzzer for apartment fourteen.

You don't know him well enough to be visiting. Turn around, leave, and forget the idea for the book.

Ella glances back towards the sunlit square, then looks down. Her finger hovers over the button. She presses it. Nothing happens. There is no sound and no answer.

Bruce is almost certainly busy, writing, hunched over a typewriter, a glass of red next to him on an antique desk in a quiet, shaded corner of the room. Writing, in his own world, the intensely private world of the writer and his work. And I'm interrupting him. I don't want to press the buzzer again. Fuck. I can't do it.

Ella turns and walks away back down the quiet, dark street, emerging into the brightly lit Plaza de Merced once again.

She walks past a Japanese schoolteacher who is smiling, talking and waving directions at a line of rigidly smiling Japanese schoolchildren, obediently posing for the camera alongside a bronze statue of Picasso, hunched in solemn contemplation on a white bench in the corner of the square. The teacher beckons to the children to follow her and they leave the silent bronze man alone, deep in thought. The sun is like a weight, pushing all life back into the shadows.

An almost intangible tingling on the back of her neck and a feeling that someone is watching her compel her to turn around.

Leaning against the railings of a balcony on the second floor is a man, barefooted, wearing jeans, a loose white cheesecloth shirt and drinking a glass of red wine.

For a moment Ella stands rooted to the spot in the brilliant sunshine. She adjusts the brim of her hat and continues looking up at him. He notices her, tilts his head to the side slightly, and smiles.

'I was…er…hi Bruce…' she says, raising her voice so she can be heard.

'Hi, Ella,' he says, smiling and raising his glass.

'I was just wondering if you…I'm here, in Málaga for a bit…'

'So I see,' he continues, beaming at her from the balcony.

'I…er…could we? Is it OK if…?'

'There's a bar just down below on the corner. Right in front of you. Tita Conchi. I'll see you there in five.'

'OK…thanks. Thank you. Thanks,' She smiles up at him.

Ella realises she's already standing in front of Tita Conchi. She takes a seat under the awning and nervously picks up a menu. She doesn't feel like eating or drinking but she stares at it anyway. She scans the list of dishes and drinks, but the words merge together nonsensically.

Then she looks up and Bruce is walking towards her with his light, springing gait and a big grin on his face.

'Ella! Hi!'

'Hi, Bruce.'

She stands up and they kiss on each cheek, perfunctorily.

'I hope I'm not interrupting you. I hate people interrupting me. I was literally just passing through and noticed that this was where you were staying.'

'You're not interrupting.'

'Oh, good. I thought you might be busy…um…writing or something.'

Bruce laughs. 'Actually, I was doing nothing of the sort. I was attempting to find some glue,' he explains, pulling out the chair next to Ella to sit down.

'Oh…glue…'

'But I don't want to rifle around. It appears that Maria's apartment may in fact be a glueless one. At least on the surface.'

'What do you need glue for?'

'To repair a key fob. It's one I've had a very long time. I've grown quite attached to it.'

The waiter, Miguel, approaches the table bearing a silver tray, perched on one hand.

'Señor Bruce! How are you this morning?' he says, grinning at Bruce.

'Fine and dandy. Muy bien. I'll have the usual please,' replies Bruce, grinning back.

'Excellent. And for the señorita?' asks Miguel, turning to Ella.

'I'll have a sparkling mineral water, please,' says Ella in Spanish.

The waiter disappears inside and returns almost immediately bearing a tray. He puts a glass and a bottle of water on the table in front of Ella, the green glass frosted and coated with tiny beads of cold water. He opens a bottle of red wine and ostentatiously pours a small amount of wine into a glass, placing the bottle before Bruce with a smile and a very slight bow.

Ella pours a glass of the cold water and then simultaneously, she and Bruce raise their glasses to one another.

'Cheers,' says Bruce.

'Cheers. I would normally have joined you for one. Or five,' says Ella, taking a sip of water.

Bruce smiles, noncommittally, waiting for her to continue.

'But I stopped.'

'Did you really? How long ago?'

'Recently. Last week, just before I came over here. But I know that's it. I've had it.'

'What made you decide to stop?' he asks, taking a first sip of his wine.

'Well, my partner, Zack, a mate of his died a couple of weeks ago. Accidental overdose. Booze. Choked to death on his own vomit. Curtis Christ he was called.'

'How very sad. Curtis Christ…'

'Yeah. That was his real name, too. Didn't know him that well. But he was lovely. It came as a bit of a shock. And it got me thinking, what if Zack died? What would I do? Would I be making phone calls and arranging the funeral? Or would I be collapsed in a puddle of Prosecco, unable to do anything because I was drunk with grief?'

'Yes, that would be a problem,' says Bruce, thoughtfully.

'I mean, I tend to be a stress drinker, and normally it would be Zack picking me up from that puddle. But what if he weren't there and my best friend was having to arrange everything for me? I mean, how's that gonna work?'

'Is she...um...reliable?' smiles Bruce.

'She's a total pisshead, too,' says Ella, grinning.

'Might be tricky,' says Bruce, nodding, sagely.

'So I played the video in my mind right from hearing about his death and grabbing that first bottle of wine, then watched the fucker right to the end. His death, what a mess I'm in, the funeral, embarrassing everyone because of my drinking, and I could see quite clearly that I wouldn't be in a fit state to organise a piss-up at a funeral because I'd be hammered before I even got there.'

Bruce smiles. 'I see. Yes, I take your point.'

'So I thought I'd better stop....'

'Right.'

'I wouldn't say I was an *alcoholic,* of course. I don't like that word, anyway. It smacks of AA and twelve step programmes.'

Bruce looks at Ella, levelly, half smiling.

'Sorry. That's a bit rude. I read somewhere that you attend. It's got its place, I guess. It's just not for me. I prefer the term "alcohol addict." Like "drug addict". Because alcohol's a drug, after all. Isn't it?'

'Well, whatever you want to call it. I know that I'm an alcoholic. You...' Bruce raises his eyebrows, quizzically.

'I don't know what I am. I know I was trying to control it. It's like anything. If you have to develop a strategy to hide your actions, then they're out of control. Thing is, when I controlled it, I wasn't enjoying it. And when I was enjoying it, I wasn't controlling it.'

'Did you find it easy to stop?' asks Bruce, taking another sip of his wine.

'The day after Curtis died, I just thought, I can't do this to myself anymore. I had what they call, in inverted commas,' Ella flicks two fingers of each hand in a bunny ears motion next to her head and immediately wishes she hadn't, 'a moment of clarity, I guess. And stopped.'

Bruce looks at her thoughtfully. 'For me, it's booze that *gives* me those moments of clarity. I don't think I've ever sat down to write without having a head full of red.'

'So you always drink and write?'

'I drink red wine when I write for exactly the reason that you're not allowed to drink and drive. Because if you drink two bottles of wine and you're in a thirty mile an hour limit, you're going to exceed the speed limit and probably bugger something up, but that same sensation you get when drink driving is why I drink when I type, because I can exceed the speed limit. I don't have to stay in thirty. I'll do ninety sometimes. Brakes off, foot on the gas.'

'So you've never written anything sober?'

'Actually, I did give up for six and a half years. In the mid-nineties. I wrote *Thomas Penman* during that period.'

'I think it's the best thing you've ever written.'

'My wife thinks so, too.'

'And you wrote it sober…'

'Yes. Lara pointed that out to me, as well.'

Ella looks over at the square and sighs.

'When abusive parents twist you out of shape, substance use is just a desperate way to attempt to twist yourself back to normal, really. For those few seconds when the drug first hits your system, you feel overcome with relief at being momentarily untwisted, as it were.'

Bruce looks at Ella and smiles.

'It's true. The man I thought was my father certainly twisted me out of shape. "A loud mouthed little cunt" is a very dangerous assembly of words to lay on what is ostensibly your son.'

'I know, that's terrible.'

'He brought me up under the set condition that my sister was highly intelligent, and I was stupid. You start believing it. When I say in *Thomas Penman* about "Playing tennis with my childhood", it's actually true.'

'I could tell.'

'I keep meaning to stop drinking. Turning it over in my mind. Lara is at her wits' end, I think. Or maybe not, I don't really know. Maybe she's even more in denial than I am.'

Ella looks at Bruce then away, back at the square.

'Denial is the glue that holds us together. It's at the core of all our drinking. All that "I'm not as bad as so and so. *They're* on three bottles of vodka a day. That's a *real* alchy." In other words, "I might be making a prat of myself to all and sundry and behaving like a tedious drunken bore, but I just like to have a drink and occasionally it gets out of hand," kind of thing. We've all been there, Bruce.'

Ella glances back at him. He's looking at her intently, studying her face as she talks. She looks away again.

'All I can say is that since I stopped,' she looks upwards and gestures with her hands towards the tops of the trees, exploding with life all around the square, 'The sky is bluer, the clouds seem whiter, the trees glow with green. Everything's better without booze.'

Ella pauses, continuing to stare up at the trees and sky, then glances again at Bruce.

He's looking at me as though he thinks I'm completely and utterly bonkers. Is he amused? Bemused? No idea. I don't care. I love this place. I love being with him. It feels right, all of this. As though it were meant to happen.

Two youths walk past the table, dressed in baggy shorts, t-shirts and trainers. The shorter of the two does a double-take when he sees one of his favourite directors, Bruce Robinson, looking curiously at the woman sat next to him.

'You're the bloke that did *Withnail and I!*' he shouts, pointing at Bruce. 'Fucking love it! Sick film!'

Bruce looks up, raises his eyebrows and smiles, looking slightly nervous.

'Scrubbers!' shouts the youth, quoting the seminal *Withnail* line, putting his arm around his friend and grinning wildly.

'Yeah, we've come on holiday by mistake!' exclaims the other one, and both laugh uproariously.

'We'd get a selfie but we ain't got our phones!' shouts the first youth.

'Yeah man! Bottom of the hotel pool!' laughs the other one, by way of explanation.

They stick their thumbs up at Bruce and Ella as they walk away, who look from the youths back to one another and laugh, wryly.

'Do you get that a lot?' asks Ella.

'Now and again. Never fails to bemuse me.'

She shakes her head, smiling and a silence falls between them.

Ella looks down for a moment, then across at Bruce. 'There's a place...down the coast a bit...I don't know how busy you are...I don't want to interrupt your glue hunt, but it's beautiful, the tables are right on the edge of the sea. And no English people. All locals. Do you want to go?'

'I should ring my *wife...'* says Bruce. 'Only I don't have a phone either...' he laughs.

'You can ring her from mine. Tell her the author's taking you to a secluded blue lagoon.'

Bruce looks at Ella, his smile fixed into a nervous grin.

'Kidding. It's just a beach bar. You get the bus over on Paseo del Parque, just opposite the university. Fancy it?'

26
THE SEA

'BUT BOSS, DON'T YOU THINK I SHOULD, LIKE, HANG OUT here for a while?' asks Adriana, looking worried.

Juliette kicks off her high silver stilettos, marches through the open French windows to the balcony and stands glaring out at the ocean. Its very vastness seems to mock her feeling of utter futility.

Here I am, breathing in and out my tides, covering three-quarters of the planet, harbouring a world alien and unseen to you beneath my glassy surfaces, churning foaming waves onto the edges of your tiny world, and you can only stand and dream of everything unknown which lies within my ceaseless belly. You, a thin and fragile splinter, against me, the very womb of the earth, roaring silently since the beginning of time.

'I'm going nuts. It's like the fucking ocean is talking to me. I've got it inside my head, like something from a movie script.'

'Whaddaya mean?'

'I dunno. It's so big. The ocean. I mean, look at it. And that's just the bit we can *see. The surface.*'

'Sure, it's big alright. Are you, like, OK?'

'Yeah. I just don't want you around when Micky gets home. 'Cause I just know things are gonna go to shit.'

'Shouldn't I just be here, boss? I feel kinda protective, yanno?'

Juliette sighs, deeply.

'Yeah I hear ya, Adriana.' She turns and looks at Adriana with a pained expression.

'I just gotta do this by myself.'

'OK. Whatever you say. But I'm not splitting downtown. I'll be at the surf bar, OK? I'll sit right there and catch up on some stuff on my laptop. Just in case you need me.'

'OK. Thanks.' Juliette reaches for Adriana's hand. She squeezes it briefly.

'I'm worried, boss.'

'What, that he's gonna kill me?'

'Well, like you just said, things could go to shit.'

'I'll be fine. Go.'

Juliette replaces her heels and turns around on the spot for Adriana, her short red dress twirling.

'How do I look?'

'Hot.'

Juliette examines herself on her phone, pouting and posing, moving to get the best light and taking a few selfies.

'OK. You'd better go. He'll be here in ten.'

Juliette reaches out to Adriana with both hands and pulls her close, hugging her tightly.

'You're so good to me. I don't know how I'd manage without you. I know that, *technically,* you're like, an *employee,* but you're pretty much my best friend, you know that?'

Adriana hugs her boss back, before pulling away and smiling.

'We...well...we make a good team,' she says, shyly.

As Adriana drives away, she glances in her rear-view mirror and sees Micky's convertible pulling in off the Pacific Coast Highway. A knot tightens in her stomach.

⁂

Juliette wasn't planning to drink. But with Adriana gone, she realises she can't do this sober.

She opens a bottle of Prévost and pours herself a glass, then retreats out to the balcony again. She downs the whole glass of champagne in one, places the empty glass on a table, then stands and looks out at the sea.

She hears him before she sees him.

'I've been stuck on the PCH for *sixty fucking minutes!'* he yells as he walks in through the door. 'Why the fuck did we have to meet here? It would have been quicker to get to Los Feliz!'

Juliette turns around, her back to the sun and the sea, and smiles nervously.

Micky stands in the middle of the room holding a leather holdall, which he drops on the floor in front of him.

The pair stand staring at one another for a few seconds. He approaches her cautiously, like a nervous animal.

As he gets nearer, he can smell her. And she smells, and looks, intoxicating.

He reaches out and draws her towards him, burying his face in her long, auburn hair.

'Oh God. You smell amazing. You *feel* amazing. God, I've missed you, Juliette. *I have missed you.* I've never missed anyone like this as long as I've lived.' He kisses her hair, her neck, and turns her face towards his with both hands.

'God I love you. God, just look at you. You're *gorgeous.'*

He starts kissing her deeply on the mouth.

Every fibre of her being wants him to fuck her. He smells so good and the feel of him is incredible after long months apart. She feels so aroused it's almost painful. But after a momentary kiss, she finds the strength to pull herself apart from him and step back, out of his arms.

She flashes him a warning look.

'I think…yanno Micky…I think we're going a little too fast here,' she says, trying to edge any warmth out of her voice.

'Baby, what are you talking about? I've missed ya!' he says, grabbing her by both shoulders and pulling her roughly towards him.

'Quit!' she says, firmly, pulling away again, glaring now, fire shooting from her eyes.

'Jesus! What the fuck is *wrong* with you?' he shouts, the heat of his passion igniting into anger.

Juliette stares at him with pure hatred. '*You* are what's wrong! You and fucking *Freya Stephens!'*

Micky stares at her, incredulously.

'*What?* Not that fucking *horseshit* again! I am fucking *sick* of this *crap!* Me and Freya Stephens, me and Freya Stephens, *me and fucking Freya Stephens!'* he mimics her in a whiny playground taunt.

'Fucking Freya Stephens! You said it, not me.'

'Don't you get sick of the sound of your own *voice,* whining all the time? I don't wanna hear this tired old *bullshit* the minute I *walk through the fucking door!* Do you even know what I've been *doing* for the last four months? *Do you?'* he yells, the volume of his voice rising with every sentence.

'No? Well I'll fucking tell you!' He jabs a finger at her face. 'I've been stuck in the middle of a fucking *mosquito-infested forest* in the *middle of fucking Bulgaria* for four. Fucking. Months. *Working my sorry ass off!'*

'Working your sorry ass off fucking Freya fucking Stephens!' yells Juliette.

'What, are you fucking *crazy? No! I haven't! Nothing* happened with her! Nada! Zilcho! She's a dumb stuck-up bitch! *I hated her!'*

'Well how come you looked so goddamn cosy on Instagram, then? Not only are you fucking her, you're spreading it all over the fucking internet for the entire world to see! Me and Freya Stephens, hey everybody, look at us! Look at what a great fucking time we're having, fucking the fucking tits off each other!'

'You are so fucking *stupid,* Juliette. So fucking *naive! Instagram? She* did that, not me! To make her boyfriend jealous because he's been *fucking the maid* whilst she's been on location!'

'Oh well. That's just great, isn't it! Yet another man who can't keep it in his pants! You're all the same! This planet would be a much saner place if all the fucking men just dropped dead!' screams Juliette.

Micky reaches out and grabs Juliette's bare upper arm and shakes her violently. His scarlet face looms and disappears from view as her head snaps back and forth.

'You hysterical fucking *cunt! Quit,* will ya? I don't need this when I get back from months of *fucking shit* on the other side of the *fucking planet!'*

Juliette pulls away from him. She can feel the sea again, behind her back. She can feel its quiet, unfathomable power. It is as though an invisible spirit has risen from its depths and she has breathed it in, filled her lungs with it, and she is now flooded with a magnificent strength and unearthly calm.

She picks up the champagne bottle from the table next to her and brandishes it in one hand.

'Keep your fucking hands off me. If you touch me again, I will kill you,' she says quietly.

There is something in her voice Micky has never heard before and it fills him with dread. He doesn't know whether she's crazy or possessed. But suddenly, he's scared.

He shrugs in a studiously casual manner and walks back into the house, heading for the kitchen. He yanks open the fridge, helps himself to a tin of beer, cracks it open and takes a slug, trying to calm the shaking of his hands.

'I'm done with this shit. I'm taking a shower,' he announces in a firm voice, concealing the dread inside him and filled with gratitude that he's able to hide his sense of utter defeat.

Juliette walks back out to the balcony, turns her back to the house and pours herself another glass of champagne. She looks down at the lights popping on, one by one, along the shoreline, as dusk falls. Methodically, she lights candles on the glass tables and feels the unearthly calm which entered her earlier continue to flood powerfully through her body as each blackened wick bursts into life with a tiny flame, illuminating the space around it.

Micky returns after a few minutes, wrapped in his favourite white towelling bath robe. Unusually for him, he has the bath robe belted tight shut.

Juliette returns inside and stands with her back to Micky, still looking out to sea.

'So where is she now? Freya Stephens?' she asks, coldly.

'Back with her dopey husband in Brooklyn. Pair of assholes.'

Juliette turns to face him. 'How do you know what he's like?'

'She told me.'

'I see,' says Juliette, flatly. 'So she filled you in on her broken marriage. Cute. My husband's an asshole. That old story. I know that one from cover to cover.'

Micky sits in the middle of the vast sofa, puts his feet up on a recliner and continues to drink from the can, saying nothing.

'So. I never got a response from you about my meeting with The Pork Chop. Gigantic kudos to see you returning so full of sympathy for me, Micky. Nice to see that you're so on my side.'

Micky gives an exaggerated yawn.

What the fuck is her game? Maybe she'll offer me a spread of sushi poisoned with a piece of lethal blowfish? Or maybe she's gonna whack me with the champagne bottle when my back's turned. One thing's for sure. The bitch has lost her fucking mind.

'Yeah, well, I thought I'd wait till I got back to talk about that in person.'

'So...'

'Look. He's a pain in the fuckin' ass, OK? Everyone in the industry knows that. *Everyone.*'

'But he's not *just* a "pain in the ass", Micky. Other artists have been talking about him.'

'Yeah, right. Gossip. What's new? This town is full of gossip. You ignore it. I didn't witness any of it so it's none of my business.' He shrugs his shoulders and peers at his can of beer, running his finger around the Budweiser logo, through the cold misty droplets on the chilled exterior.

'Gossip? You know what "gossip" is, Micky? It's a word bandied around by men, to belittle women for sharing information, often about the crimes that men have done to them. So you call it "gossip" to trivialise it. Bella George has been saying that Montana *raped* her!' says Juliette, her voice rising in anger. 'Is that gossip, Micky?'

'*Bullshit.*'

'What, you think she's making it up?'

'Of course she is!'

'Why would she make something like that up?'

'I dunno. Attention?'

'Micky, rape is the *pinnacle of humiliation! I*t's a violation not only of your *body* but also of your *mind!* You don't just say someone's *raped* you for *attention!* Are you *fucking serious?* For *attention? What fucking planet are you on?*'

'Bella George would,' he snorts, derisively, draining his can.

'*No,* Bella George *wouldn't.* And Winter Green said he made her watch him shower whilst he was jerking off...'

'Who's Winter Green?'

'She's in that new all-female cop show on Netflix.'

'Jesus. Wall to wall pussy. In uniform, too. Nice.'

'Wall to wall *talent,'* hisses Juliette. 'How many shows are wall to wall fucking *men?* With the odd female role thrown in as the token sex object or maid or murder victim splayed out legs akimbo covered in blood? Huh?'

'What the fuck has gotten into you?' Micky starts shouting, his voice rising again as he gets up and heads back to the kitchen to fetch another beer.

'How come suddenly you've turned into some *hysterical fucking feminist? T*his isn't the woman I married! You'll be shaving your head and wearing fucking dungarees, next!'

'Don't be so fucking crazy. I'm just telling you what other actors have been sharing with one another.'

Micky rolls his eyes. '*Sharing.* Yeah, right. Like I said. *Gossip. Rumours.* First thing you learn as a man in this town. Don't fall for women peddling that shit. 'Cause it will only get you in deep fucking doggie-doo. And who's the victim then? Huh? Reputation ruined by a bunch of dried-up bitches who need ten cans of Bud and a good *fuck!'*

Micky returns with another can and slumps back down on the sofa, cracking the can open and taking a swig.

Juliette takes a deep breath. 'You are disgusting. You are not only fucking disgusting. You are also fucking *wrong.* So, let's get this straight. What you're saying is, don't listen to actors who speak out against bullying and abuse because they're desperate to be fucked? Are you fucking *serious?'*

'I'm trying to lighten the atmosphere with a bit of humour, Juliette! Jesus! Gimme a fuckin' break with the feminist libtard shit!'

'It's only funny if it makes people laugh. Nobody's laughing.'

'For chrissakes. Whaddo I know? Seriously. Yeah, I've heard the rumours about The Pork Chop. Everyone has. But you can't listen to every little rumour you hear. Bottom line is, there's a whole lot of actors out there pissed at him for not getting parts in his movies. And the ones that do get parts are pissed with the low quotes they're on…'

'The unequal wages they're on, you mean…'

'Whatever. It's the easiest thing in the world to like, accuse Montana of some "misconduct" or other.'

Juliette's eyes flash and she jabs a finger in Micky's direction.

'"*Misconduct?*" That fucking word! It's not "*misconduct*"*!* We're talking about *sexual abuse* and fucking *rape* here, Micky!'

'Sure,' he yawns, exaggeratedly. 'Hey, if every woman who threw herself at *me* protested about it afterwards, they could accuse *me* of being a multiple rapist.'

Juliette glares at him. 'What's that supposed to mean?'

'I'm talking about BJ...'

'*Blow jobs?* Are you fucking *serious?*'

'Before Juliette,' he announces, smugly. 'When, in the past, boys will be boys, and I'd pretty much take what was offered up to me! That ain't rape! These cunts were *throwing* themselves at me! Have you any idea how many fucking desperate teenage groupies there are out there? Once you're even slightly famous, they're *everywhere,* like a fucking *groupie plague*, a groupie fucking apocalypse! Messaging you, turning up unannounced at your hotel, all wanting you to fuck them. To be honest, it gets kinda fucking tedious. Sometimes I wanna just kick back with a beer and watch the game. But if it's put on a plate in front of me, I'll eat it, even if I'm not hungry. Not my fault. It's the way men are.'

Juliette glares at him. 'So living, breathing, flesh and blood women are *food,* huh? Well in that case Wayne Montana is a fucking *predator.* He hunts 'em down, shoots to kill and *drags 'em behind a bush to devour 'em!'*

Micky yawns. 'For fuck's sake, you're just being a total drama queen. Sure, the guy's an animal. But what about his *art?* He gets *movies* made. *Great* movies.'

'So that's an excuse? He's a fucking *artist?* What about all the *art by female artists* that never even got made because those *artists* were too traumatised to work again because men like Wayne Montana had *raped* them and totally *fucked up their lives?'*

'Yeah, whine whine whine. That's how these gold-diggers make a fast buck, Juliette. Whining over nothing. Over a groped fuckin' tit. Over a pat on the fuckin' ass. It's how the world fuckin' works for chrissakes! Men are men, and women are women. It's nature! It's fucking *biology!* So, maybe Montana pushes the envelope a bit. So what? Jesus. There's more important things to worry about. Bitches need to fuckin' grow some.'

He nonchalantly finishes his beer, keeping a close eye on his wife as she walks towards him.

Juliette leans over her husband and hisses '*Wayne Montana assaulted me.* He grabbed me by my arm, *just like you did.* He called me a cunt. *Just like you do.* All the fucking time. And now you're *defending* him? If you were *any kind of man at all* instead of a *going-to-seed shit-for-brains,* you'd be round at his place right now *beating the crap* out of him! But look at you!' She stands up and glares at him.

'Lying there on the sofa like Homer fucking Simpson, knocking back beer and defending that fucking *monster!* You're *pathetic!* You're a *small, little, pathetic man.*'

Micky carefully puts his can on the table in front of him and stares at Juliette, his jaw dropping open slightly, as she stands over him, a coiled spring of loathing and resentment.

She shakes her head slowly.

'Actually. I just summed it up in one word. Didn't I? *Pathetic.* You're *pathetic.* How the fuck I brainwashed myself into thinking I ever loved you is a *complete fucking mystery.*'

He stares back at her, his jaw slackening further.

'Don't look at me like I just dropped your dreams on the floor,' she says, glaring at him.

'There's literally thousands of women and girls out there who *totally idolise you,* Micky. And you know what? I feel *sorry* for them. For their *naivety.* They have no fucking idea that crawling around in the shadows behind your carefully constructed public image is just a selfish, vain, *misogynist.*'

Her voice softens into a tone of slightly depressed resignation.

'It's actually, just really sad.'

Micky nevertheless keeps an eye on the champagne bottle which, with some relief, he can see, out of her reach, beyond the open glass doors on the balcony.

'So whaddaya gonna do? *Divorce me?*'

She lifts her chin up and looks down at him as if he were a piece of shit on her shoe.

'Yeah.'

He looks back at her, steadily, and sits up on the sofa.

'Now you're acting *crazy.* Come on, baby. This is gonna cause all sorts of fucking shit!'

Juliette glares at him. 'Well why don't you call *Gary* and get him to come and fucking fix it for ya, huh?'

'Gary's out the country.'

'I am kidding, you asshole! Gary can't fix our marriage. What are you, crazy?'

'We just had a *fight*, that's all. We do it all the time. Divorce? Are you *serious?*' 'A fight? A *fight?* I haven't even started...' says Juliette.

Turning, she picks up her phone and calls Adriana. 'I'm on my way.'

She grabs her bag, sunglasses and keys and without a word, walks out of the house, leaving Micky looking blankly out towards the ocean. Dazed and confused.

27
El balneario

BRUCE STICKS HIS HAND OUT TO FLAG DOWN A CAB. A white taxi appears almost immediately, and he and Ella both climb in.

'El Balneario, por favor,' says Ella. The driver nods an acknowledgement.

The sea comes into view on their right, sparkling in a flat expanse of silver and turquoise. Nestled in the hills to the left lie the chic apartment blocks of Pedregalejo.

'Isn't it lovely, Málaga?' asks Ella.

'Beautiful,' says Bruce, gazing out of the window.

After a few minutes, the cab pulls up outside a stone arch, above which a sign painted in white and blue marks the entrance to El Balneario. A dusty path lined with trees quickly gives way to a broad, tiled walkway leading to the restaurant.

'What a lovely place,' says Bruce, stopping at a small table right by the sea's edge, adjacent to the column where only a few days before Ella had photographed the boy.

'I was here the other evening. For a party. It's lovely at night. All lit up with strings of lights, reflecting on the sea. This table OK?'

'Sure.'

They sit facing one another with the sea to their sides.

'I'm using this as a location for my book,' says Ella.

'How's it going? The writing?'

'I'm still at the making notes stage. So, terribly. I'm struggling. I find the whole process extremely difficult.'

'Whoever says writing a book is easy is lying. It's fucking hard. And it's even harder when you're not doing it.'

'This one's still all in my head. Just the thought of starting it is terrifying, so yes, even harder than actually fucking writing. Anyway, I think I told you all this in my last email.'

'You probably did. I told you, I'm not good at emails and the internet. Hate it all. Whatever happened to the art of letter writing, eh? No-one writes letters anymore.'

'More's the shame.'

'No-one has time. Because they're all too busy on their bloody phones.'

'My phone is in my bag. By the way,' says Ella, laughing.

'I hate them. They are ripping asunder the very fabric of our society. Constantly buzzing away, interrupting everyone. There's no peace anymore. I threw mine out the fucking window.'

'They're a drug. Everyone's addicted to them. Including me. First thing I do when I wake up in the morning is switch it on and the last thing I do at night is turn it off. How sad is that?'

Bruce picks the menu up, peers at her over his glasses and smiles.

'Not for me to say. Are you hungry? Shall we eat?'

'Yes, their artichoke salad's lovely.'

Putting down the menu, Bruce picks up the wine list and starts reading through it.

'Artichokes. There's something very wonderful about a good artichoke heart, don't you think?'

'Mmm. Something quite mysterious.'

'Almost magical...they've got some nice wines, too,' he says, running his finger down the list.

As if on cue, a waiter approaches and puts a basket of bread sticks on the table.

'Would you like to order?'

'A bottle of Viña Ardanza Crianza please,' says Bruce in Spanish.

Ella orders a sparkling mineral water. The waiter scribbles on a pad and disappears.

'How come you suddenly speak Spanish?' asks Ella.

'Well, I don't, really. I've just picked up a bit here and there.'

'Because you're a genius,' she teases.

Bruce looks at her evenly and laughs. 'Well our chickens might think so. Not sure about anyone else.'

'How many have you got?'

'No idea. There seem to be dozens of them running around the yard. Ducks, too.'

'Lovely. We have chickens.'

'How many?' asks Bruce, looking straight at her.

'Only two now. We lost three of them to a fox a couple of weeks ago. Heart-breaking.'

Bruce shakes his head, sadly. 'Well, it's nature. We've got a stream running through the farm and at one point we lost all of them to a mink. Total massacre. Chickens, ducks, the lot.'

'Oh no...'

'Well, you start getting bloody fond of them, don't you? Giving them names and all that.'

'Yes. Ours have got names. And their own personalities. Zack says he can tell them apart just by their voices, even when they're right down the garden.'

Bruce laughs. 'Really?'

'Yeah. He loves the girls more than he loves me.'

Ella picks up a bread stick from the basket, nibbles the end of it and looks at Bruce questioningly.

'Who looks after yours, then?'

'My wife,' answers Bruce, selecting a bread stick and smiling. 'She's the overseer of our extensive menagerie. I stick to writing.'

'Sometimes I think I actually prefer chickens to people. Sitting with the chickens at dusk, just before they put themselves to bed, in the stillness of the evening air, them making their happy little noises, chuntering away, I feel happier than I do at almost any other time.'

'Better with a glass of red though,' says Bruce, grinning.

Ella says nothing and looks out at the expanse of sea, sparkling in the sunlight. They sit in silence for a while.

The waiter returns with the drinks and pours them both a glass. Ella orders a tomato salad and Bruce the artichokes.

'I had so much to ask you. But now we're here, none of it seems necessary,' says Ella, looking at Bruce then back at the sea. 'Zack's not over the moon at this book, you know. At your being my *muse,* so to speak.'

'Oh, really?' says Bruce, looking slightly worried.

'Yeah. He's young. He can be a twat.'

'How old is he?'

'Thirty-seven. Old enough to know better I suppose. He's quite up his own arse. Musician,' adds Ella, grimacing.

'Sorry. Your son's a musician, right?'

Bruce smiles, 'Yeah but, you know. Every walk of life has its arseholes. They're ubiquitous. Arseholes everywhere.'

'True. But people tend to hide their bad sides. And technology facilitates it. I mean, I think more and more that we're all hiding behind these fake internet representations of ourselves. The best sides of ourselves, seen only through selfies taken with flattering filters.'

'I'd rather not have anything to do with any of it.'

'I suppose, before the invention of the camera, this false representation was previously reserved for royalty, right? Didn't Henry the eighth commission an artist to paint Anne of Cleves before he met her, so he could see what he was letting himself in for or?'

'Yeah. Hans Holbein. Tempted by the portrait then when he saw her in the flesh ran squawking round Rochester Castle "I like her not! I like her not!"'

'That's right! I remember, now!'

'A murdering, sadistic despot, Henry the eighth.'

'Yeah, Henry the eighth was a total cunt. But I mean generally, it must be such a disappointment. To meet someone in the flesh when all you've seen is a fake representation of them, whether it be in a fine oil painting, or a filtered selfie. You know, people age. That's life. None of us look as young as we once did. Why is everyone so obsessed with youth, anyway? I love getting old. It brings wisdom. My face is a map of all the crap I've been through. Why would I want to get a surgeon to stick a knife into my face and stretch out all my experience so you can't see it anymore? Is it so frightening to men for a woman to look experienced? Are we all meant to look naive and innocent? Is that what's really attractive to a man?'

'I looked like a fucking renaissance prince when I was younger,' laughs Bruce. 'I'm old now but fuck it.'

'Yes but Bruce,' says Ella, leaning slightly over the table. 'Men can get away with looking older. No-one looks at Keith Richards, with his lined haggard face and thinks "God he looks old and ugly", do they? They think "What a geezer. Look at that face, he looks like a roughly chiselled diamond, how's he still alive after all the drugs he's necked? That's a face that's been lived in. Fuck me. Amazing."'

'Nice bloke, actually.'

'But Brigitte Bardot, say, arguably one of the most beautiful women on the planet in her youth, is now widely derided for her looks, simply because she looks - just as Keith Richards does - old. Basically, it's just never cool for a woman to look old.'

'I've never thought it's particularly easy being a woman.'

'It isn't. It's shit. Women are treated like the arseholes of society.'

Bruce looks at her thoughtfully. 'I've known some lovely women. And some unlovely ones of course...like my mother.'

'Yeah. I read all about that. Your mother keeping your real father a secret from you, even on her death bed. Terrible thing to do.'

'I've forgiven, I suppose. Life's too short to be eaten up with bitterness. It corrodes one from within. But I will never, ever forget.'

'I find most humans tend towards wickedness rather than loveliness. I don't like people much. Amazing I feel so compelled to write about the fuckers, really.'

Bruce toasts the comment with his glass. 'Me too. I'll drink to that.'

Ella looks out towards the sun, sparkling on the sea.

'I love the sun,' she says, glancing over at Bruce.

'I do, too,' he says, smiling.

'I could live in a sunny climate.'

'Me too.'

'I hate England, sometimes.'

'So do I. Awful, dank, cold island. And Yorkshire can be a bit bleak, even for England.'

'I've heard, yes. I'd love to feel the sun on my skin every single day.'

Ella turns her face upward and closes her eyes.

'I miss it, too. It makes me feel alive. I think I may have that S.A.D., that Seasonal Adjustment Disorder,' Bruce says, laughing ruefully.

Ella looks at him and smiles. 'I think I might have that too. You can get light bulbs for it, can't you?'

'Horrible fuckers. I wouldn't sit under one of those. I'd rather be in the sun.'

'Me too. They do get some spectacular storms here, though. When they have storms here at El Balneario, the waves crash right up to where we're sitting now. If there was a storm right now, we'd be underwater.'

'We'll all be underwater before long with the climate crisis,' says Bruce, glancing at the cloudless sky. 'But yes, I love storms. I was out in one just the other day in fact. Quite magical.'

'They frighten me. Being struck by lightning…'

Bruce drains his glass and immediately pours another.

'Shit. You said you wanted to call your wife. You can use my phone to Facetime her if you want. We do it with my mother. She refuses to have anything but an old landline. So every time we visit, we Facetime the entire family from my phone. She thinks it's like science fiction.'

'I'm not quite *that* out of touch.' says Bruce, laughing. 'Lara uses her mobile all the time. It's just something I personally don't really want or need. That extra level of interference in my life. I'll call her later.'

A group of musicians files into an empty area by the bar entrance and commence setting up their instruments. After some quiet talking, laughing and tuning up, they begin to play a mid-tempo Bossa Nova.

One by one, the diners rise and start to dance in the dappled shade of the willow and fabric canopies.

The waiter returns with the salads. Bruce and Ella eat in near silence, glancing out to sea and at the smiling dancers.

'Do you fancy walking on the beach?' asks Ella when they've finished eating.

'We could do. I have yet to actually put my toes into the Med since I arrived.'

They pay a passing waiter and descend the short flight of worn, concrete steps onto the wet sand, stopping to remove their sandals at the edge of the sea.

The out-of-town beach is sparsely populated. Just a few local Spaniards, sunbathing, sitting and talking, eating and drinking under their umbrellas.

'I like it that this beach isn't packed. I can't stand packed beaches, people crammed together like tinned sardines,' says Ella.

'Me neither. I have seen some quite horrible things on beaches.'

'Like what?'

'Oh, back in my youth.'

'You mean, like horrible grubby old men preying on young boys? You mention that in your book.'

'That kind of thing, yeah.'

'Yeah, beaches can be shit. That bloke over there on his phone, sitting by the rock. Shitty things could be happening right there. Right now. Only we just don't know about it. The world is just full of shit and shitness.'

'People ruin everything,' says Bruce, smiling.

'We do create art, though.'

'To reflect the ruin,' he laughs.

'Art reflects beauty, too.'

'Isn't that what life's all about, really? When it comes down to it? The pursuit of beauty amongst the endless ruins?'

'Yeah, then when you think you've found it, everything turns to shit. I mean, look at what fame does to people. It kidnaps things of beauty and strips them of their inherent worth,' says Ella.

Bruce smiles. 'Quite. The ravening hyena of fame, devouring the beauty it has maimed and then slaughtered. T'was ever thus.'

'But you know, it's funny how it's the fame which attracts people. Because it glitters, like gold. And yet it's the *work* which is the gold, not the fame.'

'Well yes, I suppose it is.'

'You know the score. You plug into the source and if you're lucky, the gold flows out through you and into your work. But in a way, the work never came from you, you were merely the conduit. The gold came from somewhere else, somewhere *up there.* And then other people want the gold. They think that by meeting you, they'll be able to *touch gold.* But the gold is in the *work,* untethered from its conduit.'

Ella glances over at Bruce then back at her feet as she walks in the sand. 'You know what I think? Feeling the gold coursing through your veins is the only way to transcend your humanity. And then, you know, once the flow stops, you're back to being *you* again, just a person with faults and failings. And it's fucking shit.'

'Yeah, well, nothing matches the gold.'

'Quite.'

'Except the red,' says Bruce, looking across at Ella and grinning.

'Which gives you access to the gold, I guess.'

'Which is why I drink.'

They continue walking in silence along the beach.

After a few minutes, Bruce looks over at a white wall facing the sea, painted with a long stretch of high lettering.

Fuiste, eres, y siempre seas mi mas bonita casualidad.

'What does that graffiti mean, over there, on the wall? Do you know?' he asks.

'It's only just appeared. Wasn't there last time I visited. It's only just appeared. Wasn't there last time I visited. It translates roughly as… hold on…let me think, um, you can't translate this literally. I guess in English it means "Meeting you by chance was, is and always will be the most beautiful coincidence."'

'That's lovely. I wonder who wrote it, and for whom?'

'I know. Lovely, isn't it?'

'It is.' He lapses into silence, still looking at the graffiti.

Ella turns back to the sea, then glances at her watch before turning to look at Bruce.

'I could stay here forever. But we should go, I guess.'

'Yes, I suppose I should continue trying to repair my key fob,' he says, smiling.

'The eternal quest of the artist. Creating beauty from chaos.'

Bruce's eyes light up as he laughs. She watches him, trying to take in every movement of his face.

They walk back to the steps leading to the restaurant, then back along the dusty path and out through the entrance arch onto the palm-lined avenue where several cabs are waiting in the afternoon heat, their drivers smoking and chatting in the shade of the trees.

On the journey back to the city centre, a warm, easy silence descends between them.

I had hours in front of me to talk to him. Now there's only minutes left. I still want to ask him so much. I don't want to break the silence, though. It's nice.

They pass the journey without speaking, both gazing out at Málaga, baking in the sun, until they disembark back at Plaza de Merced, from where they started out earlier in the day.

Standing on the hot pavement, Ella shelters her eyes from the glare of the sun.

'Well, good luck with your glue hunt. It's been lovely meeting you. And thanks for taking the time to see me.'

'My pleasure,' says Bruce, grinning.

Ella steps forward to kiss him politely on either cheek, but he throws his arms around her, unexpectedly clasping her to him in an affectionate hug.

She lamely attempts to continue the civil ritual of polite cheek kissing, wishing, too late, she'd had the nerve to embrace him as naturally as he had embraced her.

He releases her and steps back. They smile and he walks away towards Tita Conchi and the apartment block above, then turns back and calls cheerfully with a big grin, 'I'll email you! When I've stopped drinking!'

With a wave, he walks out of sight into the building.

Ella feels a dizzying surge of emptiness, as though something momentous has just happened in her life which she doesn't have the capacity to process or comprehend. So seemingly insignificant. Yet so gargantuan.

She stands at the corner of the Plaza de Merced, looking at the spot on the pavement where he was and now isn't, a spot so full just moments ago and now so bare.

This is just too much. I can't deal with these feelings. I need to start writing them down.

Turning, she walks away across the square.

28
Fiction

'IT'S LIKE GROUNDHOG DAY, ISN'T IT? HERE WE ARE again,' sighs Lara, reading *The Sunday Gazette* on her phone, facing her daughter Hazel across the big wooden table in the kitchen.

'Another Sunday morning with you. Another story about your father in the papers. It's *absolutely ridiculous,'* she continues, an air of exasperation creeping into her voice.

'Well I've already read it, Mum, and Dad wouldn't have said any of that. It's all made up crap,' says Hazel, decisively. 'Don't get too upset. It is *The Gazette,* after all.'

'Well as soon as we can get hold of him, we'll find out.' Lara finds the article and reads the headline out loud.

'Luvvy Lush,' she rolls her eyes, 'Bruce Robinson Can't Control His Passion for Instagram Star Maria Aranda. Wife Is Apoplectic With Rage.'

She looks up at Hazel, who grimaces, widening her eyes in sympathy.

'Wife actually couldn't give a shit,' says Lara, sardonically, continuing to read aloud.

'*Withnail and I* writer and director Bruce Robinson has been enjoying holidaying in Marbella with dusky Instagram Influencer, 27 year old Maria Aranda, much to the fury of his wife, 65 year old Lara Robinson.

'The lovely Maria - a slender size 8 - whose sultry pics have attracted over 750,000 Instagram followers and earn her a six figure annual sum from her net savvy sponsorship deals, has been seen in the millionaire playboy's paradise of Marbella in the arms of a very drunken Robinson, known as much for his foul-mouthed rants as for his cult film *Withnail and I.*

'Only recently *The Gazette* reported on his calling literary festival goers "a bunch of UKIP c**ts". It seems it's not only his drinking he can't control though, judging by the intimate exchanges between him and Ms Aranda. He seemed barely able to keep his hands off her beach-perfect body in the sweltering Spanish sun, and was overheard by a source slurring "I love you Maria. Give us a kiss!" to which she responded "Let's go to bed you crazy Englishman!"

'Who knows where this will end? A close friend of the thirty-five years married *Withnail* couple, who wishes to remain anonymous, says "I'm very worried for both Bruce and his wife. I've met Miss Aranda and she's irresistible. This could lead to some serious trouble for the couple."'

Accompanying the article is a photo of Maria with one arm around Bruce, him seemingly whispering in her ear.

Lara shakes her head.

'Absolutely *bloody ridiculous.*'

'I know, Mum! It's laughable! I spoke to this Maria on the phone the other day and to be honest she sounded lovely.'

'I'm sure she is. "Wife is apoplectic with rage." Do Gazette readers even know what "apoplectic" means? Honestly. Put the kettle on, would you Hazel? *Ridiculous.*'

Hazel's phone rings. She picks it up and grimaces.

'It's Maria,' she says to her mother, raising her eyebrows expectantly, her eyes unsmiling, and answers the call.

'Hello?'

'Hello Hazel, this is Maria. I am ringing to ask if you have seen the newspaper?'

'Erm, yes, I have. Bit crazy, really. What happened?'

'*Nada!* Nothing! I am so sorry! It is not true! I am so upset! It is all wrong! Lies!'

'Right...'

'It's so much lies, Hazel! It is true that I tell your father, "We have to get you upstairs" because he was, you know, a little bit drunk. But that newspaper, it says I was trying to take him to bed! That is such a terrible *lie!* Terrible! Your dad, and me, it is not like that! I love Richard! Me and Richard, we are very happy!'

'Look, we know the press...er...the newspapers, that they lie, OK? Especially *The Sunday Gazette.* Don't worry about it.'

'But I do. I have been so upset! And my mother has been crying too! And my sisters, my brother, my cousins and my aunt and uncle in Murcia. All the family have been calling me asking about it. It is a shame terrible on our family! Please give to your mother my apologies!'

'Yeah, well, I'm sorry Maria, but don't worry too much about it. Look, I don't suppose my dad is there, is he?'

'Yes! He is standing right beside me! Here, you can talk to him!'

Maria wipes tears from her eyes and passes the phone to Bruce.

'Hazel?'

'Hi Dad. I'm at home. I'll pass you onto Mum, she's here. You OK?'

'Yeah, Pickle, fine. Fucking press. You OK?'

'Fine, Dad. Here's Mum.'

Lara gives her daughter a weary look and takes the phone from her. She composes herself for a moment before forcing a smile.

'Hi darling.'

'Hi darling. Fucking arseholes,' says Bruce, testily.

'I know. So what happened?'

'I dunno. A couple of days ago, I spent the afternoon at this café under the apartment block and the last thing I remember is sitting in the sun, reading. I vaguely remember Maria appearing after a couple of hours and suggesting I go upstairs for a siesta. Think maybe I was getting a bit sunburnt or something.'

Lara hesitates for a split second too long. 'Sunburnt. And then?'

'Well, I just crashed out in my room. Woke up the next morning.'

'How did you feel?'

'Not too bad. Didn't have a hangover or anything. Got a vague memory of some little bastard pointing a camera at me. That was it, really.'

'So it's just the usual invented crap then? Typical *Gazette?'*

'Yeah. Really could do without it. Pain in the fucking arse, actually.'

'Yes I know. Well look, I'll field any calls from this end. It's only just appeared on the *Gazette's* website.'

'Just put the answering machine on, Lara. Go for a ride or something. With Hazel. Today's news is tomorrow's chip paper, it'll all blow over in twenty-four hours. No one really gives a shit, anyway.'

'True. And yeah, exercising the girls with Hazel is a good idea. Get some fresh air.'

'What's the weather like over there?'

'Lovely. Sunny. Bit of a breeze…although, you know, I'm starting to regret not going out there with you.'

'It's OK. I'm fine.'

Lara takes a deep breath.

'So, how did the rest of your time with the author go?'

'Oh, we didn't stay there long after I spoke to you. Got a cab back to town. And I went to buy some glue and fixed that key fob that keeps breaking.'

'Oh, you finally fixed it. Lovely. It's only been two years.'

'Yeah,' Bruce laughs.

Lara pauses again.

'So, what's she like, then? This author.'

'She's nice. Seems confident but insecure underneath, I think.'

'Bit like you, then.'

'Bit like most writers, I'd say. Anyway, what about you? What have you been up to?'

'Working, mainly. Trying to get *Dreamer* into shape for the exhibition deadline. Can't see me making it, to be honest.'

'You will. Just keep at it, darling. It'll get there.'

'I will. OK, well, I'd better go. This is Maria's phone.'

'She's terribly upset with all that crap in the fucking *Gazette.*'

'I'm sure she is. It must be horrible for her. Give her my love. Tell her it's OK.'

'I will. Bye darling.'

'Bye, darling.'

Lara clicks off the phone and looks across at Hazel, pointedly.

Hazel looks back at her mother.

Both of them raise their eyebrows and roll their eyes.

Bruce hands Maria back her phone.

'Thanks, Maria. What a fucking massive ball ache.'

'What is it? A "Ball ache"?'

'Pain in the arse.'

'Ah, sí, I know what is pain in the arse. *Coñazo!*'

'Coñazo. Great word. Yes, all this shit, it's just one great big coñazo.'

The front door slams and Richard walks into the lounge, grinning. He drops a bag of shopping on the lounge table, two long baguettes protruding from the top and throws a copy of *The Sunday Times* on the table.

'So! I've got some absolutely amazing fresh figs. Thought we could have them for breakfast! See what *The Sunday Times* has made of their interview with me!'

Seeing Bruce and Maria's faces turned towards him pointedly, his grin vanishes. 'Oh…have I missed something?' he asks, looking slightly worried. 'You've not already seen it, have you? I hope they haven't done a bloody *hatchet job* on me. I haven't even *looked at it* yet!'

He looks from Bruce to Maria. 'They haven't, have they? No? What then? Are the photos completely dreadful? Oh no. Of course, you don't subscribe to *The Times*. Of course you haven't seen it.'

He frowns and looks questioningly at them. So, what is it? Tell me!'

'Some bullshit story in *The Sunday Gazette* about me.'

'Oh *God,'* says Richard. 'What have you done *now?'*

'Oh it's just utter bollocks,' says Bruce, looking irritated. 'Whilst you were up the coast on that shoot, I spent a delightful afternoon in the café downstairs, reading. And some bastard reporter from *The Gazette* spotted me and started taking pictures.'

'Pictures of you doing *what,* exactly? Reading?' He smiles uncertainly.

'Going upstairs. With Maria.' He glances at Maria who is staring at Richard without expression.

'Well? And what happened? I mean, what's so interesting about *that?'*

'I was pissed.'

'Ah. Grist to the muckraker's mill,' says Richard, sagely.

'And *The Gazette* have made out that I was trying to seduce your girlfriend. Utterly ludicrous.'

'*What?'* Richard bursts out laughing, looking from one to the other. He takes his phone out of his pocket and finds the story. His smile fades as he starts reading through it. 'Oh for crying out loud! It's utter tosh!'

'Yeah I know.' says Bruce. 'What gets me is the amount of fucking paper and ink being wasted *printing* this load of balls. I mean, who even *reads* this shit?'

'Well, quite. It's *utter gibberish.*'

'It is not true, Richy! I was just trying to help Bruce,' says Maria, wrapping her arms around Richard.

'I know, sweetie. I understand,' he says, continuing to read. He finishes the story then puts his phone down on the table, dismissively. 'Total failure on their part not to even mention *me!* I mean, I *am* your partner, after all!' complains Richard, looking irritated. 'They don't bother doing their research, do they, these gutter hacks?'

'This is *The Gazette.* It'll be all over the real gutter press in an hour or two. Recycled effluent. Be grateful you're not mentioned,' says Bruce.

'Yes, I suppose I should be,' muses Richard, unpacking his shopping and fetching a plate on which to arrange his pile of figs. 'But really, it should have been *me!* Not poor Maria! If *I'd* gone down to fetch you back, *I'd* be in *The Sunday Gazette!*'

'Yes, but Richard! Instead you were doing a photo shoot for your big magazine!' objects Maria.

'*The Sunday Times* travel section, no less,' he affirms. 'But I could have theoretically cornered the nation's Sunday breakfast with two different stories about me in Málaga in both papers, not just one! Two completely different readerships. Contrasting demographics! It's a travesty! A completely missed opportunity!'

Bruce tops up his espresso from the cafetière on the table and smiles wryly to himself.

Richard serves up figs, bread and fresh orange juice then sits down at the table to read *Artists in the Med,* the double page spread in *The Sunday Times.* Maria drapes her arm over his shoulders, leaning over him to read the story as Richard narrates.

'The Costa del Sol is Once Again On Point - Actor and Perfumier Richard E. Grant relaxing in the beautifully unspoilt village of Nerja.'

He continues reading out loud, enthusiastically.

'On the site of a ninth century Arabic fortress sits the spectacular Balcon de Europa, jutting out over the rocks overhanging the sea and one of the loveliest Miradors this region has to offer. The perfect location for *Oscar-nominated* actor Richard E. Grant to relax before filming on the nation's beloved *Downton Abbey* resumes. Sporting a vibrant Stüssy t-shirt, inky blue Versace jeans and classic silver-rimmed Rayban aviators, Grant perfectly embodies the cultured actor in repose. Our series continues next week with Phoebe Waller-Bridge in Sanxenxo, Galicia.'

'Oh Richy! I love the photos!' coos Maria. 'You look so elegant!'

'Thank you. Yes, they've done rather a good job, haven't they? Although personally I fancied a shoot of me wearing my favourite fedora, sat outside El Pimpi right here in Málaga. Perhaps with someone like, oh I don't know, Antonio Banderas, say. More *urban chic* and less *Englishman abroad.* It's a bloody shame he's in China filming that action movie actually. A double page spread in *The Sunday Times* travel section with me and Antonio eating tapas on the terrace at El Pimpi would've been *perfect.* Followed by me getting snapped by the paparazzi at that bar downstairs with Bruce, plastered all over the tabloids. It would show that I'm getting into the *spirit of Málaga,* you know, *actually part of the fabric of the city!'* His eyes shine with wild enthusiasm.

Bruce looks at Richard evenly over the top of his spectacles, picks up a fig and begins eating it, the soft flesh yielding easily to his bite.

'The idea of *bonding* with this city is so *romantic,* so *bohemian! I love it,'* finishes Richard, opening his palms expressively, before returning to peering at the photos in *The Sunday Times* magazine.

'Have you ever met Antonio Banderas, Richy?' asks Maria. 'Do you know him?'

'No I haven't, actually. Always wanted to, though. Heard he's a very nice chap, actually,' he says, glancing back at Maria.

She smiles, smugly. 'I was at school with his niece, Gema Banderas. I meet Antonio lots of times. He calls me "Chinchilla" because I always wanted a pet chinchilla.' Her face clouds. 'But of course they are not suitable as pets. So I never had a pet chinchilla,' she adds, mournfully.

'Poor you. Chinchillaless Maria. Did it ruin your childhood?'

'Not really. We got a Chihuahua puppy instead. I was happy with my Pippi. Anyway, I have to go and get ready. I have a shoot of my own soon!'

'Oh? Who with?' asks Richard, only half interested.

'The photographer who today photographed you, Javier Ojeda!' announces Maria, triumphantly.

'How the *hell* did you get a shoot with *him?'* demands Richard.

'He follows me back on Instagram! Now we are friends!'

Richard shakes his head. 'Right. Well, good for you. Enjoy it. He's a lovely bloke, got to say.'

'Now I've got to get ready.' Maria kisses him perfunctorily and returns to her room.

Richard glances at her retreating figure then picks up a fig.

'Succulent little buggers, aren't they? Never the same when you're in England.'

'Mmm. Yes. Mysterious things,' says Bruce, biting into another fig. 'I had some lovely artichokes yesterday, too. Again, never the same in England, not half so plump and juicy.'

'Where was that?

'A place just down the coast, El Balneario. Lovely. Right by the sea.'

'Never heard of it.'

'Ella, the author told me about it.'

'The one who's writing a book about you?'

'Yeah,' says Bruce, picking up another fig. He breaks it open with his fingers and examines the dense, sweet, gooey insides. 'But it's not *about* me as such, I believe. She has a character…'

'Don't get too involved with her!' exclaims Richard. 'She's a *writer* for God's sake! In fact, *avoid her like the plague!* Here, I'll check her Instagram for any more mentions of you. She could be a stalker, she might have some *peculiar obsession with you!*'

'Like you had with Barbara Streisand as a teenager?' quips Bruce, smiling.

'Completely different! That was pure, unadulterated *love!* That was *worship!*' declares Richard, grinning. 'I told you, I think the author worships *you…*' he adds, smiling.

'I hardly think so,' answers Bruce, smiling back and looking at Richard over his glasses. 'I actually met her, yesterday. We had a drink downstairs together.'

Richard's face assumes a mask of horror. 'You *what?* Are you *completely out of your mind?* She's going to *write* about that! She'll turn it into some *ridiculous* Mills and Boon, chic lit fantasy before you know it! To writers, *everything is material!* You should know that, Bruce. *Everything!* You are simply *material* for her! She's *harvesting* you!'

Bruce looks calmly at this friend with a degree of amusement. 'Well, Richard, *you're* a writer. What about your film diaries? In which, if I remember rightly, you talked at some length about working with me, amongst other things?'

'Yes but that's different. That's factual. That's *non-fiction!* You've openly handed this woman *carte blanche* to fictionalise your life and turn you into some ridiculous Heathcliff figure to her Cathy!'

'What on *earth* gives you that idea?'

'I could *sense* it. Outside the glass museum. She had something of the *praying mantis* about her.'

'Well, I've spent some time with her and I don't see her like that at all. In fact we had a quite lovely conversation, walking along by the sea.'

'By the *sea? By the sea?* What have you been doing *by the sea* with her? You're *insane!'*

'She took me to this place I was telling you about, El Balneario. Old nineteenth century spa. Now a restaurant, right on the sea. It's stunning, absolutely lovely. You should take Maria there.'

'You went *together?* How did you get there?' asks Richard, incredulously.

'In a *cab!* How do you think we got there? In a fucking *pedalo?'*

'Well I know you wouldn't have caught a bus because you're such a snob.'

'Like you ever get buses…'

'I get *the tube!* I *regularly* travel on the Bakerloo line to my agent's! Anyway, how come I don't know about this Balneario place?' demands Richard.

'I've got no idea, Richard. Apparently it's not really known to tourists. Place for locals. Ella's been a few times.'

'Well *she's* a tourist.'

'Not really. She's got friends here. They're like her second family. She's been coming here for donkey's years.'

'What did you talk about? Was she interrogating you about your *life?* Mining for nuggets to chuck in her pot-boiler?'

'No. In fact she was very forthcoming about her own life.'

'Bending over backwards to try to *impress* you, no doubt. Put you off-guard.'

'Not at all. We discussed lots of things.' Bruce pauses and looks Richard in the eye. 'I like her. She's OK.'

'God! You're not *smitten,* are you? She's not *lulled you into some false sense of security* has she?'

'For fuck's sake Richard. She's just a woman who had an idea to write a novel with me as one of the characters.'

'*Stalker!*'

'She's actually a very sweet person. And very genuine. And, I'd say, not a little insecure. To be honest I'm quite flattered, actually!'

'I don't trust her. Run a mile!' exclaims Richard, waving his hands around dramatically. He leans towards Bruce and lowers his voice. 'Do you honestly think it's a *coincidence* that you're both in Málaga at the same time?'

Bruce laughs. 'Of course it is! How on earth could she have any idea that I'd be in Málaga?'

'Well I don't know, do I? These investigative authors have their methods, don't they?'

'What do you mean, *investigative author?* She's just a woman who writes books!'

'Well. Be careful when you get back to England is all I can say.'

'Oh for God's sake. What's she going to do? Camp out in a field outside my house with a pair of binoculars? Wait for me to have a piss in the woods then *write about it?*'

'Quite! She could find out where you live!'

Bruce is quiet for a second. 'She already knows.'

'Oh my God! How?' Richard shakes his head in disbelief.

'Because I gave her my address,' says Bruce, flatly.

'You *what?* Are you completely *mad?*'

'She wanted to send me a copy of her novel.'

'Novel? Which novel?'

'Her latest one, *Fake Smiles.*'

'*Fake Smiles!*' declares Richard, triumphantly, slamming his fist on the table. 'Says it all!'

Bruce finishes his coffee and looks at Richard, calmly and with amusement creasing his eyes. 'You're just jealous she's not writing a book about you, Richard,' he says, laughing.

Richard's face breaks into a grin. 'I *am!* Why haven't *I* got a fucking author stalking *me?* Where's *my* fucking stalker?' He bursts out laughing and shakes his head.

'As I said. She's not a stalker. She's lovely.'

'See?' says Richard, fondly. 'Heathcliff. Cathy.'

Bruce smiles. 'If you say so.'

29
Facetime

EIGHT AM. ELLA WALKS ONTO THE ROOF TERRACE, already warmed by the sun, the sea sparkling in the distance.

Her phone bleeps. Zack.

Got another phone. Are you awake?

She messages back.

Yeah call me.

She sees the incoming call, hesitates for a second then clicks accept. Zack's sleepy face fills the screen, yawning and smiling, his eyes still blurry with sleep.

'Morning darlin'.'

Ella forces a smile. 'Morning darling! You got another phone, then? How come?'

'Benjy had a spare. Half a day without a phone, nearly done my bleedin' nut in.' He scratches something beyond the edge of the screen.

'I'm relieved. How did the gig go last night, then?'

Zack makes an "O" with his thumb and forefinger. 'Amazing.'

'Any of the London crowd there?'

'Yeah. Notting Hill Scarlett was there. Off her fucking tits.'

'Really? After what happened to Curtis?'

'Same old, innit? Cherry and Jim were there too. Asked after you.'

'What did you tell them? That I'm falling to pieces with despair, self-loathing and insecurity trying to write this book?'

'Nah. Told them you're on holiday. Cherry asked when you'd be back, said we should get together, grab a few beers.'

'I don't drink anymore.'

'Well whatever. You can still go to a pub and socialise,' says Zack, rolling his eyes.

'Well, we should see Cherry and Jim, it's been ages. We don't do enough socialising, do we? It's always my book readings or your gigs. Never just the two of us.'

'Whaddya mean?' He looks instantly defensive.

'I mean, we need to do more lovingly gazing into each others' eyes over a romantic meal, that kind of thing. We don't do that enough.'

'We don't. You're right, babe. We should do more intimate stuff…'

'Yeah…'

'Intimacy…' sighs Zack, looking at Ella and smiling.

'Yeah.'

'Miss you.'

'Miss you too.'

'So, what was the most intimate moment you've ever had?' asks Zack.

'Easy. The most intimate moment I've ever had is when we first kissed. What about you?'

'First guitar solo at the 100 club. No fucking contest.' He looks heavenward and smiles, beatifically. 'Felt like I'd been invited to join a select club. By the mistress of *rock*.' He looks at Ella, deadpan.

'Fuck off!'

'Kidding.' Zack grins. 'It was when I first wanked over your tits. I mean, you don't do that with just anyone, do you? You don't do that at, like, a job interview...'

Ella smiles. 'You're so funny. I miss you.'

'I miss you too,' says Zack, his eyes shining with love.

'What am I doing? You know, over here. When I should be at home, with you, just enjoying my life?'

'You're writing a book. Catching up with your mates. That's your life. Enjoy it. So, what happened with Brucey, then?'

'He was all over yesterday's *Gazette*. You didn't see it?'

'We had a *gig*. And I don't read the fucking *Gazette*. Why was he in *The Gazette*, anyway?'

'Because the gutter press are a bunch of fucking cunts, that's why.'

'So what happened when you met him?'

'We had a drink. Then went to that place up the coast I told you about. He was lovely. I fucked it up.'

'What do you mean, you fucked it up?'

'I should have asked him more about his life. He's not like I envisaged. I wanted to write a love story, but it has to feel real. And he's not about to fall in love with some gorgeous American journalist. It's not gonna happen. Ever. It's just not him. Fuck it, he could be gay for all I know.'

'I thought you said he was married with kids.'

'You can be married with kids and still be *gay*, Zack. It happens all the fucking time,' says Ella, pointedly. 'Anyway, I know fuck all. I can barely even remember what we talked about.'

'Well you're sober now. You must remember some of it.'

Ella turns away from the screen, looks out to the sea, then back at Zack.

'I do remember, he was standing by the sea, throwing his head back with laughter at something I'd said. The man behind the funniest film ever made.'

'Bit like Keith Richards admiring your guitar playing,' says Zack, raising his eyebrows. 'So you were walking by the sea? How long were you with him, then?'

'About four hours.'

'*Four hours!* So you must have had *something* to talk about!'

'I can't remember. It's all a blur. And now I just feel miserable.'

'Why?'

'I felt so happy last night. Afterwards. You know, I'd spent some time with the subject of my book. And he's a great bloke. We got on. But, now it's like, *obsessing* me.'

'You're *obsessed?* What do you mean, *obsessed?*'

'Just, I can't stop thinking about him.'

'Right,' says Zack, flatly, staring at the screen.

'For the book, obviously.'

Zack's eyes are cold. 'So you want to fuck him.'

'No, I don't want to *fuck him!*'

'Well it sounds like that.'

'It isn't like that. It's not...physical. It's *cerebral.*'

'Right. *Cerebral.* Of *course* it is,' says Zack, rolling his eyes. 'So... what, are you *in love* with his *brain?* His *intellect* gives you a moist gusset?'

'Of course not! No! I'm trying to write a fucking *book* about him! It's what *happens!* You get obsessed with your characters! Only my protagonist happens to be a *real person!* It's just like when you and the band are in the studio recording a new album, I've seen it, you get *obsessed!* It's all you can fucking talk about! Actually it's fucking *boring.*'

'Oh, that's right. Turn it onto me, now. It's all *my* fault. I'm *boring* so you've gone and fallen in love with *Bruce fucking Robinson.*'

'I'm not in love.'

'Well you fucking sound like you are, Ella.'

'I'm *conflicted.* Being *in conflict* isn't the same as being *in love.*'

'Well what are you *in conflict* about?'

'Where do I fucking start?' says Ella, shaking her head, sadly. 'Throwing away my time with him by not asking enough questions? Sounding like a fucking idiot blethering on about nothing? Knowing I'll never get to see him again?'

'Why the *hell* do you need to see him again? You've already met him *three times.* Isn't that enough for you? You should just get on with writing the fucking *book!* That's what it's all about, isn't it? The *book.*'

'I *thought,* as a moderately successful artist yourself, that I could talk to you honestly about this and that you'd actually *get it.* But obviously you don't. You just resort to fucking *mansplaining.*'

'You mean, I'm right, and you're wrong. Why are you being so defensive?'

'I'm not. I've seen the way girls suddenly materialise in your dressing room after a gig. Standing there wearing next to nothing and drooling over you. And you fucking *love it,* Zack. And I don't even go to all your gigs. So fuck knows what goes on half the time. But I don't question you about it because *I trust you.* As you should trust me.'

Zack silently stares at Ella.

'And we think differently, because I'm a woman and I'm not obsessed with fucking *sex* like men are. A woman obsessed with a man she's writing a book about does not mean that she wants to *see his fucking cock,* for fuck's sake!'

Zack's face remains impassive. 'No, Ella. It's worse,' he says, quietly.

'Oh don't be so *fucking stupid!* I'm going! I'm depressed enough as it is, and this is just making it *worse!* I was hoping you'd be *supportive!*'

'Well I'm so fucking sorry that I can't be more *supportive* of the fact you're obsessed with another *man.*'

'He's an aged, married alcoholic who describes himself as a paranoid freak. I'm hardly weighing him up as a potential partner,' sneers Ella.

'Oh, so now we're talking actual *relationships,* are we? And there's me simply concerned about a casual *trophy fuck!'*

'Oh do fuck off, Zack. Trophy fuck? I have *never* regarded men in that way. Remember when I went on tour with The Lemonheads? I was there as a *fucking photographer!* What am I going to do, start working my way through the band? And let's not forget that in those days Evan Dando was one of the most gorgeous men on the fucking planet! But *he had a girlfriend,* Zack, and *I have principles!* Trophy fucking is what *men* do. So don't tar me with *that* fucking brush!'

'You've got a real way of making a man feel great about himself, you know that? First you shove Bruce Robinson down my throat and now it's Evan fucking Dando. Unfuckingbelievable!' He stares at Ella for a moment then adds, 'Whose latest album is shite, by the way. Totally past his best.'

'This is sapping my energy. Why am I even bothering? I'm going for a run along the seafront.'

'Great. Enjoy your day. As I will enjoy mine.'

'Fine. Bye.'

The screen goes blank. Ella puts the phone down and stares out at the sea.

Wanker.

30
HUSKS AND FREAKIN' DUST

'I HATE THE RAIN,' SAYS JULIETTE, WEARILY, LEANING over her glass of champagne and stirring the bubbles with one finger.

'Don't do that, honey. It'll froth over. Then where will you be?' says Susan, smiling.

Juliette sighs, then removes her finger from the glass, lifts it to her lips and swigs back the champagne in one.

'I shouldn't even be drinking. I don't think it's the best course of action right now.'

'Probably not. A bottle's not a great place to hide.'

Juliette looks up at her friend and her eyes widen and fill with tears.

'I can't help it,' she says, her voice coming out in a squeak.

'I know, honey. You're going through the shittiest time. But booze won't help. You don't need me to tell you that.'

'It just feels like I'm caught in the middle of all this fucking bullshit, everything at once.'

'I know. I understand. This is a tough time for you. So you need to toughen up, honey.'

'They made the announcement this morning.'

'I noticed.'

'Did you see the actual video?'

'No, not yet.'

Juliette takes out her phone and opens a video, handing it to Susan. Juliette and Micky are standing next to one another in front of a pair of vast, gleaming glass and metal doors with a bunch of microphones, each bearing a different news logo, thrust in front of their faces.

'We're not thinking of this so much as a separation, but of us both moving forward graciously and with love on our mutually respectful unentwined paths,' says Juliette, coolly, to the congregated press.

Micky leans into the forest of mics and adds, 'That's right. We love one another so much we're gifting each other the greatest gift of all - freedom. The freedom to each fulfil our individual potential. We both feel that's the greatest gift.' He glances at Juliette. 'Such a great gift to give. The greatest, in fact.'

Juliette stops the video.

'What a crock of shit,' she says. *'Asshole.'*

'So you keep saying.'

'What, so, you don't believe me?' asks Juliette, incredulously. She picks up the bottle to pour herself more champagne and frowns when only a few drops trickle lamely into the glass. Glancing up, she catches the eye of her favourite server across the patio of the Desert Rose. The server hurries over to Juliette and Susan's table.

'Another bottle, please,' says Juliette, quietly.

'No problem,' smiles the server, picking up the now watery ice bucket. 'I shoulda kept that bucket refreshed with ice, ma'am, I'm so sorry. I'll make sure the next one is topped up.'

'You can call me Juliette, it's OK,' says Juliette, sadly, smiling. 'I come here often enough.'

'And it's always a pleasure to see you…Juliette,' replies the server, grinning broadly before whisking away the ice bucket and empty bottle.

Susan leans forward. 'Of course I believe you. Come on. You know he and I have never really hit it off.'

'So you always knew he was a total asshole? Is that what you're saying?'

'Juliette, don't put words into my mouth. I'm not saying that. I'm saying we didn't click. He always seemed a little…I don't know…a little off to me…even more arrogant than the usual shit fucks.'

'You should have said something!'

'Well I'm hardly going to say to one of my dearest friends that I think her husband is a total *asshole,* am I?'

'So you thought he was arrogant *and* an asshole? And you never told me?'

'Look, I've always been here to listen, Juliette. And sympathise. I hoped things would get better for you both. But it wasn't my place to tell you everything that I thought about the guy.'

'But you always knew he was an *asshole.'*

'Well, I guessed it might not end happily and I'm real sad for you that it hasn't worked out, OK? You're my friend. I wanted you to be happy.'

'Yeah, well, I'd like to see where he is in ten years' time, with the amount of Oxy he's packing away…'

'He's still using?'

'Yeah. I haven't mentioned it for months because he gets so defensive. But it's been going on for fucking years. It's written all over him.'

'Well, ten years can wreck a man. But those years all boil down into that one split second when the fateful decision is made, whatever it might be. To take that job, to take that drug, to hit that woman. And the second after? You're on the road to ruin.'

'Yeah, well, he can live happily ever after with fucking Freya Stephens now, can't he? They can both run down the fucking rainbow road to la la land together, hand in hand,' says Juliette, bitterly.

Susan pours herself a glass of Pellegrino and looks up at Juliette, thoughtfully.

'I'm not so sure there's gonna be a happily ever after for Freya Stephens.'

'Why? Not that I give a fuck.'

'She's considering going public about something Montana did to her, apparently.'

'What?' Juliette's eyes narrow at the mention of Wayne Montana.

'Getting her over to his hotel room for a so-called "script meeting", then making her watch him take a shower. And then, when she tried to leave the room, raping her.'

'Jesus! Her too? What the fuck is *wrong* with him? He's a fucking *monster!* This fucking shit is endemic!'

'He has a juvenile sense of sex and sexuality, coupled with the overbearing power of a famous, rich man. One of the worst possible combinations. Powerful men with the brains of adolescent boys. Now that *is* endemic. Not just in *this* industry. But *every-fucking-where.* It's not just Montana...'

'You know, years ago, when he got married to Emma, it crossed my mind that maybe he'd like, actually fallen in love for real. I was actually under the delusion that the Pork Chop was an actual fucking human being. Jesus!'

'Wayne Montana is not only incapable of loving anyone else, he doesn't even love Wayne Montana. The man is full of self-loathing. He hates himself. He hates the world. Everything about him is sociopathic manipulation,' says Susan.

'He *is* a sociopath. And you know what gets me? All the fucking men in this town just turn a blind eye. Micky feels *sorry* for him! Says there's a witch hunt against him and that he's a target for women accusing him of "misconduct".'

'"Misconduct" is turning into a handy euphemism for rape, huh? "Misconduct" sounds like "misplaced." Like it's a sloppy *mistake* or something. "Oh sorry, my penis accidentally slipped into your vagina, what a clumsy *oaf* I am." "Misconduct" totally minimises what these men do.'

The server returns with a freshly filled ice bucket and another bottle of Cristal, which she pops open before pouring Juliette a fresh glass.

'Thanks,' says Juliette, flashing her a broad smile. She waits until the server has left, furtively glances around her then drains the glass and pours a refill.

'You know, if we were both characters in a work of fiction, we'd fail the *Bechdel Test.* All we ever discuss when we get together is *men,*' says Susan, smiling.

'I just left my husband. I'm not gonna sit here and discuss *politics,*' snaps Juliette.

'Marriage *is* politics, honey. It's *all* political.'

'Yeah, I know you're like, really into politics and everything. But I think it's a mistake to *politicise* stuff all the time.'

'There's a lot going wrong in this country. The actions of so many people in power - and you've been a direct target of that with the way Montana treated you recently - they're a reflection of some of the deepest failings in our society. This country was founded on the genocide of Native American Indians and on the backs of slaves and I don't think we've ever really dealt with that.'

'But, yanno, when these men get into powerful positions, why can't they just be kind? They don't have to be so awful and ugly!'

'Because with a lot of these men, it *takes* being awful and ugly to *reach* these positions of power. And also, I think there's a lot of men out there who simply believe that women are innately inferior. It's like a fundamental part of their belief system. And they sure don't like that being challenged. Especially by a woman. I mean, woe betide you if you attack a person's belief system. People wear them as protective skins against the world. Puncture the skin and the bile comes out. People can get nasty. They need that insulation, that armour.'

'Do you think I should go to rehab?'

Susan shrugs. 'I don't know, honey, that's for you to decide.'

'But do you think I've got a problem? With all this champagne?'

'Well, here's the thing. You wouldn't be asking me that question if you didn't think yourself that you had a problem. So yeah, it's possibly something to think about.'

Juliette looks up at the giant stained glass rose gleaming in the sunlight now that the rain has passed. She smiles. 'I like this place.' She glances at her friend. 'Thanks for being there for me, Susan. You don't know how much I appreciate it. I know I'm not always the greatest company. And I'm not as clever as you or anything. But I do love you.'

'Love you too,' says Susan, smiling.

⁂

Brandon and Adriana both lean forward to peer down through the glass case at the face of the Egyptian mummy lying before them, his dark face taut and stretched like dirty leather.

'Rhanubkheper. Male aged 35-40 years,' reads Brandon from the information plaque. 'Man, Rhanub sure looks older than that.'

'He looks really, like, dead,' says Adriana, bemused.

'He sure does. Power and status. Who's gonna give a shit about what he thinks now, huh? How much power has he got, lying there all shrivelled up like a dead cicada?'

'Art has power. Art lasts forever.'

'Sure it does. Not after the climate crisis heats the fuck out of everything and the globe *fries.* Trust me. It'll all go. Art, the internet, everything. You think Plato's work'll be around forever? Fuck that. Everything gets swallowed up by everything else. It all turns to husks and dust, baby. Husks and freakin' dust. And the dust in your coffin will look exactly the same as everyone else's. We're just tiny little specks on a little blue ball in a tiny galaxy on the edge of a great swathe of galaxies which in turn are just a speck in an even more unimaginably vast structure of these entities, which may as well go on forever, they're so beyond our comprehension. Plus there's an invisible mirror version of the whole lot too. Dark matter.' He glances at her. 'Fucked up shit, huh?'

Adriana smiles at him, reaches out and ruffles his hair, tenderly.

'Your mansplaining is fucked up shit. I *read* Scientific American, remember?'

He looks nonplussed. 'Did I actually know that?'

'You do now...'

They turn and look at the shrivelled, darkened corpse lying silently under his white spotlight, then wander aimlessly around the exhibition.

Adriana walks past the cases of Egyptian artefacts - urns, cat ornaments, bowls, knives and hairpins - and sighs.

'Shall we see if it's stopped raining, yet?'

'Sure.'

They leave the cooled air of the museum and head back out into the sunlit warmth of the LA morning.

'You know the big fountain? Down by the rose garden?' asks Adriana.

'Can't say I do. I haven't really been here since high school.'

'There's some benches. Down there. We could sit and watch the water.'

'Cool.'

Adriana leads the way along the grass verges in between the stands of yellow and pink rose bushes, towards a large circular fountain spraying tall jets of glittering water into the blue sky, surrounded by granite paving furnished with wood slatted benches.

As they arrive, a pair of teachers shepherd away a small group of school children, leaving the fountain area empty.

Adriana sits down on a bench and Brandon sits beside her, close enough that their hips touch. The cascading water sounds with a rhythmic shush, almost drowning out the screech of the parakeets overhead.

The couple stare at the water in silence for a minute.

'I love it here,' says Adriana, quietly. 'Fuck the coast. This is one of my favourite places in town. It's just so tranquil. And the water's so mesmerising. Don't you think?' She turns to look at Brandon.

'Yeah,' says Brandon, staring ahead at the water. 'I wanna get out of here one day soon. Travel.'

'Where to?'

'I dunno. Australia, Thailand, Cambodia. Do that whole Far East thing, yanno? Maybe work on a farm up in Queensland. Just, something different. Something more real than this.'

'This is real. Us. Sitting here. You and me.'

'I don't mean us. I mean LA. Is there anywhere more fucking fake than Hollywood? Fake speeches, fake tits, fake faces and fake smiles. It's all *bullshit.* I've just had it with this place.'

'I don't have fake tits. Or a fake face. For what it's worth. In case you hadn't noticed. I mean, not that I wanted you to notice or anything.'

Brandon looks across at her.

'I know. You're natural. You're beautiful. That's a rarity.'

'I think you're beautiful too.'

She looks at him and neither look away.

'I just…' starts Adriana. Brandon leans towards her, cups her face in both her hands, and gently kisses her on the mouth. And carries on kissing her.

After she shyly pulls away, she smiles at him. 'I've been wanting you to do that for weeks and weeks. And actually months.'

'I've wanted to, as well. But what with us both working for Juliette...'

'Yeah.'

Adriana reaches over and takes his hand in hers and they carry on looking at the fountain in silence.

'Well, we both have the rest of the day off…' says Adriana after a few minutes.

'You want to come back to mine? I can fix us some tacos.'

'You can cook?' Adriana exclaims in surprise.

'Sure. Yeah. I was a cook back in Brooklyn.' He looks at her.

'Really?'

'Yeah.' He laughs. 'You think I just, like, *drive* and that's it?'

Adriana laughs. 'Of course not. But, you can really, really cook?'

'Yeah. I can really, really cook.'

'OK. Then you can really, really cook for me.' She grins and swings her feet.

'And then…' smiles Brandon, pulling Adriana towards him and gently kissing her nose and her cheek.

'And then…' whispers Adriana into Brandon's ear, 'You can fuck me.'

31
The Black Dog

ELLA SITS ON THE TERRACE NEXT TO THE SLIDING doors, glumly looking out to sea.

Three o'clock. That row with Zack has completely fucked up my day, I've not even tried to write yet.

The front door slams and footsteps echo on the staircase leading up to the attic.

Isabella appears at the top of the stairs, her face a mask of fury.

'It is freezing cold! I cannot stand this cold in my house!' she shouts, forcefully sliding the patio doors shut in Ella's face.

Ella watches Isabella's retreating figure through the glass, then stands up, slides open the doors again and walks through into her room. Isabella has thankfully returned downstairs.

Ella shouts into the empty stairwell, 'I'm sorry, Izzy! It's just that to me this is hot weather!'

Isabella's shrill voice rises up the stairs. 'No it's not! Not for *Spain!* You are in *Spain* now! Anyway, we have to get ready to get ready to meet Juan and Emile! I don't want to have to wait for you! When I'm ready, *we go!*'

'OK!'

Ella quickly gets changed then runs downstairs, not wanting to further upset her host.

Isabella is standing by the front door, rattling her keys and staring at Ella. She raises her eyebrows questioningly.

'We go?'

'We go,' nods Ella, smiling.

In the Jeep, Ella glances at Isabella as she drives. Her sunglasses are pushed up on her head, and she is sporting thick, long fake eyelashes. Her nostrils are wet, and there is a speck of white powder on the side of her left nostril.

'I like your eyelashes,' says Ella, meekly.

'Yeah. They are extensions. I had them done yesterday afternoon while you were out. What were you doing all day, anyway?' She sniffs then screeches the tyres as she pulls onto the roundabout.

'I met up with Bruce.'

'Who?'

'Bruce Robinson. I told you about him. The author. The one I'm writing a novel about.'

'I'm sorry but I don't know him, I told you!' snaps Isabella.

'Well, he's very well known in England. He directed a film with Johnny Depp. Johnny loves his work.'

'No-one knows him in Spain! Is he famous in Spain?

'I don't think so.'

'Pah!' says Isabella, dismissively.

'Well it doesn't matter, really, does it? He wrote one of the greatest comedy films of all time. That's why Johnny loves him.'

'You talk like you know Johnny. Do you know Johnny? Have you met Johnny?' barks Isabella, accusingly. 'I don't think so.' She waves a hand dismissively.

'Well, no. I'm just using the familiar forename because he's familiar to Bruce. Who I do know. Well, a bit.'

Ella stares at the fleck of white at the side of Isabella's nose, which is running slightly, so that the white is now caught in a small smear of mucus, glistening beneath her nostrils.

Isabella pulls the Jeep into a side street at the edge of town and parks across an entrance, ignoring a sign reading 'No Parking' in Spanish.

She gets out of the Jeep and glances at Ella who is staring through the windscreen, despondently, deep in thought.

'Are you coming?' barks Isabella. 'Or not? You can stay here if you want while we all have tapas together without you.'

Ella climbs out of the car and walks alongside Isabella.

'You seem to be very on edge,' says Ella.

Isabella looks askance at her friend, her eyes alight with anger.

'What do you mean? On edge? I am not on edge! I am relaxed! Look at me! Very relaxed! It is *you* who are on edge! Asking me if I am on edge! *That* is being on edge! You!' She pulls her phone out of her bag and starts scrolling through it as she walks ahead, pointedly ignoring Ella.

The women reach a set of steps leading down from the street and onto a shaded seating area in front of a run down little bar. The sign above the door reads El Perro Negro. The Black Dog.

Isabella sashays ostentatiously over to a table. Removing a mirror from her bag, she checks her face, surreptitiously wiping her nose with the back of her forefinger, finally erasing the trace of white from her nostrils.

Ella sits next to her and glances at the white table in front of her, which is bare but for a trail of cigarette ash across its plastic surface.

A short menu is chalked on a board attached to the wall. The air is thick, hot and still.

There are only two other customers in the café, both youngish men on their own, looking down as they silently scroll through their phones.

The server, a large, miserable looking woman, approaches and lifts her chin in greeting, without smiling, then bends over to firmly wipe the table with a wet cloth.

'I want the usual,' says Isabella, addressing the server. 'What do you want?' she asks, turning to Ella.

'Um. I'll just have patatas bravas. And an agua con gas. What are you having?'

'Pata negra. It is the best jamón ibérico. *I love it.*'

Ella smiles without saying anything.

Two men approach the table. One is in his sixties, with a deep suntan and short-cropped, salt and pepper hair, wearing a black vest emblazoned with a golden tiger. The other a beautiful looking boy in his twenties, with a head of tight blonde curls, wearing a neatly pressed short-sleeved checked cotton shirt in lemon and peppermint green.

Isabella jumps up and throws her arms around the older man, her first sign of warmth all day.

'Cariño!' She kisses him on either cheek.

The man kisses her back, perfunctorily, smiles curtly and sits, glancing at Ella disinterestedly. The boy raises his eyebrows slightly and looks over at the other patrons, sitting alone, before also taking a seat at the table.

'How are you?' asks the man.

'I have been so busy! I am living the crazy life, preparing for my book tour!' says Isabella, with a wave of her hands, before looking around for the server. 'Where is she? It's not even busy here!'

'Hi, my name's Ella, what's yours?' asks Ella in Spanish, addressing Emile.

'I am Emile. This is Juan,' replies Emile, coolly appraising her.

Juan smiles quietly and nods a greeting, without saying anything.

'This is Ella. She's English. But she speaks Spanish. She understands *everything*,' says Isabella, finally introducing her friend and glancing at Emile, pointedly. 'So are you eating?' she adds, sweeping her hand towards the men.

Emile shakes his head. 'We've just had tapas with El Gordo.'

'El Gordo! El Gordo? I haven't seen El Gordo for *months!* I thought he must be *dead!* Or in *prison!*' she laughs.

Emile's eyes flash a warning and he looks from Isabella to Ella and back again. 'He has been in Morocco,' he says curtly.

'So, how do you know Isabella?' Ella asks Emile.

'We go back a long time.'

'So do we. We knew each other as children. Marbella is like my second home.'

'You speak Spanish very well,' he says, glancing down at his t-shirt and flicking a speck of something from the tiger's tail.

The server appears at the door of the café, lifts her head and stares at two small speakers attached to the wall. Music starts playing and she nods to herself before returning to the bowels of the interior.

'*El Camarón!*' announces Isabella, grinning. She jumps up and twists her body into a flamenco dancers' classic pose, one arm in the air, wrist flicked. 'El maestro!' she shouts. She purses her lips into a tight pout and stamps her feet in time to the music, then starts singing along to the song at the top of her voice.

'She loves Flamenco,' says Emile, flatly, by way of explanation.

'I love Flamenco, too. It's a great art form.'

'How can *you* love Flamenco?' interrupts Isabella angrily, seating herself once more at the table. 'You don't *know* it! You don't *feel* it in your *soul!* How *can* you? You're *English*!' she sneers, accusingly, waving one hand dismissively towards Ella. 'Flamenco is *not in your blood*.'

'Have you ever been to England?' Ella asks Emile, ignoring the slight and attempting to change the subject.

Emile laughs, a sharp bark. 'No. It is too cold for me. And you have terrible food in England, yes?'

'Well, I don't know. We have Yorkshire Pudding. And fish and chips.'

'Fish and chips. I like fish and chips.'

'Fish and chips is for *guiris*. In Málaga we eat sardine kebabs,' spits Isabella with disgust, her face masking over in a frown again.

'Well, I'm practically vegan now anyway. I don't eat meat or fish anymore.'

Juan looks nervous. Emile looks confused, his hard eyes narrowing with suspicion.

'You don't eat meat? Or fish? How strange! Why not?'

Before Ella has a chance to answer, the dour server brings a plate of thinly sliced Spanish cured ham to the table.

Immediately, Isabella grabs a piece of flesh and thrusts it into her mouth. She closes her eyes rapturously and smiles to herself. It's the first time Isabella has looked truly happy since Ella's arrival in Spain.

'Oh! It is so good! I love it! I love this! Oh, it is so wonderful!' she coos.

'So, why do you not eat meat?' persists Emile.

'Well, animal agriculture is destroying the planet. And killing animals is cruel.'

'But plants have feeling too!' sniffs Emile, sneering derisively.

'Well in that case, you'd better give your bougainvillea a shot of anaesthetic next time you trim it,' says Ella, smiling.

Juan giggles and Emile shoots him a look of disapproval.

'But you need to eat meat and fish to survive!' protests Emile, tapping the table with a thick finger.

'Well, look at me, I'm alive, aren't I? I eat very healthily, actually. I just choose not to eat the corpses of murdered animals,' Ella says, shrugging.

Isabella glares at Ella, her eyes flashing. She thumps her fist on the plastic table. '*Enough*, Ella! Stop talking about this! You are being disgusting! You are ruining my lunch!'

She devours the rest of the tapas and licks her lips with relish. 'It is *delicious*. You are so *stupid*, with these crazy foreign ideas about *not eating meat*,' she says with disgust. 'In Spain we eat meat and fish. You are in *Spain!* I go to the bathroom!' she announces, suddenly, getting up from the table and walking off towards the interior of the café. After a minute, Emile stands up and follows her.

The server returns and dolefully places a dried-up looking dish of patatas bravas in front of Ella, who stares at the food, mournfully.

Ella looks up at Juan, who is gazing forlornly at her food. He glances up at her and meets her eyes, then looks away with a nervous smile.

Isabella and Emile are gone for a full ten minutes. When they return, Emile beckons to Juan, who stands up. 'We must go. Goodbye, Ella.'

'Bye, Emile. Bye, Juan.'

'I see you on Friday, yes?' asks Isabella, kissing each of the men on either cheek before they leave. Emile nods.

She sits down again, her eyes shining, and smiles at Ella, benignly, seemingly refreshed and suddenly good-humoured.

'It is good, here, yes? The food is amazing, I told you! How was your patatas bravas?'

'Bit dried up to be honest. I've had better.'

'It is *fantastic* here. *I love it.* No *guiris!* Apart from you!' she points at Ella and laughs.

She removes a cigarette from the box in front of her, purses her red-lipsticked lips and lights the cigarette, before squinting and exhaling a plume of smoke in Ella's face.

Ella recoils. 'Please don't do that, Isabella.'

'Do what? Oh, the smoke? Sorryyyyy' she says in English, and laughs.

After lunch, Isabella sits on her sun bed on the roof terrace, rolls a large spliff, throws off her t-shirt and lies topless under the sun, smoking.

'I love the sun,' she sighs, rapturously, to nobody in particular.

After quietly smoking for several minutes, she stands up groggily with her eyes half-closed.

'I am going for a siesta,' she drawls needlessly to Ella.

Ella sits alone on the terrace, opens her laptop and finally starts to work on the chapter plan for her novel.

Around eight o'clock Isabella reappears on the terrace, a large, ice-clanking gin and tonic in one hand and a small metal tray of spliff-making materials in the other.

'You are still here?' she asks curtly.

'I've been working. Finally.'

'On this novel?'

'Yeah. Well, just the chapter plan at the moment.'

'And how is your work going?' Isabella asks, disinterestedly, sitting down on her sun lounger to roll a spliff.

'I don't know, really. It's too early to say.'

'You're not feeling any fire?' asks Isabella accusingly.

'The creative fire? Yes, I can feel it. I feel passionate about Bruce, about trying to capture something of his essence and get it into the book.'

'Bruce! Again!' wails Isabella. 'Why don't you use your imagination?' She taps her forehead, glaring at Ella, her eyes almost bulging. 'Instead of being obsessed with this *Bruce* person? Whom nobody has even heard of!'

'That's not true, Izzy. A lot of people have heard of him. He's got lifetime achievement awards coming out of his arse. But I'm not writing a book about him because of his renown. I'm writing a book about him because he's brilliant. And funny. And perceptive. And self-deprecating. I admire him.'

'That is a stupid reason for writing a book!' sneers Isabella, lighting her spliff and taking a deep toke. 'And anyway, *I don't know him,'* she grunts, trying, with a massive effort, to keep the smoke in.

'I did meet someone the other day who you might have heard of. She *is* well known in Spain. Well, right here in Málaga actually.'

'Who?' asks Isabella, accusingly. 'Who do *you* know here?'

'She's called Maria Aranda.'

'Who?'

'Maria Aranda.'

'I don't know her,' spits Isabella dismissively, flapping her hand.

'She's an Instagram star. A model. She promotes fashion and make-up lines. Instagram influencers, they call them.'

Ella shows Isabella Maria's Instagram.

'Her? I've seen her around. Never spoken to her,' she grimaces. 'She thinks she is something special. So *that* is what she does! Precisely *nothing!*'

'Well, I only met her briefly, but I thought she was really nice.'

'Pah! She is *nothing!* She does *nothing!* She has no *value*! Unlike *me!* She will get old and have a face of *plastic!* But my books will never get old! They will be reading *Gazpacho en Verano* on the moon in five hundred years' time! My art will live forever! Like *Cervantes!*' she says, waving her hands in the air.

'I don't think humans will be here in five hundred years' time, Izzy.'

Isabella ignores Ella, puts on reading glasses and peers at a photo of Maria and Richard together, screwing up her face suspiciously.

'And who is he? Richard Egranté?' she asks, reading the text underneath the photo.

'An English actor. Richard E. Grant,' Ella corrects.

'Another one I've never heard of. Talk to me about someone *interesting* for a change. In fact don't. I need to clear my mind. To think. You, you can go back to your *work*,' she says, dismissively.

Isabella tops up her gin and tonic with more gin at regular intervals, gulping back the drink before re-filling her glass.

Ella turns back to her phone and spends an hour reading the news, absorbed in the outside world.

Suddenly, a drunken Isabella looms over her, eyes flickering between open and closed. She thrusts her phone in front of Ella's face.

'Have you seen this?'

Ella glances at the Instagram feed on her screen.

'No, I haven't. I told you, I'm trying to keep off social media.'

'You haven't seen it? Why not? It's me in my Mexican sombrero! Three thousand likes!'

'Lovely.'

'My fans! They *love* me! I have readers *all over the world!*'

Ella recoils as Isabella's face moves closer, her coke-speckled nose only a few inches away from Ella's own. Her breath reeks of alcohol.

'They *love* me! Adore me!' she slurs.

'I'm sure they do. Lovely.'

'But you don't understand how much they *love* me! I am like a *goddess* to them!'

Isabella stands upright again and sways towards the edge of the roof terrace. She notices the moon, rising over the sea on the horizon.

'The *moon!*' she yells. 'Look at *the moon!* It's so *beautiful!* Come here, *now!* Come and see *the moon!*'

'I can see it from here, thanks.'

'But look at it! *Look at the moon!*' Isabella thrusts a splayed hand out towards the silver disc of the moon, looming over the horizon, far out to sea.

'Yes, it's quite beautiful.'

'But it's the *moon!*' insists Isabella, shouting into the sky.

'I love the moon, yes.'

'But stand up! Come and look at it! How can you see it properly, sitting there! Come and look at the moon!'

'Really, I'm fine Izzy. I can see it from here and yes, it's lovely.'

'Pah!' snorts Isabella, then grabs her phone and sways over to the edge of the terrace again, pointing it waveringly at the sky.

'The moon! *I have to instagram the moon!*'

32
Return

'IT'S IN HERE,' SAYS LARA, GENTLY. THE DOOR STICKS slightly as she opens it, revealing a cavernous barn lit by high windows.

The sparse room is dominated by a life-sized stone statue of a small boy, standing alone in the centre on a large wooden carving bench. His face is inclined, looking upwards towards a huge roof window which bathes him in a dusty beam of summer light. The figure's loose hoodie and trainers seem incongruous with the smooth, almost translucent white of the alabaster from which he is carved.

The air in the barn is cool and still. Tom looks around him momentarily at the dusty rafters, blocks of alabaster and shelves of stone, before resting his eyes on the statue.

'It's not finished yet, of course. I'm getting there, though,' says Lara almost apologetically, wiping a strand of hair from her face with the back of her hand.

Tom walks towards the carving bench and glances at a long linen pouch of blue-handled knives and chisels lying on the scored wooden surface, then looks up at the statue and slowly walks around it. He glances across at Lara and smiles.

'It's stunning,' he murmurs.

'Thanks. Like I said, there's still a long way to go,' says Lara, shyly, walking over to the statue and standing near Tom.

'You're so talented, Lara.'

She catches his eye and smiles back. He continues to look into her eyes, once again, as before in the kitchen, holding her gaze too long. She looks away and runs her hand down the child's arm, feeling the cool touch of the stone beneath her fingers. A pained expression fleetingly crosses her face as she shakes her head, wearily.

'I…thanks…I…it's just…you know, I just wanted to capture the sadness in one soul. I don't know whether I've managed it yet. That's for the public to decide when I show it, I guess.'

'Well I love it already. It's beautiful,' Tom says, quietly.

Lara glances back at Tom and smiles, uncertainly. 'Thanks.'

The sound of Charles barking excitedly in the yard outside disrupts the dry silence.

'That'll be Bruce I expect.' Lara laughs, embarrassed by her relief at the interruption. 'Charles can hear the car from miles away. Back in one piece, I hope,' she grins at Tom.

Bruce's Land Rover pulls into the yard and stops beside the excited dog, who jumps up at the driver's door. Charles throws himself at Bruce, his tongue lolling as he pants with glee. Bruce smiles and hugs the dog, burying his face in his neck. 'Charles! I've missed you old boy. Where's Lara? Hmmm? Where is she?'

The dog, still panting with excitement, looks over towards Lara's studio. Bruce walks over to the barn.

Tom and Lara turn towards him as he enters. Lara grins and walks over to her husband, putting her arms around him and holding him close.

'Bruce. I've missed you so much.' She draws away and glances over at Tom.

'Tom just came to deliver some cables for James's studio.'

'Hi Tom. Is it finished yet? Been going on ages.'

Tom scratches his head, avoiding Bruce's eyes. 'Yeah, just about. Been a bit more complicated than we expected.'

'Right.'

'Lara was just showing me her studio. I've always been interested in sculpture.'

'Yes. Fascinating art form, isn't it?'

'Absolutely, yeah, amazing.'

'Do you have a preference? A favourite sculptor?' asks Bruce, smiling.

'Oh, the usual. Henry Moore, Michelangelo, you know. I'm not really up on modern sculpture. I just kind of like what I see, you know. Your wife's really good. I love her stuff.'

Bruce raises his eyebrows and smiles. 'She is.'

'If I see it and like it, then I just like it,' adds Tom, unnecessarily.

The room falls into silence, as everyone looks at the sad figure on the table.

'Anyway, I'm gonna shoot. Tell James I'll give him a bell.'

'Thanks, Tom. Are you still dropping by next week with the other speakers?' asks Lara.

'Yeah, when they arrive.'

They file out into the sunlit yard, dazzling after the half light of the studio.

'I'll just take my stuff in. See you later,' says Bruce to Tom, heading to the car to fetch his luggage.

Tom looks after Bruce then turns back to Lara, smiles warmly, then steps forward and kisses her on the cheek.

'See you next week.'

'Sure.' She smiles back, watching him as he heads to his van parked at the other end of the courtyard. She follows it with her eyes as it disappears through the gate.

As she stands in the empty yard, chickens slowly wander across the cobbles. Comet snorts and nods her head at the stable door. Lara looks across at her and smiles, then follows her husband into the house.

By the time Lara returns from walking Charles in the woods, the house is silent again. The door to Bruce's barn is open. Inside, Bruce is sat at his desk, moving piles of paper around. He looks up as Lara enters the room.

'Have the fucking chickens been in here?' he asks, testily.

'Not that I know of, darling.'

'There's fucking *chicken shit* on my *desk!*'

'Ah. Um. No idea how that happened. I'll have a word with them,' says Lara, suppressing a smile.

Bruce stands up and points at a pile of papers which are topped with a dry mound of chicken shit.

'Fuckers. I really don't like the fucking chickens in here, Lara, I've told you that before.' He picks up the bottle of red standing next to his typewriter and opens it with his favourite corkscrew, a spiral of metal attached to a gnarled piece of ancient French grapevine, its surface polished to a golden patina through years of use.

'Ah, I know what happened. I came in for something a few days ago and left the door open for a few minutes. One of the girls must have got in then. Sorry darling,' says Lara.

She walks over to Bruce and puts her arms around him.

'I really missed you. Didn't think I would as much as I did. Place was so quiet without you.'

'I missed you too. You know I wanted you to come to Spain.'

'Let's not go over that again, Bruce. I'm just saying I missed you.' Lara pulls away and looks at him.

'Fucking crapping on my desk. Fucking chickens,' says Bruce, irritably, pouring a glass of wine. He looks sideways at Lara and smiles, eyes creasing.

'I'm cooking soon. Are you staying here or coming back to the house?'

'Think I'm going to catch up on things here for a bit. Made quite a few notes in Spain for *The Block*, I'd like to type them up whilst they're fresh in my mind.'

'OK darling, fine. Call me if you need anything.'

Hearing a noise on the stairs, Lara puts her book on the bedside table and looks at her watch.

The bedroom door opens and Bruce stumbles in.

'Time is it?' he asks with a slur.

'Midnight. Aren't you tired after travelling?'

'Yeah. Tired.'

He awkwardly takes his clothes off, struggling with sleeves and trouser legs, then climbs into bed.

Lara turns to him and strokes his hair as he lies on his back.

He stares at the ceiling, then his eyelids slowly close and his breathing becomes heavy.

He's asleep.

The window is open, and the scent of night jasmine permeates the air.

Lara sighs. She continues running a hand through his hair and gazes at him, lovingly.

'I remember...when we used to make love all afternoon. Do you remember that, Bruce? You used to tell me I was the most beautiful woman you'd ever seen. And you've met some beautiful women. So

I always took that as such a compliment. Because I don't really think I'm beautiful at all. You used to know that. Do you still know that? That I don't feel beautiful? I did, once. But now, I just feel tired, if I'm honest. And a lot of the time, I feel lonely. Tired and lonely. You know I never really bought into that idea that another person can somehow complete you or make you happy. So no-one else is going to make me happy. Not even you. I know it has to come from within me. If I can't be happy with myself, nobody else can change that. And I'm trying, Bruce. I'm trying very, very hard. But I don't want to feel little sparks of happiness inside me caused by another person. By someone else. I want it to be because of *you.* Sometimes, I don't think you have any idea just how much I love you. I don't want anyone else, Bruce. I want you, *you*, my husband.'

A tear falls from Lara's face onto Bruce's cheek, and she watches it travel slowly across his skin towards his mouth, which opens slightly with a silent snore. The tear stops just short of his lips. She can smell the booze.

She lays her head down on her pillow and falls asleep, grateful that he is home again.

❧❧❧

It feels early when Lara wakes up. She's instantly aware that she's alone. She checks her phone. Seven o'clock. She climbs out of bed, pulls on a dark blue silk dressing gown and some slippers then stops by the full length mirror. Her long silver hair is all over the place. She pulls it back into a bun with a large, matte silver hair clip, before going downstairs to look for Bruce.

The house is silent. Guessing he must already be in the barn, Lara crosses the yard to check.

Charles lollops playfully out of the barn towards her, sloppily licking her face as she bends down to greet him.

'Hello Charlie boy! Is he working already? He hasn't even unpacked, yet, has he?' Charles hangs his tongue out and pants, looking up at her hopefully.

The door to the barn stands open. She walks in, followed by an eager Charles, tail wagging.

Bruce is sitting at his desk, staring at a sheet of A4 sticking up from the typewriter bearing half a page of dialogue. An open bottle of red stands by the typewriter alongside a full glass.

He turns around and grins at Lara.

'Hi, darling.'

'Hi.'

'I was going to take Charles out for the "W" word in a minute.'

'It doesn't matter. If you're busy. I'll do it.'

'Thanks. I am kind of engrossed,' says Bruce, peering over his glasses at the page before him.

'I can see.'

'So, I'll be in for breakfast in a bit,' says Bruce, turning back to his work.

'OK.'

Bruce resumes staring at his typewriter. Lara stares at his back, remaining standing by the door.

Sensing she's still there, he turns round again and smiles at her, a charming grin on his face.

'What?'

'Well, you know, I don't want to interrupt you, but...you've only just got back from Spain, Bruce. And well...we haven't even talked yet.'

'Yes we have.'

'No, Bruce. We haven't. I mean, actually sat down and had a chat. Actually talked. I haven't seen you for a week!'

He looks puzzled. 'You've spent weeks on end not seeing me when I've been away on a shoot. What's the problem?'

Lara sighs, heavily. 'There isn't a problem as such. It would just be nice to sit down together and have a conversation. It's already sunny out there. I thought maybe we could sit in the sun and have breakfast together.'

'Yeah, OK. Great idea. I'll just finish this scene. I got the idea for it in Spain. Been struggling with it for weeks. Just need to get it out and on paper, OK?'

'Fine. As I said, I don't want to interrupt you.'

'You're not interrupting me,' says Bruce, becoming slightly irritated.

Lara returns to the house, pours herself a chilled orange juice and goes upstairs. She gets changed into some sweatpants and a t-shirt and spends half an hour doing yoga in silence.

When she returns downstairs, she can hear the *clackety-clack* of Bruce's typewriter from across the courtyard.

She makes herself some muesli and goes out of the back door to sit alone at the wrought iron table on the rear terrace. She looks out across the tiered cottage garden she has so lovingly planted up and tended over the years. The bright blue cornflowers, vivid red poppies and spikes of multi-coloured lupins always make her feel happy.

Her phone pings. Tom.

so lovely to see your work yesterday, thanks for showing it to me - speakers have been delayed a few days, not sure when i'll be over now, will let you know...tom xxx

Lara feels a pang of disappointment and her mind starts whirring.

Why are you feeling disappointed? What, you're so desperate to see him again? He's a fucking kid! You don't need him in your life any more than he is already!

I know. I know that. I don't want him in my life. It's just the attention, I guess. If I'm honest with myself, I like the attention. And flattery. That's it. Attention and flattery. It's not him at all. He could be anyone. Fuck it.

'Fuck it,' says Lara out loud to herself. 'What I really want is to have fucking breakfast with my husband, sitting here in the sun. Why is that such a seemingly *impossible goal to achieve?*'

She slams down her spoon, leaves her half finished bowl of muesli and marches through the house, back out across the courtyard and steams into the *clackety-clack* of Bruce's barn, seething.

Bruce pulls a sheet of writing from the typewriter, turns round and looks at Lara, grinning.

'What?' she demands. 'What are you fucking grinning for?'

''Cause I'm happy,' replies Bruce, nonchalantly, his grin fading only slightly.

'Why?'

'Well, I've just drunk a bottle of Château Haut-Trion and the voices are here. It's a great feeling,' he replies, his grin fading completely now that he can see how angry his wife is.

'Well that's great, Bruce. Really, that's fantastic. I'm so happy for you.'

'What's wrong?' he asks, warily.

'Everything.'

'Can you be a bit more precise so I'm not clutching at straws? I mean, *everything* obviously isn't wrong. The house isn't on fire. A meteorite hasn't just struck the earth, destroying humanity,' he says, smiling hopefully. 'Or has it?'

'For fuck's sake, Bruce! This is what I mean! You're so *evasive!* You're impossible to pin down! You just give that...that...charming smile, you make some witticism and think everything's going to be alright, but it isn't!'

'Well tell me what's wrong! What have I done?' he asks, exasperatedly.

'It's like you're stuck at age *thirteen!* It's like you've got arrested development or something!'

Bruce looks hurt and stares at Lara, nonplussed.

'Well, that's a bit harsh. Where has all this anger suddenly come from? You were fine, earlier.'

'It's come from the fact that I'm sitting alone having breakfast! Again! Instead of with my husband, who said "Yes, let's have breakfast together", but who's in here, as usual, fucking working!' And…' She stops herself, but glances again at the bottle.

He ignores her glance. 'Well, that's what I do. I'm a writer. You knew that when you married me.'

'Of course I fucking know you're a writer! But writers *eat*, don't they? Are you simply *incapable* of joining me for breakfast? What's *wrong* with you, Bruce?'

'Nothing! I was just finishing this scene, I told you!'

'But how long's that going to take? Until lunchtime? By which time it'll be too late for breakfast!'

'We could do brunch.'

'I don't want fucking *brunch*, Bruce, I want fucking *muesli*! On the *terrace!* With *you!* Half an hour ago!'

'Right, well, you should have said it was *urgent.* I'll stop what I'm doing and join you, then. Alright?'

'But it's no good, now! You've ruined it! I'm not going to enjoy breakfast with you now we're in the middle of a fucking *row*, am I?'

'Well, what do you suggest I do?' asks Bruce, smiling and opening another bottle of wine. 'To make amends.'

'You know what? Sometimes I think that mentally, you're even younger than Tom is.'

'Who?'

'Tom. James's friend.'

'How old is he? Tom?'

'Thirty-seven.'

'I wish. I would *love* to be thirty-seven again.'

'That's not the *point*, Bruce!'

'Alright, no need to yell. How come you know how old he is, anyway? You and this…this *Tom* seem to have been getting quite close recently.'

'Not that it would bother you, would it?'

'Well, yes, of course it would bother me. So *have* you been getting close?' asks Bruce, pouring himself another glass of wine and taking a slug.

'No, not really. But he finds me attractive. I can tell that much.'

Bruce stares at his wife, not quite knowing how to process this new information.

'I see,' he says, quietly. 'So he fancies you. OK.'

'*See?* You don't even *care!*'

Bruce smiles and looks affectionately at Lara. 'Well, I'm hardly surprised he fancies you. You *are* gorgeous, after all.'

She stares at him before replying. 'How long is it since you've told me I'm gorgeous?'

'No idea. Last week?'

'No, Bruce, not last week. About five fucking years ago.'

'Really? Is it that long? I could've sworn it was last week.'

'Well it wasn't. Women take note of these things. They're *important.* They're as important as your *work.* Even more so, actually, if you want to keep a bloody marriage together.'

Bruce raises his eyebrows at Lara, not quite sure where this is going and not wanting to say the wrong thing at the wrong moment.

Lara looks out at the yard. 'I could have had a thing with him. If I'd wanted,' says Lara, trying to sound casual.

Bruce stares at her blankly.

'Is that what you want? A "thing"?'

'No. No it isn't,' she replies calmly, without looking at him.

'Well why bring it up, then? Why use it as a threat?'

She meets his eyes. 'Because, Bruce, I'm feeling *neglected. Lonely.*'

'I really don't understand. Neglected? Seriously? I pay you attention *all the time!*'

'Not *enough* attention.'

'Well how much do you need?'

'More than I'm getting. I know where my place is in the pecking order. Work. Wine. Me,' says Lara, bitterly.

Bruce looks at Lara for several seconds, then stands up and walks over to her and pulls her gently into his arms. 'That's not true. You and the kids are everything to me. We've discussed this a million times. You know the score, Lara. I'm an alcoholic. It's a disease. And we agreed long ago you would never beat me up for it.'

'I know,' says Lara, her anger evaporating. 'I'm not beating you up for it.'

She pulls away from him, strokes his hair and looks into his eyes.

'I just want us to have breakfast together,' she adds, softly.

'OK…'

As Bruce opens his mouth to continue, the phone rings. Bruce picks it up.

'Wayne…really? Right…' He glances over at Lara and rolls his eyes.

Lara stares sadly at Bruce, then turns and walks out of the barn into the sunshine.

Charles appears in front of her, still panting and wagging his tail, his lead already in his mouth as he looks up at her expectantly.

'OK Charlie boy, let's go,' says Lara, flatly.

33
MICKY'S MOROCCAN PALACE

MICKY VALLANCE SLOWLY SNORTS A HUGE LINE OF OxyContin from the carved mahogany table, then jerks his head up. Shards of jewel-like shadows splay across the white marble floor, creating a sprawling psychedelic mosaic at his feet. He leans back on the crimson velvet sofa and smiles beatifically.

The haunting sound of the early afternoon Dhuhr floats through the open windows from the nearby Mosque. Its sad, lonely tone, seeping through the warm air fills him with longing for a life he knows has slipped away through his fingers. A life of companionship and love with one of the most beautiful, feisty, determined and talented women he's ever met. His love, Juliette. And, despite the euphoric golden sunset rush of the Oxy, he is filled with a sadness which penetrates to his very core.

Reaching out slowly, he picks up his favourite briefcase, its brown leather worn soft and pliable after many years of travelling. Opening it, he removes a sheaf of papers, printoffs of his early emails to Juliette, from when he was trying to make sense of the new love flooding his body and mind with delirious confusion and almost intolerable passion.

He reads, barely able to believe that he actually wrote the words before him.

'Basically, I'm making a crappy attempt to escape being in love with you and it's not working. Every time a traffic signal changes from red to green that is a sign to me to text you. But I know I can't because you'll think I'm hitting on you. I want to though. I want to just talk to you. It's like a physical need. The way you looked at me when we said goodbye at the wrap has only happened now and never before in my entire life. Your soft, warm eyes enveloped my soul and I flew on their trusted wings to a place which, when I had to leave it, wrenched my heart from my body. A body, which, because I'm married, will never feel your touch. The feeling between us is like a delicate flower. Its petals, glowing vivid with sunlight shining through their translucence, so delicate they could be crushed by the gentlest touch. This is how I feel about you, Juliette. This is how you've turned my life upside down.'

Tears run down Micky's face as he turns the pages. He finds another one, written when both had escaped their doomed marriages but were forced to spend weeks apart on their respective movie shoots.

'Oh Juliette, where do you reside? In that dizzy land beyond the reach of my physical embrace, somewhere out there in space and time, separate to me, so far away you may as well be dead, I've got no idea where you are, what you're doing or saying right now, and yet you rage alive inside me, a burning fire igniting and exploding my heart into the ether in search of your body and mind.

'I love you, is all that I know now. Maybe we'll die in separate lands, march on to the end of time half forgotten, a dream barely remembered. And my fingers touch your pillow, my tears sink in your soil as the trees bare their trunks to the wind and shed their leaves just one more time. And I will lift into the clouds away from you, the feel of your skin a distant memory I cannot touch. Just sweat and nightmares and blaring gales to remind me of your love. Oh how I wish I could hold you forever. More precious than gold. More precious than life, your love, and you.'

He puts the papers back into the case and collapses back onto the sofa, looking up at the ceiling.

The tears run freely and turn into deep sobs which rack his body.

Wiping his eyes with the back of his hand, he sits up and picks up his phone. Her latest Instagram post is of Juliette and Susan Sarandon at that place she seems to love so much, The Desert Rose, both of them grinning into the camera. He zooms in on Juliette. So beautiful. So fresh-faced. So gorgeous. So fuckable. The post is captioned *catchup with my bbf Susan before the party tonight! #girlz #party #bestfriends #lalife*. It's got 33,000 likes already.

'Whose party? And where? Fuck it. Fuck her. I need to call Gary. Gary will fix it. Gary fixes everything.'

In the heat of the Moroccan night, Micky gnaws at chunks of marinated roast lamb, carved from a spit-roast set up by the riad's staff on the roof terrace which overlooks Essaouria's medieval sea walls, a glittering line of white and gold against the roaring darkness of the Atlantic beyond.

He belches contentedly. The girls will be here soon. He ordered five of them. Should be enough. He sits on the roof terrace, his fingers sticky with grease and pungent, spiced marinade. Oblivious to the hired staff, he cuts and snorts a line of Oxy, then takes out his iPad and scrolls through the latest posts on the Flat Earth Society forum.

'If we were living on a giant ball, an airplane would constantly have to dip its nose. If not, it would find itself at over 80,000 feet in just half an hour and soon it would be floating around in outer space. #nasalies'

Micky solemnly nods in agreement, completely engrossed.

'Water mountains are what ships disappear behind in the sea. Ball Earthists are just too stupid to recognise them, so they claim it's evidence of a Ball Earth. Sheeple.'

'Fuckin' A,' he mutters to himself.

The rasp of crickets pierces the white noise of the Atlantic surf. The staff sit in the darkness, smoking and talking softly as they half watch the rich, crazy American.

Around ten o'clock, the rumble of a lorry grows louder, stopping outside the gates of the riad. Micky peers over the parapet but his view is obscured by a stand of thuja trees.

He can hear muffled female voices in hushed tones. He grins to himself.

The housekeeper, a small, slender, middle-aged Berber dressed in a black djellaba, appears on the roof terrace. He bows slightly.

'Sir, your guests have arrived,' he announces discreetly, and gestures for Micky to follow him.

They walk down a narrow, worn stone staircase, open to the sky and stars, to the expansive courtyard, in the middle of which stands a large stone fountain on a blue and white mosaiced plinth. Around the courtyard, large arches bordered by huge potted date palms conceal cool, dark rooms draped in rich, jewel-coloured fabrics.

As Micky descends the staircase, he sees the girls. He counts eleven of them, lined up in a row, all smiling alluringly. They are dressed identically in flowing, sequinned chiffon skirts, revealing their legs to their thighs. Their flat young midriffs are exposed, jewels in their navels. Firm adolescent breasts are tightly squashed into spangled, satin bras. As requested, all have long hair in shades of blonde, brunette and black. No redheads.

An elegant middle-aged woman dressed in a smart navy blue linen skirt suit, smiles at Micky and approaches him respectfully.

'So lovely to meet you, Mr Valance. My name is Nicky. We have a selection of our very top girls for your perusal. None are over fifteen years old. Please feel free to choose as many as you like.'

'Yeah. Nice to meet ya, Nicky. Tempted to say I'll take 'em all.' He laughs, mirthlessly. 'I kinda had five down as a good number though, right? My lucky number, in fact.' He grins.

Nicky smiles politely, her eyes like flints. 'Would you like the girls to dance for you, perhaps? To help you select your chosen ones?'

'Sure, yeah. Go ahead. Nice touch.' Micky sweeps a hand towards the girls.

He nods to the housekeeper. 'Fetch me a brandy, huh? Make it generous.'

The housekeeper bows and shuffles off, his sandals slapping the clay-tiled floor.

Nicky clicks her fingers and after a brief pause, some music starts to play. Some kind of Moroccan hip-hop. Without hesitation, the girls gyrate to the music, all of them looking longingly into Micky's eyes.

Micky makes a mental note to have Gary fix this up for him at least once a week, no matter where in the world he is.

He points at a blonde. Then another.

'Yeah, I'll have her,' he grunts, thickly. 'And her. And that one. And…those two at the end,' he says, grinning, as he makes his final selection.

Nicky clicks her fingers again. The music stops. She gestures for the other girls to follow her. They file out, staring ahead silently, without expression. The last one, a girl with alabaster skin and raven black hair, glances over her shoulder longingly at Micky. He notices her and shrugs, grinning.

'I'd have ya baby, but five's my lucky number. What am I gonna do? Gotta stick to my limit. Discipline, baby. Ciao, sweetheart. Have a great life!'

Her eyes smoulder as she looks away from him and vanishes into the darkness.

Outside, the night air is still hot. The crickets chirp incessantly in the fragrant darkness.

The girls talk to one another in hushed, disappointed tones as Nicky opens the back of the lorry and ushers them in. She barks orders in Russian and the girls disrobe in the dusty interior of the lorry, handing their clothes back to Nicky before finding their own clothes in piles strewn in corners, pulling on scruffy hoodies, tracksuit bottoms and trainers and scraping their hair back into scrunchies with their fingers. Alabaster girl defiantly wipes her lipstick across her face leaving a clown-like red smear on her chin. Nicky clicks her fingers, gestures for the girl to come towards her, and slaps her hard across the face, hissing something in Russian. The girl bursts into tears but as she turns away from Nicky her eyes are glacial and full of resentment.

Nicky slams the door of the lorry shut and shouts to the driver, before walking over to a black jeep and climbing in next to a man in a dark suit. The lorry drives off kicking up a trail of dust behind it. The jeep sits in silence, awaiting the empty lorry's return. Nicky and the suited man smoke and stare into the darkness.

As the moon rises over the distant Atlas Mountains, Micky sprawls naked on a pile of plump, brightly embroidered cushions, watching a huge screen upon which plays a Blu-Ray of *The Hooded Claw*, the Wayne Montana produced movie which first catapulted him to A-list movie stardom.

A low brass Moroccan table next to the cushions is covered in lines of coke, Oxy and rolled up 100 dollar bills.

A naked blonde girl is sucking his cock. One of the brunettes is standing naked by a carved mahogany dresser, mixing cocktails, and another is plopping chunks of pineapple in syrup into his mouth. The two remaining girls are lying next to him, one stroking his balls, the second running a hand over his chest whilst using the other hand to wipe white powder from her nose.

He smiles contentedly.

Nothing can beat this. Not even love. Fuck Juliette.

By 6am the sun is already rising, gathering heat. Micky is still sprawled naked on the cushions, asleep. The girls are all lying together on the huge bed, their arms draped over one another, cuddled up together like soft puppies.

Micky's eyes flicker open and struggle to focus as he slowly remembers where he is. Much of the night before is a black haze, with certain scenes popping out in lurid colour. He smiles as he remembers the blonde sucking his cock. And that spectacular scene in *The Hooded Claw* where he did his own stunt and leapt off the roof of that burning car.

His back is aching. He looks over at the mound of sleeping, naked girls on his bed.

'Hey, get over here,' he says at no-one in particular. The cock-sucking blonde opens her eyes, looks blearily over at him, then wriggles across the bed and slides down onto the floor next to Micky.

'Hi,' she says, smiling, reaching across to stroke his chest and then moving her other hand down to his crotch to fondle his cock.

'How is Micky feeling this morning?' she purrs in a heavy accent.

'Like shit,' he says sleepily. 'Fetch me some water, wouldja?'

The girl stands up and walks over to the dresser. She pours a glass of water from a jug, then brings it over to Micky.

He knocks it back in one then glances over at the brass table, still scattered with white powders.

'Take a shit for me, then snort me a line of coke, 'cause I can't be fucking bothered to do either,' he says, laughing at his own joke.

He looks at the girl. 'What were you called, again, sweetheart? Katie?'

'Katya,' she replies, her head on his chest.

'Katie'll do. You can be called Katie.'

'You were calling me Katie last night.'

'There ya go, then. So, didja have fun, hun?'

'Sure. You were the best fun. Very funny fun,' says Katya, resuming stroking Micky's cock, which fails to respond to her touch, remaining limp and inert.

'You'd say it was fun even if it wasn't,' says Micky, looking down at Katya and smiling.

'I would tell you truth,' she protests, lifting her head.

'Nah, you wouldn't. You're fuckin' paid to say yes. Correct?'

'And you, you never hear "no", correct?' smiles Katya, teasingly.

'I don't want to hear "no". "No" is a diarrhoea bomb in my face. I want to hear "yes".'

'What is diarrhoea?'

'Shit. Fast shit. Comes out fast and sloppy.'

'But life is full of your fast shit. If you never see any fast shit, you living pretend life. Like if the clouds are white and pretty all the time. Is not real. No storms.'

'No shitstorms,' he muses

'No shitstorms,' she repeats.

'Well honey, I got plenty of shitstorms, believe me. I'm an artist at the top of my fucking game and my whole fucking life is a fucking shitstorm.'

'Your life, it looks very nice to me. You have everything you want, no? But is it real? Is this real?' She gestures around the luxurious room, sunlight streaming in through the open windows and falling on the naked girls.

Micky grabs Katya's backside and squeezes hard.

'This is real. This is fucking real, baby. Stop talking. I haven't paid for a fucking shrink, I've paid for a piece of ass.'

Katya smiles, wriggles closer to Micky and resumes fondling his cock, which is finally starting to awaken with the day.

Leaning over the brass table, Katya snorts a line of coke then wipes her nose.

'Try some Oxy if you like,' offers Micky.

'No, I won't, thanks.'

'Have whatever you want. Mi casa es tu casa.'

Katya resumes her position next to Micky on the pile of cushions, whilst the other girls slumber on, blissfully unaware of the new day.

'I am fine. I like the coke. It is good. Is not often we get good coke.'

'You're gonna get a huge tip, too. You've been the best company, Katie. Real good company, y'know?'

Katya smiles wanly.

'Thank you. A tip would be very nice. We don't get paid much. And they took away our passports.'

'Are you serious? You are fucking *kidding* me!' exclaims Micky, looking down at Katya, genuinely shocked.

'Please. Don't tell Nicky I say that. She will kill us all,' says Katya, gravely.

'What kind of fucking *bullshit* is that? Taking away your fucking passports!'

Katya shrugs. 'It happens.'

'The girls I use in LA are all in control of their lives. Fucking top of their game. So you're saying you're all, like, fucking *sex slaves?*'

'Sure,' says Katya, glumly.

'I didn't fucking pay for *slaves.* I paid for *high class hookers.* I'm gonna be asking for a fucking *refund.*'

'Please, please, do not say anything. I beg of you. I am serious. They will kill us all.'

'I'm gonna fix you some fucking passports, don't you worry about it.'

'Really? You could do that?'

'I can do fucking anything I want, baby. Like I said. No-one says "no" to me. Nobody.'

The other girls start stirring. 'Fetch 'em some drinks and give 'em some coke,' says Micky, reaching for the remote to put another movie on. 'Let's party.'

***

As the sun descends towards the Atlantic, Micky awakens from a deep sleep.

A warm breeze drifts in through the open window, bringing with it the scent of the ocean.

He looks around him in the shadowed room. The girls have gone. So have all the bottles, glasses and food trays. The brass table is clean and shining gold in the last rays of the sun.

The bed has been freshly made.

Next to the bed, the printoffs of his emails to Juliette are stacked in a neat pile.

Micky reaches for his phone.

'Gary? I need you to get me some passports. Five.'

34
Over

THE STORM WAS FORECAST FOR THE AFTERNOON, BUT by 11am the sky is heavily overcast and the air is humid and thick with electricity. Sunbathers are packing away their belongings and leaving the beach, whilst shop owners on the Paseo Maritimo are reeling in the awnings above their shops.

An intermittent low rumbling from the sky grows louder and the first heavy drops of rain start to fall, spotting the dry pavements.

Ella stops walking along the paseo, takes shelter under a palm tree and stares at the increasingly deserted beach as the sky darkens. Plump raindrops start falling on her head from the palm tree above and then with a sudden hiss, the rain comes in a heavy deluge, trapping her under the tree.

She looks at the rain pounding the beach, cratering the dry sand and bouncing from the paving slabs.

As she stands watching, imprisoned by the rain, a single thought comes into her head.

It's over.

The first thing Ella notices as she walks up to Zack's micropub is the new sign. 'Shoreditch Alehouse' is prominent in gold lettering on a green background. It looks good. She stares silently at the sign for a moment then walks down the narrow side passage leading to the rear of the premises.

Zack glances down from the ladder where he's perched, measuring the top of the pergola he's partway through constructing.

'Ella!' He climbs down to greet her, hopping off the third step of the ladder. He wraps his arms around her before kissing her on the lips. 'Have a good trip?'

'Yeah. Sorry I didn't ring before. Both chargers ran out.'

'S'OK. We've been busy.' He stands back to give Ella a better view.

'I can see. The sign out front looks great.'

'Cheers. Yeah, I'm well pleased with it.'

'Hi, Benjy!' Ella waves across the courtyard towards Benjy who is bent over, shirtless, sawing a large log in two. His torso is tanned and slightly flabby around the waist; his blond hair flops over his face.

'Watcha Ella! Looking gorgeous, babes. Holiday's done you good.' He brazenly looks her up and down.

Let's hope all that frantic sawing does the same for you.

'Great to have you back, darlin'. What you up to today?' asks Zack.

'Unpacking. Just came round here to see how you were getting on.'

'Should have the pergola finished by tonight. Fancy going out for something to eat afterwards?'

'Yeah, OK.'

'Isabella sad to see you go?'

'No idea. She's away with the fucking fairies, Zack. I'm relieved to be back, to be honest' says Ella, looking at the half-finished pergola. 'The fame's completely gone to her head. She was being a complete dick.'

'I hope you told her that.'

'I should have done, but I've known her my entire life. We're meant to be soul mates.'

'Right. Well you might have been soul mates when you were five years old playing on the beach, but from what you've told me the drugs have obviously got her now. She's a loser, Ella.'

'Bit of an exaggeration. How can she be a loser when she's one of the greatest writers in the Spanish language? The whole of South America adores her.'

'Except Brazil.'

'Portuguese,' says Benjy, helpfully.

'Whatever. The point is, she's a massively fucking successful author.'

'Doesn't stop her being a *loser*,' says Zack.

'What, just because she takes a bit of coke now and then? So do you!'

'I'm a musician. It's a requirement. Writers are meant to stick to booze and lock themselves away in a hole feeling suicidal, not cavort all over Europe snorting their way through kilos of blow making arses of themselves.'

'When has Isabella cavorted all over Europe making an arse of herself?'

'Meant to tell ya. Saw it in an old Hello mag in the dentist's. Got in a fight in some restaurant in Paris with some film producer's wife.'

'I don't know anything about that. Which film producer?'

'Can't remember. The wife was hot though. Emma something.'

'Well, Izzy didn't say anything to me about that.'

'She wouldn't, would she.'

Zack's eyes flit over to the other side of the courtyard.

'Benjy, mate, do that smaller one next, yeah?' he shouts.

'Anyway, I won't be going back,' says Ella.

'You do right, babe. So did you see your new best friend Bruce again?'

'Of course not. We've only just *met.*'

'You're gonna keep in touch, though, right?'

'Maybe. He said he'd email when he stops drinking.'

Zack smirks. 'Well that's gonna happen *tomorrow*, isn't it?'

'It's a turn of phrase, Zack.'

'Fuck's sake, Ella. He knows he's never gonna give up drinking. That's his way of saying "Don't call me, I'll call you."'

'Well, that's not how it made me feel. He seemed very upbeat about it. I'm sure he'll be in touch.'

'I wouldn't get your hopes up for meeting him again darlin'. He's probably one of those *really private people* who don't socialise with anyone apart from people they've known really well for years.'

'He probably is, yes.'

'Which ain't you,' says Zack, winking. 'You're just a speck in the distance. A little boat, sailing away towards the horizon of his life before it vanishes over the edge.'

'Cheers Zack. Really reassuring.'

Zack grins, smugly. 'Face it, Ella. The truth is, he means a lot more to you than you mean to him.'

'Well, I guess it's true that our lives are on separate paths.'

Zack walks over to where Benjy is still sawing, bends down, lifts a large tree branch at one end and drags it across the courtyard, dumping it at Ella's feet. He rubs his hands together and looks at her.

'You're like a dandelion seed. Floating past his open window then disappearing on the breeze. Just like that,' he says, flicking his fingers.

Zack turns away from Ella to drag the heavy branch up the ladder. With an effort, he hoists the branch into its position and picks up a drill.

'Thanks. A speck on the horizon. A dandelion seed. Nice. And there's me actually thinking we'd made a connection, that our lives are now somehow, I don't know, *inexplicably entwined.* What a fool.'

Zack holds the drill in mid-air and stares down at Ella.

'For *you.* Not for him, darlin' He's your *muse.* But *you,* on other hand, are not important to *him.* You're not even part of his life. You're just...' he looks upwards, searching for the words, 'background hum.'

'And background hum, too. Excellent.'

Zack climbs down the ladder and walks towards Ella, pulling her close. He hugs her, then pulls away to look into her eyes.

'Stop obsessing about Bruce fucking Robinson. Forget about him. Just write the book.'

'But Bruce *is* the book. He's the whole inspiration for it.'

'Bruce is just a bloke in a fucking barn out in the sticks up North. It's getting *boring,* darlin''

'But I set out to write a love story. And now I don't even know what I'm doing.'

'Write about *us.*' Zack affects a pretentious theatrical voice. 'Their love was like a mountain stream, tumbling over rocks, splashing everywhere, before becoming a slow, powerful current, deep and full of mystery.' He laughs, wields his drill and pulls the trigger twice, making it whirr into action. 'Song in there somewhere.'

Benjy walks over, grinning.

'Love's about banging. End of.'

Zack studies his drill, adjusts the settings and then looks over the half-built structure spanning the length of the courtyard.

'Yeah well, maybe with the women you bang, Benjy, but me and Ella love each other. We'd love one another even if we were incontinent paraplegics, wouldn't we, darlin'?' He smiles, glancing over at her affectionately.

'What a lovely thought,' says Ella.

'True though. Real love isn't about passion. Or sex. It's about caring, devotion and sacrifice,' adds Zack, archly, as he fires up the drill again, holding it like a gun.

Benjy stares at him and laughs.

'I'd better get on home and finish unpacking,' says Ella, wearily.

She walks down the side passage and starts to cry.

Back in the courtyard, Benjy looks at Zack with a smug smirk.

'I know you love her, mate, and she's fucking fit an' all, but you would not love her if she didn't have no legs and she was shitting her brains out all over the bed. Don't tell me you are seriously gonna stick around to fuck *that*.'

'You are a fucking animal,' says Zack, handing Benjy a pack of screws. 'Hold these.'

35
DUI

JULIETTE STARES AT MICKY'S WEEK-OLD MESSAGE FOR perhaps the fiftieth time.

'I still love you, Juliette. I totally fucked up. But I've learnt from it and I've changed. Please come out to Morocco without the kids. I need you.' The last three words linger in her mind.

I was doing so well. We're divorcing. And he's still screwing my life up.

Juliette rolls across the bed and sits upright on what used to be Micky's side. At the very back of Micky's old bedside drawer is a small white screw-top bottle containing three tablets. She knows what they are. She should have thrown them out when Micky first left. Instead, they've been squatting in her life ever since, just asking to be swallowed one day.

She looks at the message one last time and throws the phone on the bed. Pulling open the drawer, she reaches in for the bottle. She stares at it for a few moments, then unscrews the bottle top, tips out the three tablets into her hand, picks one out and swallows it without hesitation, then returns the remaining two to the bottle.

I can't take any more pain and bullshit. What harm can it do?

'I don't even wanna look. It's gonna be more than a couple a hundred hits, right?'

'It's gone viral, honey,' says Susan, gently.

'Whaddaya mean *viral?* How viral?' asks Juliette, switching her phone onto speaker as she adjusts the towel on her lounger.

'Multiply your couple a hundred by a few thousand.'

'Gimme the figure. How many? I'm not goin' on YouTube till I know exactly how bad it is.'

'Well as of this morning, it had one point two million views,' says Susan, flatly.

'Shut. Up. You are shitting me.'

''fraid not.'

Juliette stares at the blue water undulating in the pool in front of her.

One point two million people have seen me getting busted by the cops. Get your head around that, Juliette. One point two million. Fuck.

'It's a whole new level of dumb, huh?' asks Juliette, knowing the answer already.

'It's probably not your greatest ever move, no.'

'I dunno why I even took that fucking pill. And as for driving to the mall. It's the dumbest thing I've ever done.'

'Well look, you learnt your lesson.'

'Yeah.'

'Are you gonna watch it?'

'How humiliating is it?'

'Like I said, not your greatest move. Gimme a call back once you've watched it, honey. Don't do anything foolish in the meantime, OK?'

Juliette opens up the YouTube video. It's got one point three million views.

Fuck it. What's a few thousand people more seeing what a complete fuck-up I am?

She presses play.

The view is evidently from the dash-mount camera in a California Highway Patrol car. The patrol car's lights strobe harshly, illuminating the scene. A cop is approaching a car, pulled over at the side of the freeway. A woman can be seen struggling to get out of the driver's side door. Juliette's heart sinks.

That's me. Fuck. I'm completely out of it.

The cop walks over. The audio is muffled. But she can still make out the voices. Which means the other one point three million viewers will be able to make them out, too.

'Oh, my back. My back's hurting,' moans Juliette.

'Hello M'am, would you step out of your car for me? What's going on? What's wrong with your back? Is something wrong?'

Juliette clambers out of the car with some difficulty, makes a pointed effort to stand up straight and slumps slightly against the side of the vehicle.

'Some of the discs in my back kinda crunched into each other,' she says, by way of explanation.

'OK. So you're not able to walk?'

'Well, no.'

'Are you in pain?' the cop asks, watching her carefully.

'Uh huh.'

'What's your name, please M'am?'

'Juliette Janesson.' She enunciates her name carefully.

'Your name is Juliette Janesson? The movie actor? Is that correct?'

'Yeah.'

'Have you taken any pain medication, M'am?

'Uh huh.' Juliette nods slowly, staring at the cop, glassily.

'OK M'am. With your back being in such pain is there any way you might be able to do some voluntary sobriety tests?' the cop asks, his voice emotionless.

'What do I have to do?' she mumbles, eyes unfocused. She puts a hand behind her, as if checking the car is still there.

Fuck. Fuck. Fuck. I am so obviously completely fucking wasted.

She sways slightly, as though she's having trouble standing up.

'Just step forward away from the car, M'am,' instructs the cop. 'Because you're a concern. I understand that you're injured. But because you've taken some medication now, I need to make sure that medication is not impairing you. Like alcohol. Does that make sense? That means you're OK to drive. That way I'm comfortable with you driving away from me. Would you be able to do some of these tests, M'am?'

A slow, deliberate smile spreads across Juliette's face. She nods slowly.

What the fuck am I smiling at? I'm smiling, for fuck's sake! Shit, I don't remember any of this!

The cop approaches Juliette, stops in front of her and holds one finger up in front of her eyes.

'Keep perfectly still and follow my finger with your eyes. Do you understand, M'am?'

She nods.

The cop moves his finger slowly from left to right in a horizontal line, then back again. Juliette moves her head from side to side, entranced by and struggling to focus on the disembodied digit floating through space in front of her eyes.

'We do this in yoga,' she says, casually, staring in front of her.

'What's that?' asks the cop, confused.

'Move our heads from side to side. We do it in yoga class. Slowly. Real slow.' She looks at the cop, wide-eyed.

The cop stares at Juliette, expressionless.

'Keep looking, M'am, please.'

He looks into her eyes and a dubious expression settles on his face as Juliette tries, with obvious effort, to remain static and upright.

'Do you know your alphabet? Do you know your abcs? Can you say the alphabet without slurring the letters?'

'Sure!' says Juliette, brightly. She leans her back against the side of the car and starts to slide slowly down the door.

'Might be a little easier if you stand up.'

Juliette hoists herself to an upright position and starts reciting the alphabet, intoning each letter carefully and deliberately, 'a, b, c, d, e, f, g…'

The cop studies her carefully the whole time. As she gets to 'z' he says, 'Can you take half a step away from the car for me?'

'Sure.' Juliette pushes herself away from the car door and lifts her right leg as if stepping over a ditch.

'Thank you M'am. OK. So what I'm gonna have you do is I'm gonna have you tilt your head back as far as you can, OK? Then I'm gonna have you close your eyes. Then I'm gonna have you estimate thirty seconds inside your head like a clock, OK? Then when you're done with that passage of time, I want you to open your eyes, tilt your head forward and tell me to stop. You have any questions with that?'

'You're gonna be talking?'

'No, M'am. I'm gonna let you concentrate. So put your hands by your sides for me. Tilt your head back as far as you can. That's it. OK? Close your eyes.'

Juliette closes her eyes. A gentle smile settles on her lips. The cop stares at her, watching as the seconds invisibly flow by.

After a minute or so, Juliette opens her eyes.

'That took a little more than thirty seconds,' says the cop, with a concerned tone.

'Yeah. I was just high.'

'*High?*'

'Yeah.'

'You been drinking any alcohol today?'

'No.'

'Have you taken any prescription medication?'

'Yeah.'

'OK, Juliette. I have some concerns, OK? There's a lot of tests on here that you've failed. Would you be willing to accompany me to the precinct to submit to a voluntary test by a drugs recognition expert?'

'Sure.'

'OK. I'm gonna see if we can do that. Unfortunately I believe that you are under the influence of some kind of powerful prescription medication and I think it's prohibiting you from driving, OK? So because of that I have a process I have to follow, OK? So I'm gonna place you under arrest for driving under the influence of prescription drugs, OK?'

Juliette looks at the cop blankly for a moment, then says flatly, 'Sure.'

'You have the right to remain silent. Anything you say can and will be used against you in a court of law. You have the right to have an attorney. If you cannot afford one, one will be appointed to you by the court. With these rights in mind, are you still willing to talk with me about the charges against you?'

'Yeah, I guess.'

'OK.'

'Are you gonna take me somewhere, now?'

'Yes M'am. Because of your back injury I'm gonna handcuff you in the front and I'm gonna put you in my car.'

'OK.'

'And my car's not that comfortable.'

'OK.'

'Do you have any weapons on you? Needles, knives, firearms or similar?'

'They don't ask that at yoga.'

'We're not at yoga, M'am. I've just read you your rights and I'm placing you under arrest. Do you understand what's happening to you?'

'Sure.'

'OK. Hands out of your pockets. Stand right here for me. Now hold out your arms. Like this.' He holds out his arms horizontally.

Juliette raises her arms. The cop runs his hands up and down the outside of her sweatpants and sweatshirt. He glances up at her. Her face looks slack and compliant, like a kid who's having its clothes changed and has wordlessly acceded to all the seemingly endless pushing and pulling, patiently waiting for it to end so they can go out and play.

'I'm just making sure you don't have any weapons on you, OK?'

'Yeah.' Juliette looks along her outstretched arm and waggles her fingers.

'OK. We're gonna make our way over to my car. Then I'm gonna help you in because of your back injury, as we don't wanna make that worse. Then we're gonna handcuff you, once you get in the car. Is all that OK?'

'Yeah.'

'OK. Let's go, Juliette.' He takes hold of her right arm, just above the elbow, her face bleached intermittently by the strobing lights.

Juliette walks unsteadily towards the camera, weaving like a drunk, her eyes bleary and unfocused, before disappearing from view. The video stops playing as she walks out of shot.

Cut. Fuck. This isn't a fucking movie, Juliette. This is real. Fuck.

Juliette bursts into tears. And cannot stop crying. Her tears turn into sobs, great heaving convulsions which wrack her body. She cries for half an hour.

Once she stops, she looks into the mirror and barely recognises the blotchy red face before her.

She washes her face, composes herself, then calls her friend.

'Susan? I just saw it. It's pretty bad, huh?'

'Well, it is what it is.'

'Face it. It's what I've become, huh?'

'This is a mistake. One that does not define you. You're so much more than this, Juliette. It's humiliating, for sure, but you'll get over it. And those YouTube viewers will already be watching someone else.'

'Yeah. Instead of me. I don't want anyone watching me for a while. I feel like ditching the whole fucking thing.'

'Ditching what?'

'My entire career. The acting. Being stared at like a fucking exhibit in a zoo.'

'Maybe it's time to get out of town for a while. You've got that place in Brooklyn, right? Why not go there for a while? Do some theatre or something. Have a change of scenery.'

'Brooklyn, yes. Theatre no. I don't want that BS right now. I need some privacy. Some me time. Some peace and quiet.'

'Yeah. And no more pills.'

'Never. Ever. Again. In fact no more booze either. I'm done.'

'That's great to hear. Look, why not try your hand at producing? I think you could do it, honey. You know how it works by now.'

'I know that assholes like The Pork Chop get their way by terrorising and raping women. I know how *not* to do it. But d'ya think I could? Go into production?'

'Sure. Why not? You're obviously gonna do what the hell you want anyway.'

'Yeah.'

'So why not make it productive and go into production?'

'I've always dreamt of producing, it's true.'

'Don't dream it. *Be it.* You've got this.'

Juliette pauses, her stomach still heaving with shame.

'The *yoga* thing though…'

'I know,' says Susan, warmly.

'D'ya think one day I'll be able to laugh at that?'

'Who knows. Maybe this was meant to happen. Sometimes matters of seemingly passing concern take on a whole lot of significance when fed through the insane blender of time. Maybe one day you'll see this was just what you needed to turn your life around.'

'Uh huh.'

'You OK, honey?'

'Yeah…'

36
Intimacy

HI BRUCE, I KNOW YOU SAID YOU'D EMAIL AFTER YOU GAVE up drinking but as it's been a couple of months, I guess that didn't happen. It's none of my business whether you stop but all I can say is, it's been a couple of months for me and it's the best thing I've ever done.

Anyway, I just wanted to say that after meeting you, I wasn't able to write that love story. Your character, falling in love with this American journalist and having this mad affair and then it all going tits up. After meeting you in Spain I realised it just isn't you. I couldn't just conjure up some fake love story, I knew I had to write about something real.

So I went ahead and started working on a novel about a writer, struggling to write a novel about Bruce Robinson. I've been writing every day since I got back from Spain and almost finished the first draft.

Anyway, look, if you can be arsed to meet up with me again, it would be brilliant. Let me know if you're in London at all and can spare an hour or something.

And thank you for Spain, it was lovely, meeting you.

Ella x

Bruce walks down the dark hall, out into the afternoon sunlight of the courtyard.

Comet stares at him from the open stable door as he crosses the worn cobbles.

He enters his peaceful, book-lined sanctuary, walks past his desk and looks out at the apple tree in full leaf beyond the window, before talking out loud to himself.

'Be arsed? *Be arsed?* It's not a question of being *arsed* or not being *arsed!* You're lovely! But you're writing a book about me! You could write *anything!* And *I'm married!* You've already got some way into my head and I'm not keen on the fact I appear to be in yours so much that you want to meet up with me again!'

He starts pacing up and down the worn, deep red rug running the length of the barn.

'Why would you even *want* to meet up with me again? Whatever for? What do I have to offer? Precisely *nothing!* I'm a greasy ghost half the time, waxen with anxiety and paranoia. Why would you want *that* in your head?'

He paces up and down then pauses to look out at the tree again. Turning, he crosses to a tall bookcase and peers closely at a row of ancient hardbacks, in varying states of musty preservation.

'I mean, what am I, precisely? A man who's only really fluent before the sun is at its apex and whose destination is a muddy quagmire once the sun declines the day in preference for its setting bed. What is there in me for you to want to *see* exactly? I don't want you to see inside my *head! I* don't like going in there. It's not a place of sanctity, refuge or joy. I'd rather the devastation remain unseen, only glimpsed through the window of my work. See me in my books! That should be enough!'

Bruce crosses to his desk and takes another swig of wine before returning to the bookcase. He removes one of the books, its orange cloth cover worn and tattered. He looks at the gold lettering on the spine. *This Side of Paradise* by F. Scott Fitzgerald.

Opening the book at a random page, he reads out loud.

'They slipped briskly into an intimacy from which they never recovered.'

'Well, that's not us, is it Ella? I mean, I would certainly say we *connected* with one another and I spent a thoroughly pleasant afternoon with you yakking about this and that. Beyond the farthest reaches of small-talk, yes, I'd concur there. But I wouldn't call it *intimacy,* exactly!'

Bruce resumes his slow pacing, still addressing himself and the absent Ella.

'There *was* a level of intimacy. I'm not usually so forthcoming about the vino situation. Not with anyone. And I was very honest with her about that. She kind of...drew that out of me. But there's the thing. She's trying to write a book.' He pauses, looks up and notices a small spider, sitting in a web spanned across two ancient beams of wood above his head. 'A book,' he announces to the spider.

He looks back at his bookshelves and sighs, heavily.

'Writing books is a complete fucking nightmare. An endless curse of obsession, despair and insecurity. You could cut the poor woman some fucking slack if she feels she needs to see you again.'

He continues pacing up and down the barn, pausing before the window again and gazing at the apple tree, trying to keep apace with his mind.

'*No!* Don't ever see someone because you feel sorry for them! *Rule number one!*'

Bruce walks back along the rug, pausing at the door, open to the courtyard. The bright golden light of the late summer afternoon glows beyond the dark, ancient wooden frame of the doorway, illuminating the cobbles, the old stables and the fields beyond.

As if growing tired of the voice to which she has been listening across the yard, Comet lifts her head and looks away from him disinterestedly.

Bruce steps out into the dazzling sunlight, shading his eyes after the cool gloom of the barn.

'But I *don't* feel sorry for her. She's *lovely.* I actually *would* like to see her again.'

He walks over to the Land Rover, peers through the driver's window and contemplates going for a drive.

'But I probably *shouldn't,* all things considered. Too unpredictable. What with 'a', her being a woman who isn't *my wife*, and 'b' my being an alcoholic. Too many opportunities to say or do something unquantifiably *terrible.*'

Comet is staring at him again, her eyes soft and penetrating. He catches her eye. This time, she doesn't look away.

'I know what to do,' he addresses the horse. '*Nothing,* that's what. If in doubt, *don't do anything.* That solves the problem,' he says with finality.

He walks over to the stable and looks the young filly in the eye. Close up, he can smell her warm, earthy, animal fragrance, not an experience to which he is particularly partial.

'I'm not afraid of you,' he says, pointing at her soft, velvety muzzle. She lifts her head and attempts to nibble his finger. 'And I've already said sorry,' he adds, accusingly. 'It's a level playing field, now.'

Comet turns her head away and backs away from the stable door into the dark interior. A last, contemptuous snort emerges from the shadows.

Bruce stares into the dark stable for a few moments then looks up as a taxi appears, its tyres kicking up a cloud of dust. It comes to a halt in the middle of the courtyard and a young woman climbs out of the back. She is slim, tall, with long legs, big blue eyes and long blonde hair loosely tied in a messy bun.

Bruce grins in recognition. Winter, James's girlfriend.

'Hey y'all!' says Winter, grinning and circling a hand in front of her face. She retrieves a small, overnight case from the interior of the cab.

'Hi Winter! How are you?'

'Great to be back in the UK, I'm worn slap out,' she says with a slow, South Carolina drawl.

'You and Lara OK?' she enquires politely as they embrace lightly.

'Splendid! All fine here!' he says, brightly. 'How's LA been?'

'Oh, yanno, awesome, crappy, amazing, cool, uncool,' she shrugs and laughs. 'The usual.'

'Yeah. The first three days in LA are great. Then it all goes to shit, I find,' says Bruce, picking up a large, gnarled piece of dried grapefruit peel from the cobbled courtyard and turning it over in his hand, examining it.

'Yeah. Uh-huh. Yanno,' says Winter glancing at Bruce shyly. 'There's some real *assholes* out there, for sure. It's the whole thing. The oil that runs the engine. Yanno, all the *crap*.'

'Are you still working on that Bowie thing?'

'The glam rock bio-pic? All the Young Dudes? Yeah,' says Winter, pulling a face of disgust.

'Oh dear, things not going well?'

'They would be if Wayne fucking Montana got swallowed up by a black hole.'

Bruce looks at Winter evenly.

'Do I want to ask?'

Winter shrugs. 'He tried to make me watch him take a shower.' She looks at Bruce calmly but with obvious pain in her eyes.

'He fucking what?' says Bruce, appalled.

'Yeah. Well he needs to shower frequently. He smells bad enough to gag a maggot. I don't wanna watch him doin' it though.' She shrugs her shoulders. 'Yanno, a lotta people have no idea what he's really like. What a *monster* he is. They think he's just a great big fat bully. But it's much worse...' she says, tailing off and bending down to pick up her case again.

'I'm really sorry,' says Bruce. 'I had no idea…'

'Whatever. Shit happens. So where's James? I so wanna see him!' She smiles a perfect smile.

'He'll be over in his studio. I think it's finished now. He's been dying to show you. You know where it is, don't you? The old barn the other side of the swimming pool.'

'Sure. He showed it to me before they started work on it. I'll go check him out. Catch ya later, Bruce!' she says, smiling.

Bruce looks after her for a moment then down at the piece of dried grapefruit peel he's been turning over in his fingers.

He notices Comet staring at him from her stable and walks across to her. She lifts her head to sniff at the dried peel in his hand.

'Wayne Montana, eh? Strange man. Always had him pegged as a complete and utter cunt, so no surprise there.' He pauses, then adds, 'What do you think?'

The horse flares her nostrils at him and looks away, whinnying softly, the whites of her eyes showing.

'I'll bring you an apple later, OK?'

Comet looks back at Bruce tenderly through the large lashes fringing her eyes, as though she understands him.

'First proper conversation we've had to date,' says Bruce, smiling with satisfaction, before turning and heading back to the tranquillity of his barn, with Comet looking after him in silence.

James looks up from his keyboard to see a figure silhouetted in the doorway. Winter sashays into the studio, her pale blue chiffon dress shot through with silver stripes, shimmering as she walks. He leaps from his seat and rushes over to her, throwing his arms around her and clasping her close to him.

'Winter!'

'James. I thought I'd just come straight over to see the studio,' she says, burying her face in his neck and breathing in the scent of his skin. She draws away to look at his face and then kisses him deeply on the lips before pulling away and tenderly touching his face. 'It's so lovely to see you. I've fucking missed you so much, man,' she murmurs.

'Me too. Let's not leave it three months next time, eh?'

'Fuck, I've been so busy. This is honestly the first week I've had free since the start of summer!' exclaims Winter.

She looks around the studio, now kitted out with a huge mixing desk, sound booth and synths, but still with an aroma of sawdust and wood shavings.

'It looks amazing! That guy Tom built all this?'

'Yeah,' says James, standing up. 'Wanna meet him? He's out the back, having a piss.'

'I totally needed to know that,' says Winter, rolling her eyes.

'Tom! Come and meet Winter!' James yells through the open door towards the field round the back of the studio. A muffled shout drifts in by way of response.

After a few moments, Tom appears in the doorway. He stops as he sees Winter standing in the middle of the studio, one hand on her hip, looking at him with her head tilted slightly, smiling.

'Hi, Winter. Pleased to meet you,' he says, sticking a hand out to shake hers and grinning at her with his most charming smile.

Wow. That, I have to fuck.

He catches her eye and holds her gaze.

Winter smiles back, all glowing Californian tan and white teeth. 'Great job you've done with the studio, I love it,' she says, looking away from his steady gaze.

'Cheers. Yeah, I'm pretty pleased with it.'

'James!' Lara's voice sounds from the direction of the house.

'Be right back,' James says to Tom and Winter as he heads out of the door.

Tom looks at Winter.

'So, James says you live in LA? Which part?'

'Los Feliz.'

'Oh, Los Feliz, cool.'

'D'you know it?'

'Yeah sure. Stayed there loads of times. I've gotta girlfriend over there. Shannon. She's, you know, a bit crazy.'

'Uh huh. Crazy how?'

'She's kind of possessive. It's been dragging on for ages. I should end it, really.'

'Right.'

'But there's this other girl in London, Flip.'

'Flip?'

'Yeah. Philippa. Everyone calls her Flip.'

'Uh huh,'

'They're models. Fucking gorgeous, both of them. At the same agency. Shannon at the LA branch and Flip the London branch. And Shannon hates Flip. And Flip hates Shannon. They kind of, hate each other. You know, it's kind of awkward.'

'So you've got, what, a double girlfriend kinda setup?'

'Yeah. Kind of. Not really. Just a bit, like awkward at the moment. I'm a bit of a ladies' man. It makes the women crazy. Hating on each other, you know? Proper mess.'

Winter stares at Tom in disbelief.

A ladies' man?

'Oh honey, bless your heart. A ladies' man. OK. So, watch out ladies, yeah? Here comes Tom!' she says, repressing an urge to burst out laughing.

'It can get messy,' says Tom, earnestly.

What a dumb ass. I thought I'd seen it all. He thinks the sun comes up just to hear him crow.

'Okaaaay. So, you, like, don't believe in love, kinda thing?'

'Oh yeah. Love. I'm in love.'

Winter picks up an apple from a bowl of fruit on the table and bites into it, still gazing coolly at Tom.

'James would never put fruit on the table. Lara's done this,' she laughs. 'I really love Lara. She's *wonderful*.'

Tom stares at Winter but says nothing.

'So,' Winter asks casually, 'Which one of them are you in love with, then?'

'All…I mean both of them. I'm in love with both of them. That's the problem. I think you can be in love with several women at the same time, only in different ways.'

'OK,' says Winter, looking at Tom curiously. 'Doesn't work for me personally, but if that's your jam, then cool. I'm into loving one guy at a time,' she adds with a firm smile.

'Hey, I'm actually in LA next week. To end it with Shannon. Face to face, you know. She deserves that much. When are you back out there?'

'Next week.'

'Cool. We could hook up for a coffee or something if you like?'

'Sure! If the good lord's willin' and the creek don't rise I'm sure we can do that. I'll check our schedule with James.'

'James is going?'

'Yeah, didn't he tell you?'

'Yeah he probably did actually.' Tom looks at Winter and shrugs. 'I'll see how things pan out. I'm gonna be really busy.'

'Sure thing. Stay in touch,' trills Winter airily. Turning, she leaves the studio for the sunlit field, her dress swishing as she walks. Tom watches her moving gracefully through the long grass towards the house.

Totally wasted on James. So fucking hot.

Before he leaves, Tom walks out to the pool to look for Lara in order to say goodbye. The sun is just setting behind the trees, spreading a burnished golden haze across the fields.

He finds Lara standing in the shadows, looking down into the pool, glass of wine in hand.

'Hi, Lara,' says Tom, stopping to stand beside her.

'Hi,' says Lara warmly, looking up at him and smiling. She takes a sip of wine. Already it's forming a sticky web around her mind. 'I only just got back from Harrogate. Did you bring the speakers over, then?'

'Yeah. Just fitted them. They sound great.'

'So it's finished now? The studio?'

'Yeah, that's it now. Oh, I met Winter, James's girlfriend.'

'Oh, she's here already? Yes, she's lovely, isn't she?'

'Aye, nice lass,' says Tom, evasively, looking up at the sunlit trees.

'So…I guess…you won't be coming round here again any time soon, then?' asks Lara.

'Well no, I guess not. Not now the studio's finished.' Tom looks at Lara intently, as though waiting for some kind of response.

Lara takes a sip of wine and thinks for a minute, not knowing what to say. She looks down at the calm water and then back at Tom.

'Yeah.'

Tom smiles, trying to sound casual. 'I suppose, to be thorough, I should pop over again in a couple of weeks when I get back from LA. Just to check everything out.'

'You're going to LA?' Lara looks at him inquisitively.

'Yeah. Got a few meetings lined up. Got some business to attend to,' says Tom a little furtively, the slight widening of his eyes giving away his lie.

'Ah. I see. So you'll be coming back here, then? After attending to your business in LA?'

'Well, I could do. Probably should, actually. You could show me how your sculpture's coming on. We'd have more time, then…' he says, looking into her eyes. Once again, he holds her gaze too long.

'Right,' says Lara, nervously taking another sip of wine. 'Look, Tom. I've just got to say…' Lara takes a deep breath and looks into the distance to avoid his gaze. 'You know. I'm married.' She glances quickly back at him before looking away again.

'Yeah. I know,' says Tom, still looking at her earnestly.

'And I don't do affairs or anything.'

'Yeah. Of course…' he says, on guard now, staring at her.

'And to be honest, you know, you're very *young*. I mean, I don't mean that as an insult. You can't help being the age you are. But young men…they…they don't understand women. They think they do. But they don't. They haven't a clue how to treat a woman. They… shag around. It's just…it's not personal…it's just what they do at your age.' She bites her lip, choosing her words carefully. 'So, as an older woman, getting involved with a younger man is just asking for trouble.'

Tom continues to look at her intently. Lara glances away as she's talking to avoid his eyes.

'I'm just saying that it's not the fact I'm *married* that's the issue, here. I mean, if I were single, nothing would happen either. That's all I'm saying. But it's not that I don't like you. I do.'

Tom's face clouds over momentarily with a flash of childlike anger which he immediately tries to suppress.

'Nothing would happen? Between *us*, you mean?' he asks, defensively.

'Yeah,' says Lara, sadly, glancing over at him. 'I'm just saying, there's obviously some kind of…feeling there.' She shrugs her shoulders. 'The way we've been talking. You know, the way you look at me and everything. And I'm just trying to be honest and clear the air.'

'I've banged plenty of older women,' blurts out Tom.

Lara stares at him, incredulous, trying not to laugh.

'You've *banged plenty of older women?*'

'Yeah.' He nods and tries to look nonchalant.

'Right. I'm sure you have,' she says, looking at him with a mixture of astonishment and repressed mirth.

'So. You fancy me, then?' asks Tom, his eyes widening with deliberately faked incredulity.

'I've tried to explain. You're obviously attractive. But I'm married. And you're too young. Nothing, in a million years, is ever going to happen between us.'

Tom stares at her.

'But you wanna bang me. Yeah well, I had no idea,' he says, flatly. 'I thought we were just mates, you know. And you're James's Mum. Like, James's Mum who was becoming a mate, kind of thing.'

Lara can feel the sky slowly descending upon her and crushing her with anxiety.

Just walk away Lara. Walk back to the house. Now. Do not give him a chance to say another word.

'I don't want to hurt your feelings or anything,' says Tom, archly. 'But you've totally misread the situation. Sorry, Lara, I'm like this with everyone. This is just me. I'm just very at ease with women,' he adds, shrugging his shoulders, still looking at Lara intently. 'I can't help it, it's just the way I am. Sorry you've misinterpreted that and got the wrong end of the stick. Wishful thinking on your part, maybe. But I've only ever thought of you as a *mate*.' He stares at her, challengingly.

Lara silently, invisibly, takes a deep breath. She glances at Tom and in that split second suddenly sees him completely. Where she thought she had been talking to an attentive, mature man, she realises she is now faced with a sulky, immature boy, whose arrogance and clear-eyed coldness are breathtaking.

Tom continues to stare at her, defiantly, hoping through his wounded pride that his defensive barbs have met their mark.

Lara raises her chin slightly and looks at him evenly.

'I'd better crack on in the studio. Bye, Tom,' she says quietly, and turning, walks away from the swimming pool, leaving him standing alone, watching her retreat towards the house.

37
Micky's harem

JOLTING HIM OUT OF HIS AFTERNOON NAP, THE housekeeper appears on the roof terrace in front of Micky, bearing a tray with a silver pot of mint tea alongside an array of jewel-coloured glasses engraved in gold.

'Mr Gary is here, Sir.'

'About fucking time!' Micky jumps up from his cushions and strides across the terrace where Gary appears at the top of the spiral staircase, wiping sweat from his brow with a handkerchief.

'Hey buddy! You made it!' says Micky, grinning.

'You owe me one Micky boy,' says Gary in a thick Australian accent. 'I was meant to be on me way to fuckin' Alaska not the edge of the fuckin' Sahara, mate. Fuck's sake.'

'Get your ass over here in the shade,' says Micky, ushering Gary to the tented seating area in the corner of the terrace.

They sit facing one another as the housekeeper pours them tea.

'It's like The Mad Hatter's fuckin' Tea Party, ain't it?' says Gary with a guffaw, loosening the collar of his shirt. 'Could ya bring me a cold one instead of the tea?' he addresses the housekeeper.

'A beer. Could ya bring us a couple of cold beers?' explains Micky. 'Do you wanna go and change into something more comfortable, first Gary?'

'Nah I'm fine. Get down to business, first, then I'll get the safari shorts on later and we can share a few tinnies. So,' he says, rubbing his hands. 'You wanna buy a bunch of prossies. That right?'

'I want to liberate them from their suffering, Gary,' says Micky, earnestly.

'Yer not planning to cop a root with all of 'em at once, then? I know what you're like when you get going Micky, I mean good on ya, if I was a fuckin' Hollywood star I'd do the same. I don't blame ya mate.'

'Yeah well, I've had some time to think, over here, since splitting with Juliette.' Micky looks sadly at the silver teapot in front of him and pours himself a glass of cold mint tea whilst he awaits the beers. 'Have you heard about her charity work?'

'Can't say I have.'

'She's representing this organisation, LongaVita, she's trying to wipe out poverty or something, I dunno.'

'Fair dinkum,' says Gary, nodding.

'And I just thought...'

'That you could beat her at her own game?'

'Well, no, not quite.' Micky takes a deep breath. 'I had a bit of a party here last week. And I woke up alone. I didn't feel good. I mean, everything had been cleared up.'

'Whadaya mean, cleared up? You chucked a few pizzas on the pavement?'

'I didn't *barf* Gary. I can handle my *booze.* I mean, the girls were gone, everything was quiet. The birds were twittering outside in the trees, yanno, it was like the whole fucking party had never happened. And I just felt like such a douche. There was this girl, Katie.

Katya, actually. The one that told me they'd had had their passports confiscated, you know, like I told you on the phone. And I couldn't stop thinking about her.'

'What, you got the hots for her?'

'No way, it's not like that. And there was another girl. I didn't choose her, actually. I thought five was enough.'

'Yer a greedy bugger, ya cunt,' says Gary laughing.

'Anyway, she looked so sad, when I didn't choose her. And I remember I said to her "Have a great life!" And it's like, come back to haunt me, kind of thing. What a jerk.'

'So you've been on a massive downer, then.'

'Yeah, kind of. I just got to thinking what a shit life she's having. I mean, these are not your high-class hookers I'm used to ordering. These are sex slaves, Gary.'

'And you wanna free 'em from their slavery. I get it, Micky. Fair play to you, mate.'

'So, did you broach it with that Nicky woman yet?'

'I fuckin' did. She said eighty thou a piece and I knocked her down to a round fifty.'

'I guess I don't wanna ask how you bargained that one.'

'You don't, mate, that's right.'

'So it's fifty thousand dollars? Per girl?'

'Yeah. Seems like a lot to pay for a fuckin' sheila, but...'

'It's worth it. So there's eleven of them. Half a million bucks. OK.'

'And the passports on top of course. And then there's what we're gonna do with 'em, you thought about that? Are you gonna just hand 'em the passports and wish 'em on their merry way? They'll just fuck off back to fuckin' Russia, mate.'

'Why don't we ask them? Maybe we can help 'em get to where they want?'

'OK. Well, I'll give Nicky another ring, we'll get the girls over here tomorrow, and in the meantime, let's grab a few tinnies and get down the fuckin' beach, yeah? You got any thongs?'

At nightfall the next day, the same black jeep as the week before pulls up outside Micky's riad, followed by several black SUVs.

Nicky gets out of the jeep and beckons to the drivers. The same girls pile gingerly out of the cars. They're all wearing brand new sports casuals - Nike, Rab, Adidas and North Face.

Gary strides over to Nicky and slaps her on the back, making her almost jump out of her skin.

'Nice doin' business with ya'.'

He looks at the girls suspiciously, counting them in his mind.

'Hold on, there's only ten of 'em. We paid for eleven.'

'Unfortunately, one of them is not available. We have already issued refund of fifty thousand dollars.'

'What do you mean, she's not available?' asks Gary, suspiciously.

'No longer available,' says Nicky, firmly, staring into Gary's eyes.

'Hope we don't need to send any of the others back for a fuckin' refund,' says Gary, staring back at her.

He turns his back and ushers the girls into the riad.

'Alright, ladies, follow me.'

Katya is the first to emerge at the top of the stone steps, followed by the other girls. Micky stands up when he sees her. She runs over to him, grinning.

'Micky!' She throws her arms around him. 'Is it true? Are we going to be free, now? I cannot believe it!'

The girl with the raven hair and alabaster skin walks up behind her.

'Thank you, Micky. This is more than we could ever dream about.'

The other girls file up to Micky and hug him, one after the other.

'Streuth, it's like the fucking *Godfather*!' laughs Gary.

'Well, I couldn't have done it without you,' says Micky.

'I didn't come over here to fuck spiders, ya cunt, I came over here to get the fuckin' job done.'

Micky laughs.

'So do you all speak English?' he asks of the girls.

'We all understand. Some of us speak better than others,' says Katya.

'OK Katya, so here's the deal. Gary's gonna take your passport photos, you're gonna rest up here for a few days and then we're gonna give you your new passports. Then it's up to you where you go.'

'America!' says Katya, grinning.

'Hollywood,' says the girl with the raven hair and alabaster skin.

'What's your name, baby?' asks Micky.

'Oksana.'

'Nice to meet you, Oksana. Why don't you all tell me and Gary here, what your names are? Let's get acquainted,' says Micky, addressing the girls in unison.

'Acquainted? You mean...another party?' asks Katya.

'No, honey. No more parties. Well, not that sort, anyhow.'

'So, you wanna go to America?' asks Gary, looking at the girls.

'Yes!' 'America' 'Yes, would be good,' they all agree.

'You sure?' says Micky 'With a ludicrous tangerine installed in the White House?' he adds, laughing.

'He will be gone soon. But we will stay,' says Katya, with determination.

'All that's shiny isn't gold, girls,' says Gary. 'But if you wanna give it a go, we can get you all on the plane over there.'

'Yup. Fix 'em up with my agent, Gary. Get 'em all some film work and somewhere to live.'

Katya smiles at Micky. 'I can't believe you are doing this for us. Why are you doing this? Is this trick? Are we going back to sex trade again?'

'Well, let's put it this way. We'll set you up over there, OK? But you gotta put the legwork in. Download fuckin' Duolingo. Study

English. Go to auditions. It's hard fuckin' work. And if anyone tells you you gotta fuck 'em to get a part, you tell 'em to go fuck 'emselves and walk out. You'll pick it up, honey.'

'LA is full of bastards and mongrels, girls. Just like anywhere else. But you got us on your side. Dunno how good that's gonna be for you. Couple of drongos like us. But there ya go,' says Gary.

'What is it? Drongo?' asks Katya.

'Stupid people. In this case who are trying maybe to educate themselves a little bit. Anyway enough of that soft shit. We need to get you all some thongs and get down on that fuckin' beach!'

'I have thong,' says Katya, smiling.

'He means flip flops. He's from Australia. They talk weird.'

'In Russia we also have many weird words. We teach you,' says Katya, laughing.

'Ten passports and ten pairs of fuckin' thongs, Gary.'

'No worries.'

38
CREPUSCULAR

ELLA SITS AT A SMALL WOODEN PATIO TABLE, SHADED by a red parasol, scrolling through her phone.

Zack pokes his head through the patio doors. 'I'm off out.'

'Where?' she asks, disinterestedly.

'The Alehouse. Got the press in tonight.'

'I thought that was tomorrow?'

'Change of plan.'

'So, you're not arsed whether I come or not, then?'

'It'll be boring. You wouldn't enjoy it. All those journos and Instagram influencers. They're all cunts.'

'It'd be nice to be asked.'

'It's an industry do, babes. Really, Ella, you'd be bored shitless.'

Ella stands up and adjusts the parasol slightly now that the sun has moved lower in the sky. She stares at Zack.

He's fucking someone. I knew it.

'You mean, you've got a girl coming. Or something.'

Zack stares back at her and sniffs, before wiping a tiny white speck from his right nostril with his forefinger.

'Don't be ridiculous. This is fucking *work*, tonight, babe. *Graft*.'

'Bye then,' she replies, rolling her eyes.

Zack retreats from the patio and back into the house. A few seconds later, Ella hears the front door slam shut and then, once more, the house falls into silence.

She sits at the table and opens Instagram. The page for The Shoreditch Alehouse is teeming with glossy, upbeat, edgy photos of craft beer pumps, latte art and chalkboard menus. All posted by a user called Flip. Ella clicks on her profile.

It's her. 'Flip.' The model. Friend of Benjy's, according to Zack. What's she doing taking promo shots for The Alehouse? You know what? I don't fucking care. Leave them to it, Ella. Focus on your own stuff.

She searches Instagram for posts with the hashtag #brucerobinson. The most recent one is a photo of Bruce and another bloke with glasses, both standing at a bar, grinning. The description says 'Great meeting up with #brucerobinson @thenightjar last night!' The photo has been posted by @markmeadows of Weft Films and is geotagged as Hoxton, London.

Right round the corner. A stone's throw away, yet a million miles. We could have met up for a drink. He was almost certainly too busy having the important meeting with Mark Meadows of Weft Films though. Oh God. He'll probably never even reply to my email.

Ella walks over to the pond and stares down at the fish. Little streaks of golden light, flitting through the dark water, completely unaware of her world above them.

'Hello fish.'

They ignore her. She hears Venus, one of the two remaining hens after the fox attack, giving her singular 'I've laid an egg' call. Ella walks over to the chicken run where she sits on a bench in the dappled sunlight as the hens mill around her feet, pecking at the ground.

Her phone bleeps with an email notification. Bruce. Her stomach jolts with excitement.

sorry not to reply - been in Los A for a few weeks and had no email equipment available, plus i only look at this fucking thing once a week anyway. good to meet you in spania, hope all going well with book and that ink isn't acidic BR x

Ella stares at the words for a minute.

'Acidic? *Acidic? I adore you!'* she says out loud, before silently reading the email again, word by word. She looks at the chickens, who both look back up at her, expectantly.

He doesn't want to see me again. It's taken him weeks to even answer my email. He probably hated me. I'm not intelligent enough for him. He probably uses words like 'crepuscular', not only in his work, but in his everyday life as well. I'd never even heard the word 'crepuscular' until yesterday. He probably walks around his house talking to himself in Latin. And he doesn't drink boxes of plonk from Aldi like I used to. He drinks fine wines, almost certainly curated in a musty, vaulted cellar. He's cultured and intellectual. And I'm not. I do have to email him back though. But I've got to be honest. Honesty is the best policy. In fact, I should put it in a letter! He hates emails!

The chickens look at Ella, making happy, contented noises.

'See you later, girls,' she says, before walking back to the house. She rummages in an old wooden cupboard where she fishes out a sheaf of hand-made writing paper the colour of pale peppermints. She takes her favourite, black, glossy book signing pen, sits at her writing desk next to the French windows and starts to write, the pen audibly scratching as the ink flows carefully over the textured paper, the whole process feeling unfamiliar, so long it is since she last wrote a letter.

Dear Bruce,

Thank you for your email. I know you hate emails so I thought I'd write you a letter instead - I hope you're able to decipher my fairly rubbish handwriting.

Yes, everything is going well with the book. The writing has been pouring out of me like blood from an artery. Meeting you by chance in the glass museum was a huge inspiration for me.

And of course the book won't be acidic. I have nothing but respect for you and this novel is coming from a place of love. I do want it to be real though. So I hope we can meet up again. I feel like I need more time taking in the essential youness of you. Pheromones can't be communicated through either emails or letters.

Well, the light is becoming crepuscular so I will leave you here.

Bonum nocte, Ella x

Ella stares at the letter for a few moments then folds it in half and carefully places it in an envelope, copying the address Bruce gave her in Spain.

That's it. He'll think I'm a fucking nutjob now and I'll never hear from him again - this letter will almost certainly put a full stop to all communications between us.

Her hand slips as she's placing the stamp so that it ends up attached to the envelope at a sad little lopsided angle.

I am a fucking idiot.

She puts the envelope in her jacket pocket and leaves the house. The sun has set and darkness is falling. She can sense autumn in the evening air with its hint of a chill. She walks briskly to the post box down the road then stands, staring at its gaping slot, waiting to swallow up her letter. The snail-mail equivalent of the 'send' button. Once posted, she will never be able to retrieve it. But, for once, the ever-critical inner voice is silent.

It doesn't matter what Bruce thinks, Ella. Or Zack, whose opinion has completely ceased to matter. But then, it doesn't matter what anyone thinks, does it? You don't want to be lying on your death bed thinking 'My only regret is that I wish I'd given more of a shit what other people thought of me.' You're coming from a good place. Post it.

She slips the envelope into the post box, pulls the collar of her jacket up around her neck and begins walking back home.

❧❧❧

The golden September sun is comfortingly warm by early afternoon, illuminating the bucolic idyll of the dusty courtyard with rich honey tones and soft shadows.

Lara descends the stone steps to the musty chill of the cellar and selects a bottle of Château de Camensac for Sunday lunch. As she walks back up from the cellar she feels the air around her gradually becoming warmer with each step. She emerges into the kitchen and hears Bruce's voice, talking on the phone.

'I'm really not comfortable about this, Wayne. Look, somebody's waiting to talk to me. I've gotta go.' He hangs up then notices Lara.

'About time you told that heinous ogre to fuck off.'

'He just wouldn't take no for an answer. The man is a law unto himself.'

'After what Winter told us, the man is a complete and utter cunt and I don't want him ringing this house.'

'He won't ring again,' says Bruce, gently, smiling.

Lara places the bottle of wine on the kitchen table. 'Has the washing machine finished?'

'Um, I'm not sure.'

She walks over and inspects the machine which is still and silent. She puts the washing in a large wicker basket and takes it outside to hang on the line.

Bruce stands by the table, opens the bottle of wine, pours himself a glass and begins flicking through his copy of *The Observer.*

Lara takes the empty basket upstairs. She picks up a pair of underpants from the bathroom rug and places them in the basket, followed by the contents of the laundry hamper in the main bedroom, then returns downstairs.

She walks out of the house and across the courtyard to Bruce's barn and enters, casting a cursory glance around for items of discarded clothing for the next wash.

A handwritten letter on a pile of books next to his typewriter catches her eye.

This must be the letter he told me about, from that author, Ella.

Lara stares down at it, reading out loud the careful script on the pale green, textured paper.

'And of course the book won't be acidic. I have nothing but respect for you and this novel is coming from a place of love…'

She rolls her eyes slightly and shakes her head with an indulgent smile, then picks up one of Bruce's faded denim shirts from the armchair, drops it in the washing basket and walks out of the barn and across the courtyard.

As she heads back towards the house, she notices Bruce, standing at the stable door, glass of wine in hand, talking to Comet, the horse he supposedly has no interest in.

'I know you hate me. You can't hide it, you know,' Bruce accuses, looking at Comet's warm, velvety muzzle.

Maybe I should have a go at stroking it. Nope. Probably not.

'*She* loves me, the author, she wants our fucking pheromones to mingle over a mochaccino latte or something or other,' he continues, casting a casual glance at Comet as she stares back at him enigmatically with her brown eyes.

'Look. I am genuinely sorry about the off-licence incident. I really am genuinely remorseful. It wasn't the real me. I had no idea that trailer was attached. Even less that you were fucking *in it.* Sorry. *OK?* And sorry about not bringing you that apple. Are we *quits* now?'

Comet snorts at him, looks away and stares into the middle distance.

'She said "I want more time to take in the youness of you." What do you think about *that,* then? Not very often I get that said to me, I have to say.'

The horse continues to ignore him and looks down at two chickens who have wandered over, hoping for food.

'Not really bothered, are you?'

Comet's eyes widen and the whites show as she looks sideways at him, suspiciously.

'The "youness of you". What does that even *mean?* What the fuck is my "*meness*"? The essential distilled spirit of my being? Even *I* don't have a fucking clue what that is.'

Comet looks at him guardedly. Bruce takes a risk and sticks out his hand towards her muzzle. She shies away. Bruce drops his hand. 'You're never going to forgive me, are you, you brute?'

Lara appears at the front door of the house and calls over.

'Lunch is in about half an hour, darling. Richard's on the phone. Do you want to take it in the barn? I'm catching up with *Woman's Hour.*'

Casting a last glance at Comet, Bruce turns and walks into his barn. He picks up the phone and hears the extension from the kitchen click off as Lara hangs up.

'Bruce! How's it going?'

'I was just outside, having a discussion with one of the horses.'

'I thought you hated them?'

'I do.'

'Well why are you talking to them, then?'

'I dunno. They make more sense than most of the people I speak to. I'm starting to understand why Lara's so crazy about the bloody things.'

'Good God, she'll have you kitted out in riding boots and jodhpurs in no time,' laughs Richard.

'I don't think she will.'

'I don't think she will, either,' Richard continues to laugh at the image in his head. 'So how was London?'

'Great. Had a meeting with Mark Meadows.'

'Weft?'

'Yeah.'

'How'd it go?

'Not sure. They're interested in making *Penman*.'

'Really? That's *fantastic* news, Bruce! *Marvellous!* About time *Penman* made it to the screen!'

'Yeah, well, just the perennial stumbling block of finance in the way apparently.'

'The usual. Well, you know I think that's one of your best works to date.'

'Even though you're not in it,' says Bruce, laughing.

Richard laughs along with him.

'Actually, that reminds me,' says Bruce. 'That author, Ella. She told me she's putting *you* in her book.'

'*Me?* Really?'

'Apparently so.'

'She only met me for five minutes. She knows nothing about me!' Richard pauses. 'How big's my part?'

'Well, she hasn't discussed the ins and outs. But it's a cameo, apparently.'

'A cameo? So, a walk on part.'

'That's the general idea. She asked me if she could have your email address actually. Said she doesn't want to contact you through your fragrance Instagram. Whatever that is.'

'Well quite. I have enough perfume groupies as it is. *Don't* give her my email. I'm too busy for emails. And too busy to read her book when it comes out.'

'Well you can download it on one of those Kindle devices and skip ahead to the bits about you to save you reading the whole thing,' says Bruce, tartly.

'I would *never* do that to a book!' replies Richard, outraged.

'Yes you would.' Bruce laughs, followed by a loud exclamation and a thumping sound, after which the phone goes silent.

'Bruce. Are you alright?'

A series of nondescript muffled noises follows, before Bruce comes on the line again. 'Richard? You still there?'

'Of course. What happened?'

'Oh, nothing. Just tripped over this fucking piece of carpet. It keeps coming up at the edges. I keep meaning to stick it down.'

'OK. Well, take it easy, OK?'

'I'm fine.'

'Look, I know we have an unspoken *gentleman's agreement* that we don't discuss your…you know…the vin rouge…but I do worry about you sometimes.'

'I'm fine. Never been better. Hardly drinking anything now, not since that silly article in *The Gazette* when I was in Spain. Can't even go for a few drinks without it ending up in the fucking press. *It's ridiculous.* Anyway, Ella. I nearly forgot. She wrote me a letter.'

'*A letter?*'

'Yeah. An actual letter. Sent through the post.'

'*No-one* writes letters any more. What's up with her?'

'I thought it was quite touching, actually.'

'What did it say?'

'She said she wanted to meet up again. So that she could soak up my pheromones, as she put it.'

'She fucking *what?*'

'Yeah.'

'Is she batshit *crazy?* I *warned* you!'

'She also said "I want time to take in the youness of you," or something.'

'*Jesus H fucking Christ* Bruce. That's a fucking *love letter!* The woman is half in love with you!'

'She's not in love. I understand totally where she's coming from. She's writing a fucking book. You get obsessed. *I* got obsessed. With that cunt Jack. Writing the Ripper book. Ate him, slept him, dreamt him. My mind a swarm of nightmares, day and night for fucking years on end. It's what happens.'

'Well she'd better not fucking fall in love with *me*. I'm spoken for!'

Bruce laughs. 'How is Maria, anyway?'

'In Seville. Doing a photoshoot for her Instagram with Antonio Banderas.'

'Lovely.'

'She works too hard. Everything's got to be Instashootable or whatever. She can't even eat a plate of fucking tapas without photographing it. She was asking after you the other day, actually. Sends her love.'

'Lovely girl. She really is, Richard. I liked her a lot.'

'She's a handful and a liability but yes, I like her a lot, too. Getting more and more fond of her, actually,' says Richard, grudgingly. 'Anyway, it was just a quick call. My cab's coming. Talk soon old boy.'

'No doubt we will. Take care, Richard.'

'You too. Bye for now. Bye.'

'Bye.'

'Bye. Byebyebye.'

The heat of the day has evaporated by early evening, and a refreshing chill has descended on the fields around the house.

Bruce refills his glass and walks across the courtyard and field to the swimming pool.

He stands, staring at the surface of the water, which gently ripples in the breeze. It looks cold and slightly eerie in the diffuse evening light, as though a gurgling phantom might emerge from its pellucid depths.

Lara crosses the courtyard and heads round the back of the stables to fetch more chicken feed. She can see Bruce in the distance, peering down into the water. A surge of protective love rises up inside her.

She puts her hands into her jacket pockets and finds a wine cork which she must have absent-mindedly picked up from the kitchen table. She turns it over gently in her fingers as she silently watches her husband.

Deciding not to disturb his thoughts, she picks up a bag of chicken feed and walks back to the courtyard where she tops up the chicken feeders. Returning to the house she notices an opened bottle of wine on the kitchen table. She pours herself a small glass and takes it to her studio.

Outside, darkness has almost descended and the light of a brilliant silver moon streams through the skylight, a soft spotlight illuminating *The Dreamer*, which stands finished on a plinth in the centre of the room.

The curves of the child's form gleam dully in the moonlight, the sad stone eyes expressing a fathomless pain.

Lara takes a sip of wine and feels the exhilarating warmth gently spreading through her body.

39
Bermondsey Belle

I HOPE YOU DON'T MIND MY CONTACTING YOU OUT OF the blue. I saw you at the ICA a couple of months back and was knocked out by your work. I wondered if you fancied performing at my spoken word night, West End Lights. We're at the Soho Theatre second Tuesday of every month. Let me know if you're interested.

Best Wishes

Felix Glebe.

'Fuck! Felix Glebe's emailed me!'

'And?' says Zack, coldly.

'He saw me at the ICA! He was in the audience! Mind you I don't know what he looks like, I wouldn't have recognised him anyway.'

'You were arseholed, you wouldn't have noticed if Ryan fucking Gosling fell through the ceiling,' says Zack through a mouth full of food as he lays stretched out on the sofa, flicking between channels.

'God, I love his work. Felix. He's *amazing*.'

'Benjy knows him. Told me the bloke's a complete dick.'

'Benjy, that arbiter of good taste.'

'You're so fucking cynical, Ella.'

I wonder what he looks like? Earnest, I imagine. I mean his poetry's teeming with darkness and death.

Ella opens Instagram and searches for Felix Glebe.

One result. Felix Glebe, Poet. Bingo.

She clicks on his profile.

Oh shit, he's gorgeous. Wasn't expecting that. He's got a thousand yard stare. I wonder how he got that? What's he been through? Fascinating.

She looks up from her phone, stares at Zack pointedly then replies to the email.

Hi Felix,

I'd love to perform at WEL, heard great things about it. WhatsApp me if you want, my number is 077 9003 7539,

Cheers,

Ella.

ps I love your work too.

'You've not told him you'll do it, have you?' asks Zack.

'Yeah. Maybe you'll be free this time to actually come and see me perform.'

'If we haven't got a gig. So is he on Insta?' says Zack, wiping tomato sauce from his chin then yawning.

'Dunno. I'll have to check.'

'I would. He's probably a complete perv. Seen what a hot mess you are when you're performing wankered and figured he'll clean up after the gig.'

'Cheers. Not a chance he actually *liked my work*, of course.'

'Those nerdy poet types are all total flakes. If they had anything about them, they'd grow some balls and get a fucking guitar.'

'Like you, you mean.'

'They dunno what they're missing. That crescendo of bliss from the perfect fucking guitar solo. They'll never realise that of course, 'cause they're too busy fannying around on fucking hillsides, staring at the fucking clouds, scribbling their neuroses on scraps of paper then regurgitating it as fucking so-called *poetry.*'

Zack sniffs and wipes his nose, which is running slightly.

Ella gives him a withering look then picks up her phone which has just pinged with a message.

Great. How about meeting up at the Bermondsey Belle for a drink tomorrow to discuss, are you free at 7pm? F.

Sure. Well, I don't drink. But a pub's fine. And so is 7pm tomorrow. E.

I don't drink either. Nice garden though. See you there. Fx.

Great. Ex.

She looks out of the window and smiles to herself with satisfaction.

'You're not messaging him, are you? That poet?'

'The scribbling neurotic? Yeah. I'm meeting him tomorrow to discuss performing at WEL.'

'Oh I see, "WEL" now, is it?'

'You know what I mean.'

'Where are you meeting him?'

'The Bermondsey Belle.'

'Shit pub. Beer's warm.'

'No it isn't, Zack.'

'How would you know, you don't drink! And you never drank beer anyway, you were too busy floating your eyeballs in fucking Prosecco.'

'Well I don't now, do I? And nor, for that matter, does Felix. Times are changing,'

'Why aren't you meeting him at The Alehouse? We do soft drinks,' asks Zack accusingly.

'Because Felix suggested The Belle. And it's got a nice garden.'

'*We've* got a nice garden! Me and Benjy fucking *built it.* You should be supporting our new venture, not taking your custom to sub-par rival establishments like *The Belle* for fuck's sake!'

'Look Zack, it's organised now. What do you want me to do, message him and say we can't meet at The Belle because my boyfriend doesn't want us to? Don't be so fucking ridiculous. Grow up.'

'You see, you're doing what you always do, Ella.' Zack adopts a whiny, patronising tone. 'You're losing focus. Diversifying. You're meant to be writing this novel, and now you're wasting your time chasing some fucking poetry dream, meeting up with this complete loser. You're distracted. You're never going to be successful without focus.'

She turns to stare at him.

'What is success, Zack? Being a best-selling author? Being a world-acclaimed poet? A rock-star with groupies dangling their tongues at your crotch?'

Zack smirks involuntarily. 'Well with Benjy it's tongues *and* titties.'

'"Titties"? You are fucking disgusting.'

'Just sayin''

'Is that *really* your idea of success? *Honestly?* Success is happiness, Zack. And you get that by working hard, living healthily and treating people with respect. It's not rocket science.'

Zack stares at Ella, then stands up and yawns, stretching his arms above his head.

'I preferred you when you were a pisshead. You're boring sober. I'm off out.'

She stands up to face him.

'What, to meet *Flip?*'

Zack's face clouds with barely repressed fury.

'Don't tar *me* with *that* brush! Just because you're sniffing round this dickhead poet doesn't mean that Flip and I have anything other than a professional working relationship.'

'My arse. You're fucking her.'

'Think what you want. You're being hysterical and paranoid. I'm going.'

'Well I'd like you to take all your stuff with you. This relationship's run its course. You're an abusive wanker, Zack. I'm done.'

Zack glares at her.

'*I'm* abusive? *You're* abusive.' He jabs a finger at her.

'I've never done anything other than be supportive to you! The very fact you've been living rent free in my home in fucking Shoreditch *is* supportive! How the *fuck* am I abusive?'

Zack leans his face closer to Ella's and sneers 'You're *boring. That's* fucking abusive. It's abusive to my *mental fucking health.*'

'Get out. You can pick your stuff up another time. And I want my keys back.'

'You'll get your keys back when I've picked up my things,' says Zack, coldly, glaring at Ella. 'You're a cunt. You know that, right?'

'If you don't hand the keys to *my home* back to me *right now*, you will seriously regret it, Zack. I will carefully pack all your things up then drop them off at The Alehouse tomorrow. Give me the keys,' she says, quietly.

Zack rummages in his jacket pocket, pulls out his keys and throws them at Ella. They hit her in the cheek then fall on the tiled hall floor with a clatter. He walks out of the door, slamming it loudly behind him. Ella puts her hand up to her face and pulls it away. Her fingers are covered in blood. She goes to the bathroom, cleans the minor wound and applies a couple of steristrips. She looks at herself in the mirror.

Cunt, cunt and cunt.

Back in the lounge, Ella looks out through the open French windows into the back garden. The air is becoming crisp and cool with the approach of autumn.

She shuts the doors and returns to her laptop, staring silently at the screen for a few minutes, then begins to type.

40
Kimono

THE ACTOR SITS SELF-CONSCIOUSLY ON AN ACACIA lounger by the poolside, looking nervously around her for signs of human life. There is no-one to be seen. Her long hair trails over her bare shoulders as she stares fixedly at the gently rippling blue water of the pool.

Wayne Montana emerges from the house, carrying an ice bucket with a bottle of champagne and two glasses. He sits down heavily on the double day bed beside her, its wooden base creaking in protest.

'You look nervous!' he says, half-accusingly, as he opens the bottle and fills both glasses. 'What's up?'

She looks him in the eye. 'You know I wanted Jeanie here with me.'

'That piece a shit? I don't trust her. She's a fucking gossip, I told ya that before. No fucking assistants, this thing is bona fide confidential! Just you and me, OK?' He grins but his eyes are cold. 'Like old times,' he adds, staring at her challengingly.

She looks at him warily.

'Relax, baby!' he says soothingly as he hands her a glass of champagne, still grinning, his eyes not leaving hers.

She takes the wine from his hand and forces a smile as she takes a sip, the smallest she can. She needs to stay in control.

'Yeah, well, I don't actually feel very relaxed. I dunno why I'm even here, to be honest. I feel as though I've been summoned by the fucking principal for being a naughty girl.' She rolls her eyes.

'I'm sure you *are* a very naughty girl with that man of yours,' chuckles Wayne, plucking a ripe apricot from a bowl next to him and taking a bite, lasciviously. 'He's a lucky guy.'

'Shut the fuck up, Wayne. Why am I fucking here? Let's just get down to business,' she says, coldly.

'OK OK. No need to be like that,' he purrs, still grinning at her with piggy, flint chip eyes.

She notices a tiny fleck of golden apricot flesh stuck between his top teeth and represses a shudder.

'Look, I'm really busy, OK? I just got back from a long shoot. I'm busy and tired. Me and Jeanie have, like, a zillion and one fucking things to catch up on. This had better be good,' she says, her eyes hooded with boredom and exhaustion.

'Believe me, it is. It's the most amazing part I've read in the last decade.' He leans towards her and lowers his voice. 'Bernie Carter. Astrophysicist turned Save the Whales campaigner. So there's your sensitive fucking liberal planet-hugger box ticked right there. We need her to have an IQ off the scale to pull this off. Plus, of course, bombshell looks. So, you're perfect. You've got it all, baby. You were born to do this,' he beams.

'"Liberal planet-hugger", huh? Is that how you see me and my husband, now we're setting up our global foundation?' she asks, pointedly, an angry spark flaring in her eyes.

'Well no, it's a great cause, baby. Climate change is on all of our minds, every day. All the days. I think about it constantly.'

'No, Wayne, you don't. Let me see it, then.'

'*Please.* Forgot your manners now you're Hollywood Royalty, huh?' he admonishes, wagging a finger in front of her face. 'You're only as good as your last movie, baby. Remember that. And parts have a habit of just dribbling through the cracks once you get to your age.' His shark-like grin reappears, underlining the implicit threat.

'Bullshit. I'm not out of my twenties, yet.'

'Sure. Exactly what I mean,' replies Wayne, casually, handing her a few pages of script.

She stares at him for a second as he hands her the script, then takes them out of his hands and starts reading. A smile spreads across her face.

'Wow, this is great dialogue. Who's the writer? Anyone we know?'

'Can't say at the moment. It's totally under wraps. But this script is fucking *volcanic*.'

'So, have you got the whole thing?'

'Are you serious? You've seen enough. I could tell by that cute little smile on your face when you were reading that you fucking love it already though. So are you in, or are you out? You're hooked, am I right?'

'Come on! I can't commit to a whole movie on the basis of a couple of pages of script. Jesus!'

Wayne picks up another apricot and stares at it. He pushes both thumbs into the flesh and prises it apart, carefully picking out the stone, which he tosses into the pool before glancing up at her and smiling, a smile which vanishes almost as soon as it appears.

He puts the mutilated apricot into his mouth and begins chewing, slowly, then licks his fingers, one at a time, whilst staring coldly at her.

'Are you saying "no" to me, sweetheart?'

She looks around her nervously, suddenly feeling frightened.

Wayne picks the last apricot from the bowl on the table and digs his nails into it, breaking it apart, all the while looking into her eyes. His shark grin has gone, leaving only a cold mask in which burn the two flint shards of his eyes. The threatening silence is broken only by his breathing, heavy through his nostrils as he stares at her.

A young female voice from the house calls out 'Mr Montana! A delivery! Won't let me sign! They need you to sign!'

At the sound of the voice, the cold fire in his eyes vanishes.

'I wanna get some of that whippy cream stuff,' he mumbles to himself. He drops the apricot back in the bowl and heads towards the house.

The actor pulls out her phone and quickly sends a message, checking the patio doors to the house for his reappearance.

pork being a total asshole. dunno whether this whole thing such a good idea…

'Why didn't ya fucking tell 'em, then?' Wayne's voice booms from the house. '*This is your fucking job you cunt!*'

She winces at the threat of violence in his tone of voice and stares at the brutalised apricot, prised half open, lying alone in the bowl.

Are you gonna do this, or not?

She glances back towards the house, checking the coast is clear, then takes a small plastic insulin syringe out of her bag and carefully dispenses a measure of liquid into the flesh of the apricot.

She leans back again and stares at the apricot, sitting there in the bowl, glistening in the sun.

Is he gonna notice it looks different? He's gonna suspect something. Shit…

'*You fucking greaseball whore piece of fucking shit!*' yells Wayne at the unseen maid from within the house. Something smashes and a female voice whimpers in fear or pain.

He storms back out to the pool area carrying a tin of aerosol cream, his face red with fury, mouth hanging open in a snarl.

Levering himself onto the day bed once again, he reaches for the last remaining piece of fruit, aims the nozzle of the can at it and hoses the apricot with a thick dollop of whipped cream.

He holds it up between his fat fingers, tilts his head back, opens his mouth wide and plops the apricot in. A smile of satisfaction spreads over his face as he chews contentedly. He swallows the treat, then glances at her, all warmth and bonhomie, the menace momentarily quelled.

'Apricots and whippy cream. Food of the fucking gods,' he says, smugly.

'I wouldn't know,' she says coldly. 'Anyway, I think we've covered everything, I have to go. I'll be in touch.'

She stands to leave.

'OK baby. You're gonna do it, yeah?'

She looks down at him. 'Whatever you want, Wayne.' She smiles a strange smile, as if about to laugh, then turns and walks away across the lawn.

Wayne stares at her retreating figure.

Long time since I've had that piece of ass. Time I had it again. Fuck her. She's gonna do this movie. Nobody says no to me. Nobody.

He lies back on his day bed and closes his eyes. Her strange smile lingers in his mind as he drifts off to sleep.

A terrible, deep rumbling penetrates his foggy mind as he rises from the depths of sleep then splutters, crying out fearfully as he surfaces into consciousness. It takes a second or two to realise that it's the sound of his own snoring. He shakes his head and rubs his eyes as the waking panic recedes.

He reaches for another apricot and realises they've all gone. He looks at the empty bowl, picks up the can of aerosol cream and sprays a thick blob on his finger then licks it off. It tastes strange. Kind of metallic.

He goes for the can again, this time spraying a huge mound of cream into his palm and licking it off in one great big blob. The white goo feels greasy, as though it's sliding around on a journey of its own between his tongue and the roof of his mouth. He swallows it nevertheless. The metallic tang lingers in his mouth.

He rests his eyes on the water rippling in front of him. The sun sparkles on the glassy surface, creating mesmerising patterns on the pool floor. As he stares at it, the water slowly starts to grow, swelling up into mounds of moving glass which stretch a few feet above the surface of the pool then recede again to their previous level.

The ripples start singing to him. Like a choir. All in harmony.

He can smell the music from where he's lying. The smell has a name. *Rhinestone.* He can smell rhinestones, all around him, twinkling in the sun, clumping together to form heaps of moving glass then exploding into tiny shards of crystal which melt into the deep blue swarm of water seething in front of his eyes.

The sweetness of the whippy cream lingers on his tongue and sounds like a rainbow.

I'm sick. I've been poisoned.

He grabs his phone and rings his lawyer.

'Something's wrong…get your ass over here…oh God…in a fucking what?…oh shit…a meeting?…oh shit…get the fuck over here I'm fuckin' dyin'…'

Wayne lies down again and stares up at the Chinese fan palms surrounding the pool. He recoils in horror. Their spiky green leaves have morphed into huge, writhing green spiders. His mouth opens wordlessly as he stares, bug-eyed, at the trees.

I need to get indoors.

He rubs his eyes then looks around for his flip flops. He sees them, lying on the decking next to his day bed. As he stares at them they start to hop across the deck towards the pool, all by themselves, leaving a trail of dancing flip flops in their wake.

He screws up his eyes, trying to focus and force the world return to normal.

But it won't.

For the first time in his entire adult life he feels a strange, new sensation.

Fear.

I can't move!

The panic has completely immobilised him, a fat, bronzed slab, lying on his day bed on the decking of his house on Rodeo Drive, Beverly Hills, Los Angeles, South California, U.S.of A.

The American Dream.

She floats towards him, a long red kimono emblazoned with an embroidered dragon flapping softly around her as she moves, gliding, not walking. She hasn't got any feet. She's just...hovering, silently drifting nearer and nearer to him.

She has straight black hair and he can see eyes and a nose and a mouth but no discernible face. She's like a mannequin, blank and cold.

He looks on, terrified, stranded on the day bed, eyes popping out of his head with fear.

Now he's grasping for his phone but it's bouncing around in mid-air, laughing at him in an irritating little squeak, darting away from his pudgy, outstretched fingers.

The blank eyes stare at him and the mouth speaks in a deep, gravelly, accusatory tone.

'Hello, Wayne. It's me. Don't you recognise me? In 1997 you raped me at Cannes. I was nineteen years old, Wayne. Nineteen.'

'Wah?' He can barely speak now, his tongue feels grafted to the sticky sweet roof of his mouth.

'Remember me, Wayne? Don't recognise me, huh? I don't have a face, right? I don't look quite the same, huh? Like you'd even remember.'

He writhes around helplessly on the day bed, eyes glazed with terror, as he stares at the vision in front of him.

'How many women have you raped, Wayne? Hundreds certainly. Thousands of us probably. Any that stand out in your memory? Or do all of us faceless victims blur together in one poisonous mess inside that shit-dump of a brain?'

Her voice echoes as though she's shouting across a mountain range.

'That's all we are to you, isn't it, Wayne? Meat. You'd eat us if you could. Gnaw on our flesh and spit out the bones.'

His mouth opens and closes like a fish stranded on the river bank.

'Then toss the bones to the dogs. Which reminds me. *Bones*, Wayne. The ones you had killed and who were left to rot. How many of us did you *order to be killed* Wayne?'

He tries to lift himself up from the day bed to escape, but the ground is edging towards him and receding away again and he flops heavily onto the decking, a loud trombone announcing his fall in a single, muted, elongated note.

'Former actors. Now flight attendants, truck drivers, lecturers, prostitutes, childminders. There've been a fair few of us, haven't there? Who threatened to blab and couldn't be paid off? Three bodies recovered so far in Long Island alone.'

The disembodied lips snarl and the eyes narrow, moving towards him in tandem, whilst the red kimono billows as if caught in the winds at the edge of a storm.

'Long Island, Wayne. Not too far from that palatial home of yours in the Hamptons, huh? Once those tests come back from the lab and they join up those little DNA microdots, your secrets are gonna come tumbling out the closet like hoarded shoes. We know what you did, Wayne. It's aaaaaall comin' out now. Your name is shit, boy. You're *done*.' The final word echoes like thunder.

He looks down. Somehow the phone is in his hand. His eyes are like saucers, his fingers like fat sausages, scrabbling over the screen, desperately trying to make the call to his lawyer.

'So you've got a choice, Wayne. This is option one. Live in disgrace till the end of your days, shunned and abandoned by a film community that once embraced you and provided cover for your vile crimes. And also shunned by your wife. Who's just filed for divorce, by the way. And who has three of her favourite gigolos on rotation. You did know about that, right, Wayne? You didn't? Hey, too bad, buddy.'

His eyes dim with confusion, his fingers desperately struggling with his phone.

'Whilst you've been away fuckin' and gettin' those "problem" women whacked, she's been in your bed gettin' fucked by men half your age and twice as pretty. No, make that, um, hundreds of times as pretty. Taken a look in the mirror lately, Wayne? Pretty gross, huh? Ugly, fat, balding and old. You wouldn't fuck a woman as ugly, fat and old as you, would you Wayne? Specially one with no hair on her head. And no woman, no matter what she looks like, wants to fuck you either. They only fuck you because you terrify 'em into submission and clamp 'em down. Such a ladies' man, huh, Wayne? Such a stuuuuuuud.'

Wayne lies on the decking, his mouth open, his eyes wide with terror, and grunts, unable to speak.

'Where's Mr Fixit gone, Wayne? Can't find him? He's hiding right there, behind that big green blob on your phone. He's so shy, Wayne, he doesn't want to come out. See him peeping from behind that big green blob? Can't see him? He's there, Wayne, he just doesn't want you to find him right now. Look real close. Can you see him now, Wayne? I wonder why he doesn't wanna talk to you, Wayne?'

Wayne opens and closes his mouth, his eyes bleary with the effort of trying to focus.

'You're impatient, huh? I get it. OK let's move on to option number two then, shall we? Option number two is an interesting one, and the option you might just want to take. Option number two involves *death*.'

Wayne starts to writhe around on the decking now, his fat hands flapping from side to side in front of his face, his eyes becoming bloodshot.

'Death,' the figure repeats, the word echoing in Wayne's skull. He leans over to one side, trying to prop himself up on one arm, but immediately collapses back onto the decking with a jubilant fanfare of horns.

'Because let's face it. Maybe it's better you just flip off this mortal coil right now, huh? Better for you. Better for your wife. Better for your many, many victims. Better, in fact, for everyone. Yeah. I actually think that's the preferable option, Wayne. There's no place on this earth for monsters like you. You belong in hell. Do you fancy a little trip to hell, Wayne?'

Wayne is thrashing around on the decking now, his lips flapping together, spittle flying as he struggles.

'Yeah I think that's probably the most sensible option, all things considered. You're getting pretty excited down there, Wayne. You like the idea of that one, huh?'

The Pork Chop's eyes take on an hysterical desperation.

'Oh! Silly me. It's not excitement, is it? It's *panic!* You're panicking slightly there, Wayne, huh? Frightened you might lose your way, there, boy? Get lost en route to *hell?*'

He limply reaches out his hand to her, stretching his fingers towards her.

'Google Maps not working for you, Wayne? Oh, you're still on the green button to Mr Fixit, sorry, I missed that.'

His eyes fill with tears.

'Don't worry your big ugly head about it. I'll tell you the way, Wayne. It's pretty easy to remember. You're not gonna forget this one like you forgot all those women you raped and had whacked. Don't worry, this one's gonna be emblazoned on that fat, flabby brain of yours. Forever. And for you, forever isn't long.'

Wayne looks up at her, piteously, waving his hand towards the hem of her kimono.

'The road to hell, Wayne, is right there, about a foot in front of you, boy. Right there by your feet. There's the gates, open and waiting.'

Wayne turns his head and looks down at the pool.

'The blue gates of hell. Your swimming pool, Wayne.'

She reaches out and stabs a bony finger into his upper arm, where it dimples his soft flesh. He feels himself being dragged across the decking towards the water, the texture of the wood rasping against his skin, right to the edge of the pool, the water lapping at his bloated, paralysed body.

'Fancy a little dip, Wayne?'

41
Pheromones

'I WON'T HEAR FROM BRUCE AGAIN,' SAYS ELLA, SADLY.

'Why not?'

'I emailed him a few months back, told him I wanted to meet up with him again. That I needed more time "taking in the essential youness of you," I think I said. Something totally ridiculous like that. He never replied. I'm not surprised. He probably thinks I'm completely nuts.'

'I'd love it if a beautiful woman told me she'd like to spend time "taking in the essential me-ness of me",' says Felix, smiling.

'I'd love it if I wasn't such a dick.'

'You're not a dick, Ella. Far from it.'

'Well, I got the book finished.'

'I know. And well done again. I'm really looking forward to reading it. I can't believe you've written it so quickly.'

'All those months of worrying. Such a waste of time and energy. In the end all I had to do was put bum on seat and write the fucker.'

'Yup. That sums up the process very well. Bum on seat. Write. But those months of worrying weren't a waste, Ella. The final words on the page are the tip of the iceberg. That huge dark mass, looming unseen beneath the surface, that's the real work.'

'Well, it's done, now, out of my hands and with my agent. So I can perform at your night. If you still want me.'

'I very much do want you, Ella. And I've been looking forward to seeing you again. Face to face.'

'Yeah. I'm sorry it's all been on Facetime lately. I just haven't felt up to seeing anyone. Just wanted to hibernate and write.'

'Well, it'll be great to see you in person again. Facetime's OK, but pheromones can't be communicated through a screen.'

Ella holds up her phone and stares at Felix.

'What did you say?'

'I said that pheromones…it doesn't matter.' Felix smiles and brushes a strand of dark hair out of his eyes.

She looks at him and smiles. He smiles back.

'Hold on. The door. Can I call you back?' says Ella.

'Sure.'

She opens the front door to the postman and takes a parcel and letter from him. Putting the parcel down, she examines the black, spidery ink on the letter, smiling in recognition at the hand-writing. She opens it and pulls out the letter, written on textured handmade paper and bearing Bruce's address: Lilythwaite Farm, Horsehouse, Coverdale, North Yorkshire.

Dear Ella, I hope my letter finds you well. I have had an absolutely nightmarish fucking fortnight stuck in Japan with the fucking flu. Have you ever been stuck forty-two floors up in a fucking skyscraper in Tokyo with flu? It's a fucker and I hope I never have to endure such utter misery again. Anyway, thank you for your letter. Sorry not to reply sooner. I'll be in London sometime in December. If you want to meet up to yak about your book you can get hold of me then. Love Bruce x

Ella stands staring at the letter, then calls Felix back, aware that a huge grin is plastered on her face.

His face appears on the screen, still smiling.

'Hi.'

'Hi. Sorry about that. Postman.'

'You look ecstatic. Must have been something good.'

'Yeah,' says Ella, still grinning. 'A letter. From my friend.'

42

CHRISTMAS IN BROOKLYN

THE NEON LIGHTS OPPOSITE BRANDON'S BEDROOM window in LA's Chinatown are flashing on and off in a sickly green.

'Nice view you got here,' murmurs Adriana, smiling, lying on the bed next to Brandon.

'Suits me. Sometimes I just lie here and try and memorise all those Chinese characters. I've always wanted to learn Mandarin.'

'You should start. There's no time like the present.'

'I never seem to have the time to do the things I wanna do.'

Adriana props herself up on one arm and looks at Brandon's face as he gazes up at the stationary ceiling fan gathering dust above his head.

'You and me both.'

'I dunno. It sometimes drives me a bit crazy, living in this room.'

Adriana starts singing. 'If I could be you, and you could be me, would we behave so differently?'

Brandon smiles, warmly, his eyes creasing at the corners.

'Remember that song?' asks Adriana.

'Those lyrics just fuck with my head, man,' says Brandon, turning his head towards Adriana to look at her. 'I don't even get it. If I were you, wow, I'd behave totally differently. I mean, for a start, I'd just spend all day at home running my hands over my breasts. Imagine actually having breasts.'

'Loads of fat guys have man breasts. And guess what? They're allowed to have 'em on show wherever the fuck they want, even though precisely no-one wants to see 'em.'

'The world's a fool…'

'If I were a man, I wouldn't spend all my time at home touching my dick. Although I guess a lot of guys do spend a lot of time doing just that.' Adriana laughs.

'I've spent a fair amount of time doing that myself, since you came into my life,' says Brandon, looking at Adriana lovingly.

She picks up a pillow from the bed and swipes him, laughing.

'Is that meant to be romantic?'

'Kinda.'

Adriana smiles, gently. 'Actually that is sorta romantic. I like the idea of you thinking about me like that.'

'Ever since the first time I set eyes on you,' says Brandon, wrapping his arms around her and pulling her down to him.

'For real?'

'For real.'

'I had no idea.'

'I didn't want you to have any idea.'

'Why not?'

'Because I'm Juliette's driver. And I don't think she'd have been wild about the idea of you and me making out.'

'You could have given me a little clue. A hint,' says Adriana teasingly, stroking the hair curling around his neck.

'I thought you'd probably just…know, you know?'

'I didn't know. I had no idea. I thought you had me down as some shallow Valley girl type.'

'Sure. With you sitting in the back of the car quietly reading Proust. Yeah. Some Valley girl. No, Adriana, I knew everything I needed to know in the first second I laid eyes on you when I picked you up from the house.'

'Really? Go on,' says Adriana, leaning in and gently kissing Brandon's neck as he speaks.

'I saw you, and a whole new world appeared in front of me. I knew you were beautiful inside and out. Your soul shone out from inside your body. You just radiated something. Love, beauty, unattainability. Like the most beautiful flower I'd ever seen, its petals glowing in the sun, promising a heavenly scent if only I could get nearer, but sitting just there, out of reach.'

Adriana laughs. 'Shut. Up! Get the fuck outta here! Are you for real?'

'I am,' smiles Brandon back, lovingly tracing a finger around the curve of Adriana's chin.

'Yeah.' Her smile fades as she looks into his eyes. 'You are, aren't you? Guys never talk like that. They're all like, trying so desperately to be cool. But you just don't give a shit, do you?'

He shrugs. 'Nope.'

'Well whatever you've been doing, it's working. 'Cause I'm not out of reach. I'm here now.'

'You sure are,' smiles Brandon, and pulls her towards him, kissing her.

Adriana's eyes glaze over with love and desire as she looks into his eyes.

'I'm gonna miss you so much when I go to Brooklyn with Juliette.'

'Yeah. Me too.'

'Wish to hell I didn't have to go.'

'Yeah, me too.'

'Gotta do what I gotta do.'

'Yup.'

'New York is like, literally so fucking far away.'

'When you're there New York is the gold at the end of Flyover Rainbow. But you'll be back. I'll wait.'

The stone balustrades and iron railings leading up the steps to the porch of the Brooklyn brownstone are swathed in thousands of tiny white fairy lights, shimmering in the chill night air. The snow has been falling all afternoon, big soft heavy flakes settling on the handrails and the windowsills above.

The heavy crimson curtains in the front room overlooking Prospect Park are drawn shut.

Juliette lies on a long, midnight blue velvet sofa, staring at the piece of paper in her hand. *Bacchus Umbra Productions* is emblazoned across the top in large black letters.

Her own production company. No-one else calling the shots. No-one else making the decisions. No-one else hiring or firing. No-one raping her.

Adriana pulls the curtain aside slightly and peers out. 'It's snowing again, boss. Do you think we'll be like, totally snowed in for Christmas?'

'Who cares? Snow the fuck outta this town. I couldn't give one. I wanna be totally out of contact.'

'Really?'

'Yeah. And I'm sick of hearing stories about Micky. I forgot to tell you. Bella George rang me the other day. Get this. Micky told her he's a changed man, that he's been inspired by my charity work, and that he's working for some anti-trafficking organisation and he just fixed it to get passports for this entire family, a whole bunch of 'em, ten of 'em or something.'

'Shut up!'

'Yeah. That's what he told her.'

'So how come he's not been tweeting his ass off about it?'

'Oh, he's keeping a *low profile* on it for their safety. Or something.'

'No shit.'

'I mean. If he's trying to impress me, he's a day late and a dollar short. I don't wanna hear about it. I just want some peace and quiet. So, I'm just gonna hang here for the next week and chill with the kids. That's my idea of heaven.'

'I don't blame you,' says Adriana, warmly.

'So, where would *your* idea of heaven be at Christmas?' asks Juliette, inquisitively.

Adriana looks over at her and shrugs her shoulders.

'I dunno. Paris, I guess. With Brandon. In fact, anywhere with Brandon. Just, Brandon.'

'You wanna go to Paris with Brandon for Christmas?' asks Juliette, looking up and smiling.

'Is that an offer or like a general feelings question?' asks Adriana, laughing.

'It's a fucking offer, Adriana. Do you fucking wanna go to fucking Paris with fucking Brandon or not?'

'What, all of us? Like, and the kids and Nanny Frances too?'

'I *mean* just the two of you. You and Brandon. You book it, I'll pay. My Christmas present to you both.'

'Are you shitting me? That'd be super amazing!' says Adriana, breaking out into a huge smile. 'Thanks boss! You sure you can, like, manage without me?'

'Sure. And I'm turning my phone off. I'm having an assistant-free, screen-free Christmas. Just me, the kids and that pile of scripts,' says Juliette with determination, gesturing towards a table in the corner of the room covered in paperwork and packages.

'Three kids and a pile of scripts might not be such a focusing experience…' says Adriana, doubtfully.

'Nanny Frances and the kids are arriving tomorrow. I'll switch my phone off after she gets here. But then no screens at all. I will be uncontactable. It's the future. Being out of contact. Everyone just expects everyone else to be right there on the other end of a fucking phone. Well this Christmas, I'm not doing it.'

'You're setting up a production company and you wanna be out of contact?'

'It's only for a week, but what I need is *solitude* right now. Sometimes it's what everyone needs. Just some quiet time to think and reflect. Life's too fast. Need to slow it *way* down.'

Juliette walks over to the table and unwraps a jiffy bag containing a book, addressed to Bacchus Umbra Productions. 'See? They want me. And what I wanna do, Adriana, is fucking *read*.'

'I think that's a great idea, boss,' says Adriana, smiling.

'Call me Juliette. I'm *Juliette*, now.'

'OK, Juliette. I'll see ya after Christmas,' says Adriana, smiling fondly and picking up her bag.

The two women spontaneously hug.

'I love ya Adriana.'

'I love you, Juliette.'

43
Weft

BRUCE'S HEAD RESTS ON HIS FOLDED ARMS. HE OPENS his eyes.

It's gone dark. But is that afternoon dark, or evening dark? Hard to tell, considering it's dark all the fucking time right now.

He looks at the empty wine glass next to his elbow and then notices the letter lying next to it. He lifts his head to read it.

Hi Bruce,

Regarding our recent phone call about the possibility of developing your novel The Peculiar Memories of Thomas Penman into a film with ourselves. I wanted to let you know that…

The text moves in and out of focus as he reads to the end of the letter.

He looks out of the window at the apple tree, gaunt in its winter dormancy.

'Fuck…'

THE GOLD

If you enjoyed reading this book, please leave a five star review wherever you bought it.

Find Jude Calvert-Toulmin online @judeauthor and her books at www.judeauthor.com.

Other novels by Jude Calvert-Toulmin:

My Adventures in Cyberspace
Drowning
Labrats
Mother-in-Law, Son-in-Law
A Passion for Classic Cars
A Hidden Passion for Classic Cars

FLEUR DE LYS

Printed in Great Britain
by Amazon

71210731R00231